THE VICTIM

Jane Bidder

Published by Accent Press Ltd 2015

ISBN 9781783751396

WINDSEA GAZETTE

Police warn against new spate of car thieves. Owners urged to lock doors and report any suspicious activities.

ONE

Portfolio. Check. Wallpaper swatches. Check. Fabric samples. Check. Mobile phone. Check.

Georgie prided herself on being organised. You had to be in this business, if you were going to be taken seriously. There were already too many 'mothers-turned-interior-designers' in this wealthy part of Devon. Anyone who wanted to be someone had to stand out from the crowd.

So far, Georgie told herself, swinging her legs out of the Volvo while clutching her various bags, she'd managed to do that. Touch wood. Feeling rather stupid, she looked around for something wooden. The security fence around the Hon. Mrs David Romer-Riches' extensive front garden was made of metal but there was a tree by the gate where you had to press a button to announce your arrival.

Blast! In an effort to press the button and hang onto her things, she'd gone and dropped her handbag and portfolio. Papers were flying everywhere. *And* it was raining. Her purple reading glasses (a regretful nod to early middle age) lay on the verge. Those notes for today were already getting damp. The rain, as if in conspiracy, became heavier. Georgie put her hands over her hair (how lucky to still be a natural blonde after all these years!), hoping the weather wouldn't mess it up. The damp always made it frizz slightly.

Two magpies flew past, just above the head of a youth in a maroon hoodie, hands in pockets. A middle-aged man cycled by on the other side of road, eyes straight ahead. Then a young

3

mum with a pushchair bent down to hand her one of the pages that was flapping in the breeze.

'Thanks,' said Georgie gratefully, glancing at the little bundle in blue inside with a globule of snot running down its nose. Then she dashed down the road in pursuit of the rest of her notes. It took her a few minutes to gather them up.

How annoying! One or two had got muddy. Still, a quick wipe with the Wet-Ones that she kept in her handbag – something she always carried even though Ellie and Nick were way past that stage – and they'd just about pass muster.

Just as well. Mrs R-R, as Georgie privately called her for brevity's sake, was a new client and, judging from local gossip, hard to please. The other rival interior decorators in town had been trying to get hold of her ever since she moved here from London. Knightsbridge – or so it was rumoured.

Georgie pressed the button by the gate to announce her arrival, as instructed.

'Yes?'

The voice at the other end was tinny. Matter of fact.

'Georgie Hamilton.'

Why, every time she said her name, did she feel like a fraud? Everyone's like that, her childhood friend Lyndsey used to say. No one really likes their name.

'Enter.'

It was a command rather than an invitation. Why did she have to park outside the gates instead of driving up, she wondered as she made her way up the gravel drive. Still, clients could be very odd. Especially new ones, until they'd got to know you better. Besides, she didn't want to annoy this one: it would be awkward for Sam who had, in effect, got this commission for her.

A warm feeling went through her despite the rain which had become more of a drizzle now. Her husband had been incredibly supportive since she'd told him that if she didn't find something now the children were virtually grown up, she'd go stark raving mad. In fact, she'd gone perilously close to it. Until

4

then, she'd ignored women's magazine articles about empty-nest syndrome, dismissing them as histrionic. But when Ellie and Nick had sauntered off to university with a year between them, she'd felt completely lost – especially as her son was due to start a sabbatical term in the States in the spring.

'How about doing a degree yourself?' Sam had said in a tone which suggested that if he was her, that was exactly what he would do. Her husband's one fault was an inborn conviction that if only the rest of the world thought as he did, everything would be all right. Still, after everything he had done for her, it seemed a small price to pay. Even so, a degree …

'My brain isn't what it was,' Georgie had replied, recalling, with a slight pang, how she might have gone to uni if she hadn't been so keen to do a post-A-level gap year. 'I can't even do the crossword any more, let alone remember the minutiae of the Thirty Years' War.'

Sam had bent his head quizzically, pushing his hands deep into his pockets as he often did when making a point. His hands had been one of the first things she'd noticed about him. Strong, capable hands to match the strong, capable jawline. The second thing she'd noticed had been his height. Six foot two and a half inches, he'd informed her when they knew each other better. Tall enough to look after her. The third thing had been his hair. Over the years it had thinned somewhat, although he was still an attractive man judging from the heads which turned when they walked down the street. Thank goodness, Georgie often thought, that she'd married a man who would never look at anyone else. A man whose only concern was his family and how to help each one fulfil their potential. At times, she couldn't help feeling that it was all a bit too much. The children certainly did.

'You've always been good with colours,' Sam persisted. 'What about Fine Arts?'

'Like everyone else, you mean?'

It was becoming a joke in the local dinner party circle that other empty-nest mothers had applied for mature degrees in

History of Art, a course made popular by the young Royals.

Sam had given her a warm cuddle. He was good at that. Sometimes she felt it was nicer than sex. Less demanding. Easier, especially when one was tired. Comforting, too. Joly had never cuddled her. Instead he had ...

'Look at all this!' Sam waved around their sitting room, indicating the Designer Guild curtains with their rich blues that set off the pale yellow sofas and matching carpet.

'What about it?' said Georgie, frowning in case anything was out of place. At times, it was hard to live with a perfectionist. At other times, it was comforting. As long as she was with Sam, nothing could go wrong again.

'Remember how you used to do up people's homes when we first got together?'

So much had happened since then. With two young children and a busy ex-pat life – Australia, Singapore, the Cayman Islands – there hadn't been time to work.

But now, thanks to head office, they were back in the UK – something she still wasn't happy about. 'It's a no-brainer,' Sam had said. 'The money's good so the kids can go to decent schools and we can afford a nice house.'

'Only if it's nowhere near Yorkshire,' she'd insisted.

Sam had shot her a knowing look. 'You still feel that way?' She'd nodded.

'The south-west would work: many of my clients will be in Exeter and Plymouth.'

So Devon it was. They'd bought a large, rambling, white-bricked Victorian house with a beautiful garden (stuffed with peonies, lupins, Canterbury bells, and old-fashioned roses) that ran down to the river which 'fed' the sea a mile down the road. Georgie – finding it hard to adjust to the UK after so many years away – had diverted her fears by becoming a dedicated homemaker.

When the children were at school, she'd spend hours scouring local auctions and newspaper columns for antique fireplaces to replace the original tiles that had been ripped out.

Her greatest coup was finding a second-hand navy-blue Aga through eBay and then discovering rich terracotta flagstones from a house that was about to be pulled down round the corner. Instead of employing decorators, she took a painting course and did everything herself.

The result was stunning. One of their new neighbours, who freelanced for a glossy homes magazine, had even featured it as House of the Month.

It all helped to obliterate the demons.

'If you can do this to our house,' said Sam, cutting into her memories, 'you can do it to others.'

And so Gorgeous Georgie's was born. The name was Ellie's idea. ('You need something catchy, Mum!') and although at first she'd thought it was a bit tacky, it had taken straight off. Word of mouth helped, when she'd started to meet people through the tennis club and a local 'Women in Business' group. Then, after a chance meeting with a journalist at a dinner party, she was featured in a local upmarket glossy magazine. Her flattering profile was picked up by *Tatler*, which resulted in almost more work than she could handle.

Apparently it was the *Tatler* profile which had swayed the Hon. Mrs David Romer-Riches. 'I showed it to her husband,' Sam had said the other week. 'He came to me for tax advice, said he wanted to bring his business locally now he's down here. Nice man. although he did say that his wife was very "particular".'

He'd given her a quick, warm squeeze that smelt of the expensive cinnamon after-shave which she'd put in his stocking last Christmas. (In turn, he had hidden Chanel No. 5 in hers; a luxury he had introduced her to in the early days.) 'I know you've got a lot on but you can't turn this one down. And don't be worried about the "particular" bit. You're more than capable of holding your own.'

Was she? Georgie looked cool and confident on the outside though; the local magazine picture had certainly inferred that, with its shot of her sitting on the edge of a sofa, facing the camera with her newly blow-dried blonde bob neatly in place and classic pearl earrings. Georgie was a classic kind of girl.

Or so, she thought uncomfortably, everyone said.

'Mrs Hamilton. Thank you for coming.'

A tall, slightly haughty-looking woman stood on the doorstep, her left hand held out in greeting. She was younger than Georgie had expected from Sam's description. Roughly her age, in fact. Handsome, rather than pretty, with short, dark hair (cleverly feathered); the country trademark upturned powder-blue shirt collar, and soft-looking creamy flats. Despite the loosely cut linen trousers, it was clear she was painfully thin. Georgie, who worked hard in the gym to maintain her size-ten figure, couldn't help thinking her new client would benefit from a few extra pounds.

From her icy grey eyes, it was clear she was taking in Georgie's damp appearance. There was almost a hint of amusement. 'I hope you found somewhere to park in the lane. It's a new drive, you see, and the builders advised us to let the stones settle.'

Really? In her experience, the more you crunched down on a drive, the quicker the bedding-down process took place, but Georgie wasn't in a position to argue.

'Do you mind taking off your shoes?'

Her new client eyed Georgie's little red suede summer boots with disdain. 'We're a shoe-free zone inside. Much more hygienic, don't you think?'

Clearly, Georgie told herself, following her new client in, the Hon. Mrs R-R was one of those fussy types. No shoes in the house. No 'clutter' in the front drive although there was – wow – a gypsy caravan in the back garden, next to a small water fountain. Now that was unexpected.

'It was a wedding present from my father. Do you have family nearby?'

Georgie was taken aback for the second time in as many seconds. Normally, clients didn't get to the personal level so quickly.

'No,' she replied crisply.

'I gather you have a step-daughter.'

What relevance did that have? Briefly, she felt slightly cross with Sam for having talked about his family with a client.

'I do, although to be honest, I don't see her that way. I've brought Ellie up since she was small.'

'You have a son of your own too?'

On paper, such a conversation would sound friendly, but on the strength of a two-minute acquaintance it felt like an interrogation.

'Yes. What about you? Do you have children?'

A shadow passed across that impeccably made-up face. 'No.' There was a brisk irritated gesture of the hands, suggesting the personal conversation had been Georgie's initiative and not hers. 'Let's not waste time. What would you suggest for the morning room?'

She looked around. First impressions were crucial; both of the house and the client. The latter, it had to be said, was odd. There was something about the Hon. Mrs R-R that she couldn't put her finger on it. But the first was stunning.

Georgie loved classical Georgian houses like this, with big square rooms and wide picture windows which let in lots of light. But there was no getting away from the fact that it was boringly bland with all those cream walls and beige carpets that were crying out for colour. Even the sofas were off-white.

'I thought I'd start with a blank canvas but it hasn't quite worked out the way I thought.' The Hon. Mrs R-R was standing now, her arms folded and those cold, grey eyes focussed on Georgie as though she was about to interrogate her. 'What are your views?'

'Actually,' said Georgie brightly, getting out her pad and pen, 'I need to see the rest of the house first.' She fixed her client with a mirror gaze – a phrase she'd learned from a psychology book on how to start up in business. 'Be respectful but at the same time don't be afraid to show your experience. If faced with a challenging look, return it or else you could be seen as ineffectual.'

'Then,' Georgie added with a smile that she didn't really feel like making, 'I think it would help if we got to know each other better. That's important if I'm going to come up with the kind of home that would work for you and your husband. It might be helpful if I could meet him too.'

Two small, vertical frown lines between the eyes suddenly sprang to attention. 'Not possible.' The tone was crisp, as if Georgie had asked whether she could go through the Hon. Mrs R.-R's underwear drawer. 'David is away a lot and besides, he wouldn't want to be consulted on something so trivial.'

A home is not trivial, Georgie was about to say before stopping herself. It took all sorts. Just because she didn't warm to this client didn't mean she had to scotch a lucrative business connection. 'Do you see it as trivial too?' she found herself asking.

'No.' For the first time since meeting, a trace of uncertainty crossed the other woman's face. 'Otherwise I wouldn't have asked you here, Georgie.' Her eyes took on another challenging look. 'May I call you that?'

It was exactly the opening she needed. This Mrs Hon. David R-R business was ridiculous. 'Certainly. And do you mind if I call you by your first name?'

'Actually, I do. Now, let's go into the kitchen, shall we? I'd like some advice on that too. I'm thinking of changing the colour of the Aga. At the moment, it's the wrong shade of cream. I favour buttermilk, myself.'

Three hours later, Georgie was drained. She never wanted to see any shade of beige again. Talk about unimaginative! Then again, any woman who wore cream linen trousers without so much as a crease or mark on them was no candidate for a kindred spirit in Georgie's view. Although she tried to draw a line between clients and friends, it made it so much easier if she got on with them.

Clearly this wasn't going to happen with the Hon. Mrs R-R.

'I'll be in touch with sketches and swatches for each room within the week,' she promised, hoping that her gurgling stomach wasn't too audible. The woman hadn't even offered her so much as a coffee.

'Better make a date now.' Crossing to the table, she picked up an iPad Georgie recognised as the very latest model. 'I can do Tuesday at 11 a.m. but that's it, I'm afraid.'

Georgie gritted her teeth. 'I'll re-arrange my diary to fit that in.'

'Good.' There was a curt head nod. Apart from the gypsy caravan = providing that initial brief insight into her new client's life = she had gleaned absolutely nothing about the woman, thought Georgie walking down the drive. In fact, for two pins, she almost felt like turning down the job. The money was important but not as much as the prestige, that feeling she was doing something worthwhile with her time, instead of playing tennis four times a week like some of her friends.

Unzipping the side part of her portfolio and reaching in, Georgie's hands closed around ... nothing. A cold, sharp chill went through her. Impossible! She'd put the car keys there when she'd got out of the car. Hadn't she? She normally kept them in her soft navy leather handbag but after she'd dropped it, she'd placed the latter in the boot = too much to carry! – away from prying eyes.

Frantically, Georgie began to rifle through her pockets. Nothing. Then her portfolio case. That was empty too. Perhaps she'd dropped the keys by the driver's door. Running now towards the road, she stopped dead.

The Volvo wasn't there.

'Impossible,' Georgie told herself as her heart began to beat itself into her throat. What were the chances of her dropping the keys, only for them to be picked up by a thief who had made off with a car? Oh my God. Her purse had been in the handbag too.

Thank heavens she still had her mobile on her. It was in her portfolio case. She'd remembered checking it when she'd got out of the car. The portfolio case which had then fallen from her

11

arms, scattering pages …

A wave of sickness followed by disbelief swam through her as she unzipped the case on the ground and found … Nothing. She couldn't have lost the phone too. She just couldn't. There had to be a mistake, some simple explanation.

Struggling to remain calm – and failing – Georgie ran the last few hours through her mind. When she'd dropped her things, people had been walking past. The young mum who'd helped her. The youth in the maroon hoody with hands in his pockets. The middle-aged man cycling past.

It had to be the youth in the hoodie. He would have seen her and come back in the hope she'd dropped something precious.

Georgie's heart began to race. At the same time, she felt a sickening weight building up in her stomach. What should she do now? She could go back to the Hon. Mrs R-R, but that would look incompetent. Losing keys and a phone, not to mention a car, definitely wouldn't give the right impression. Yet without any of these 'necessities', she felt as if she was standing naked in one of the best residential roads in town.

Not sure what else to do, Georgie began to walk. Maybe she'd bump into someone who would lend her a phone. But there was no one. No sign of any of the people who had walked past when she'd arrived, or anyone else for that matter. It was way past school run time and not early enough for nursery pick-up (although she guessed that in an area like this, there would be au pairs or nannies to do that).

Great. Now it was beginning to drizzle. Putting up the collar of her crisp white shirt (she'd left her jacket in the car too!), Georgie stumbled on miserably, towards the main road. Her little red suede boots – not made for walking – began to pinch.

Wait! There was a phone box on the corner. Her spirits lifted only to fall again when she remembered she didn't have any spare change for a call. Still, she could reverse the charges! It had been years since she'd done this. Her mother had thoroughly scolded her at the time ('Do you realise how much that cost?') even though she'd been stranded in town after

12

missing the last bus.

She'd never have done that to her two.

Georgie had to try several times to dial Sam's number, even though she never usually had trouble in remembering. It was as though the theft had centrifuged her brain, rendering her incapable of thinking clearly. Was the last digit a six? Yes!

'Hi. This is Sam Hamilton on Monday July 12. I'm in a meeting until 3 p.m. but leave a message and I will come back to you shortly afterwards.'

Her husband was always so precise. 'How could you lose your keys?' she could almost hear him saying. 'That's not like you.'

What was she going to do now? Her eye fell on a sticker advertising a free number for a taxi. Someone had scribbled on it, but the number was still readable. Thank God.

Fifteen minutes later ('There's a bit of a wait, love'), a silver Fiesta pulled up. By then, Georgie was in such mess that she could hardly get in. All her credit cards had been in the purse. She needed to cancel them but how could she, without her phone which had a copy of the passwords on them (stupid, she could see with hindsight, but at the time it seemed the easiest option). And what about all her contacts? They were on the phone as well. Ellie had promised to back them up on the computer but had never got round to it …

Somehow she found herself babbling this all out to the young taxi driver with slicked-back hair.

'You can borrow my phone, love. Use Google to get your bank's emergency number.' He shook his head. 'You've got to stop those bastards. Soon as they get your cards, they're quick.'

It was all she could do not to throw up. She'd have to try to remember her passwords …

'Your call is important to us …'

Come on. Come *on*.

'No luck?'

The driver glanced sympathetically at her in his mirror.

Tearfully, she shook her head. How could they take so long!

13

She'd have to do it at home. They were here now anyway.

No. This couldn't be right.

'My car's there,' she said out loud.

There was an uncertain glance via the mirror. 'Thought you said it had been nicked.'

'That's what I thought.'

She could sense his suspicion. Feel the sympathy evaporate only to be replaced with a growing wariness. 'My mum does things like that sometimes. Forgets she's done things. Maybe you didn't take it in the first place.'

'But I couldn't have got there any other way.' Georgie heard her voice coming out in a slightly hysterical scream. 'I told you. My house keys were stolen too. And my purse. And my phone ...'

'Maybe you left those behind too.'

'But I didn't!' She ran her hands through her hair. 'I'm sorry. I didn't mean to shout. But none of this is making sense.'

The startled look in the lad's eyes suggested he felt the same.

'It's all right,' she added, forcing herself to be calmer. 'I've got money inside so I'll be able to pay you.'

'Ta.' He looked relieved. 'Want me to come in with you, just to make sure everything's OK?'

Stammering her thanks (Georgie hadn't stammered since she was a child), she walked hesitantly down the path, past the blowsy peonies and straight lines of delphiniums.

'Looks like you left the door open.' There was a pitying edge to the young man's voice.

'But I didn't. I never do ...'

'Perhaps we ought to call the police first, then.'

Too late. She was in. Her heart beating so loudly now that she could hardly hear him, Georgie stared around the wide spacious hall. It had been the first feature that she and Sam had fallen in love with when they'd seen the house. It was virtually a room in its own right, with enough space for the nineteenth-century pew that had come from Sam's family home and a rich red mahogany rocking chair and marble hall table where they kept their keys in a bowl.

Both the car keys and the house keys were in it.

On the pew was her navy blue leather handbag. With her matching purse sitting on top. Georgie's heart took another leap. 'I had that this morning,' she stammered. 'I know I did. I had to get petrol on the way.'

'Better check your credit cards then.'

Frantically, she unzipped it. 'They're all here. So's the money I withdrew from the hole in the wall this morning.'

He shrugged. 'That's all right then.'

No it wasn't. Her phone, she realised with a sinking thud, was nowhere to be seen. And besides, none of this explained how the car arrived back here before her.

Georgie's stomach began to churn like the drum of a washing machine on spin. It was like a trailer to a weird psychological film that she and Sam had seen at the cinema the other month. The plot had featured a woman who was losing her mind.

'Looks good,' her husband had said.

'Not for me,' she'd shuddered.

And now it was happening to her. Perhaps someone was here, in the house, right now! Or maybe that person had been and gone, having burgled them.

Glancing through the door of the sitting room, she took in the pictures on the walls and the pink cranberry vases that Sam's mother had left them. It didn't look as though anything had been taken, although part of her almost hoped that it had, if only to prove that she wasn't going crazy.

Meanwhile, the driver with the slicked-back hair was waiting to be paid. She pressed a ten-pound note into his hand. The boy had done more than enough.

'Ta.' His tone was slightly mollified by the tip. 'Don't take this the wrong way, miss, but I'd have a bit of a lie down if I were you. Perhaps you've been overdoing it.'

TWO

I've done it. Did what I was told.

Dead simple, really.

All I had to do was keep my eyes open. Knew it was my lucky day when I saw those two magpies.

Usually, I bump into someone or almost run them over. Of course, I make out it's my fault. I say 'Sorry' so much that they start saying sorry themselves. It's only afterwards that they realise their purse or bag or phone is missing.

And by then, I've legged it.

They've also taught us to ask people for directions. Even better if you've got a map. You hold it right up to them and while they're busy trying to help, you pick their pockets.

Sometimes, if we're on airport duty, we're given a partner. You ask someone something to distract them and then the other person nicks their bag. That one works well in hire car depots, especially late at night. I had a French couple the other day where the bloke was loading the cases into the boot and the woman had put her handbag onto the driver's seat. I asked her some questions that didn't make sense – putting on a silly accent – and while she tried to understand what I was saying, my 'partner' sneaked in the other side and got her bag. Bit risky, that one, but we were lucky. We got a passport; an EHIC card; a phone; three credit cards; and five hundred euros in cash. You'd be amazed what they fetch on the black market. As for the euros, we kept a few and passed the rest onto the boss. He's not to know, is he?

Talking of luck, today's was a doddle. I didn't have to bump into that woman with the blonde hair and posh accent. Or ask her the way. She did it all for me by dropping her phone just as I happened to walk by. It was like picking an apple off a tree. I couldn't believe it when she dropped the car keys too. Sat Navs are the icing on the cake. A dream come true.

Home.

What a giveaway.

Don't take anything, they said. But it was tempting when I opened the boot and found that bag with the purse inside. Four lots of twenty-quid smackers.

I touched them, just to feel the crispness.

One day, I'm going to have a stack of notes under the bed. And a phone. I would have kept that one if I didn't need the money so badly.

One day, I'll have a runner of my own to do the dirty work.

'When will I get paid?' I asked my brother.

'When they're ready.'

'Who's they?'

I reeled as the blow hit my cheek. 'Don't ask and you won't be able to tell.'

OK. OK. I get it. Maybe now wasn't the time to tell him about selling on the phone. Or taking one or two other little things.

'Want me to do anything else?'

There was a snort. 'Another geezer will take over now.'

After that, it will be someone else and then someone else. It's the way it works on the estate. You start at the bottom and one day, you won't have to touch the stuff – whether it's money or drugs. Then you can tell the Pigs you had nothing to do with it.

Like I said, I'm going to be at the top one day. That's cos I take risks. If you don't, everyone else will tread on you.

And no one's going to do that to me.

THREE

'Who's that?'

Georgie froze at the sound of footsteps clattering = very deliberately = down the stairs from the third floor.

Sweat streamed from under her arms, sweat she didn't know she was capable of producing. She felt an urgent need to wee. And her voice refused to obey as she tried to scream. 'Stop. STOP!'

Stumbling to the door, she opened the front door to call the taxi driver back. But he'd gone, a flash of silver grey disappearing round the corner.

'Mum?'

Georgie's chest filled with relief as she whipped round, taking in the tall, slim girl with long, dark hair tied up in a casual ponytail. Ellie had always called her Mum. It was, the child psychologist had said, a sign that she needed stability. Not surprising given what she'd been through. Correction. What they'd *all* been through. When a teenager goes off the rails, it affects the whole family.

'Ellie! Thank heavens. I thought we had burglars.'

Her daughter's normally smooth forehead = that complexion was to die for! = creased with confusion. 'Really? I was looking upstairs for you. When I got home, I saw the car was unlocked and found your handbag in the back. So I brought it in. You must be more careful, Mum.'

None of this was making sense.

'But I put it in the boot = not the back.'

'Are you sure?'

Georgie waved her question aside. 'Anyway, why was the door open?'

'Was it?' Ellie bit her lip. 'Sorry. I was so worried about you that I must have just run in and forgotten to shut it.'

Georgie began to feel cold again. 'Not again,' she murmured.

Ellie sighed heavily. 'I wish you and Dad would stop going on about that. It was only the once. And anyway, it was ages ago.'

Once was more than enough, she had to stop herself from saying. She and Sam had gone away for the night, telling themselves that the psychologist was right. They had to learn to trust her. Besides, as Ellie had argued, she was seventeen years old! More than capable of looking after herself for twenty-four hours. But when they'd got back, the back door was swinging in the wind because Georgie had 'forgotten to shut it properly'.

The fact that she and a friend were completely plastered in the cellar 'den', was not entirely unrelated. Nor were the strange-smelling roll-up ends that lay littered around them, not to mention the empty bottles of vodka.

Georgie didn't even want to think about those dark days when, at times, she'd begun to despair that a rebellious Ellie would even get through her A-levels. Yet here she was: a beautiful, composed, 'clean' young woman, about to embark on a PhD. Psychology had seemed a fitting subject, given the amount of help she'd had.

'It's all really weird.' Georgie sat down at the kitchen table next to the comforting warmth of the Aga. For a summer day, there was a nip in the air. Or maybe it was because she couldn't stop shaking.

Ellie put a slim arm around her. She smelt of soap – such a welcome change from the BO-heavy days when she'd refused to change her jeans, let alone have a shower. 'How come you left the bag in the car? Where have you been?'

Her voice began to falter. How to explain? 'I went to see a

20

new client and I *know* I drove there. I had so much stuff to carry that I left my bag in the car. But when I came out, my keys weren't in my portfolio.'

Ellie drew back, frowning again. 'What do you mean?'

Georgie was beginning to feel foolish now. 'It had gone. I had to get a taxi back and ...'

'But the Volvo's outside. I saw it when I came home. Unlocked, like I said. That's why I thought you were in the house.' Ellie's hand tightened on hers. 'I know it's hard now with Nick and me gone but ...'

'It's not like that!'

For the second time in less than an hour, Georgie found herself shouting. What was wrong with her?

'Sorry.'

Ellie's hand began to stroke hers in lovely, slow, comforting circles, just like she'd done with her daughter as a child when she'd had nightmares. 'I know what it's like when you're stressed. You begin to imagine things.'

'But I couldn't. I didn't. I ...' Then she gasped. 'In fact, I can prove it.'

Leaping up, she grabbed her purse, pulling out the receipts until she found the one she wanted. There it was. 'See! I stopped on the way to the client's house to get petrol. It's got the time on it.'

Together they stared at the credit card receipt. There was no doubt about it. The date was clear enough. So too was the time. Just ten minutes before her appointment with the Hon. Mrs R-R.

'And my phone isn't here. You didn't borrow it, did you?'

It wouldn't have been the first time. But Ellie was shaking her head, still looking at the petrol receipt.

'I don't know what to say,' she faltered. 'I'm sorry. I didn't mean to doubt you. It's just that I remember when I imagined things ... when ...'

'It's all right.' Georgie wrapped her arms around her daughter. 'Don't go there. Blank it out.'

21

Don't, she found herself praying fiercely, don't let this make her regress again.

'I'm sure there's a logical reason behind this.' She forced herself to laugh brightly. 'Maybe I'll give your dad a ring. See what he makes of this. I'll ring the bank again too. Just to make sure no one's taken anything. And cancel the phone.'

It took ages. Why hadn't she written down her passwords on a piece of paper instead of on her missing phone? But eventually, it was all done. A kindly voice from the 'Lost or Stolen' option at the other end of the phone confirmed that no one had taken money from her cards in that short time they'd gone missing. Thank heavens. She decided there was no need to cancel them.

'See,' said Ellie, giving her a comforting hug. 'It's all right. Mind you, it might be an idea to call the police to tell them about the phone and the money.'

No. Not the police. For most of her adult life, she'd tried to avoid any unnecessary form filling. Anything that might draw attention to herself. It wasn't worth it. Not this time.

'Maybe later,' she said.

Ellie gave her a worried look. 'Are you sure you're OK, Mum?'

'Fine.' She mustered a smile. Didn't parents always have to be strong? Wasn't it part of their job description? But as she freshened up her make-up (thank goodness she hadn't left her new Yves Saint Laurent lipstick in her bag), Georgie felt as though she'd been mentally violated. Someone had picked up her car keys and somehow found their way back to the house.

No one had broken in and taken anything – both she and Ellie had done a good search of paintings and silver – but it was, to put it mildly, unnerving.

But the missing phone really upset her. When you were freelance, contacts were gold dust. It had nearly all her numbers! How was she going to get hold of her clients without it?

'Idiot,' she told herself crossly.

Meanwhile, Sam was in a meeting. Nothing new there. Be reasonable, she told herself, driving to his office. There might or might not be an economic upturn in the country's finances – depending on which paper you read – but financial advisors had to be sharper than ever. 'There are a lot of wealthy people still about,' her husband would often say. 'But they're also aware that there are far more consultants hoping to make them even richer.'

Wasn't this one of the reasons she had gone out to work? It might have started out as pin money but now her contribution was an important part of the mortgage repayments. They were both working too hard, Georgie told herself as (miraculously) she found a space in the 'Free after 6 p.m.' parking zone. Not for the first time she wished they had stayed put abroad. Life had seemed easier there. More money. A maid. A busy social life to block out the past ...

That's why it was a good idea to take Sam by surprise tonight. Go out for a two-for-one Italian so they could talk. Much as she loved having Ellie come to stay, there were times when they needed some time alone. And this was one of them, especially after an unnerving experience like this.

'Sam's meetings should be over by 7.30,' his secretary had told her.

So here she was. Just in time from the look of things. There was her husband, walking briskly down the stairs, blue tie slightly dishevelled round his neck; mobile phone in his hand, texting as he went. As always, his dark looks were almost a mirror image of his daughter's. Both were stubborn too but with huge reservoirs of love and compassion – sometimes at unexpected times. Georgie had often wondered if it was their similarities which made each so impatient of the other.

'Hi!' There was a happy-surprised look on his face. 'I was just letting you know I was on my way home.'

He waved the phone in front of her as if she needed confirmation. Rather touching, really, even though it was Sam who was the needy one in the emotional department – despite

23

the way he tried to hide it. Even though his mother was dead now, she'd had left her mark, not the least because she'd packed him off to boarding school at the age of eight. 'I never really knew her,' he kept saying after her death. 'You can't have a relationship with someone if you don't know who they are deep down.'

His words had made Georgie shiver.

Now, pushing that memory impatiently to one side, she took her husband's arm. 'Something really weird happened today. I tried to call you but ... Well, I thought we'd have dinner on our own to talk about it. Is that all right?'

His voice tightened. 'Ellie's back?'

She nodded. Ironically, she got on better with her step-daughter than her husband did. Friends joked that it was normally the other way round. Perhaps it was because she was a woman. Or maybe it was because she ...

No. Don't go there.

'What kind of weird?' Sam's question thankfully diverted her. 'Ellie hasn't done anything stupid again, has she?'

Already, Georgie was beginning to wish she'd kept all this to herself. Unlike her, Sam wasn't so keen to accept that his daughter had finally turned the corner. 'No. it's not her. In fact, I was beginning to wonder if it was me. But it can't be, because of the garage receipt ...'

They were approaching the Italian now. Music was spilling out and couples were going in, arm in arm. Others were living normal lives where their cars hadn't disappeared and reappeared. A tantalising smell of garlic reached out to them as they pushed open the door.

'What are you talking about?'

'I'll explain.' For the second time that day, Georgie found herself shaking. 'When we're sitting down.'

The waiter found them their usual table by the window. Normally she loved this position, looking out into the high street. Windsea was a busy market town, justly deserving of its reputation for Regency buildings on the sea front which hadn't been ruined by the developers. But tonight, even the sight of a hen party walking past – complete with giggling girls wearing pink sashes and not much else – couldn't divert her.

Briefly, she explained what happened.

Sam's face looked as though she'd just run out to join the hen party. 'Someone must have taken the car. Someone who knew you'd parked it there.' He put his head in his hands. 'You do know what that means, don't you?'

'No.' Georgie's voice was firm as if trying to convince herself. 'I don't think I do.'

'But she's got a spare key.'

'She lost it. Remember?'

It had been the one blip last month. Ellie had asked if she could borrow the car and come back, having 'dropped it somewhere'. It could have happened to anyone, Georgie had argued in her daughter's defence.

'So she said.'

'But why would she do that?'

'To make trouble? Remember what the consultant said. Cannabis can sometimes do that. Tip you over the edge. Make you act unpredictably.'

'But she's clean now.'

'Are you sure?'

'Yes. Besides, Nick says that …'

Sam put down his pasta fork. 'Nick would say anything to defend Ellie.'

It was true. Nick – as blonde as Ellie was dark – had always adored his big sister. When the ambulance had come that awful night, it had been him who had refused to let her go, screaming until he'd been allowed to follow in the car with them. Only later did Georgie discover that Ellie had persuaded Nick to hide her stash in his wardrobe.

Sam had never forgiven her for that. Maybe that's why he couldn't accept her 'change of heart' now.

'I honestly don't think it was her,' said Georgie slowly, pushing her *salade niçoise* away. Suddenly she wasn't hungry.

Maybe this wasn't such a good idea after all.

'Then we'll agree to disagree. But we'll need to keep a sharp eye on her.'

Georgie nodded reluctantly.

Then he sat back as if making a conscious effort. 'Tell me about your new client.'

Grateful for the change in subject, she told him about the aloof Hon. Mrs R-R. 'Are you on first-name terms with the husband?'

'Sure.' Sam looked as though that was a daft question. 'Maybe she's lacking confidence. In my opinion, people like that want to keep a distance from others.'

Georgie spluttered into her green tea. 'I don't think so. In fact ...'

'We're getting married in the morning!'

'Great.' Sam put down his coffee. 'Looks like the hen party lot are coming in to finish off their celebrations.'

'Finish off!' The chubby brunette with the silver and white 'BRIDE' sash, ruffled his hair in response. 'We're just starting, mate.'

Georgie couldn't help giggling. Sam could be extremely traditional. It was one of the reasons she'd been attracted to him. The sight of a blowsy brunette with a chest that had to be at least a 38 DD almost – but not quite – distracted her from the mystery of the car and the keys.

'I'll pay,' she offered.

That was the nice thing about earning. It made her feel more independent to be able to settle the bill every now and then. Rather naughtily leaving her husband to the attention of the hen party, she made her way to the counter.

'Sorry, Madam.' The manager frowned at the screen. 'Your card has been declined.'

Georgie felt a cold chill running down her back as she looked at the 'Payment Refused' notice.

'It can't have been. There's plenty in the account. In fact, I only used it this morning at the garage. Can we try again?' She keyed in the number, wondering if she'd got it wrong the first time.

PAYMENT REFUSED.

'Do you have another card?'

'No. It's all right. I'll ask my husband.'

Slowly she returned to the table. Sam appeared to be more relaxed now, even asking the bride how long she'd known her 'intended' as he put it.

'Darling.' She touched him on the sleeve. 'There seems to be a bit of a problem ...'

Ten minutes later, they marched back to the car; Sam, his mouth set in a tight line while Georgie's fingers flew across the phone. Thank heavens for telephone banking. Option one for a balance. There had to be a mistake. Maybe the machine wasn't working. Maybe ...

'You are £1,300 in debit,' announced the automatic voice.

But she couldn't be. She was more than that in credit!

'Overdrawn?' demanded Sam grimly.

She nodded.

'By how much?'

She told him numbly. 'My purse. I told you. It was in my bag in the boot of the car.'

'Ring the police.'

'No. Not yet. If we do ...'

'If we do, she'll get her just deserts.'

She. She. Sam had been unable to use his daughter's name when they'd gone through all that stuff before. Would he feel the same about her one day, when – if – he knew more about her?

No. That could never happen.

Georgie began to flounder desperately. 'You don't know for definite that Ellie used the card.'

She stressed his daughter's name deliberately, watching him wince. 'Yes I do. At least put a stop on the bloody thing or she'll try and get more money out of you.'

'It can't be her.' Hot tears stung her eyes. 'Ellie told me to

27

report this to the police. If she was behind it, she wouldn't have suggested that.'

Sam stood by her car, his hands on her shoulders, his eyes heavy with sorrow. 'Please, Georgie. When are you going to face the truth? Ellie banked on you thinking that way. She's taking the piss out of us. Always has done. And always will. It's about time we got tough again. Don't you think?'

Maybe he was right. Maybe ...

Then it hit her. If her daughter had taken her card and her phone, what else had she taken? She always carried so much in her bag. Little things as well as big. It would be so easy for something to go missing without her realising.

'What are you doing?' Sam watched, shocked, as she tipped the contents onto the pavement, sifting her way through them. It had to be there. It had to.

'What are you looking for?'

'It doesn't matter.' Panic made her spit out the words. Her hands were shaking now. She couldn't live without it. She just couldn't. It had been with her through thick and thin. Never would she find another. Never would she find the person who had given it to her all those years ago.

A couple walking past stared at her as she went through everything one more time, to check it hadn't got caught up with something else. 'For pity's sake, Georgie. Tell me what's gone missing.'

How could she?

'Nothing,' she said fighting back the tears. 'I thought I'd mislaid something. That's all.'

'You're upset.' He laid a hand on her arm. 'It's no wonder. Come on. Let's go home.'

Mechanically, she allowed him to help her onto the passenger seat. But all she could think about was her shell. The pink and white shell which was no longer in her bag.

WINDSEA GAZETTE

Fifteen-year-old 'joy-rider from good home' cautioned after breaking into car.

Judge warns that he won't be so 'lenient' if there's a second offence.

FOUR

'I didn't do it,' protested Ellie, rubbing her eyes.

She'd been asleep when they'd got back from the restaurant and even though Sam had been all for waking her up and demanding 'an explanation', Georgie persuaded him against it. Instead, she'd spent hours on the phone trying to cancel all her cards. She still hadn't sorted out everything. Why hadn't she written her passwords down instead of storing them on her missing phone? Thank goodness they were in code.

Nor was she certain (a fear she kept to herself) that all the store cards were there. There were so many of them. John Lewis, House of Fraser ... She should have had them insured by one of those financial services, like her friend Jo who ran a 'shabby chic' antique shop in town.

By the time she finally got to bed, Georgie was exhausted. When she woke, it was to the sound of her daughter and husband arguing in the kitchen.

'I didn't do it,' repeated Ellie. 'Why would I bother trekking out to one of Mum's stupid clients and nicking the car, just to use her credit card? If I wanted to do that, I'd just use it, wouldn't I? It's not as though she bothers to hide her stuff. As for the phone, I've got my own. I don't need hers.'

Georgie stood at the bottom of the stairs, listening. *Stupid clients?* That hurt. So did the '*hers*' bit. So impersonal. So cold after everything she'd done.

'Because you made it look as though there'd been a theft.' Sam's voice was steadily furious.

'You just can't trust me, can you?' There was the sound of something being dumped on the table. A plate, perhaps?

Hopefully not from her bone china set. Not that this mattered in the grand scheme of things.

'Just because of that one incident ...'

'*One* incident? You used my card to buy a grand's worth of drugs.'

This time it was the dishwasher lid that was being slammed shut. 'I paid you back, didn't I? And I'm clean now.'

There was a snort of disbelief. 'So you say ...'

That was enough.

'Please. Both of you.'

They turned towards her. Same dark looks. Same defensive expressions. For the first time in a long while, Georgie felt like the outsider. What had Ellie's mother been like, she had often wondered. What had really made her give up her child? Was it because no one listened to her either? Was it because she was fed up of keeping the peace? Or was it because, as she'd said, she just hadn't been able to cope?

Pretending to be calmer than she felt, Georgie put the kettle on and reached up into the duck-blue Smallbone cupboard for a new packet of ground coffee beans. The rich smell from the packet helped calm her. No wonder people became addicted. Not just to coffee but other substances too ...

'We don't know anything at this stage but ...'

'Have you rung the police like I told you to?' Sam's terse voice, rode over hers in his deep, assured, public school accent.

'No. I told you. There's no need. I've cancelled my cards. The police can't do any more.'

'But that doesn't explain the car being "hijacked".' Her husband's eyes were flashing at Ellie's. 'If she's telling the truth, it means that someone else took it, so the police need to be informed.'

'*If* I'm telling the truth?' Ellie squealed.

'Did you take anything at all?' asked Georgie in a low voice.

'No, Mum. I *told* you.'

There was a thud on the mat, making the dog jump off the rocking chair as he did every day when the papers arrived. No one took any notice.

If ever there was an opportune time for the phone to go, this was it. Georgie dived for the landline with relief. At barely 7 a.m., this had to be reasonably urgent. 'Yes. This is Georgina Hamilton speaking. Yes, I'm happy to run through security checks.'

'Is that the bank?' demanded Sam.

'Not ours,' she hissed, waving at him to be silent so she could hear. 'Mine.'

Apart from their joint account, she had another, purely for work. (Sam did the same.) It would, her accountant had explained, make it easier to keep track on business payments. It was this one which had been used to withdraw the money.

Walking into the sitting room for some peace – the two of them had kicked off again – Georgie sat down on the ornately carved Chinese sofa which she'd shipped back from Hong Kong and ran through the usual polite interrogation.

Date of birth. Mother's maiden name. Fourth letter of her password. Why hadn't she kept the same one for each card? On the third attempt, she got it right.

'Thank you, Georgina, you have passed your security check.'

The voice made it sound as though she had flown through an exam. But the uninvited familiar use of her full name stung in view of the argument raging next door. Was it any surprise she was feeling tetchy? 'Actually, it's Mrs Hamilton if you don't mind.'

Instantly she was reminded of the Hon. Mrs R-R yesterday. Perhaps she'd been wrong to expect her client to welcome her on the same level. Boundaries had to be set. The kitchen voices rose again. Providing they were fair.

With one ear on the argument in the kitchen and the other on the voice at the other end, Georgie found it hard to concentrate. 'Gather you cancelled your card at 11.05 last night … Unfortunately withdrawals made before you did so … Name on card doesn't exactly match our records ... Georgina spelt with a 'J' ...'

What? Jumping up, she dashed over to the Victorian roll-top desk in the bay window where she kept receipts. There it was. Last month's full statement. At the top was her name. Jeorgina ...

'Someone's made a mistake,' she gabbled into the phone. 'Yes. I'll check the card.'

Where was it? Tearing up the stairs to the bedroom, she grabbed her bag, flinging out cards from the purse. Costa; Network Rail; Oyster for rare trips to London; Waterstones credit voucher ... here it was. Sparkling new with her signature freshly written on the back.

Georgina with a G.

Jeorgina with a J, on the front.

Why hadn't she noticed when it had arrived the previous week to replace the old?

'I will still be covered, won't I?' she gabbled.

'I'm afraid I can't answer that until I've made further enquiries.'

Georgie's hands began to sweat on the phone. 'But it's not my fault if some idiot has made a mistake!'

Even as she spoke, she realised she was hardly endearing herself to the authorities. For that's what this woman was! Someone who held the upper hand; the other cards, so to speak. The pun might have been funny at any other time.

'Just a minute,' she said suddenly. 'You said my card had been used. Presumably that was on the phone?'

'I can confirm that it was not a telephone transaction,' replied the voice primly.

Not? 'Then it was used in person?'

'That's correct.'

So why hadn't she said so in the first place? Georgie bit back the question. Far better to get this woman on side, like she did with tricky clients. 'I'm so sorry if I sound snappy. It's just that this is a really worrying time for me.'

The voice softened. 'I understand that.'

'Can you tell me what time the card was used and when?'

'4 p.m. in Croydon and then again at 10.50 p.m. in central London.'

'But I had the card on me then! I got it out to read the number over the phone when I cancelled it.'

The voice was low. Warning. 'I'm afraid it's possible for cards to be duplicated if they are out of someone's possession, even for a short time.'

Three hours. That's how long she'd been at the Hon. Mrs R-R's. Add another hour by the time she'd got back home to find her purse sitting 'safely' inside her bag at home. Was that long enough for someone to make a copy?

'Like I said, Mrs Hamilton, we will look into it and be in touch.'

Helplessly, she made her way back to the kitchen. Something had changed. Ellie was sitting at the table, her arms folded, looking smug. Sam seemed almost − but not quite − repentant. 'My business account has been looted,' said Georgie flatly. 'And apparently it might be my fault because the name was misspelt on the new card and I didn't check.'

She sat down heavily. Beano − their much-loved dog whom they'd got from a rescue place soon after arriving 'home' − started madly licking her hand as if sensing her distress. 'It was used − in person − by someone in Croydon and then again in central London last night, when we were all home.'

'See?' Ellie leaped to her feet. 'Then it couldn't have been me.'

'The woman said people could duplicate cards,' added Georgie reluctantly.

'So *you* don't believe me either?'

'I didn't say that ...'

Ellie was brandishing the local paper in front of her face. 'Look! Some kid has been done for nicking a car. He apparently made a key to get into it and then used the Sat Nav to park it outside the owner's house. Did it for kicks. Now one's done it, others are going to do the same. Even Dad concedes that.

Maybe that's what happened to you.'

Could that really be possible?

They both stared at her. Ellie furious. Sam resigned. It had been like that at the beginning, Georgie suddenly remembered – back in the early days when it had taken her time to understand how a small child ticked. It was only in the teenage years that Georgie had come through – able to understand adolescent angst in a way that Sam (despite his own issues with his mother) had been unable to.

But that didn't matter. Not now. There were more important things to deal with.

'I'm calling the police.' Sam's voice echoed the same thought in her head.

'I'd rather you didn't.' Even as she spoke, Georgie realised it sounded odd.

'Dad's right,' said Ellie tetchily.

There was nothing for it. It took almost as long to get through as it did to the credit card people. Still, this was scarcely a 999 call. Briefly, Georgie explained what had happened.

'Nothing we can do about the credit cards, Madam,' said the kind of voice you might expect behind a teacher's desk from her days at school. 'But we'll file a report on the car. Registration number? Name of registered owner?'

So many details. So much to remember. Such a vast amount of personal data in order to live! No wonder some people just gave up and led simple lives. An institution, at this very moment, seemed quite appealing. Someone else to make all the decisions. Someone who would make sure that her secret was safe. It would be all too easy for one check to lead to another …

Thank heavens her passport hadn't been in the bag.

'I'm going out.' Ellie's eyes flashed.

Georgie felt a tremor of alarm. 'Where?'

'To steal another car.'

Sam groaned. 'That's not funny. I said I was sorry.'

'No you didn't.'

36

'Well, I'm sorry now.'

'Too little, too late. You forget, Dad, I'm studying people like you at the moment. BMs, we call them. Bloody Minded. Unable to see further than their own noses.'

Georgie had to hurry to catch up with her daughter by the front door. 'Did you borrow anything from my bag?' she whispered. 'Like a shell?'

'A shell?' Her daughter gave her a strange look. 'What do you mean?'

'It doesn't matter.' Ellie's face was all the answer she needed. If anyone had taken it, it wasn't her daughter. Perhaps she'd dropped it somehow. The thought made her heart sink with self-reproach.

'Don't blame Dad,' she said to Ellie. 'It's difficult for him.'

Those beautiful almond-shaped eyes swallowed her up, taking her back to that small child who'd arrived so unexpectedly. 'It's not Dad I'm disappointed with. It's you.'

Those eyes flickered. 'For a moment, you doubted me too. Don't deny it. I saw it on your face.' Her hand reached out and touched hers. 'But there's something else troubling you, isn't there? Why didn't you want to call the police?'

How long had she been preparing for this question, or something like it? Why hadn't she told Sam the truth all those years ago? How could she have hidden something so big for so long?

In a way, it would be a relief to shed the burden. To come clean and take the consequences, come what may. 'Actually,' she began, shepherding her daughter back into the privacy of the house, but before she could close the door, there was the sound of a car outside.

'Mrs Hamilton!'

This time her name was said with a joviality that, after all their sessions, would surely earn the right to use a more informal address. After all, the computer man had come highly recommended by Jo, who'd used him to set up her laptop connections in the shop. Some of the others in the local

Women's Business Network used him too.

'Sorry I'm early but I had a cancellation!' The small, bearded man beamed at her. Dimly, Georgie recalled the appointment which was written in her beautifully-formed calligraphy style in the diary.

'I was going to run a check on your hard drive. Remember? See why it's running so slowly.'

Ellie was already by the gate now, heading down the road. At least her daughter's absence had got her off the hook. For the time being.

'Please, come in,' she said to the computer man. 'Just go straight to the office. I'll be there in a minute.'

At the same time, the landline rang. This was getting mental.

'Georgie?'

'Jo! I was just thinking about you.'

'Have you got a second?'

Something was up. She could sense it.

'Remember when I paid you for the job directly into your bank account?'

She remembered the job all right. Jo had wanted a new look for the shop and Georgie's idea of differently coloured themed walls had proved quite a lure for customers. She'd also got some editorial in *Shop Beautiful* as a result, great stuff for her portfolio.

In return, Jo had given her a heavy discount for a beautiful pine wardrobe that she'd bought for Ellie.

'Yes. I think so …'

'My bank has just rung. Apparently you've been taking money out of my account.'

'Me?' Georgie froze. 'That's impossible.'

'Well, I knew you wouldn't have done it.' Jo's voice was warily reassuring. 'But someone posing as you has done it. Don't ask me how. But I need to warn you that my bank's security people are going to be in touch if they haven't already.'

'Is there any way that someone else could have got my bank details from you?' continued Jo tightly. 'Remember when you bought the wardrobe? I asked you to pay it into my private account because of the discount.'

'Yes. Yes, I do. But ...'

Oh my God.

'What?'

The notebook. The small one that she kept for customer details together with their bank account details. That had been in her bag too. Breaking out into a sweat, Georgie dashed back up the stairs to rifle through her bag again.

It wasn't there.

'Georgie? Georgie? Can you hear me?'

Make a paper note, the computer man had advised during his last visit. *'Not that I want to put myself out of business but sometimes the old-fashioned ways are best.'*

'Yes,' she said numbly. 'I'm still here.'

FIVE

I like this bit. Using the card, that is. I don't get to keep all the cash, of course. Only some of it, though they're not to know that.

After all, I've got to have something for taking chances.

Between you and me, I'd do it anyway. There's something about putting a stolen card in the machine and putting in the pin number that gives me a real thrill.

It's almost addictive. Like walking along a cliff edge. Wondering if someone is going to jump out and say 'What do you think you're doing?'

Some people live on adrenaline. That's me. Otherwise, life just gets too boring. Who wants a nine to five job? It would drive me nuts.

Hacking is a great career. You just have to know what you're doing.

I started off on the bottom level, like the kid who picked up the key. That was the stage I was at a few years ago. But then they realised I was a bit of a geek and got me onto the copying stage instead.

All you need is the right machine and there you go. Different card. Same number. Pretty impossible to tell the difference. Don't ask me how we get the pin. One of the other lads does that.

'What did you do before this?' you might ask me if I was on the telly.

Funnily enough, I tried to get straight when I was sixteen. It was when my mate got six years. I thought, 'Do I really want this?' So I got a job at the bookies, but it was always the same. Miserable old men coming in and hoping that their life would change if they got a winner. When they did, they'd only bet it all again and then lose.

Did my head in, it did.

In between punters, I began playing round with the computer. Then one day, this bloke parked his Merc on a double yellow outside and came in to place a bet.

He won a grand. But he didn't get all excited. He just acted as though it was his right. That impressed me, it did.

The next Tuesday, at 3 p.m. – always the time when my boss left me in charge = he placed another bet. Here we go again, I thought. Stupid idiot. You'll only lose everything you got last time.

But he didn't. He won two grand this time.

Once more, he acted like it was nothing special. So I got straight back on the computer. Like I said, I've always been good with figures. When he came in the next week, I told him that I'd worked out how he'd done it and I was going to shop him.

It wasn't true of course. It's not as simple as that. My guess was that he'd bribed the other jockey – the one that was tipped to win = but I couldn't prove it.

I could bluff, mind you.

'Shop me?' He'd laughed, fingering the gold chain round his neck. His eyes narrowed. 'I could do the same to you. I've watched you cream off the odd tenner here and there. My mates have been observing you, see.'

That threw me. It was more than the odd tenner, you see. Maybe he was bluffing too. Maybe not.

Then he ran a finger down the side of his nose. Did I mention it was crooked? The way he touched it made me think that if I didn't play fair, I might end up with broken nose too.

'Why don't you come and work for me and we'll call it quits?'

And that's how it all started.

SIX

Jo, who was always nice to everyone, was blanking her.

Not surprising, really. Not after Georgie had had to tell her that someone had stolen the book with all her clients' banking details. It was just one more puzzle in this increasingly complex nightmare.

'Why did you leave it in the car?' her friend had demanded when Georgie had gone down to the shop to explain the theft face to face. Jo pressed her lips together in distress. Ironically, she was wearing a pretty apricot shade of lipstick which, only the other week, Georgie had helped her choose.

'I was carrying too much.' It seemed silly when she said it out loud. 'I was worried about dropping it.'

Jo took off her glasses, rubbed them furiously against her Phase Eight silk top as if erasing Georgie's crime, and then replaced them. 'It might have been better if you had. Why didn't you store it on the computer instead?'

You couldn't win, thought Georgie miserably as she apologised for the umpteenth time, horribly aware that the bunch of stargazers she'd brought with her were a pretty pathetic apology. If you kept everything electronically, you could lose it if your computer messed up.

But if you wrote them down, someone could take them. Her friend Jo wouldn't be the only one, the police had warned her when she'd finally summoned up the courage to call them. She'd probably find that other clients would have their accounts tapped into.

'Best ring each one of them,' the officer had told her on the phone. 'Give them a chance to change their details before something happens – if it hasn't already.'

So before calling in on Jo, she'd called each customer on her newly bought phone (Ellie had helped her go back through her website's emails to find the details) to explain what had happened.

Reactions varied from confused ('What should I do?') to downright angry ('If I'd known this was going to happen, I would have used one of the proper firms in town.')

Only one person understood: one of the girls in their Business Network group whose laptop had been hacked. 'It's a horrible thing. You'll probably find you lose clients, I'm afraid. Bit of a learning curve. So unfair too. After all, it wasn't my fault.'

But this was hers, Georgie told herself as she finally finished making all those calls. She had to take the blame for her stolen identity.

After all, hadn't she committed a similar crime herself, all those years ago?

She'd been eighteen. Nearly nineteen. Not much younger, really, than Ellie. Rebellious and deeply resentful of life in general. In particular of her mother.

'You always said you'd never marry again after Dad,' she had raged when Mum had announced, out of the blue, that she'd been seeing 'someone else' and that she hoped Ellie would be happy for her.

'Your father died before you were born.' Her mother's strong Yorkshire accent sliced through the furious air. As if she needed reminding! Hadn't she felt different from all the other girls over the years? 'Don't I deserve some happiness now?'

Georgie had gripped the side of the cheap yellow plastic kitchen table to steady herself. It was stacked with the remainder of her A-level textbooks. At least Mum had had the decency to drop the bombshell *after* the exams. The worst thing was that she had a point. Why should she be alone for ever? Even so …

'I'm not going to college if you marry some stranger,' she found herself saying.

Her mother's eyes widened in shock. Georgie felt an unpleasant flash of pleasure. All her mother had ever wanted was for her daughter to get a degree like the girl next door. Well, it was all changing now.

'You don't mean that,' Mum had said, moving towards her.

'Don't try and touch me! Yes I do.'

In truth, Georgie had simply intended to shock when she'd first made her threat. But now it was snowballing and she couldn't take it back.

Mum was folding her arms now, shooting her a defiant expression. So much for the conciliatory approach. 'What will you do then?'

Georgie looked away. As she did so, her eye caught the cover of her Geography textbook. Asia sprawled out across the page in vibrant pinks and blues. Colours had always grabbed her more than words. It was why she'd been insistent on studying fashion instead of a 'more academic subject', as her teachers had put it.

'I'll go to Thailand,' she said with more certainty than she felt inside. 'For a gap year.'

'A gap year?'

The apprehension in her mother's voice was almost worth it. Girls in her neighbourhood didn't do gap years. They either went straight to work after school or straight to college. No luxury of lounging around for 'people like them'.

'Why not?'

Her mother had turned her back now and was fussing with the tea towels; neatly folding them as if the action might sort out her daughter at the same time. 'Who's going to pay for that then?'

'I'll use the money Gran left me.'

'That's for emergencies.'

Georgie snorted. 'What do you think this is?

Then she slammed the door behind her in what felt like a very satisfactory exit.

It took a while to sort out things like tickets and visas: a period during which Georgie knew she was doing the right thing. You only had to look at the arrogant, cocky man whom her mother was planning on marrying (a salesman!), to know that she couldn't have stood living there another day.

'He'll only be around in the holidays,' her friend Lyndsey had pointed out. 'Couldn't you cope with that?'

But no, she couldn't. The very thought of Mum with a near-stranger in her bed made her feel sick. Besides, Lyndsey was just upset because she was going to do her degree in London too, near St Martin's where Georgie had a place. She couldn't bear to be parted from Georgie. Not after being at primary and then secondary school together.

'I'll only be a year behind you by the time I get back,' Georgie had pointed out.

'If you get back.' Lyndsey had given her an I-know-you look. 'You won't want to return once you get a taste of freedom. That's what my mum says.' She put a hand on Georgie's arm. 'I'm just upset because I'll miss you. I'd love to go, to be honest. But Mum wouldn't let me.'

Won't want to return? Lyndsey's mum had been right. From the minute Georgie stepped off the boat (after a long coach trip from Bangkok), she knew she'd made the right decision. Mum and her stupid bloke were another world away here on this remote Thai island, though funnily enough, Dad was closer than ever. She might never have seen him, but he was always with her.

'I always wanted an adventure,' he seemed to whisper inside her head. 'I'm proud of you, girl.'

That was all very well but inside, Georgie was shaking. Where was she going to go now? She'd told her mum it was 'easy' to get a job out there and Mum, not knowing any better, had swallowed it.

But here she was, in a line at a bottled water stand, along with loads of other teenagers her age – all chattering in groups – without any idea of where to go.

'Where are you going?' asked a voice behind her.

Georgie swung round – and gawped. The girl behind her was so similar they could almost be twins. Same height, around five foot six. Same blonde hair. Almost the same pert noses except that hers had a slight kink in it from a childhood fall on her bike. They were even wearing the same shade of turquoise top, although she'd run hers up on her mother's old machine and the girl's looked much better.

'I saw you on the bus,' said the girl. Her voice was higher than hers, noticed Georgie. Better spoken too. 'On your own, are you?'

She nodded, trying to find her voice. Dad had been from London. Maybe that's why she had always made a conscious decision not to speak like her mother. Anything to bring her closer to him …

'Where are you going then?'

Georgie took a deep breath. 'Not sure yet. Thought I'd get my bearings first.'

'Good idea.' The girl got out her purse. 'I'm meeting up with friends on the beach. It's a sort of commune. We do various jobs and share our earnings.'

Sounded like another world. One she was excluded from.

'Next,' barked the small, short-sleeved shirt man at the counter.

Georgie handed over some money and received a cool bottle. She stepped aside to take a drink, which was wonderful.

Her friend, meanwhile, had bought her own bottle and had come back to join Georgie. 'You can come with me if you like.'

The invitation took Georgie by surprise.

'Really?'

'Sure.' The girl's eyes flickered up and down. 'We could do with another pair of hands after Louisa …'

Her voice tailed away.

What happened to Louisa, Georgie wanted to ask, but something held her back.

'My name's Georgina,' said the girl, putting out her hand.

'Really? Mine too, but they call me Georgie.'

She could have added that a fancy name like Georgina (her great-grandmother's name) had made one boy tease her at primary school which was why she'd promptly abbreviated it at the age of eleven. But something held her back.

'Wow. What a coincidence.' The new Georgina's eyes sparkled. 'What's your surname then?'

'Smith'.

'Georgina Smith.' Her new friend repeated both names as though she'd said something miraculous.

Then she gave a sort of half-laugh. The kind which posh people gave.

'There's no need to be rude,' Georgie heard herself saying.

'I'm not.' The girl reached out and touched her arm as though they were already good friends. 'I'm just a bit taken aback. My name's Smith too, you see. Well, Peverington-Smith, actually.'

She stepped back as though appraising her. Suddenly, Georgie felt very scruffy after travelling, in comparison with this vision before her. They might look rather similar from a physical point of view but this girl's confidence and way of carrying herself – such poise! – instantly set her apart. It was the kind of self-belief which money and class gave you, thought Georgie rather enviously.

'What brings you out here?'

None of your business, she almost said. But partly because of the heat, which made it hard to think straight, and partly because her new friend's face was so open and kind, she found herself being utterly honest. 'Mum's marrying someone else. I just wanted to get away.'

Georgina Peverington-Smith (what a mouthful!) nodded sympathetically. 'Do you like him?'

'No.'

'My parents are both dead.' She announced this in a matter-of-fact way as if this wasn't unusual.

'I'm sorry,' she said. 'My dad's dead too. I don't even remember him.'

But both remarks were lost in a high wolf-whistle that was coming from – goodness! – Georgina's long, elegant fingers at her lips. 'Joly! Over here.'

'Come on,' she said, grabbing Georgie's arm. 'The boys are here. With any luck, there'll be just enough room in the van.'

The mobile hummed in Georgie's pocket, catapulting her forwards twenty-two years to her beautiful Smallbone kitchen.

'Hello,' she said, in an accent the old Georgie would never have recognised.

'Georgie?' For a minute, she thought it was the original Georgina speaking with those assured vowels. 'It's Mrs Riches-Romer here.' The tone was cool. Aloof. 'Have you forgotten our appointment?'

But it wasn't until next week!

'I've got 11 a.m. on my iPad.' The voice spoke as though there was no other possibility.

'I've got 11 a.m. for next week,' said Georgie hesitantly.

'Well, one of us is wrong. It's not me, I assure you.' There was an irritated cluck at the other end. 'If you're here within the next twenty minutes, I'll make time to see you. Otherwise I think we'd better call the whole thing off, don't you?'

It wasn't so much a question as a statement.

Looking wildly round the kitchen for the plans she'd started, Georgie grabbed the car keys. 'I'll be there.'

There was silence at the other end of the phone. Either they'd got cut off or the Hon. Mrs R-R didn't believe in goodbyes.

The phone rang again. She'd spoken too soon. 'I'm just on my way.'

'Mum? It's me. Nick.'

Nick. Georgie paused mid-flight. Nick rarely rang unless

something was wrong. His loan had run out. He needed picking up from the station. Or – as on the last occasion – he needed his cricket stuff posted to him by the next day. All the way up to Durham, where he was staying on for the summer holidays to be with friends and then travel round Europe for a month, before going back to uni. It hurt that he wasn't home right now although Sam, with his years of boarding school experience, said it was 'natural'.

She could see their boy now. Small and slight in frame, with that blond floppy fringe that he refused to cut. A deliberate way of talking, just like his father. A geek but not in an unattractive way. Someone in the family who specialised in IT would be very useful, as Sam was always pointing out.

'Darling, may I ring you back?'

'This is important. Are you near your computer?'

Georgie began to feel uneasy. 'Why?'

'I got a random email earlier with a YouTube link in it. I'm sending it to you now. There's something you ought to see.'

SEVEN

It's incredible how easy it is to extract bank details if you know what you're doing. Frankly, I'm amazed anyone's daft enough to do online banking. It's like putting all your money outside the door of your flat and asking people to help themselves.

People who know what to do with it, that is.

I was a bit of a loner at school. Don't mind admitting it. Computers were my saviour. Not that we had one of our own. But there was a teacher at school who let me into the computer room at break time.

'I didn't have many friends myself at your age,' he told me.

Who needs friends when you've got something to do all day? There are times when I get so carried away that I don't know where the time goes.

And to think I get paid for it as well.

There's only one thing that makes me feel uncomfortable. I don't know who my paymaster is. I suspect I'm not the only one working on this particular project. When they emailed me my brief, they mentioned some kid who'd pretended to help some woman who'd dropped her stuff and then stolen her key. An amateur, apparently. Someone new to the job.

There are others involved too. Including some bloke who used to work in a betting shop.

That made me feel a bit uneasy. I don't want to be mixed up with those kind of criminals. We're a cut above that. Intelligent crime. That's us. Or rather, me.

Amazing how fast it's evolving. The buzz word on

everyone's lips is 'mental manipulation'. We make the victim imagine that the crime is their fault. Take the car, for instance. Someone lower down than me nicks the car key and then calls us. We drive it somewhere safe, copy the credit card, and then – thanks to Sat Nav – drive the car back home.

The important bit (and this is crucial), we don't do what other gangs do and clean the house out. The boss is really clear on that. Even if there's a window open, we just park the car nearby and beat it. This is the dangerous bit but so far, no one's been caught.

'You've got to make it look like no crime's been committed.' That's the golden rule. Engraved right on my wallet, it is.

With any luck, the victim's family accuse her of imagining she's driven the car back herself and 'forgotten'. (I say 'she' because this approach works best with women. More emotional, in my view.) Then because the card is still in the bag, the victim is lulled into a sense of false security. This buys us time to use the duplicate before the number's stopped.

Clever, eh?

Then of course you can embellish it. Put stuff on the internet. Play a few games. It makes it more fun …

You'll see.

EIGHT

YouTube? Georgie wasn't particularly technical but panic made her determined to sort this one out. Especially as Nick had rung off with a hurried 'Must go or I'll be late for lectures'. Otherwise, she'd have got him to talk her through it.

Google. YouTube. Now what? 'Check out your name,' Nick had said.

Georgina Hamilton.

When she'd got married, it had been such a relief to have a new name. A clean slate. A fresh future. But then, however much she tried to stop them, the doubts kept creeping in. Now, as she turned on the laptop which she kept in the kitchen for easy access, she felt wary.

Oh my God.

Mouth dry, she took in the pout. The pert bottom pushed out behind as if she was in a yoga pose. A face that was hers but which didn't match the said bottom – or the breasts which were voluptuously straining to escape from the kind of low-cut top which she wouldn't be seen dead in.

Someone had taken her face and matched it with other body parts.

Stunned, Georgie read the text which had emerged and was now swimming down the page.

DO NOT TRUST THIS WOMAN. SHE CLAIMS TO BE AN INTERIOR DECORATOR BUT SHE'S AN IMPOSTER.

Below was a logo.

The same font as hers on her headed paper. The same

colours: blue and sage green.

But instead of saying *Home with Style*, it was *Sex with Style*.

Thoughts raced round her head just like before. It couldn't be happening. It just couldn't be. Was it linked to the car; to her bag; to her credit cards? To her stolen mobile?

There had to be someone she could ring. Someone who could make this kind of filth disappear. Oh my God. Nick. He had seen this. What would he think? Was this why he had got off the phone so fast?

And if *he* had seen it, who else had?

Sam. She needed to tell Sam. But then again, was that the right thing to do in his present frame of mind? He might blame Ellie again. Insist that somehow this was her 'fault' too, along with the stolen credit card.

Maybe the computer man might be a better option. But that would mean showing him the image which was – let's face it – pretty distasteful. Just looking at what her 'screen twin' was doing with that duster …

Georgie felt sick. She had to stop this, whatever it took.

His number was actually in the family address book under Comp Help with an exclamation mark. Now the latter seemed stupid. This was serious stuff. 'It's Georgie Hamilton speaking. Something rather odd has happened to me and I just wondered if you could talk me through how to delete something on YouTube.'

Miraculously – given that he was usually booked up – he came round within the hour.

Briefly, she explained before turning away. She couldn't bear to take a second look at this woman, pretending to be her. 'Is it still there?'

'Yup.'

To her relief, he didn't seem as shocked as she'd expected although when she forced herself to turn back – still avoiding eye contact with the screen – she could see he was stroking his beard more than usual.

'Stolen identity is the modern equivalent of mugging,' he said, using more words in a sentence than she'd ever heard him use before. Usually the computer man treated the English language with scepticism. Georgie was sure that the reason people like him loved their work so much, was because it was an escape from the real world.

'Don't worry,' he continued, pressing keys that Georgie hadn't even considered before on the keyboard. 'I've seen worse.'

'How much worse?' Georgie wanted to say but then stopped herself. Of course he couldn't say. It would be confidential. If he did, it meant he might talk about her.

'I've got a customer who discovered someone had made a film of her doing it with a cow. You might know her. She lives in …'

'I don't want to know,' said Georgie quickly, cutting in. 'And I'd be grateful if you didn't mention this to anyone else.'

He frowned. ''Course I won't.'

The frown remained. Either she'd really annoyed him or something wasn't right.

'You can get it off, can't you?' she asked.

'In theory, no. Not without reporting it to YouTube and that can take them time to contact the person responsible – even if they can trace them. Some are very good at hiding their tracks and just disappear.' More beard stroking. 'I've tried getting in touch but unfortunately, it won't let me do it at this moment.'

Why did everyone talk about computers as though they were real, living entities?

Georgie's mouth grew even drier. 'My bag was taken recently. I didn't think anything had been stolen but then someone started using my credit card.'

Georgie glanced at her watch. She should be at the Hon. Mrs David Riches-Romer's now. Correction. She should have been there nearly an hour ago. 'Do you know how much longer this will take?'

There was a shake of the head. 'Nope.'

'Then do you mind if I leave you to it, then? Only I'm meant to be somewhere else.'

'Cool.'

No, thought Georgie. It wasn't cool at all. It was a nightmare. 'Ring if you need me.'

There was no answer. The computer man was too busy clicking odd-looking icons and bringing up squares of figures she'd never seen before. If you don't go now, Georgie told herself, you'll lose a client.

'This really isn't good enough.'

Once more, the Hon. Mrs David Riches-Romer was standing on the doorstep, her arms folded as if she'd been waiting there since her phone call.

'And I thought I told you not to park outside.'

She glared at Georgie's Volvo, defiantly adjacent to the row of privet bushes, framing the pillar balustrade overlooking the lawn.

'I didn't want to park in the lane because my car was stolen last time.'

'Really?' Mrs R–R looked mildly interested. 'How did you get back, then?'

'I took a taxi.'

Georgie waited for her to say that she should have sought her help back at the house. But she didn't.

'Did the police find it, then?'

'No.' Georgie began to feel rather silly. 'It was at home. My home.'

Her new client's eyes narrowed. 'How very strange.'

She doesn't believe me, Georgie told herself as she followed her in. She doesn't think I'm telling the truth.

'Right.' There was a cluck as if there had been enough chit-chat. 'Take a seat. Let's look at your plans.'

Usually, Georgie went to a great deal of trouble, drawing the outline of the room and putting pretty swatches and watercolour stripes to indicate different colour-ways. But with the time taken up over reporting the stolen account details, she'd had to rush her presentation.

Fail to prepare and prepare to fail. That's what Sam always said. Maybe that's why failure wasn't in his book.

'Is this it?' The Hon. Mrs R-R's eyebrows rose. For some reason, Georgie wondered if she had them threaded or waxed. The other month, she'd taken Ellie to Fenwick's in London for the former.

Concentrate, concentrate ...

'... looks more like a kindergarten drawing.'

Georgie's hands tightened on the piece of paper. 'I know. I'm sorry.' She took a deep breath. 'To be honest, I've had some personal problems.'

Something softened in the other woman's face. 'Why don't you sit down and tell me about it?'

Every now and then, Georgie's clients amazed her. Sometimes it was when they came up with an incredible idea themselves. All too often, it was when they insisted on a scheme that was so horrible – like leopard-print walls – that she didn't want to put her name to it. Occasionally, it was when a seemingly-pleasant woman became thoroughly nasty (like the one who had refused to pay her bill because 'on reflection' it was too high – even though it had been agreed at the beginning.) And sometimes, it was because an initially haughty client began to thaw.

This transformation, however, was almost incredible. The Hon. Mrs R-R sat and listened sympathetically as Georgie recounted the extraordinary events of the last week. 'It's frightening what people can do with computers,' she shuddered. 'I found that someone set up a direct debit in my name last year. Don't ask me how. I didn't find it for months because I don't always check my statements.'

Looking around at the paintings on the walls, Georgie could see why. The Lowry above the fireplace, her client had already mentioned, was an original. Clearly, Mrs R-R didn't need to worry financially.

'I presume you've told the police.'

'Apparently it's a matter for my bank.'

'What about the car theft?'

She flushed. 'I haven't reported it, to be honest. My husband thinks … he thinks it might have been a personal matter.'

Mrs R-R frowned. 'What do you mean?'

If there was one thing Georgie shied clear of, it was sharing her family problems with clients. But she'd already gone too far. 'Our daughter – my stepdaughter – has had a history of … well … emotional problems.'

There was a shrill peal of laughter. 'Mental illness? I know all about that. Trust me.'

Then her eyes hardened and suddenly Mrs R-R was back to the woman she'd been a few minutes ago. 'Look, I don't normally give people second chances.'

Georgie could believe it.

'But I'm prepared to make an exception in your case.' She got out her iPad. 'We'll make another appointment for a week today. Same time.'

She spoke as if assuming this was convenient for Georgie's diary too. In fact, it clashed with another client, but she'd just have to change that. 'Let's hope you come up with something a little better than this, shall we?'

The Hon. Mrs R-R cast a disparaging look at the plans in Georgie's hands. 'Otherwise, I don't think it's going to be possible to do business. Do you?'

Georgie found herself agreeing like a naughty school girl.

'Now let me show you out.'

This time, she took her through another corridor, one which she hadn't shown her before. It was lined with watercolours on either side: vibrant pictures with bold strokes. 'They're lovely,' Georgie exclaimed. Such a change, she almost added, from the cream everywhere else.

'You think so?' Mrs R-R raised those eyebrows again. 'I used to be an art student.'

'You painted these?' Georgie was stunned. It was hard to

equate this woman with bland tastes with someone who had the vision and courage to create these landscapes: quintessentially English with those fields of buttercups you could almost pick out of the canvases.

Her client stared at her, unflinching, as if daring her to voice her thoughts. 'It was a long time ago. Part of my therapy, so to speak.'

A long time ago. Part of my therapy. The words played in Georgie's mind over and over again as she drove home. It had been a long time since she'd felt as insecure as she did now. How frighteningly easy it was to forget. Twenty-two years ago, her life could have ended. Surely her family would forgive her if they knew the truth … Then Sam's face swam into her mind. Strong. Successful. Expecting others to be the same.

Maybe not.

They were all so welcoming! Well, most of them.

'I had to get away from home,' she'd explained on the bus when one of the boys, Joly – which was short for Jolyon apparently – asked why she was travelling alone.

Georgina had nodded sympathetically. 'I get that all right. Not that I've got a home any more.'

'Fuck off,' said one of the girls. 'You've got three to choose from.'

Joly put a protective arm around Georgina, even though he was driving. 'You know what she means.'

Was this anything to do with her new friend's parents being dead? She didn't like to ask.

'Where do *you* come from, Georgie?' asked Georgina, turning round to face her.

'Yorkshire.' She spoke abruptly, looking out through the window at the fields and shacks with their tin roofs. Don't ask me any more, she wanted to say. That's why I'm here. To leave that behind.

But Georgina seemed interested. 'Do you have any brothers or sisters?'

'No.' What was this? Twenty questions? Nice as she was, this girl was too pushy. Or was it because she herself was simply being too sensitive?

'Changing the subject,' said one of the other boys – who, rather flatteringly, seemed to keep looking at her – 'what are we going to call you? We've already got one Georgina. And Georgie's too similar.'

'We'll manage,' said Georgina, flicking back her blonde hair and winking conspiratorially. She'd have given anything to have such an easy confidence! On the face of it they might look alike, but Georgina's self-assurance and beautiful skin (if only she could get rid of those spots on her own chin), not to mention her perfect teeth (hers had an annoying gap right in the middle) that made her stand out. So too did her clothes: that wrap-around skirt and halter-neck top was so much more feminine than her own homemade shorts and top.

As for Joly, he was drop-dead gorgeous, like a young Robert Redford with that blond, floppy fringe, easy confidence, and beautiful manners ('After you'). If he wasn't so way out of her league – and clearly 'taken' – Georgie would have been completely smitten. As he wasn't, she felt quite relaxed when speaking to him.

'We'll manage?' repeated the thin-nosed girl, with a sarcastic sniff. 'There we go again. You have to be in charge, don't you?'

'Vanda,' said Joly sharply, looking round and glaring.

Vanda and Joly? What kind of names were these? She'd never heard anything like them before. Her old school mates would have had a field day. She wished Joly would keep his eyes on the road, too. The drivers here were crazy. Just look at that car haring past them – and the bike with a whole family on it, complete with a pig in the woman's arms.

'I think Georgie and Georgina will do just fine,' said Joly, firmly. He screeched to a halt. 'What do you think of your new home?'

For a minute, Georgie could hardly breathe. Instead, she just stared at the impossibly white beach and the incredible blue sea stretching away like a silk counterpane with sparkling silver lights. What colours! You could almost touch the textures ...

Between the beach and the sea was a row of tents. 'They're quite comfortable,' said Georgina, noticing her expression.

'Especially if you have someone to snuggle up to,' added Joly, pulling her towards him.

It was clear the two were an item. She only hoped the boy with those staring eyes didn't presume they would be too. There was something about him that freaked her out.

'It's great,' she said, forcing herself to sound more confident than she felt.

'You can share with me if you like,' said the girl with the thin nose and lumpy ankles.

'Thanks.' For a moment, she'd been afraid it was going to be a mixed tent. They seemed just the kind of teenagers who'd do that kind of thing. For heaven's sake. She was beginning to sound like her mother.

'Or you could share with me,' said the boy who'd been staring.

Georgie smiled, trying to suggest she was taking it as the joke it was surely meant to be.

But his hand brushed hers. 'I mean it.'

He did too! Georgie's skin crawled. 'Actually, I'd rather stick to the arrangements I've just made.'

As she spoke, Georgie was aware she sounded prudish but the girl with lumpy ankles snorted. 'That's telling you, Jonathan.'

The boy gave her a meaningful look. 'Pity.'

Once more, Georgie shivered. Still, she told herself, following the others out of the van, wasn't this the adventure she'd wanted?

This is an adventure, she told herself, jumping off the van. Wasn't that exactly what she wanted?

NINE

The thing is that everyone has a past. Even posh people. I can see from the screen in front of me that I'm dealing with one of these, right now. She's got friends with names you don't get round here.

As for the sums of money, I'm quite surprised. All that just for giving people advice on how to decorate their homes? I looked her up, got to admit. I don't normally do that but for some reason, this woman intrigued me.

Quite a looker, actually. Gorgeous Georgie. You can say that again. I've always had a thing for blondes. Still, she must need her head looking at if she's going to put her picture up for any mad man to drool over. I'm constantly surprised by how naïve people are about that kind of thing.

Her house is nice too. I took a virtual guided tour from when it had been on the market. Of course it should have been taken down years ago, but there are ways of finding these things. It's another giveaway, just like the picture. Might as well slap a notice on your house, saying *Burgle me!*

Made me take a look around my own place, in fact. Gorgeous Georgie might not be too impressed by the patch of damp on the ceiling. I would get the council in but I'm not meant to be here at all. The flat belongs to my boss.

Ask no questions. It's one of the first rules of the game.

Rules are made to be broken, sometimes. 'What do you want me to do next?' I emailed after I'd given him the information he wanted.

I'm still waiting.

Meanwhile, the missus wants me to go out and get a takeaway. The kids fancy Chinese. You look surprised. Thieves – or rather organised criminals – have families too, you know. They do ordinary things. They do weekly shops at supermarkets and pay like anyone else.

But inside, all the time, we think differently. How can we trick someone? How can we siphon off their funds without them knowing?

Just as well you can't see inside our heads.

Not like the way I can see inside your bank account. Or know what your middle name is on your passport.

Scared? You should be. Nowadays, nothing is safe. Least of all, your own identity.

TEN

It had been two weeks since this nightmare started. And still there was no end to it.

'There has to be something you can do,' demanded Sam in the car on the way over to dinner with friends.

He'd said this several times already, as if repetition might somehow sort it all out. Georgie drummed her nails on the steering wheel impatiently. (She'd agreed, as usual, to drive since she was the one who'd given up drink years ago. 'A long story,' she would tell anyone who enquired, before changing the subject.)

'I've told you. There isn't. The police don't want to get involved with YouTube. They say it's nothing to do with them. And the computer man has shown me how to lodge a complaint with the administrators.'

'But surely they must be able to stop it?'

'It takes time, apparently.'

Sam's mouth tightened. 'And meanwhile, anyone Googling your name comes up with a picture of you wielding a feather duster and wearing very little.'

The barrage of questions had made her stall at the lights. 'I don't like it any more than you.'

There was a snort. 'Well, you don't seem that upset about it.'

There was a crunch as she went into third instead of first. She hadn't done that, Georgie told herself crossly, since she was learning to drive. 'Of course I'm upset. But I'm more upset about the fact that someone has hacked into my clients' accounts. Jo isn't speaking to me at the moment.'

'And remind me what the police are doing about that one?'

'Looking into it,' she replied tightly. In the end, she'd had to file a police report to satisfy the credit card companies. It had been easier than she'd thought. Too easy. Supposing they put two and two together …

'At least they haven't taken any money from your other accounts.'

'In a way, it would be better if they had.'

Sam shot her a sideways look which she sensed, rather than saw. Georgie was fastidious about keeping her eyes on the road when driving.

'Why?' he replied, incredulously.

'Because it looks as though I'm guilty.' She signalled left into Tudor Drive, where they were due in five minutes' time. 'Don't you see? If I'm the only one who's not losing money – apart from that one bank transaction – it looks as though I'm behind it. Apparently, credit card thieves usually try to buy things two or three times in quick succession before anyone gets onto it.'

She took a deep breath. 'From the way the security people spoke, they seemed suspicious it was only used once. I got the feeling they thought I engineered it somehow. And they didn't like the fact that my name was spelt with a "J" instead of a "G". They made me feel it was my fault.'

'Didn't you check?'

The implied criticism stung.

'No, all right? I know I should have done but you don't expect banks to get it wrong, do you?'

She'd stopped now, outside a handsome, detached Edwardian house. It had been the views they'd bought it for, her friend Pippa had once said – that wonderful sight of the sea. Sam's eyes were bright now with apprehension. 'They'll sort it out. They have to.'

'Maybe. Maybe not. She leaned her head on the steering

wheel. If only life could work like the tide; in and out with a reassuring, soothing clockwork pattern. 'The thing is, this is a world we know nothing about.'

'But …'

'Yes?'

'No need to snap.'

'I'm not.'

'Yes you are.'

'That's because I'm tense.'

'Clearly.'

Their raised voices made a passing dog walker stop and look.

'What were you going to say just now?' she demanded, aware she sounded totally unlike herself.

Sam shrugged. 'It doesn't matter.'

'Yes it does.'

'OK, then. It does look odd, doesn't it? The car. Apparently parked outside your client's one minute and then back at home the next. You don't think … I mean you have been working very hard recently … and you have been worried about money …'

'Sam!' She swung round to face him. 'First you blame Ellie. And now you think I've been trying to swindle my own clients.'

He refused to face her. 'No, but …'

'You do, don't you? For all we know, it might have been the joyriders in the local paper.'

Jumping out of the car, she slammed the door behind her and began walking towards their hosts' drive, leaving Sam to follow.

'It couldn't have been me. It couldn't have been,' she kept repeating in her head. Yet, wasn't she angry because Sam's words had hit a nerve? Supposing she'd never driven the car to Mrs R-R's in the first place. What if she'd got a taxi – which would explain why the car hadn't been moved. And supposing she had used the credit card herself …

No. That was crazy. Then again, wasn't that what she'd been

like after Nick's birth? Post-baby blues, they'd called it. All she knew was that she never wanted to go through that again. That inability to think or act clearly ...

Exactly what was happening now.

'Georgie!' The door swung open. Pippa, the first friend she had made after moving here, gave her a brief hug. 'How are you?'

She stepped back as if to appraise her. Georgie suddenly wondered if her black evening trousers were too smart for her friend's jeans and floaty top. A casual supper, she'd said. That was the thing about being a reasonably fresh newcomer (after five years, she was still on the fringes). You were never entirely certain of the rules. Then again, hadn't that been the case for most of her life?

'Fine, thanks,' she said, conscious of Sam coming up the path behind her.

Pippa gave her another hug. 'No, I mean how are you really?'

So she'd heard about Jo. Why did that not surprise her? Anything different was immediately latched on as gossip around here.

'Sam! Lovely to see you too. Come on in.'

She ushered them through the beautiful hall, studded with school photographs of the children, and into the drawing room where a small group hovered, glasses in hand. There was the smell of something delicious in the air – fish pie, perhaps? One of the advantages of living so near to the sea was the harbour shop.

'I'm afraid there are only six of us tonight. Jo and her husband were meant to be coming but they had to cancel,' added Pippa, blushing. So her old friend didn't want to be in the same room as her, Georgie realised with a pang.

Instantly, her mind went off on a tangent (surely her friend must realise it wasn't her fault) before realising that Pippa was saying something else.

'... would like you to meet Lyndsey Green, who's just

moved into the area?'

Georgie glanced up at the woman she'd been introduced to. She was wafer-thin with short, red hair – the thin type that revealed the odd patch of scalp. There was something familiar about her.

'Haven't we met somewhere before?' asked the woman curiously. A cold shiver of sweat went down Georgie's back as she took in the white skin and freckles.

'I don't think so.'

'I'm sure we have,' insisted the woman. 'You look very like a friend of mine who I grew up with. Georgie. Georgie Smith.'

It couldn't be. That was impossible. Taking a deep breath, she tried to concentrate on the pale turquoise wallpaper behind her hostess' back. She'd helped her choose it a year or so ago. Maybe now if she focussed on the pretty swirls and soft pink shadows that brought out the colour of the shades, she could block out the memories. Lyndsey, whom she'd hung around the local park with, talking about how they couldn't wait to get out of this place. Lyndsey whose parents wouldn't let her go on a gap year – 'I'd love to go' – and had gone straight to uni instead. Lyndsey, who hated being 'a ginger'. Lyndsey who had thought, along with everyone else, that she had just lost touch …

'Of course, you can't be her.' The woman was gripping the edge of a chair as if for support. 'I lost touch with my friend a long time ago.' Her eyes began to water. 'I just wondered if you were a relation of hers.'

Pippa was looking distinctly uncomfortable. Despite the horrendous situation Georgie had found herself in, she felt incredibly sorry for her friend. This wasn't what a hostess needed. 'A relation?' She forced the words out of her mouth. 'I don't think so. Not that I know of. My name *is* Georgie – short for Georgina – but my maiden name was Peverington.'

No need to mention the Peverington-Smith bit, she told herself quickly, hoping that Sam wasn't listening.

The woman shook herself as if coming out of a dream. 'Of

71

course. I'm sorry. It would have been too much of a coincidence, wouldn't it?'

Her voice was trembling and she was looking down at her shoes; a rather smart pair of shiny black stilettos. Exactly the kind that she and the old Georgie had dreamed of wearing. 'You'll have to excuse me.' Then she raised her eyes pleadingly. 'You never quite get over losing a dear friend, you know. Every now and then, it comes up and hits me.'

Poor Pippa, who was usually in control of most social situations, looked as though she didn't know what to say. It was awkward, Georgie conceded, for someone who was completely new to the area to be so open. Then again, that was her Lyndsey. Always one to say what she was thinking. Her heart contorted. Until now, Georgie hadn't allowed herself to grieve for the people she'd left behind. Not her parents, but Lyndsey and of course her old dog who would be long gone by now. They'd used to go on long walks together.

'Shall we go through?'

Pippa had her hostess voice on. Slightly brittle and nervous at the same time. She wouldn't be worried about the food, Georgie thought. Pippa was in catering: she ran a well-established local cookery school. No. It was the mix of guests she'd invited. Georgie could see that in her eyes.

To her relief – and yet also slight disappointment – Pippa placed her and Lyndsey at opposite ends of the table. Sam was four places down. She could hear him talking to a banker whom she knew slightly through his wife (another former school-run mum) and wondered if her husband was going to mention The Thing.

Privately, that's what Georgie had begun to call it to herself. It defied any other name. Fraud didn't even start to do it justice. As for stolen identity, she couldn't even go there … That picture of her with the feather duster kept preying on her mind, even in her dreams.

Sam's face was low now, his brow furrowed; the way he looked when talking about something serious. Was he asking advice from the banker? The man might even be partly aware of the situation already. His wife was friends with Jo, who was still not speaking to her. She desperately needed this evening to think of something else. To unwind.

All they'd thought and talked about for days was how to get out of this mess and hang onto her clients. If she could have one evening off from the strain and worry, she'd feel a lot better.

'Hello,' said a pleasant deep voice, sliding into the seat next to her.

Georgie looked up to find a shortish man with an honest, open face and a firm handshake. 'I'm Steven. My wife Lyndsey and I have just moved into the area.'

Her initial relief at finding someone new next to her – who might be aware of the wild rumours flying around – was replaced by a sense of dread. Did she know him? Frantically, Georgie searched her mind for a record of one of the few local boys she and Lyndsey had known in the small Yorkshire village where they had grown up. There hadn't been many – wasn't that why they had both been itching to leave? – but she might be mistaken …

'Have you lived here long?' he asked. 'Nearly twenty years.' Then she forced herself to face him. 'Where have you moved from?'

'Birmingham, actually. We've both been there for ages.' He gave a small, slightly disparaging smile. 'Lyndsey and I met on a post-grad course there. We liked it, so we stayed put. Not very adventurous, I know.'

'Not at all.' Georgie was beginning to warm to this nice man. Good. So at least one of them had done all right. She glanced down the table to where Lyndsey was sitting. As if sensing it, the woman met her gaze. This time, instead of being a troubled look, it was a harder, reappraising one. Quickly, Georgie looked away.

'Do you have children?' she asked quickly.

Stephen's face dropped. 'Unfortunately not.'

Instantly, she wished she hadn't asked that question. It was so easy to assume other people had been blessed in the way that she had. At the same time, Georgie felt a pang in her chest. Lyndsey had always wanted kids, more so than she had, to be honest. 'Four,' she used to say happily when, as teenagers, they planned their life in advance. 'Mum says it's a good number.'

For a minute, Georgie allowed herself to remember the busy, frantic, but always happy household that her friend had grown up in. Such a stark contrast to her own cold one. No wonder she'd spent so much time at her old friend's house rather than her own.

'But we both have our careers,' continued Stephen more brightly. 'Lyndsey was appointed head of her school last year and I was a head in an out-of-city school. So we both sing from the same hymn sheet, as it were.'

She almost felt envious at the obvious unity. 'Have you both found schools down here?'

'Actually, no. My wife has ... she's taken early retirement. In fact, we both have. I'm hoping we'll both make friends soon. That's why it was so kind of Pippa to invite us. We live next door.'

'Really?'

Georgie couldn't hide her surprise. The house next door was a beautiful Georgian building which she'd often admired, even though it was out of their price range. Teaching must be better paid than she'd realised. It was certainly a far cry from the cramped semi that Lyndsey had grown up in: an exact duplicate of Georgie's.

'Yes.' Her companion made a small face as though this was pleasant news to him as well. 'I heard you were an interior designer. Maybe you could come round some time and take a look.'

No. No.

'I'd love to,' said Georgie carefully, knowing that if she refused outright it would look rude. 'However, I'm quite busy at the moment.'

Lyndsey's husband nodded approvingly. 'That makes me all

the keener. Shows you must be good at your job.' His eye fell on her bag. 'Do you have a business card on you?'

What was the point of denying it? He'd only get her number off their hostess. 'Sure.'

He glanced at it. '"Gorgeous Georgie". I was always trying to get my pupils to understand alliteration.' Then his eyes twinkled and once more, Georgie felt an unreasonable stab of jealousy. What a difference twenty-odd years had made. Ordinary Lyndsey with her conscientious attitude to life and her fear of adventures had emerged sunny-side up. True, she didn't have children and she had 'health issues', whatever they were.

But at least she wasn't living a lie.

Thankfully, after the main course, Pippa announced that 'everyone must change places to get to know each other better' and Georgie found herself sitting – not next to Lyndsey as she'd feared – but to Pippa's husband who chatted amicably about that new drama on television. She had seen it, hadn't she? No? Really? It was all about this woman who woke up one day after a coma to discover that her husband had been responsible for her accident and that ...

Georgie let the conversation wash over her. It gave her the opportunity to appraise Lyndsey every now and then at the other end of the table. She'd just have to tell them that she couldn't take on any clients until the end of the year. Then she'd try and keep a wide berth.

But that wouldn't be easy in a small town like this. What if she inadvertently let something slip?

You can't, she told herself fiercely. You'll simply have to be careful. Just as you have been for most of your adult life.

Eventually, to her relief, people were looking at their watches and exclaiming at the time. Was it gone midnight already? Such a shame to go but really, the babysitter would be chafing at the bit or they had an exhibition to go to tomorrow or ...

'Must get back to walk Beano,' said Sam, slipping his arm around her as they stood in the hallway, waiting to retrieve their

75

coats and say their thank yous.

Lyndsey and her husband were a few feet away but immediately her eyes hardened. Georgie could hardly breathe as she zoomed in. 'Beano?' she said sharply. 'Is that your dog?'

No. *No*.

'He's a black lab,' said Sam proudly. 'Our substitute child now our children are away.'

Georgie could feel Lyndsey's eyes on her like a hot grill. 'My friend Georgie had a dog called Beano,' she said slowly. 'It died of a broken heart when she went away.'

For a minute, Georgie felt her knees threaten to buckle. Then, thank goodness, Lyndsey's husband stepped in. 'Come on, darling. Try to think pleasant thoughts. Remember?'

He shot them both a 'please understand' glance before shaking Georgie's hand. 'We'll be in touch,' he said quietly. 'My wife needs a project. It will be a good diversion.'

ELEVEN

Hi. Nice to meet you. Before you ask, I'm one of the old hands. And frankly, I don't know how we managed before Facebook.

It changed everything. There are teams of us now, everywhere, skimming through it for personal stuff. Anything that will help us crack the code that people put on their iPads and phones.

Pet names are the best. You'd be amazed at how often customers use them as passwords for their online banking.

Kids' names are next.

Husbands' names hardly get a look in. Shows you where customers' priorities lie.

'Customers', I hear you asking. Well, that's what they are, aren't they? We earn a good living from them and in return they give us their business.

Even if they don't know it.

Once you've cracked the code, the world is your oyster. You can get into their bank accounts. Check their diaries. Build up a complete picture of the owner and steal their identity – more than once.

If you've got an EHIC card or a passport as well, you're really in the money. Do you know how much you can get for them on the black market? Thought not. Right now, an illegal is giving birth on the national health thanks to Mrs Hamilton's EHIC card. I know because she's my cousin.

Sometimes, just to throw people, we leave important stuff. Like driving licences. They're one of the first things victims check. If it's still there, they think they're safe.

78

TWELVE

For the next few days after the dinner party, Georgie was decidedly twitchy. Every time the phone rang, she imagined it was that kind, boring, sensible Stephen asking if she would come round to look at the house. Or, even worse, Lyndsey herself.

She had her refusal neatly planned, of course. Even written it down as an *aide memoire* in case words failed her in the panic of the moment. 'Terribly sorry. Would love to help out. But snowed under for the foreseeable future. Can recommend another interior designer.' Etc. etc.

Anything so as not to put herself in a situation where she might find herself letting her guard down or saying something that might arouse Lyndsey's suspicions even further.

To make it worse, she kept discovering more things that had gone missing from her purse. Things she didn't think of checking before. Her EHIC card. Her Boots loyalty card. But not, strangely, her driving licence. Was it possible that she might just have dropped the first two by mistake somewhere? If they'd been stolen, surely the thief would have taken the licence.

But none were as important as the shell.

Georgie decided not to say anything to anyone. It would have made her look even more stupid. Quietly, she applied for a new EHIC card. It was a surprisingly simple process. But it wasn't so easy to calm herself down. Every time she went out, she found herself hanging onto her bag; terrified that someone might grab it.

'Stop being so neurotic,' Sam said when they parked the car in the local shopping centre and she kept checking the door was locked.

'I can't help it.'

Why didn't he understand? Surely Sam didn't really think Ellie was responsible? It was a knee-jerk reaction from what had gone on before, during Ellie's dark days. Personally, Georgie couldn't help thinking that someone out there had taken advantage of her. Someone wanted to hurt her. Someone had targeted her.

The thought made her skin prickle.

Meanwhile, there was some good news. To Georgie's relief, the computer man had managed to take down the YouTube video.

'Don't ask me how,' he'd said with a grin and an implication that he might just have done something that wasn't quite legal. 'Just keep an eye on it and let me know if anything else comes up.' Then his face softened. 'It could just be one of these random things unless someone has got something in for you. Do you think that's possible?'

'No.' Georgie found herself shaking her head before the question had time to go round her brain. Then she added 'Not that I'm aware of.'

'Not a competitor or a disgruntled client perhaps?' the computer man persisted.

Georgie tried to think. So far, she had a five-star rating on her website. The only customer who hadn't been happy was a woman who'd been firm about having maroon throughout the house and then changed her mind. Georgie, who'd been against the colour scheme from the start, found herself being blamed but – in the interest of pleasing a client in a small town where word could spread – re-decorated and bore the extra cost herself.

'Looks like you've just been unlucky then,' the computer man had shrugged.

Unlucky? Georgie bristled. She was never unlucky. That was the old Georgie. The one who had disappeared years ago. But after the computer man had gone, she took Beano out along the cliffs along the beach. And – thanks to Lyndsey's unexpected appearance at the dinner party – the past began to filter back into her mind. Ruthlessly. Without allowing her to stop it.

When her life had changed so dramatically, all those years ago, she'd hardly been able to breathe for fear of someone tapping her on the shoulder.

'Who do you think you are?'

Or – even worse – 'Georgie Smith. You are under arrest.'

She got to the point where the fear and the guilt became so great that twice – not once, but twice – she actually found herself on the point of telling Sam everything.

But each time, she'd panicked and managed to change the subject before properly embarking on it. He would never understand. Besides, the sheer horror of what had happened was so unbelievable that Georgie's mind had already started to blank it out in order for her to be able to put one step in front of the other.

The old 'her' would never have been able to cope. Funny, she often thought, how names could decide a person's character. Georgie sounded soft and friendly. A bit of a pushover, in the wrong situation. Georgina sounded bold. Able to stand up for herself. Georgina definitely came from a more privileged background.

That had helped her survive. Besides, she'd made her bed, as her mother would have said, and now she had to lie in it. As for Mum herself, there was nothing in the paper about a missing girl who had failed to return from her gap year. If she'd been bothered, Mum would have launched a big publicity campaign, surely?

That hurt. So much so, that every time she thought of her old life, she imagined a large metal gate coming down and slicing her past away from the present.

By the time she met Sam, the old shy Georgie had hidden herself in a web of lies and deceit, fuelled by terror.

'What's happened about that money that got taken from your account?' asked Ellie.

If that was an innocent question, it was well presented. Like a line in a convincing play. Georgie shot a look, first at her husband and then her step-daughter. Nick was silently texting under the table and didn't appear to hear either the spoken words or the unwritten tension behind them.

She would have told him off about the texting, but this was the first time they'd all sat round the same table eating the same meal for as long as she could remember. And she didn't want to spoil it. If someone had told her when the children were little that a family meal would, one day, become as obsolete as one of the museum exhibits she was always dragging them to, she would have relished the idea. Time on her own! In those days, that was a luxury.

Now, with both of them leading their own lives, it became an empty gap that had to be filled. Right now, ironically, this was happening all right. But not in the way she had thought it might. Stolen identity didn't just take away the hours in the day or the person you were. It also threatened the person you weren't.

'I'm still talking to the bank about it,' said Georgie carefully.

Ellie paused mid-mouthful, through a bowl of vegetarian mince. That was another thing. She'd become a vegan at the age of fifteen thanks to an enthusiastic school friend who had now = such irony – gone back to eating meat. It had meant making two different kinds of meals every time – something that strangely seemed more difficult when she visited than when Ellie had been home full time.

Not as difficult, however, as the dark look that was gathering on Sam's face. 'Due to "data protection",' he said, adding a sarcastic emphasis on the phrase, 'the process seems to be taking a rather long time.'

Nick slid his mobile into his pocket. 'What do you mean?'

'The bank misspelt my name on my new card and I didn't check it,' said Georgie tightly.

'But surely the bank is still responsible for covering the fraud?' persisted Ellie, her smooth forehead now crinkly with indignation.

Her father was studying her intently. 'You would think so, wouldn't you? You'd also think that the thief would have had the decency to hand the money back.'

There was the scrape of a chair against the floor, leaving a mark on the reconstituted floorboards which Georgie had stained herself with linseed and antique wax. 'You still think it's me, don't you?' snapped Ellie, leaping up.

Then she looked at Georgie and her lovely brown eyes watered. 'I only came back to see you guys but if you're going to talk to me like this, I'm going.'

Georgie jumped to her feet. 'Ellie ...'

Too late. Her stepdaughter had flounced out of the room.

'Leave her,' demanded Sam.

'I'll go,' said Nick quickly.

Georgie stood hovering, unable to sit down at the same table as her husband yet at the same time, telling herself that her son might be able to sort this out better than her.

'Why did you say that?' she snapped.

'Because it's true. I've been looking into it after what you said. And it's true. If it was a random thief, he or she would have used the card a couple of times. It's how they work. But because Ellie was scared she'd be caught again, she didn't do it.'

'But she wasn't in the place where the card was used.'

Sam groaned. 'Do I need to go over it again? She'd have given the number to a friend to copy. A dealer. I don't know.'

'You don't know she's doing drugs again.'

Sam reached out for her hand. 'Georgie. I know this is hard

83

to take. But have you taken a good look at her recently? She's gone very thin. She gets voraciously hungry. And her pupils are big at times …'

He stopped as Nick came back into the kitchen. 'She needs some time alone,' he said, sliding back into his place.

'So she's in her room?'

Georgie felt a sense of relief. She'd go up later and sort it out when everyone had calmed down.

'No. She's gone back to the flat. Said she'd call later.'

Instantly, she was transported back into the old Georgie who used to flounce out too. Lyndsey's house had been a haven until the gap year.

No. Don't think of that. Georgie didn't exist. She couldn't be allowed to.

Another week passed. To her relief, there was no phone call from Lyndsey or her husband. Nor, however, were there any phone calls from new clients or existing ones. Georgie began to get a growing feeling of unease. Was this because it was summer and 'everyone' was going on holiday? Or could it be that word had spread about Jo's hacked account and that awful video on YouTube?

'If that is the case,' declared Sam reassuringly, putting his arm around her as they watched a film together on the sofa one evening, 'it will pass. Have you heard from Ellie, by the way?'

That was another thing. Every time she tried to ring Ellie's mobile, it went through to voicemail. If only there was a landline in the London flat her daughter shared with another student, but not many students seemed to have them nowadays.

Usually when there was a family crisis, Georgie was able to blank it out with work. But without any, she was getting bored – and finding it difficult to sleep. Even when she did, her dreams were punctuated with dreams of Thailand and beaches and vans and 'the gang' …

'I take it from your silence that you haven't,' said Sam quietly. 'Frankly, I think it's a sign of a guilty conscience. No.

84

don't get up. I'm sorry. What's happened about Jo?'

Georgie closed her eyes for a minute, allowing the wine to take her away from all this. 'I paid her off.'

Next to her on the sofa, she felt Sam stiffen. 'You what?'

'Her bank has been as slow as mine in chasing it up and she needed the money.'

'All £10,000 of it?

Georgie began to feel nervous. 'It seemed the right thing to do.'

'You could have asked me first.'

'It came out of my business account.'

'But you've got tax to pay shortly.'

'I'll sort it. The bank should have sorted it by then, and at least Jo's speaking to me now.'

Sam snorted. 'I hope the price of friendship's worth it.'

'Did you really just say that?' For a moment, Georgie looked at her husband as though for the first time. Did she know him as little as he did her?

Sam had the grace to look embarrassed. 'What I meant to say is that if you pay off the bank's obligations, it lets them get away with it.'

'I didn't say that. I'm simply bridging the gap until my friend gets what she's entitled to.' Georgie stood up. 'And if you don't get that, there's no point.'

A look of uncertainty crossed Sam's face. 'What do you mean by that?'

For a second, Georgie was taken back to those early days. To the time when, every time she walked down a street, she feared a touch on her shoulder.

It was so tempting to tell her husband everything. To release the burden that had been weighing on her shoulders for all these years. But if she did, she might throw everything away …

'I don't know.' She sank down on the sofa again, her head in her hands. 'This is all so weird. I don't know how to cope.'

'It will be all right.' Her husband's arms were around her. 'We'll sort this out. I promise. Besides, you've still got one big

85

client, haven't you?'

'The Hon. Mrs David R-R?'

She tried to smile through her tears but instead it came out like a shiver. 'Yes. I've still got her. But she's not easy.'

'Isn't that half the challenge?'

He was right. Only the old Georgie would have been afraid. The reminder gave her strength.

For the next few days, Georgie threw herself into the new plans for Mrs R-R's lovely home. Hyacinth blue would be perfect, she'd decided, for the morning room, with a touch of pink in the swag curtains to complement the striped chaise. As for the main sitting room, which needed to be 'casual chic', she decided on a colonial look with smart stripes. Hopefully her client would approve.

Duly armed with her bag of plans and swatches – having run Beano along the beach so he would last until lunchtime – Georgie made for the front door. Just as she did so, a flurry of post fell through the letter box, accompanied by a furious barking from the kitchen. Beano always saw the postman as an intruder, even though he'd known him for years.

Georgie gave the post a cursory glance. Mainly circulars plus an update from the charity which Georgie supported for families in Africa. Just as she was about to open it, the phone rang.

'Mrs Hamilton?'

To her surprise, it was from a bank which she rarely used. She'd opened a private savings account there years ago for emergencies only. No one knew about it ...

But now this voice – after taking her through security checks – was telling her that £4450 had been withdrawn and the bank wanted to check this as it was so rare for her to take anything from her account. How could this have happened?

Dropping her bag, Georgie flew up to her office, searching frantically behind the books on the lower shelf for the small wooden box where she kept the card.

There it was. Gratefully, her fingers closed round it, shaking as they opened the lid.

Empty.

Someone had taken it.

THIRTEEN

I had some bad news today. One of my mates – from a different team – got nicked. Even worse, he got a heavier sentence because they accused him of stealing three cards instead of two.

That's the thing about fraud. When someone gets their card nicked, they tell others. Their mates. People they work with. Family.

There's usually someone who reckons they can jump on the bandwagon. Steal another card. Hope that the first person will be blamed.

That's what happened to my mate. He couldn't prove he didn't do it.

Fraud is so complicated nowadays that it's just as hard to show you didn't do something as it is to show you did do it.

Makes me shiver a bit, just to think about it.

What makes it more complicated is that there are lots of us in it. We're not one person. We're many. We might work for the same master. Or we could be independent. Rarely do we know each other. But our aim is the same.

To steal from you. To muddle your head. To make you wonder if you really put your purse where you thought you had.

You can't see us. You can't smell us. You don't know if I'm old or young. Whether I smell of sweat or aftershave or perfume.

That's the whole point. We're the modern silent assassin. But instead of your life, we're after your identity. And the money that comes with it.

There's something else too. Peace of mind.

I've got to be honest here. You're not the only one to lose that. Sometimes at night, I lie awake, thinking of all the people I've cheated. I wait for the knock at the door to say I've been caught. Every time I go down the street, I expect to find a hand on my shoulder. The other day, a police car pulled me over. I shat bricks until I realised I'd only been speeding.

'Stop tossing and turning,' the wife will say when I'm having one of my bad dreams.

But I can't help it. If I had my chance again, I wouldn't do it. Yet I'm in too deep now. And I don't know how to stop.

FOURTEEN

'When did you last put your card details online?' asked the computer man tersely.

It had taken ages to get through to him. No one seemed to answer their phones anymore, thought Georgie. You had to text and ask if they could ring. She hated texting. It was so easy to put your finger on the wrong letter and as for predictive text, it was downright rude or comical at times.

Not that there was anything funny about this. Yet for some reason that Georgie couldn't fathom, she wanted to laugh. What else was going to go wrong in her life?

'I haven't,' she now said in reply to the computer man's question. 'That's the whole point. I've never used this card. It's ... it's a sort of emergency account.'

'I know that. You've already told me.' He spoke in a rush as if his time was worth more than the £25 an hour which he charged. Maybe it was if there were other people in this sort of mess. What kind of technical nightmare had the world let itself into? 'My question is, when did you last use a card online? Any card?'

She thought back over the last year. One of her strengths as an interior designer was that she liked to source local fabric manufacturers. Usually she went in person to view and buy. Yes, she used her card to pay but not online.

'You're sure? What about Amazon or supermarket shopping.'

She always did the latter in person – so much nicer to choose your own food rather than risk someone else's judgment. As for Amazon, she usually left that up to Sam or Nick – they were the experts. Wait. Ellie's birthday. She'd wanted a particular skirt from a fashion site she hadn't come across before and which was surprisingly addictive.

'That might be it.' The computer man sounded as though he'd discovered a clue in a treasure hunt. Optimistic but still slightly puzzled. 'Do you use the same password on all your credit cards?'

'Yes.' Even as she spoke, Georgie was aware this was the wrong answer. This was confirmed by what sounded like a clucking of the tongue. 'The first thing you've got to do is change all your passwords. Use a combination of letters and numbers. Instead of a "c", use the number three. That sort of thing.'

'But what about the money that's gone from my emergency account?'

There was a tired sigh from the other end as though the computer man had heard all this before. 'I'm afraid it's a matter of contacting the building society concerned. Ring first and then follow it up with a letter. Put everything in writing.'

He gave a world-weary laugh. 'Just be grateful that the money was taken out in cash and not used to pay a bill. I had a client whose account was hacked to pay for a holiday. When it made her overdrawn, it damaged her credit rating. Then she was turned down for a mortgage.'

That was awful!

'Clever too, that your thief withdrew less than £5000. That's the limit in most building societies. Usually you have to have paper identity for a withdrawal that large. That's why they'll have done it online. Even so, they'd have needed your password.'

Georgie began to feel a mounting panic. 'So how did they do it?'

'Not sure yet. We might never know. Meanwhile, like I said, you need to cancel it.'

She had to do so fast. Before Sam got home. After all, she could hardly tell her husband that she'd had a secret emergency account 'just in case' she'd needed it. He'd be rightly suspicious, and hurt too. Her heart lurched. Sam was a good man. He was hard on his daughter but he didn't deserve to be hurt like this. He didn't deserve a woman like her either. Wasn't that why she'd tried so hard over the years to be a good wife?

'I'm sorry,' added the computer man. 'I know it's not the news you wanted to hear. If it helps, you're not the only one in this situation.

'Thanks.' Georgie bit back her tears until she'd put the receiver down. Then she sat with her head in her hands and wept. What was going on? Questions whirled round her head as the clock in the hall struck. Was that really the time?

Georgie began to sweat again. Just before the phone call, she'd rung the Hon. Mrs R-R and explained that she was going to be late because of an 'unexpected event'. Her excuse had been met with a distinct coolness on the other end.

There was late and there was late. Right now, she was on the furthest end of the spectrum. The least she could do was try to hang onto the one client she had left.

'Madam is engaged at the moment,' said the maid who answered the door. 'She would like you to wait in the morning room.'

Fair enough, thought Georgie, taking a seat by the French windows which looked out over the immaculate lawns. She was being punished. Well, she'd just use the time to lay out the sketches and arrange the fabric swatches. It would be a good exercise to exorcise the thoughts that were going round and round her mind.

Nearly five thousand pounds ... not to mention the other missing money. How could that have just vanished? And where was the card? Who could have taken it? Did she even have to ask that question? It had to be someone who lived in the house. For the first time since this nightmare had started, Georgie now began to wonder if her husband was right about Ellie. It couldn't be Nick. He wasn't materialistic. Sam was out of the question too. Or was she being stupidly naïve? Was the answer staring her straight in the face?

Georgie took a seat on the chair by the fireplace and leaned back, her eyes closed. The action worsened the throbbing in her head so she opened them again. This time, her eyes were drawn to the green and black print above the mantelpiece. It was another of those Thai paintings she'd noticed earlier. This one depicted a beach and a couple of straw huts. It wasn't a complicated painting yet the few artful strokes succeeded in drawing such a compelling eye-catching picture that Georgie felt she was back there.

Back with the crowd.

It had been so good to be accepted that at first, Georgie hadn't realised what was going on. She was too caught up with the excitement of this new world and the novelty of being in the company of the equivalent of the 'cool crowd' at school: a sector which she and Lyndsey had been excluded from because they were 'boring'.

Georgina was particularly friendly, insisting that she 'shared' her clothes: wonderful, exotic garments that fluttered in the evening breeze and made her feel like a mermaid. 'You can borrow my make-up too,' said her new friend, sitting her down in the shade under a tree. 'Look, if you put a little eyeliner here, it brings out that lovely almond shape.'

She worked deftly, her tongue showing slightly through those pearly teeth. Over the next few weeks, Georgie noticed that she did that when concentrating. Without meaning to, she began to adopt the same mannerism herself. She even found herself saying words like 'yah' and 'sure'.

They began to go on walks together. One day, they collected shells. Georgina was better than she was. 'Have this,' she said, pressing a dear little pink and white one into her hand.

'Are you sure?'

Georgina nodded. 'It's for you. A sign of our friendship.' Her hand closed over hers. 'Don't lose it, mind. Or it will be bad luck.'

Then she laughed, throwing her head back, and Georgie wasn't sure if she was teasing. Or not.

She was so kind! But the worst thing was that she couldn't help heating up inside every time Joly came near. 'He's Georgina's boyfriend,' she kept telling herself. Anyway, what was the point? A man like him – tall, blond, posh-spoken, charming – wouldn't look twice at her.

Yet he did. 'You two could be twins, you know,' he murmured one night after they'd roasted fish over the fire and laid down on the sand while the sound of a steel band floated down the beach.

Georgie would have expected Georgina to have been offended. Although they looked surprisingly alike with their hair and turned up noses, their backgrounds were like chalk and cheese. Georgina had already casually mentioned a house in 'the country' where she had grown up and a 'trust fund'.

'I've always wanted a sister,' she drawled, sucking at a cigarette that was being handed around. 'It would be so nice to have someone to share secrets with.'

A blue circle of smoke floated across the evening air.

Then she gave a little girlish giggle which might have had something to do with the empty bottles around them. 'Do you have any secrets, Georgie?'

She shook her head.

'Are you sure?' Those beautiful eyes were searching her. Georgie felt uncomfortable.

'Quite sure.'

Georgina turned away. 'That's a pity.'

'Why?' asked Vanda sharply.

'No reason.' She smiled brightly. 'You know, when my parents died,' she continued, 'I'd have given anything to have had a brother or sister to talk to. Instead, all I had was an ancient grandmother who was obsessed with her own grief.'

You'd think, thought Georgie, that Georgina was desolate from the words, yet her tone was light. Almost casual.

'You had me,' said a voice suddenly. It was Vanda. 'I was there for you.'

Joly turned to her. 'They were at school together,' he said in a low voice.

'Especially,' continued Vanda clearly, 'when they o'deed.'

So her new friend's parents had taken drugs?

Georgina's face stilled. 'I told you. It was an accident.'

Vanda rolled her eyes as though to say 'You don't really believe that.'

Had Georgina seen? If so, she wasn't showing it. Then she stretched out an elegant hand towards her, jangling with thin silver bracelets. 'But you've got to admit, Vanda. We're different. But me and Georgie ... well. We're kindred spirits, aren't we, darling?'

'Like you were with Louisa, you mean?'

There was a hushed silence. That name again – the woman who had left the commune.

'We don't talk about her any more,' said Vanda sharply. Then she passed the cigarette to Georgie. Before, when this had happened, she'd politely refused. Not knowing much about drugs – she and Lyndsey had been too scared to take part in the dealings at the back of the playground – she'd been unsure about the content of these particular cigarettes.

But Georgina's compliment – kindred spirits! – and nervousness at the atmosphere around her made her accept the rolled-up paper and inhale. Immediately she spluttered and began choking.

'Your first time,' declared Joly delightedly. 'That's what I like to see.' He took it from her. 'Watch me.'

Carefully, he put his guitar down, placed the thin cigarette inside his mouth, and then removed it, breathing out slowly. 'Your turn.'

Scarcely believing she was sucking on something that had been in Joly's mouth, she did the same. After a while, she could feel it. A warm sense of headiness overcame her. Almost immediately, she stopped worrying about Vanda. Or about how she was going to manage for money – there didn't seem to be any work out here and certainly the word 'job' hadn't been mentioned by any of her new friends.

She just felt … happy.

It was a sensation she'd never had before. And it felt good. Really good. Especially when Joly picked up his guitar again and the soft music made her soul start to sing.

'I hope you don't have plans to get rid of my picture.'

The Hon. Mrs R-R's cultured voice brought Georgie sharply back to the present.

'I happen to be very fond of it.' Her eye fell on the swatches which Georgie had artfully laid around the room. 'I suppose you're going to tell me that it doesn't fit in with this colour scheme of yours.'

'You don't like it?'

Georgie was upset but not surprised. She had a feeling that nothing much was going to please this woman. If it wasn't for the fact that she didn't have anyone else, she might have cut her losses and quit there and then.

'I didn't say that.' Her client's eyes narrowed again as she picked up the hyacinth blue wallpaper strip. 'How did you know this was one of my favourite colours?'

'Then why the cream?'

The words were out of her mouth before Georgie could take them back.

Yet instead of being offended, Mrs R-R laughed. A rather brittle, mirthless laugh. 'My husband's choice. Money men are always bland, don't you think?'

Luckily, before Georgie could answer, she carried on. 'Mind you, I might like your choice of colour but your timekeeping is another matter.' Those eyes narrowed again. 'I happen to pride myself on punctuality and I expect others to do the same. But frankly, Georgie, you've been late once too often. My time is money too, so I'm afraid ...'

'Don't'. Once more, Georgie heard herself speak before thinking it through. 'I know what you're going to say and if I was in your position, I'd do the same. But please don't sack me. There's a reason for me being late.'

Her eyes filled with tears. Now she'd really done it. This wasn't professional. It went against all her rules. Yet Mrs R- R was motioning that she should sit down.

'Take a deep breath,' she said in what was almost a kind tone. 'Start from the beginning.'

Georgie tried to follow her instructions but the words just tumbled out. 'You remember how my car was stolen? Well, it started then ...'

By the time she had finished – ending with the last catastrophe – the expression on her client's face had changed to nothing short of sympathy. 'Nearly five thousand pounds,' she repeated.

'It might not sound much,' began Georgie, 'but ...'

'But it's the principle. The feeling that someone has stolen something you've worked hard for.' The eyes hardened. 'Frankly, it's outrageous. What does your husband say?'

Georgie felt like a traitor. 'I don't want to tell him.'

There was an understanding nod. 'I know all about that.' She got up and walked towards the mahogany desk on the other side of the room. 'Who shall I make the cheque payable to?'

'I don't understand.'

'Call it a payment towards your work.'

'But it's too much.'

'It shouldn't be. You must know what your London competitors charge.'

Georgie found a cheque being pushed into her hand. Ten thousand pounds? 'I don't understand.'

'Let's just say it's one woman helping another.' She spoke crisply as if embarrassed. 'Look, I like what I've seen so far so just carry on, can you? Order the curtains. Sort out the decorators. I'm going away shortly for a month and I'd like everything sorted by the time I get back.'

Georgie tried to speak but the words stuck in her throat.

'Naturally, I expect a full breakdown when you've finished. Now, there's something else. When I said just now that my time was precious, I wasn't about to sack you as you presumed. I wanted to explain that I don't have time for a longer meeting. I've just found out that a new neighbour of mine has gone into hospital so I need to visit her.'

How wrong you could be about people! Georgie hadn't put Mrs R-R down as the good Samaritan type. 'In fact, I believe you met her the other evening. At Pippa Michael's.'

It was such a small town. There had been lots of people there. Yet at the same time, Georgie had a sinking feeling. She knew exactly what Mrs R-R was going to say next.

'Lyndsey. Lyndsey Green. She's been rushed in for emergency treatment, poor thing.'

My wife has taken early retirement. We both have. Wasn't that what her dinner companion had told her?

'What's wrong?' she said, suddenly anxious.

Mrs R- R raised her eyebrows. 'You don't know? She's got leukaemia, poor thing. She was diagnosed just before moving here. Such bad luck. And from what I can gather, it's not looking good.'

Leukaemia? Her friend Lyndsey. Lyndsey whom she'd grown up with? Lyndsey whom she'd pretended not to know the other night? Lyndsey was possibly going to die?

'I'm going to visit her right now.' Those eyes narrowed again. 'Tell you what, why don't you come with me?'

FIFTEEN

Georgina Hamilton is getting smart. She's no longer replying to emails that offer her prizes to fill in a questionnaire or from holiday companies asking if she wants to be informed of new deals.

Haven't you ever wondered about them yourself? How else do you think that people like me can tap into your accounts? The more personal details we have about you, the easier it is.

Phishing, we call it in the trade.

How do you know about Mrs Hamilton's email patterns, you might ask. Because, thanks to her computer history which I hacked into when I was in her house, I'm there. In the cursor. On the screen. When she sends an email, I see that too. It's like leaving your front door open. Without realising.

That's the beauty of my world. Nothing is hidden.

Sometimes our lot on the ground steal people's secrets too. It might be a letter from a lover in a woman's bag. Or a text message suggesting something it shouldn't. You can just imagine how the victim feels. Probably shitting bricks in case it ends up in the wrong hands. I don't go in for blackmail myself. But I know plenty who do.

Then there are the photographs in a purse. The other day I came across a faded baby snap. Maybe it was the only one they had.

That quite upset me, it did. Made me wonder if I was getting soft. Then again, it's their fault for carrying their personal stuff around with them.

They should be like me. Take just enough to see you through the day. Nothing more. Nothing less.

For some reason, it's important to me that you realise how stressful my job is. In fact, it's probably more stressful than yours, because the stakes are higher. If I want to stay out of jail, I've got to be one step ahead of you.

Even if mine are the footsteps you can hear behind.

I've always got to be there to trip you up. And I've always got to be smart enough to make sure that no one does the same to me.

Newspapers get all pious about thieves like us. But why should other people have everything just because they've been given stuff that we haven't?

All we're trying to do is spread it about a bit. It's only fair.

Don't you think?

SIXTEEN

There was no getting out of it. It would have looked distinctly un-neighbourly not to have gone. But all the time she was in the Hon. Mrs R-R's Audi TT (predictably with a personalised number plate), Georgie kept feeling that there was more to this than met the eye.

Was it possible that somehow her client knew about her past connection with Lyndsey and was trying to make her feel guilty? Or was she was one of those women with more time on her hands than she needed and who decided on a whim to visit a woman she hardly knew?

Then again, thought Georgie as the Audi took a sharp bend with breathtaking arrogance – which went with the driver – maybe she was being unkind. Perhaps Mrs R-R was more compassionate than she'd given her credit for.

'I had a friend who died of leukaemia.' The words came out suddenly after a ten-minute journey of near-silence, during which Georgie had been wanting to hang on to the door for comfort but not liked to.

'I'm sorry.' So maybe that explained it.

There was a shrug of elegant shoulders at the wheel which made Georgie feel even more nervous, especially as they were going through an amber light at the time. 'These things happen. But it can't be very pleasant when you move somewhere new.'

'I'm surprised they did that,' Georgie heard herself say. 'If it was me, I'd want to stay close to a place I knew rather than going to a strange hospital for treatment.'

'But not everyone is you.' The statement came out sharply, causing Georgie to look across in concern. 'Or like me. Or like Lyndsey, come to that. Just as well we're all different, don't you think?'

Once more, Georgie had an uneasy feeling there was much more than met the eye behind these philosophical comments. But they had, she realised, taken her mind briefly off her own situation. And now they were pulling up outside the hospital.

'Got any spare change for the machine? I only carry plastic.'

The request took her by surprise. Fumbling for her purse, she went through the zipped part where she kept coins. Nothing. It would have to be a note. Her fingers closed round something hard. She gasped.

'What is it?' Those eyes narrowed.

'My card. The one that was in the box. It's here.'

The eyes narrowed again. 'Do you think you put it there?'

'No.' But even as Georgie spoke, she wondered if she was going mad. Was it possible that she had moved it without thinking? Surely not. Yet what other explanation could there be.

'Think about it later,' commanded Mrs R-R, swinging her legs out of the Audi. They had rather lumpy ankles under the casual white trousers, noticed Georgie irrelevantly, her mind still whirling. How the hell did the credit card get into her purse?

'Look. We've got free parking for the first hour so we don't have to worry about change after all.' Mrs R-R consulted her phone. 'She's on Fraser wing. Let's go, shall we?'

Georgie had never liked hospitals. They reminded her of when she was fourteen and she'd gone in for an appendix operation. Her mother had told her to 'put up with' that aching nag which had started on the Friday night. By the time it got to Sunday, she was in severe discomfort.

'We can't bother the doctor at the weekend,' her mother had said brusquely. 'It can wait until Monday.'

But when she began screaming with agony during the night, even her mother had to concede it 'might need looking at'.

'So embarrassing,' she said, dialling for an ambulance as though all this was Georgie's fault. Even when she came round from the operation, she failed to show much sympathy. 'Peritonitis can happen very suddenly, the doctor said.' Then she'd sniffed. It was almost as though she was exonerating herself from any blame for not having called an ambulance earlier.

Georgie had stayed in hospital for nearly two weeks. 'You were very lucky,' said the fatherly consultant during one of his rounds. 'You could have died. If you ever get a pain like that – or know someone who does – act a bit faster.'

She'd been shocked but at the same time glad that her mother hadn't heard. It would only have made her cross and defensive. However, she'd told Lyndsey when she'd come to visit. 'That's awful,' her friend had said, appalled. 'my mum said your mother was negligent.'

Negligent? Really? Georgie hadn't thought of her as that. Merely cold. Until now, she'd tried to explain her mother's distance by her father's early death. Now however, she felt a coldness setting in herself. What kind of mother didn't do anything when her daughter was clearly in pain?

Maybe through guilt, her mother failed to visit her after that in hospital. Instead it had been Lyndsey who'd come in every day after school. Lyndsey who had painted her fingernails in an attempt to make her giggle, even though that hurt. Lyndsey who had assured her that the scar would fade in time and yes, of course she'd be able to wear bikinis again soon.

Now, as Georgie followed Mrs R-R through the antiseptic corridors, she found herself feeling like a complete rat. What kind of friend had she been? Yet what else could she have done? Time and time again she'd thought of getting in touch with her old friend but it was impossible. Not if she wanted to stay out of prison.

Perhaps that's why she'd never had a best friend since. If you grew close to someone, you lost them, Georgie told herself. Hadn't Georgina proved that?

'Fraser Ward,' announced Mrs R-R bossily. 'Here we are.'

Georgie watched with a certain admiration as her companion marched up to the desk and announced that they were here to see Lyndsey Green. 'Yes, I am aware we're outside visiting hours but my friend and I both work and are unable to come at any other time. I'm sure you can make an exception.'

Both work? Mrs R-R didn't seem at all fazed by the lie. Clearly her tone worked on the nurse who, after a quick phone call, announced that she would 'allow it this time'. What did it take to have that kind of arrogance?

As they followed the nurse down the corridor, her mobile rang. Unknown. 'Sorry. I thought I'd turned it off. Won't be a minute.'

Hanging back by the desk, she pressed answer. 'Georgie speaking.'

'Mrs Hamilton?' The voice was deep. Slightly rough without being common. 'This is Security. I need to ask you some questions. Is this a convenient time?'

'Yes. Yes. Thank you for calling back.' A nurse waved crossly, indicating mobiles weren't allowed. 'Can you hold on for a minute please?'

She dived back towards the lifts. 'Hello. Hello?'

Blast. The caller had gone now. And because it had been an unknown number, she didn't know how to call back. Maybe they'd ring again. Georgie waited for a few minutes by the lift but nothing happened. Something didn't feel right – and it wasn't just the nervousness of having to visit Lyndsey. It was a different kind of unease.

'*This is Security.*'

That's what the voice had said. But it hadn't mentioned the name of her bank. Wasn't that a bit odd?

Just then the lift pinged. A short, grey-haired man with a slight stoop got out. He wore a worried expression and was looking around as if out of his depth. 'Excuse me,' he said. 'do you know where Fraser Ward is?' The Yorkshire accent was unmistakeable.

Georgie's mouth went dry. For a minute, her mind shot back all those years to Lyndsey's garage where – so exciting! – her father had put up a table tennis table as a surprise for her friend's twelfth birthday. She and Lyndsey had spent hours there, batting the ball back and forth. Even now, she was still quite good. Last year, on holiday in the Maldives with Sam, she had beaten him in every game they'd played.

'Yes,' she said numbly. 'It's down there.'

He looked at her again. This time, she could see his eyes registering her. Holding a question. 'Thank you,' he said hesitantly. Then, looking as though he was going to add something else, he began to speak. 'I don't suppose ...' Then he shook his head. 'No. it's all right. I'm very grateful to you.'

And with that, he shuffled off down the corridor.

Lyndsey's father! Of that, there could be no doubt. There was no way she could go and see her friend now. She'd have to go. Ring Mrs R-R later and make her excuses. It could easily be done. The bank had rung – that was true enough, wasn't it? They needed to speak to her. They ...

'There you are.' Mrs R-R's voice rang out imperiously down the corridor. 'Surely you've finished your call now. Lyndsey's waiting to see you. She's thrilled you made the effort.' Then her voice dropped. 'Poor thing. She doesn't look well. Not good at all.'

Doesn't look well. Not good at all.

Georgie began to shake. Those words were ingrained into her mind. Exactly what Joly had said all those years ago ...

'Can you come and look at her?'

Joly's whispers pierced the darkness inside the tent.

'I hope you don't snore,' snapped Vanda when they went to bed.

'Don't be difficult,' said Joly firmly. It was clear that Joly was the leader when it came to general rules. (He'd also let slip that in her case, 'Vanda' was short for 'Vanessa'.)

In the end, it had been Vanda who snored, which was why

107

Georgie was still awake when Joly's face slid into view, framed by the moon outside.

'She's breathing in an odd way and her forehead is hot.'

No need to ask who 'she' was. Georgina not only shared Joly's tent but she also clearly shared his heart. No wonder. Her friend was utterly gorgeous (it was amazing how a slightly over-large nose and sharper chin on Georgina's part made all the difference). If it wasn't for the fact that Georgina was so kind, Georgie might have felt jealous.

Now, as she padded across the sand towards the blue canvas tent on the other side of the jetty, Georgie began to feel worried. It was true that her friend had looked pale that afternoon. She'd also been sick, although that might have been the fish which hadn't, in her view, been properly cooked over the fire. That was why she had passed on it.

But now, as she laid her hand on Georgina's soft forehead, she felt more concerned. This was definitely a fever. 'I've got some paracetamol in my bag,' she'd offered.

Joly had looked so grateful that she thought he was going to hug her. 'Wonderful. We've completely run out and I don't trust half the stuff round here. You never know what the locals are going to give you.'

Georgie flew back to her bag and unpacked the first aid kit her mother had given her. 'This might come in handy if you're determined to go,' she'd said gruffly.

Now, helping her friend to sit up, she gently coaxed the tablets down the girl's throat. 'Water,' she instructed. 'We need to sponge her face down.'

They didn't have much: the bottles were running out – so Joly brought some sea water in a plastic bucket.

'I need to ask you something,' murmured Georgina.

'Not now,' said Joly sharply.

He was right. 'Get some rest,' Georgie commanded, feeling strangely in control. 'You can take over in a bit.'

Joly lay down beside her and for the next two or three hours, Georgie held a soaked cloth against her friend's forehead. By the time Joly woke up, Georgina was cooler and her breathing far more even.

'I think she's over the worst,' Georgie said, pleased and relieved at the same time.

'You're a star, you know that?' and before she knew what was happening, Georgie found herself enveloped in a bear hug. It was only a friendly hug but as it happened, she saw a shadow outside the tent. Jonathan, the boy who had tried to make a pass at her on the first day, peered in.

'So that's how it is,' he said quietly.

'Don't be such a prat, Jonathan,' said Joly moving swiftly away.

Georgie felt a pang of loss and also hurt.

'She's been helping me to nurse Georgina.'

'Is that what you call it?'

The boy gave them both a dismissive glance before gliding off.

'Watch him,' said Joly quietly. 'He's a bit of a snake. Same story at school. None of us liked him – apart from my gullible little brother who never sees anything bad in anyone – but somehow he managed to tag along.'

'You were *all* at school together?' asked Georgie curiously.

'Sure. It was what they call a progressive.' He laughed. 'Look where it's got us. Not a decent A-level, let alone a degree, between us. Still …

He pointed up to the early morning sun, which was beginning to rise over the water. 'We've got this and that's far more important than some wanker banker job like my dad had in mind for me.'

'Joly?' There was a murmur from the sleeping bag. 'Are you there?'

Instantly, Joly was by Georgina's side, kneeling down and murmuring words of endearment. Feeling it was time for her to go, Georgie, both proud of her role and yet also redundant, padded her way across the sand towards the tent. Vanda was still snoring, but Georgie couldn't go back to sleep. Instead, she

109

drew out a postcard from her bag – which she'd bought the day before at the local shop – and began writing.

'*Dear Lyndsey,*

This is such an adventure that I don't know where to begin ...'

Lyndsey was sitting up in bed, her face pale. She looked thinner than she'd seemed last week, if that was possible. By her side was the man who had got out of the lift.

Where was her mother, wondered Georgie fleetingly as she quaked inside. Was her cover going to be blown? What if the father said something? Deny it, said the voice inside her head. Lots of people look alike. They say everyone has a doppelganger somewhere.

'How very kind!' Her old friend's eyes fell on her. 'I can't believe how nice people are being. It's not as though you've known me for very long.'

Was that a test? If so, it appeared to be said in a very easy manner. Almost too easy. The words were slightly slurred.

'I'm afraid I'm still a bit woozy after the transfusion.' Lyndsey's eyes – surprisingly bright – turned to the drip at her side. There was a clear liquid going through. Glucose, perhaps.

'I'll feel better soon.'

'How often do you have to have them?' asked Mrs R-R in a softer voice than Georgie had heard before.

'Depends on my blood count. This hospital seems to be a bit different from my old one.' Lyndsey began to sound vulnerable. 'I do wonder if I should have stayed put ...'

'Nonsense.' Her father put a comforting hand on her arm. 'You're near me now and besides, the sea air will do you good.'

Near me? Georgie's chest began to beat with alarm.

'Sorry, everyone. I forgot to introduce you. This is my dad. He's one of the reasons we moved here.'

'And your mother ...' began Georgie, unable to help herself. Lyndsey's parents had been like bread and cheese. It was impossible to imagine them not being together. She had scolded him in a way that a pair of comedians might do on seventies

110

television. It meant love rather than criticism.

Lyndsey's voice trembled. 'Mum passed away last year.'

Mrs R-R shot her a look as if to say, 'Why did you ask that?'

Instantly, Georgie felt bad. It had also been stupid. Now the attention was on her. The father was staring intently. 'Do I know you from somewhere?' he asked.

Georgie tried to look him straight in the face. 'Maybe we've bumped into each other in town. I'm an interior designer.'

Lyndsey laughed. It was good to see her smile. It reminded her of the old Lyndsey who had painted her nails in hospital. 'Dad could do with one of those. Get rid of all those sixties and seventies beiges.'

'No.' Her father wasn't smiling. 'I mean from some years ago. You remind me of someone. That old friend of yours, pet. You know. Georgie. '

Lyndsey nodded. 'That's what I thought. Uncanny, isn't it?' She smiled rather sadly. 'Georgie was my best friend. She went on a gap year but never came back.'

'Really?' Mrs R-R's voice sounded sharp.

'She went travelling. Reckon she ended up in Australia. She was always talking about that.' Then Lyndsey yawned. 'You know the strange thing about being ill is that you find yourself thinking a great deal about the past and what might have been. There's a nurse on the ward who looks just like one of my old teachers from school. Still gives me the creeps.'

Mrs R-R smiled. 'I know what you mean. I disliked school too.'

That was a revelation. Somehow Georgie had a vision of her companion giving as good as she got in the classroom.

Lyndsey yawned again. 'You're tired.' Mrs R-R stood up. 'We'll give you some time with your father.'

'But you've only just arrived.'

'We weren't even meant to be here. It's not officially visiting time.'

'I probably got away with it because I'm old,' said her father. 'You can get away with a lot when you're my age.'

Nice to see he hadn't changed, though Georgie was still filled with sadness because Lyndsey's mother had died. It brought back all those feelings which she'd tried to shut out. Not a comfortable feeling. And what about her own mother? Was Lyndsey's father still in touch with her? How could she ask without it looking suspicious?

'I'll be back in a minute,' said Lyndsey's dad, getting up. 'Just need to find the necessary room. It will give you time to say goodbye to your friends.'

Mrs R-R brushed Lyndsey's cheek. Once more, Georgie felt surprise. What a conundrum. Capable of showing emotion one minute and coldness the next. 'Call if there's anything we can do.' Then she glanced at Georgie. 'See you downstairs. I need to make a call first.'

Suddenly it was just her and Lyndsey. Georgie felt her heart beating in her throat. Tell her, said a voice. Don't be mad, said another.

'I do hope you feel better soon,' she said lamely. 'Would you like me to bring in a book for you?'

Lyndsey had been a voracious reader. They both had. The librarian used to approve of them. 'In again,' she'd say, pleased, when they went down every Saturday morning to swap their latest Anya Seton or Georgette Heyer for another.

But the woman in the hospital bed was staring at her. Ignoring her question. This time, she wasn't smiling. Just looking at her as though she could see right through her. Suddenly she grabbed her waist. Her grip was stronger than she'd thought. The action was so unexpected that Georgie didn't have time to step away. Horrified, she found her top being pulled above the line of her designer navy culottes. There, starkly obvious, was the long, thin, appendectomy scar.

'I thought so,' breathed Lyndsey. 'It *is* you, isn't it, Georgie?'

SEVENTEEN

A geezer recognised me yesterday. In the post office queue, we were. Both taking a risk, really, considering it was the same one that we did over a few years ago.

He got caught. I didn't. Should have been faster on his feet.

Still, he knew that. It's the law of the jungle. Every bloke for himself. Everyone knows that. Wasn't my fault that he got four years and I got away. Could easily have been the other way round.

Even so, I felt my heart beating when he came up to me, swaggering with his hands in his pockets and a mean look on his face.

'You're doing all right for yourself then,' he said, eying the gold chain round my neck.

I stood my ground. Made eye contact. Did the stuff you're meant to do if you want to look big. 'Can't complain,' I said.

Then he came real close. Put his mouth against my ear. 'What did you do with the stuff?' he hissed.

'What stuff?' I said, stepping away.

His face blackened. 'You know bloody well.'

I made a sign that we should step outside. Other people in the queue were looking at us suspiciously. I'd only come in to send a parcel. Didn't need this bother.

'I dropped it,' I said.

His eyes turned nasty. Cold and threatening. 'You don't expect me to believe that? There was at least a grand in the bag.'

113

I thought back to the terrified post office woman who had handed the money over. Sometimes her face haunts me. We didn't hurt her. Not physically. But she isn't there any more.

'It's the truth,' I said.

I meant it. I did drop the bag. In the lounge of my mate's house. It lasted me a few months but I was greedy and spent too much. Then I had to think of other ways of making money. Like this.

Right now, I had my fists ready. Curled up into a ball in case he got heavy. 'I'm surprised you have the nerve to come back to the same place,' he said.

Me too. But it's my local, isn't it? And 'sides, as I said, the girl has gone. The CCTV wasn't working. It said that in the local paper. And – luck's usually on my side – there weren't any witnesses. My mate only got caught because his fingerprints were on the counter and he had previous.

Right now I shrugged. 'Better get going,' I said, trying not to sound scared, 'or I'll be late for work.'

He laughed. A rather nasty short laugh. 'You've got a job?'

I grinned. 'The best kind.' Then I fingered my gold chain meaningfully. 'The type where I can't get caught. Not if I'm clever.'

I turned my back and sauntered off. But his words rang out in the air. 'Don't be too cocky, mate. It will get you in the end. It always does.'

EIGHTEEN

Georgie stood frozen to the spot.

'I knew it was you at the dinner party,' said Lyndsey, letting go of her shirt and sinking back into the bed. The previous sudden strength seemed to sap away and she looked drained.

But at the same time, she looked excited. 'I always hoped we'd see each other again one day. You were my best friend, Georgie. I've never had another one since, you know.'

Me too, she almost whispered. Me too.

Suddenly, to Georgie's horror, Lyndsey's eyes filled with tears. 'Why did you just go off like that? Why didn't you stay in touch? I mean, I know things were bad with your mother but you could have lived with us in the holidays. You had a university place, Georgie. Such a waste to give it up like that!'

Still she couldn't say anything. If she did, she'd be admitting the truth. The longer she stayed silent, the longer she had to make something up.

But it wouldn't come. Hadn't she prepared herself for a moment like this for the last twenty or so years? Hadn't she prepared alibis and excuses and stories to 'prove' that she couldn't possibly be the old Georgie Smith?

Yet now the moment had come – the moment of reckoning – Georgie felt terribly tired. Tired of living a lie. In one way, Lyndsey's recognition was a huge relief.

'It's a long story,' she said, looking around to make sure that Mrs R-R or Lyndsey's father weren't on their way back to the ward. 'It happened like this ...'

After Georgina got better, she was really grateful and told everyone that Georgie had 'saved her bacon'. Joly was all over her too; constantly putting his long, tanned arms around her and telling her she was 'incredible'.

Both Vanda and Jonathan hated this and made constant snide comments. 'It was only a mild fever. What's all the fuss about?' Seeing this, Georgina showered Georgie with even more 'favours' to prove her gratitude. She insisted on giving her clothes and, on one occasion, spent hours braiding her hair.

Her keenness to touch her as she did this – stroking her cheek almost lovingly – made Georgie feel really uncomfortable. Not only that, but she kept going on about secrets.

'Are you sure you don't have any?'

Georgie laughed to try and defuse the situation. 'Quite sure.'

She waited for her friend to express disapproval but this time, she seemed pleased. 'Good. Every girl needs her secrets, you know. It makes her more mysterious.'

Such inconsistent behaviour clearly made her even more attractive in Joly's eyes. Often, she would see Georgina pushing him away or telling him he was a 'complete prat' in a loud voice. Then, minutes later, she'd be standing on tiptoes to cup his face with her hands and pull his mouth down on hers in front of everyone. He didn't need a second bidding.

'This attention-seeking is nothing new, you know,' Vanda would say, observing her confusion. 'The trouble with Georgina is that she doesn't know what she's thinking herself. Never did. Even when her parents were alive. That girl's got past issues, if you ask me. Goodness knows what.'

How unkind! Yet it only served to affirm in Georgie's mind that Vanda wasn't very nice.

Often she thought of her old friend Lyndsey at home – with her mischievous grin and 'carrot top', wishing she was here with her. When Georgina wasn't being weird, she was really lovely. But, despite their tempestuous relationship, she was always with Joly. Often, at night, she would hear the two of them in his tent making strange noises: low moanings that would escalate into cries that worried her until she heard them ending in terms of endearment which left her in no doubt about what they had been doing.

It made Georgie feel desperately lonely.

Once, she caught Vanda sitting upright, listening too. 'Jealous?' she demanded with that sharp look of hers.

'No.'

'Louisa was jealous too. That's why she did it.'

'Did what?'

But Vanda just turned away. More worryingly, Georgie knew that this spiteful girl had seen through her. She knew Georgie fancied Joly. But who wouldn't? Just as well that she was realistic enough to know that he would never be in her league.

Even so, he punctuated her dreams. One morning, she woke up early, bolt upright, certain that he was kissing her. To her disappointment – and also relief – there was no one in the tent apart from Vanda, who was snoring away as usual.

It wouldn't be right, she told herself, for Joly to kiss her. That wouldn't be fair on Georgina. But it was so hard when he kept putting his arm around her in a friendly fashion, not to imagine what might happen if she'd been born in the other girl's place.

Feeling restless, she slipped into her shorts and T-shirt and went for a walk along the beach. It was all so beautiful! Even after over a month, she had to keep pinching herself to check she was really here. White sand that felt so soft against her feet. An azure sea that stretched on for ever. What else could she want?

Yet she knew she couldn't stay here for ever. The money was running out. She needed to get a job. Ideally, something to do with fashion, but that seemed impossible out here.

'You don't need to worry about that,' Georgina had said the other night when she'd confided her worries. 'You can share our food.'

But how did they all afford to enjoy themselves? Georgie presumed they must come from very rich families. Certainly, Vanda was always going on about Georgina having a trust fund. Georgie wasn't sure what that meant exactly but it sounded as though her friend was 'set up nicely', as her mother had said about the girl next door who had married a doctor.

Now, as she walked along the beach, feeling the sand between her toes, Georgie spotted a figure crouching in the brushwood next to a shack. It was Joly, speaking to one of the local boys! She could see from the way he was speaking that he wouldn't want to be disturbed. Something also told her to hide. She sidestepped quickly behind a tree at the edge of the brushwood, but just as she ducked out of sight, she trod on a twig and there was a sharp crack.

Instantly, from behind the tree where she was hiding, managed to peep found and see the local boy look up, his eyes widening. Joly too looked around, his eyes searching. He saw her but said nothing.

Georgie knew instinctively that she had to stay exactly where she was.

'It's all right,' she heard Joly say. 'Just an animal.'

Then he handed over a small, clear plastic bag of what looked like sugar. In return, the boy gave him a fistful of notes. Then, all in the space of a few seconds, the boy jumped up and ran off through the shrubwood.

Georgie waited behind the tree. Should she come out and say hello? Or should she pretend she hadn't seen anything? It all looked rather mysterious.

'He's gone.' Joly's voice didn't have its usual jovial tone. 'You can come out.'

Slowly she did so. Joly's face was solemn. She almost didn't recognise him without his usual smile. 'Shall we walk?'

As they strode back to the camp along the beach, he draped an arm casually along her shoulder. His touch thrilled her. She could feel herself growing damp below, the way she did when

118

she explored herself at night.

'You're probably shocked,' he said easily.

'Shocked?' she turned her face to his. They were so close that he could easily have leant down and kissed her. No, that was wrong. He belonged to Georgina. Even so, she was thrilled by the proximity that took them to a new level of intimacy. 'Why should I be shocked? You only sold him some sugar.'

Then his face broke out into a grin. 'Either you're very clever or you really don't know what's going on.' He had stopped now and his face was so close to hers that she could hardly breathe. 'We don't all have trust funds, you know. But at the same time, we don't want jobs in the city.'

He held up a hand to indicate the beach and the sea. 'Where else would we want to live? But it costs money. So we have to pay for it somehow.'

Georgie was confused. 'But how?'

Then something else flashed across his face. It looked like the pity that had flashed over Lyndsey's parents' faces when they'd visited her in hospital after the appendicitis. 'You really don't know, do you? Maybe it's just as well, in case we are caught.'

His voice had a tinge of fear to it.

'Caught for what?'

His fear was catching and she could feel herself trembling.

'Nothing. Nothing.'

He'd moved away from her now and she felt a jolt of loss. Then he began to stride along the beach and she had to run to keep up with him. 'Forget what you've seen. Do you hear me?'

She nodded. At that moment, she'd have done anything for him. 'And don't tell Georgina. Jonathan knows, of course, but there's not much I can do about that.'

Knows what, she wanted to ask. But that might annoy him. And if there was one thing she'd learned from her mother it was that you didn't want to annoy people. Not if you wanted them to love you.

They reached his tent. Inside, she could see Georgina in her sleeping bag. 'Of course,' she said softly. Then he placed his lips on her forehead.

Every bone in her body shivered with excitement.

'Thank you for understanding.' Then he paused. 'You don't pay us anything for your food, do you?'

Silently, she shook her head.

'Every now and then, I might ask you to carry a package and leave it in the spot where you saw me.' His eyes narrowed. 'But you mustn't mention it to anyone else, OK?'

'OK.'

'Good.' He hesitated. 'I trusted Louisa. She was one of us. But then she threatened to split on us so we made her leave.' Gently he traced the outline of her lips. 'I don't want to have to do that to you.'

Then he slipped inside the tent and – with a terrible ache – Georgie saw him lie down beside Georgina.

Threatened to split on us? What about? Was it possible that those packages contained drugs? Was she being naïve, Georgie asked herself. Neither she nor Lyndsey had had anything to do with that kind of thing even though the boy next door had been 'done' for it.

Meanwhile, Georgie's lips were still burning from Joly's touch. If that's what his finger could do to them, what would happen if he'd actually put his mouth against them?

A wave of excitement raced through her. Of course she wouldn't split on him. How could she?

Lyndsey's eyes were wide in her pale face. 'What happened next?'

Georgie closed her eyes. She felt tired. Telling the truth was always exhausting. She'd read that phrase in a book once and it had stayed with her.

'It's complicated ...'

'I'm sorry,' said a nurse walking briskly up. 'Visiting hours have been over for some time now. We allowed you in as a favour but I really must ask you to leave now.'

'Come back,' pleaded Lyndsey, holding out her hand. 'I can't believe we've found each together again. I don't want to lose you. It's so comforting at a time … at a time like this.'

Georgie looked round quickly. Where was Lyndsey's father? Could he have heard? 'You mustn't tell anyone,' she said quietly.

'I won't.'

The nurse was staring at her suspiciously. Instantly, Georgie knew she'd made herself even more vulnerable but there'd been no option. How could you refuse a sick woman? A woman who had been your very best friend?

On the way out, she met Lyndsey's dad waiting in the corridor. 'Thought I'd give you two some more time together,' he said, his eyes on hers.

Did he know?

Maybe. Maybe not. She could only hope that Lyndsey kept her promise.

'I'm glad that my daughter has already made new friends,' he continued, his eyes on her. 'Goodness knows she's going to need them.'

Georgie felt her throat thicken. She couldn't find Lyndsey only to lose her again. There was so much she'd wanted to ask her too. Like whether her mother was still living in the old place …

'I'll come back tomorrow,' she said.

The older man nodded. 'Just as long as she doesn't get upset.' His words cast a warning note into the air.

'Why would she do that?' Georgie managed to say.

He shrugged. 'I don't know, lass. You tell me.'

So he knew. Or at least suspected.

Go, said the voice inside her. Go away and don't come back. Do you really want to blow your cover after all this time?

'I'm sorry,' she said quickly. 'I have to go now. Bye.'

Her head was a whirl as she made her way through long corridors with that ever-present whiff of disinfectant, towards Mrs R-R's car. What should she do now?

The thoughts flying around her brain were almost enough to block out her client's obvious annoyance.

'What took you so long?' Mrs R-R adjusted her designer sunglasses as she started the engine. 'Really, Georgie. Time-keeping isn't one of your strengths, is it?'

By the time they got back, Georgie had worked out a plan. It was the only way, she told herself. The only way to keep this façade going.

'Move?' demanded Sam shocked. 'Why do you want to do that? I thought the whole idea was to put down roots after so much travelling. That's what you've always said.'

'I know, but I've changed my mind.'

It sounded weak and she knew it. 'You only have to read the property pages to see that lots of people our age are downsizing.' She clutched at her husband's sleeve, aware that she was beginning to sound desperate. 'We could use the money to buy somewhere smaller and live on our savings. You could reduce your hours and I might start a new business in a different place.'

'But that doesn't make sense. It would be hard to build up a new client base for both of us.' Sam's held her at arm's length, looking straight at her. 'What's going on, Georgie?'

'All this,' she blurted out. 'All this stuff about me! Stolen bank cards. My car which was there one minute and not the next. And now this latest thing ...'

'What latest thing?'

'Nothing.'

'No.' This time, he caught her sleeve. 'What do you mean?'

She was about to protest but then she saw Lyndsey in her head. Her old friend lying in a hospital bed. The whiff of antiseptic. Plastic meals. Time was running out for her. Time was running out for them both. All her old thoughts about hanging on to her fight were beginning to weaken.

'I had another savings account,' she heard herself say as she turned away from him. 'An emergency one, just in case.'

His eyes went steely. 'Just in case of what?'

Too late, she realised she should have kept quiet. 'Just in case.'

'You mean you had an account which I didn't know about?'

'Sort of.'

His voice took on a hard edge. 'Well, either you did or you didn't. And if you did, I'm beginning to wonder why.'

She sank onto a chair. 'I don't know. I just … I just felt safe knowing I had some savings of my own.'

'Go on.' The hurt in those two words was painful. Too late, she realised she'd made a mistake in not keeping this back.

'Someone's got to it. They've emptied it.'

'How much?'

She couldn't speak.

'I said how much, Georgie?'

'Nearly five thousand.'

He let out a sharp, disbelieving laugh. 'And you kept this from me?'

'The point is that someone's taken it.'

'That's *not* the point. The issue here is that you kept a secret from me. If you did that, what other secrets do you have?'

If only he knew!

The words came stammering out of her mouth. 'The thing is that I kept the account card in a box upstairs, but when I checked, it wasn't there. Then I found it in the back of my purse.'

Her husband's face changed again. This time it was genuine fear. 'It's like the car,' he said, moving towards her. 'You said that had been stolen. But it hadn't. You'd simply forgotten you'd left it there. Just like you probably forgot you'd put this card in your purse.'

He drew her to him. The familiar smell of his clothes made her want to weep. So too, did his change of voice. Sympathetic rather than accusing.

'You need medical help, darling. Don't worry. We'll get through this. I promise.'

NINETEEN

I've driven people mad through doing the kind of thing I do. I didn't know this till I heard about a pensioner who cracked up when her savings were emptied.

Strictly speaking, that wasn't me. It was one of the team.

But it's what we all do.

That made me feel bad for a bit. Mental illness is shit. My mother had it. She'd sit and stare into space for hours. Forget to feed me, she would.

When the neighbours found me, I weighed the same as a five year old. I was ten at the time.

Didn't even know what the word 'foster parent' meant.

Just as well.

Sometimes I try to block it out but every now and then, it comes back to haunt me. All this stuff about celebrity abuse. It almost makes me laugh.

Except that if I'm not careful, I'd cry.

Even now I can remember stiffening in bed, as my foster dad padded across the room. 'If you say anything,' he'd whisper, 'you'll go back to your mum's and not get fed.'

So I didn't say anything. I just lay there.

No point in telling the social worker. People don't believe you. I'd learned that one at an early age.

One day, I told myself , I'd get out. Meanwhile, I had to sit tight.

I don't like to think about what happened next. Maybe another time. Right now, I've got other things to do. It's how I block it out, see. Keep busy.

TWENTY

'Of course I didn't.'

Ellie's voice was rich with indignation on the other end of the phone. 'Dad's got to you, hasn't he? I can imagine him thinking I'm a thief but not you.'

Georgie felt as if she'd plunged a knife through her own chest. Why had she said anything? Of course Ellie wouldn't have done that. Despite the lack of actual blood ties, they were closer than most mothers and daughters. And now she'd blown it.

'I'm sorry,' she mumbled. 'But all these weird things are happening to me. None of them make sense.'

Instantly, she could feel Ellie's psychologist mode switching on with all the fervour of a keen student. 'Life happens like that sometimes. Certain schools of thought think it's a test that we're all put through at particular times of our lives. We have to prove our mettle by coping or else we go under.'

'Thanks.'

'Don't take it the wrong way. I'm trying to encourage you, Mum. You're not the kind of person to go under. You're strong. You'll get through this.'

Would she? Fleetingly, Georgie thought back to the time in Thailand when her world had fallen in. She hadn't thought she could get through that either, but the flight or fight instinct had kicked in and she'd fought back. She'd hoped she'd won then – after making some serious concessions – but now it looked as though she was wrong. Her past had come back to get her.

Almost as vengefully as this person – whoever he or she was – that was emptying her savings account.

'Let's get practical,' continued Ellie crisply. 'Your hidden credit card went missing and then used. But somehow it turns up in your purse. You didn't put it there. Or you don't think you did. That leaves two options. Either someone stole it and replaced it, hoping it make it look as though you were losing your memory. Or you really did use it and can't remember.'

That was the gist of it.

'So start off with a two-prong attack. Go and see the doctor. Have some checks. And at the same time, push the bank. It's got to do something. There must be a record of you or someone else taking the money.'

'They're looking into it but it all takes so long.' She sighed. 'Data protection issues; security checks; nothing happens fast.'

'Then use that breathing space to get yourself looked at. Honestly, Mum. It's not being weak. It's being sensible.'

Reluctantly, Georgie made an appointment. Her neighbour had recommended the doctor shortly after they'd arrived in the UK and she liked her. The doctor's son was in the same A-level year as Nick, and within months, they'd slipped into first-name terms ('just call me Laura') and often found themselves at the same local dinner parties.

But after explaining to Laura exactly what had happened, Georgie began to wonder if she should have booked an appointment with someone she didn't know.

It might have made it easier. Less embarrassing.

'Poor you.' Laura took off her glasses and gave her the sort of smile one reserved for a child who had fallen over and grazed her knee. 'I do think it's worth running a few tests but there's a wait, I'm afraid. The memory clinic is always busy.'

The memory clinic? 'That makes me feel as if I'm in my sixties,' Georgie tried to joke.

'You'd be surprised how early people can forget things.' Laura spoke solemnly as if she'd had personal experience herself. 'We'll also run some blood tests, in case it's hormonal.' She glanced at the screen in front of her. 'The last time you came – nearly a year ago now – you were having warm flushes.'

'Still am,' she admitted.

'Then it might be perimenopausal or menopausal. If so, there are some things we can give you for that. '

'HRT?'

'Or herbal supplements. They can work well too.'

Could it really be as simple as that? Knock back the tablets and your money stopped going missing? But it wouldn't solve the other thing. It wouldn't protect her from being exposed.

'There's something else too,' she began.

Laura waited. That's what she liked about her. She was so even-keeled. So nice. So practical. Not the kind of person who would have got herself into the mess Georgie had.

'I'm …' then she stopped.

'It's all right.' Laura laid her hand briefly on Georgia's arm. 'We're in the surgery. This is totally confidential.'

'I'm … anxious about something,' she blurted about. 'Worried about something that happened a long time ago which has suddenly come back to trouble me.'

There was a flash of curiosity in her friend's eyes, followed by sympathy. 'That's very common too, especially at our age. In fact, I've just been to a conference about it.'

She handed Georgie a leaflet. 'This might be worth following up. It's a walk-in clinic for low-grade stress and anxiety. No appointments necessary.' She faltered.

'Yes?'

'The only thing is that the doctor who runs it is married to Becky.'

Becky?

She'd been in their book group. In fact, she was one of the reasons Georgie had left. Becky had always dominated the evenings with her over-bearing views.

'Of course, there's a confidentially clause but …'

129

'Thanks.' Georgie rose, leaving the leaflet on the table. Who knew if doctors told their wives about patients? Of course they weren't meant to but it must happen. And there was no way she could risk this getting out. Maybe, she told herself as she left the doctor's, she needed to get back to the bank. Get heavy.

In the event, there was no need. After getting home and walking Beano along the beach, breathing in the fresh sea air, grateful for the diversion, she returned home to find a message on the landline. It was the security people. They wanted her to ring back.

Miraculously, she got through almost immediately. 'Mrs Hamilton?'

Why was it that ever since this had happened, her name didn't feel real?

'Before we can speak, I need to run through some security checks.'

She was used to this now. Before every conversation, tit was the same thing. Date of birth. Sometimes place of birth. Password. Etc etc.

'Thank you.' This time the security woman spoke English as a first language. Georgie felt a guilty flash of relief. She was the last person in the world to be racist – how she abhorred it – but at times of crisis it was so much easier to speak to someone who didn't talk fast or used words in an unrecognisable manner.

'We have some news.'

Georgie held her breath.

'The transaction was made in Edinburgh last Tuesday.'

Georgie felt a huge flood of relief. 'So it couldn't have been me!'

'I'm afraid that's difficult to prove. The person who withdrew it – from one of our branches – provided the correct password and correct date of birth.'

'But this can't be possible.' Georgie felt a mounting sense of panic. 'That's fraud. What about your CCTV?'

There was an embarrassed pause. 'Unfortunately it wasn't in

operation at the time.'

'But what can I do?'

'Out security team is looking into it. Meanwhile, I suggest you contact the police ...'

The police? Georgie, sat, frozen with the shock by the phone, long after putting it down. Beano pawed at her, sensing something was up. She hadn't wanted to call the police last time but had had no choice. Sam would have thought it was weird if she hadn't. What if someone put two and two together? Twenty-two years was a long time but not that long.

But now it looked as though they were going to be involved again. Some sharp cop somewhere might make the connection. Thanks to the internet, the whole world was connected. Including Thailand and the UK.

Her mobile rang sharply, making her jump. 'Hello,' she whispered.

'Georgie.'

Georgie froze.

'Who is this?'

'Lyndsey.'

'This isn't a great time.' Her voice came out as a cry.

'I'm sorry. But can you come in? I've got to have another transfusion later this afternoon and I need to speak to you. Please.'

Just as well she wasn't working. When she'd been busy, she'd never have time for hospital visiting or ringing up banks. It was, Georgie conceded wryly, one of the advantages of being the dark sheep of the interior design business in town.

Jo still wasn't returning her calls, despite the fact that Georgie had paid her the missing money.

For the first time in years, Georgie found herself wishing that she had a sister to share this with. Lyndsey hadn't had sisters either. 'But we have each other,' they'd often said. Now, as she walked towards the hospital bed, Georgie began to wonder how she could possibly have managed for all these years without her old friend.

'You came!' Lyndsey smiled weakly at her. 'It's as though we've picked up from where we've left. It's so easy to talk, don't you think?'

Georgie took the thin hand in hers. 'Yes. It is.' She looked down at the bed where Lyndsey's painfully thin form almost poked out from under the blankets. 'So you've got to have another transfusion?'

'A nuisance, isn't it, but it will make me feel stronger.'

She spoke brightly and Georgie found herself wondering if she would be as upbeat in her situation. Money, she told herself, was nothing compared with health.

'You said you needed to talk to me.'

Lyndsey nodded. 'I need you to tell me what happened next.'

She spoke like a child waiting for a story to be completed.

'Don't you see?' added Lyndsey, an unexpected bright light in her eyes. 'For years I always wondered what had happened to you. I was scared you were dead. Your mother thought so.'

Her mother …

A fleeting memory of coal tar soap mixed with disapproval wafted back to her. It wasn't pleasant.

She felt a flash of pity. So her leaving was all for nothing. 'I can't go back. I've made myself a new life now.' She glanced around but there was only one other patient in the small room. An old lady who was sleeping noisily. 'If my husband or children or anyone else finds out about this, they will never forgive me. You do understand, don't you? This has got to be our secret.'

'My dad recognised you. Or thought he did.'

'Then you'll have to tell him he's wrong.' Georgie heard her voice rise, not the kind of soothing voice one should use on an invalid. 'Do you understand?''

Lyndsey nodded and immediately Georgie felt bad. This was an ill woman. She needed handling with kindness, not anger.

'I just need to know what happened to you. I'm worried. You can tell me, Georgie. We always told each other everything.'

It was true. Georgie felt herself slipping away. Back in Thailand. Being watched by the boy with the close-set staring eyes who had seen Joly hug her.

Jonathan followed her around for the next few days until Georgie's skin began to crawl. It didn't help that the others noticed too.

'Johnny's got the hots for you,' Georgina said, nudging her meaningfully.

Joly nodded but his eyes didn't smile, Georgie noticed.

'I don't fancy him,' she announced.

Did she imagine that or did Joly look relieved?

'By the way,' added Georgina quietly. 'There's something I need to ask you.'

'Not now.' Joly's voice cut in.

'What do you mean?' Georgie turned from one to the other. Wanted to ask her what? Suddenly, she recalled her friend had said something similar when she'd been ill.

'It doesn't matter,' Georgina now said, almost sulkily.

Joly nodded. 'Exactly. Forget it.'

Forget what? Was it anything to do with the obsession that Georgina seemed to have about secrets? She couldn't imagine life now without her new friends. But they weren't like anyone else she'd ever known. It was both exciting and unnerving, as though she was treading on ground that might open up and hold her safely – or suffocate her.

The following week, when they were all sitting round the fire, Georgie had to move places twice to get away from Jonathan. Surely he could get the message? She got so frustrated that when someone circulated the joint around as usual, she took a longer drag than normal. Almost immediately, she felt warm. Slightly heady but in a pleasant way. The half bottle of wine helped too.

133

Jonathan smiled. 'Learning to relax, are we? Like the other night?'

'Be quiet,' she said fiercely. 'I told you before. It was just a hug. A friendly hug.'

'If you say so.' He blew the smoke out deliberately. 'Not sure our friend Georgina would see it that way.'

Georgie felt like shoving him, the way she'd pushed one of the boys in the playground when he'd bullied Lyndsey. 'If you don't shut up, I'll sort you out,' she heard herself say.

Jonathan's eyebrows raised. 'I like a girl with spark. Always thought you were a bit different from the rest of us even though you try to ape your idol.' He glanced at Georgina whose head was in Joly's lap.

Georgie felt a stab of longing. Why did she always get the boys she didn't want? Standing up, she took another swig from the bottle that was being passed round and moved towards her tent. 'Want some company?' called out Jonathan.

One of the other girls sniggered.

'No. Just some time on my own.'

For a while, Georgie sat there, trying to think. Maybe it was time to move on. Perhaps Jonathan was right. She was trying to ape her 'alter ego'. Georgina, who was everything she'd always dreamed of being. Pretty. Charming. Clever. Enough money to do what she wanted. Georgina, who had gone to a smart school instead of her own rough comprehensive.

At home, she'd always felt she was a changeling. Sometimes, she used to tell Lyndsey, she wondered if her mother really was her mother. Perhaps she was adopted. Where else could she have got her flair for colours from? Certainly not Mum, with her frumpy A-line brown skirts.

'You don't really think that, do you?' Lyndsey had said.

No. But she wished it was true.

The laughter had died down now by the fire. Georgie put her head out just in time to see Jonathan lead Vanda by the hand into his tent. That was a relief. She'd got rid of her two least favourite people here, in one go. For once she could have a night to herself without any snoring.

Then she jumped as the tent flap opened.

'Joly?' she gasped. 'You frightened me,'

But before she could say any more, his arms were around her and his lips pressing down on hers. Immediately, her own responded. It felt so right. so good. As though they had been doing this all their lives.

Eventually, he drew back and Georgie felt a stab of disappointment. He was teasing her. Or else he was stoned. She certainly felt woozy from all the wine and the joint.

'I know exactly what I'm doing,' he said softly as if knowing what she was thinking.

'Georgina,' she managed to say; the taste of his mouth still numbing her tongue.

'Asleep,' he retorted shortly. And then his hands moved downwards ...

'You slept with your friend's boyfriend?'

Lyndsey's voice was shocked, jerking Georgie back to the present. She let out a hoarse laugh. 'If you think that's bad, I'd better not continue.'

Her old friend's face bore the look of someone who was riveted but horrified at the same time. 'You must go on. It's distracting me. And besides, as I said, I have to fill in the gaps.'

She could get up right now and run. It wasn't too late. But something about Lyndsey's pale face made her feel she should continue. She owed it to her friend. She owed it herself. But most of all, she owed it to Georgina.

When Georgie woke in the morning, it was much later than usual. She could tell from the chatter outside and the quality of the light that streamed through the canvas. Where was Vanda? The sleeping bag next to her was empty but ... but right next to her, breathing evenly with a face as untroubled as a male angel, was Joly.

How was she going to get him out of her tent without

135

anyone else finding out?

Georgie's heart began to pound. Maybe if she left first she could pretend that Joly had somehow gone back in to call her for breakfast. or maybe …

'Georgie!' sang a voice outside. 'Want a cup of tea? By the way, you haven't seen …'

The voice faltered at the same time as Georgina's lovely long blonde hair appeared at the flap. 'Joly?' she whispered.

Georgie had never seen anyone's face drain of colour before. Appalled, she watched her friend take in the naked man and then her own nudity.

'So this,' she whispered, 'was your secret. This is your way of repaying my friendship.'

No. *No*. 'I'm sorry. I'm so sorry …'

She reached out her hand but Georgina pushed her away, uttering a muffled cry of anguish like an animal in pain. Backing out of the tent, she disappeared from view but there was no mistaking the sound of footsteps running.

By the time Georgie had scrambled into shorts and a T-shirt and run out, her friend was nowhere to be seen.

By lunchtime, she still hadn't appeared. No one else seemed concerned. Vanda and Jonathan were so wrapped up in each other that they failed to notice anyone else. Meanwhile, Joly didn't wake up until way past midday, despite her shaking him. Even though he'd declared he hadn't been 'stoned', Georgie suspected he had been. Why else would he have done things to her in the night that she had never dreamed of, calling her his 'beautiful darling'?

She might look a bit like Georgina but there was no comparison mentally. Not when it came to degrees of confidence.

'Where's my girl?' were Joly's first words when she'd managed to wake him.

Instantly, Georgie felt crushed. So she'd been right. Last night had merely been a diversion in the Joly world.

Falteringly, she explained what had happened.

136

'No one's seen her?' he repeated. Then he jumped to his feet, grabbing his shirt as he ran. 'For God's sake, everyone. We need to form a search party. Georgina's missing.'

'Did you find her?' whispered Lyndsey.

Georgie was about to speak when there was the clinking of the trolley behind her. 'Time for your meds!' called out a nurse cheerily. 'End of visiting time, I'm afraid.'

'Will you come back tomorrow?' asked Lyndsey. 'After the transfusion?'

Georgie nodded, wishing she'd said no. Why had she allowed her past to return? As she walked briskly down the corridor, she tried pulling the metal gates down just as she'd down over the years whenever she felt the memories banging on the door.

But this time, the gate wouldn't move. It was stuck. Wide open. Joly's face. Frantic with worry. Georgina's face when she'd seen the two of them together. Shocked. Betrayed. Vanda and Jonathan. Eyes only for each other. Lyndsey and her mother at home. Getting on with ordinary lives. And then …

No. No, she wouldn't – couldn't – think of that. Time to get back to ordinary life. Time to nail this woman on the head. This imposter who had used her card. Somehow, Georgie felt certain she was a woman, although why, she wasn't sure. Presumably she was responsible for the other thefts and the YouTube video, too.

Who was she? Was it a random thief or was she specifically targeting Georgie … Stealing her identity just as she'd stolen someone else's …

Switching on her mobile, Georgie climbed into the driver's seat. Almost immediately, the phone started to ring. Putting it on hands-free, she swung out of the hospital drive, straight past another car which looked – at a glance – as if Lyndsey's husband was at the wheel.

'Hello?'

'Georgie?'

It was Sam's voice. But different.

'Can you come home? Something weird's happened.'

She drew a deep breath. 'Yes, I know. Someone's been using my card. Someone in Edinburgh. I haven't been anywhere near there. But – just my luck – the CCTV wasn't working.'

'Someone's been using my card too.' His tone was flat. Yet uneven. 'But the CCTV was doing just fine.' There was a silence. 'Apparently, she looked like you.'

That was impossible.

'The woman who used the card also knew the pin code.'

'But it couldn't have been me. Not if she was in Edinburgh.'

'That's the whole point. It wasn't Edinburgh. It was in the hospital. Two hours ago. '

In the hospital ...

Georgie began to shake. Her mouth went bone dry. So she was being watched. Spied on. Someone was trying to take her life away.

'Where are you now?'

She could hardly speak.

'Georgie. I said where are you now?'

There was a hoot as Georgie only just managed to avoid hitting another car. The other driver hooted, as well she might. That had been her fault. She hadn't been paying attention.

'I've been visiting Lyndsey,' she said numbly.

'In the hospital?' His voice had a pleading quality. Please say no. Please say you were nowhere near there.

'Yes. In the hospital.'

TWENTY-ONE

You can't beat a good disguise. When my dad was little, he did jobs in my Spider-Man mask. Used to tiptoe into my bedroom, he did, and nick it from under my pillow where I'd hid it.

The funny thing is that I'd nicked it myself from this kid at school whose parents gave me stuff.

I didn't know what my dad did with the mask until later. I thought he just wanted to play.

In a way he was. Cops and robbers.

My mum told me later that he'd put it on to rob post offices.

'Spider-Man Caught at Last' said the headline. He got eight years.

Sometimes I think that if he'd been around more, my life would have been different. I read a lot, now. And all that self-help stuff says the same thing. Boys need their fathers. Makes me laugh, it does.

There are some fathers who shouldn't be allowed near their kids.

I'm living proof of that.

But let's not go there.

TWENTY-TWO

'And you are certain it wasn't you?'

The policeman looked at her in such a way that Georgie wondered if there'd been some mistake. Was it possible that she was going completely mad and that yes, it had been her?

Rubbish.

'I could hardly be in two places at once,' she remarked tartly. 'Not unless I was Superman.'

Beside her, Sam prickled. 'We're just trying to get to the bottom of this, Georgie.'

She rounded on him. 'Don't you think I want that as well?'

Fear was making her angry. She hadn't wanted to contact the police again. It would increase her chance of being found out. You read about that all the time. Criminals were caught for a past crime when they were arrested for a more recent one. The thought made her shake.

But the bank security people – who were being very sympathetic, if ineffectual – suggested that both she and Sam went down and reported the crime in person at the local police station. 'It's not unusual for more than one person in a family to have their cards misused' a kindly woman told her. 'But a disguise – if that's what it is – is another matter.'

What do you mean, 'that's what it is?', Georgie had shot back. Didn't anyone believe her? Then again, maybe she'd had her full quota of being believed in life. At the time, all those years ago, she'd been amazed to get away with it. How ironic that after all this time when she'd finally stopped looking over her shoulder, there was now a very real possibility that she might be caught.

Or was there? After all, there wasn't the technology then that there was today. Surely there had to be thousands of people like her in the world; each living a different life from the one they were meant to be.

'... be in touch.'

Georgie suddenly realised they were being dismissed. 'Is that it?' she asked her husband as they made their way towards the car, grateful to be out of the official building with its grey walls and doors that – any minute, surely – she might be taken through.

Sam's mouth was set. 'What can they do? You heard them. Fraud – both online and at an ordinary cash machine – is vast. They can't keep up. That bloke there probably can't even send emails.'

She increased her stride to keep with his. 'Something strange is going on here. Someone knew you were in the hospital and is trying to make trouble for us.' He turned round to face her. 'Can you think of any reason why that might be?'

Don't blush. Don't blush. 'None at all.'

It was frighteningly easy how quickly the lie slipped out.

'Maybe Charles can get to the bottom of it.'

He clicked open the door and she slid in, her heart pounding.

Charles had been their best man in Hong Kong. He was a lawyer – an occupation which had made her feel nervous at the time under the circumstances.

'You've told him?'

'Emailed him immediately.' Sam started the car and slid out past two police cars coming in, one after the other. There was someone in the back of one. A young boy who looked scared witless. That could be her ...

'He can see us both in his office tomorrow afternoon. They've got a special department for online fraud.' Sam's lips tightened. 'Maybe they'll do a better job than the police or our banks.'

Georgie's heart leapt into her throat. Charles had never liked her. The feeling was reciprocated. 'You hardly know Sam,' he'd said rudely when they'd been introduced just before the wedding. 'You do realise he's probably on the rebound after his engagement ended.'

Sam had brushed his friend's remarks away. 'He's not a romantic,' he had said, drawing her to him. 'Doesn't believe in love at first sight. Don't worry. You'll warm to him when you know him better.'

But she hadn't. Over the years, they had both kept each other at a distance. When Charles had returned to the UK, shortly before them, and finally settled down at forty-three with a woman called Lavinia, Georgie had hoped he might mellow.

No such luck.

'I'm busy tomorrow,' she said quietly as they drove through town.

'Busy?' Sam never took his eyes off the road. But he was doing so now. 'This isn't a lunch date, Georgie. This is possibly our only chance of getting our money back. We're broke. Don't you see? There was a story about someone like us in the *Telegraph* only last week. Some poor bloke was defrauded of fifty thousand pounds and the bank wouldn't cough up. We can't afford it. The mortgage payment is due in a week's time.'

His voice rose in panic. Sam never panicked. It had been one of the things that had drawn her to him. He was older. Settled. Secure in a troubled storm. 'What are you doing that's more important than a meeting with Charles, who's been good enough to free up a slot for us?'

Think of something. Think of something. The large hospital sign loomed up at them as they took a right, towards their home.

'Lyndsey,' she began.

'Who?'

'That woman whom we met at Pippa's. She's got leukaemia.'

'The one you were visiting this morning when the card was

143

used?'

Her words fell over themselves in her eagerness. 'Yes. I promised to see her again tomorrow. Visiting time is at 2 p.m.'

They swung into the driveway. In front of them was her lovely house with its handsome latticed windows and clematis climbing up the right hand side of the front door. Home. A home they could lose if this wasn't sorted out.

'The appointment with Charles isn't until 5 p.m.' Sam turned off the engine and stared at her hard. Something had changed in his eyes. It made her scared. 'So you can meet me at his office. Can't you?'

That night, Georgie didn't sleep a wink. What would the children say when they found out? She couldn't even begin to think how Sam would react. There had to be a way round this. There simply had to be. Eventually, she fell into a light sleep from which she was woken by the alarm clock. For a brief moment, she recalled her dream. Joly had been running with her in his arms along the beach. No one was behind them, yet there was this awful sense of urgency.

Looking across to Sam's side of the bed, she saw it was empty. Instinctively, she swung her legs over the edge and made for the window. His car was gone.

Never, in their entire married life, could she recall Sam going to work without kissing her goodbye. Georgie's chest tightened with tension. She needed to talk to someone. But her usual friends – Pippa or Jo – simply wouldn't understand.

There was only one person who might. Someone whom she'd promised to return to.

Lyndsey was asleep when she arrived. Her father was sitting by her side, watching her. Georgie felt a jolt of jealousy. If she'd had a father, would he have done the same? She was pretty certain her mother wouldn't have. If that had been different, Georgie would have come out to face the music.

You can go a lot further in life if your parents love you.

'She had the transfusion,' said the old man, as though they'd been talking just now. 'Given her a better colour, don't you think?'

He spoke as if needing reassurance.

Georgie nodded, keen to please, even though she couldn't see much of a difference herself. 'They can do so much nowadays.'

He nodded eagerly. 'That's what I keep saying.'

'No, Dad. It's what I keep telling you.'

Both turned to the woman in the bed. 'You weren't asleep at all?'

'Sort of, Dad. Just drifting in and out.' Then her eyes fell on Georgie. 'You came then?'

The pleasure in her voice was unmistakeable.

'Of course. I promised.'

Georgie became uncomfortably aware that the man's eyes were firmly on her. 'Can't get over how similar you are to this girl we used to know. Georgie. Georgie Smith.'

It was no good. She couldn't stop the blush which was spreading over her face. 'Lots of people look like other people,' cut in Lyndsey. 'Remember how everyone said you resembled that comedian. What was his name?'

'So you're saying I'm fat and bald?'

They both burst out laughing. Once more, Georgie felt a pang of jealousy. Her friend was dying. Yet she and her dad could still share a joke.

'Dad,' said Lyndsey in a more serious voice now. 'Do you mind getting me a magazine from the shop downstairs?'

He grinned. 'I can take a hint. You two want a bit of girl time together. That's all right. I'll get myself a cup of tea from the canteen while I'm at it.'

He rested his eyes on Georgie, shook his head as though he was disagreeing with himself, and then bustled out.

'He knows,' said Georgie, trembling.

'Suspects, not knows,' corrected her friend, reaching out for her hand. 'Not surprising, really. You haven't changed much.'

Lyndsey reached out for her hand. 'I can't tell you how comforting it is for me. It's almost worth being here.'

'Don't say that.' Georgie took her friend's other hand too. It was cold. 'Something weird is happening. I don't understand it.'

Quickly she explained about the credit card frauds and the missing car which had turned up again. 'The last withdrawal was done in the hospital when I was here by someone who looked exactly like me.'

Lyndsey frowned and Georgie wondered if she'd been selfish in bothering such an ill woman. 'You're not,' she said as if reading her mind. Lyndsey had always been good at that. 'It's a distraction. I reckon Sam is right. Someone is after you, trying to cause trouble. An aggrieved client, perhaps?'

'I've considered that but I've never had any complaints.'

'What about the past?'

Lyndsey was expressing exactly what she'd feared herself. Surely it had to be more than a coincidence? 'You've turned up out of the blue,' Georgie said slowly.

'You don't think it's anything to do with me?' Her friend's eyes widened.

'No but … well it is odd, you've got to admit.'

She'd hurt her. Georgie could see that. But it had to be said.

'You were going to tell me what happened.' Lyndsey sounded accusing. 'You'd promised. You were going to tell me what happened after Georgina – the real one – went missing.'

The real one. Georgie flinched. For so many years, she'd seen herself as the real one. But now she was beginning to crawl back into her old skin. The young scared girl who knew she'd done something wrong. And who was about to do something so much worse.

They searched all day, going deep into the uninhabited parts beyond the small town. The heat was unbearable.

'If she's out here, how's she going to survive without water?' Joly kept saying.

'Maybe she had the foresight to take some with her after she spotted Lady Godiva here,' Vanda said sharply.

Georgie said nothing. It wasn't fair of them to blame her alone. Joly had made the first move. He'd kissed her first! Yet is seemed churlish to try and defend herself when Georgie was missing. Maybe later when they'd found her.

They had to find her. The other option was too awful.

'Perhaps she went over there,' said Jonathan, gesturing to the shrubland on the other side of the point.

'She wouldn't,' cut in Vanda sharply. 'Georgie might be a bit naïve at times – yes, she is, Joly, don't deny it – but she's scared of snakes.'

Georgie shivered. One of the first things they'd told her was to avoid that part of the island. Even the locals didn't go there.

'Well, I'm not checking,' said Jonathan staunchly. 'Friendship only goes so far.'

'I'll go,' Georgie heard herself offer.

'No.' Joly laid a hand on her arm.

'Why not?' Jonathan glared at her. 'If it wasn't for her, Georgina would still be with us.'

'It was me too,' said Joly quietly.

'Thank you,' she muttered but he didn't seem to hear. Still none of them moved. She had to do something. Jonathan was right. She'd helped to do this, even if she wasn't fully responsible. Twigs snapped below her feet as she crossed the bridge. Once she looked behind her in the hope that Joly was following. But he wasn't.

Something moved in the dry grass beside her. There was a flash of green and then a quicker flash of red. Georgie suppressed a little scream. You mustn't disturb snakes, she'd heard one of the locals saying. If you did, they'd pounce.

On and on. Through miles (or so it seemed) of scrubland and dry grass with twigs that snapped. Please don't let there be anything nasty lurking underfoot, she prayed. Another quick look back through the hazy sun. The others were way back now. Waiting where she'd left them. If Georgie knew that Joly hadn't had the courage to join her, would she still care for him?

Another snapping of twigs. Another glimpse of red. Through the trees this time. But it wasn't moving. What had Georgina been wearing that morning? Her blue sarong? No. She'd lent that to Georgie last week. Lent it to her new friend who'd repaid her by sleeping with her man.

Ever since Georgina had put her head through the tent that morning, Georgie had tried to blank the scene out of her head. But now she saw it. All too clearly. Georgina. In a short, red sundress. Red with spots that she'd bought in the market only yesterday.

The red patch over there had white spots.

Leaving the path – something else the locals had warned her against – she crunched over the dry scrubland towards it. Something hissed. There was a snake in the grass, eyeing her. What did it matter?

Running now, she threw herself onto the ground beside her friend. Georgina's must be sunbathing. Why else were her pale blue eyes wide open, looking up into the hot, burning sky?

On her leg, there was a drizzle of blood as if coming from a small puncture.

Another hiss. The snake had been joined by another.

'Go on then,' said Georgie chokingly. 'Take me too. I don't care. Not any more.'

Then she saw it. A stain. A dark red stain oozing onto the ground. Shaking, she heaved her friend over and screamed. There was a deep wound, wide and raw like a cut in a slab of meat. It wasn't just a snake bite that had done for her friend. There was a terrible wound too.

At the same time, she caught sight of something in the woods. A dark figure running. He must have been there all the time, Georgie realised as she began to race after him. 'Stop! Stop!

Then he turned. There was a flash of light. Light from the sun reflecting on the blade which he was brandishing.

There was no time to be scared. Grabbing his arm, she

148

wrested it away from her, using a strength she hadn't known she'd possessed. There. She had the knife now. No, he was pulling it from her. But if she bent his arm like this, she could …

It was his turn to scream now. A horrible, high-pitched, agonising scream. She'd cut him! She'd scored his cheek. Then he ran. Clutching his face and leaving her behind with the knife.

Quickly. Quickly before he returned. Georgie raced back to Georgina's body. Maybe she wasn't dead, after all. Maybe …

'What have you done?'

Joly's voice roared out in pain. His eyes went from Georgina's limp body to the knife in her hand and then back to Georgina's body again.

'It wasn't me!'

Surely he must believe her?

'It was a boy. He tried to stab me too. He …'

But he wasn't listening. Instead, Joly was scooping Georgina up with a low moan. 'Don't be dead. Don't be dead.'

She had to run to keep up with him, race along behind as he made for the bridge.

Tears blurred her eyes, making it difficult to see. Vanda's face and Jonathan's dimly came into view.

'Is she all right?'

Exhausted, she fell on the dusty ground. No one wanted to know if *she* was all right, despite the blood on her hands and clothes. Instead, they were crowded round the beautiful blonde girl on the ground.

Joly had his mouth over hers, pushing her chest up and down, despite the terrible gash.

'It's no good. Don't you see that?' Vanda's voice was full of scorn. 'She's gone.'

Then she raised her face. Never had she seen anyone so devil-like. 'You killed her. You killed her.'

'No. It wasn't me. It was someone else. I –'

But Vanda was lunging at her, as if ready to tear her apart. Jonathan simply watched, his thin lips twisted into what might

149

or might not have been a smile. Joly was oblivious to everything, merely whispering into Georgina's ear.

Birds were screaming overhead. Swirling. Swooping. They knew something had happened. In the distance, was the sound of an elephant roar.

She must go! That much was clear. Gather her stuff and go home. Back to her friend Lyndsey. Find a job. She didn't belong here. Not with these people.

'Fuck.'

For a minute, Georgie thought Joly was referring to Vanda's question. Then she followed his gaze. A group of police, batons swinging at their sides, were marching towards them from the far end of the beach .

'Quick. Hide the stuff.'

She stood stock still as everyone sprang to. Bags of white powder suddenly appeared from Jonathan and Joly's tents.

'Chuck them in the sea.'

'No. It's a waste.'

Vanda stared at her. 'Give them to her. She can take the blame for the drugs.'

So that's what the white stuff was. 'That's not fair.'

'Isn't it? She murdered Georgina. They'll get her anyway. She needs to pay for this.'

Joly's eyes fell on her doubtfully.

'I didn't ...' Georgie could hardly get the words out for terror. 'I told you. It was the boy. He tried to get me too.'

Vanda's eyes swept her slim frame sceptically. 'So you fought him off, did you?'

Yes. But how to explain that she'd been given an inner strength?

The police were getting closer. Georgie's heart began to beat faster. Twenty years. That's what a French student had got last month for drug dealing. Or so rumour had it.

'Stop arguing,' yelled Jonathan. 'Run.'

No one needed to be told twice. Georgie dived into her tent and grabbed her rucksack. Where was her passport? Shit. It must have fallen out of her pocket in Joly's tent. Quickly, she rushed in to grab it.

'Run. Run separately,' said Joly outside. Crawling under the back of the tent, she headed for the hills. On the other side, she knew, was the harbour. If she was quick, she might just get a boat.

Yes. A fishing boat was about to cast off. Georgie recognised him as one of the local fisherman who often gave them a ride to get provisions.

It wasn't until she was safely on the other side = where were the others? – that she put her passport safely away in her rucksack. There was a piece of paper sticking out. As she took it out, the page fell open.

Georgina Fenella Venetia Peverington-Smith.

Georgie froze. She'd taken her friend's passport by mistake.

But there was something else in her rucksack too. Something hard at the bottom.

The shell. The one that Georgina had given her.

'A sign of our friendship,' she had said. Maybe this was a sign that Georgina understood; that she knew why Georgie had had to run. Perhaps the shell was her friend's way of saying she would always be there still.

Georgie opened her mouth and howled.

TWENTY-THREE

I had a best friend once. It was at primary school. Carl, he was called. It was his idea to cut that girl's hair with the play scissors. Can't remember her name but I do remember the hair. Red, it was.

Or was that the blood?

After that, we both had to go to different schools. We lost touch for a bit. Years later, we both ended up in Wandsworth together.

I knew it was him cos he still had the scar down his cheek that his brother had given him for a birthday present.

'Great to see you,' I said clapping him on the back.

But he didn't seem so pleased to see me.

I didn't realise then that there was a pecking order in prisons. I was only small fry. It didn't suit Carl to be seen in my company.

'You've got to do something bigger,' he said one day in the gym when his mates weren't around.

So I did.

TWENTY-FOUR

'You'd taken your friend's passport,' said a voice behind her in a strong Yorkshire accent. 'And I suspect, lass, that you also took over her identity.'

Georgie jumped. She hadn't noticed the old man coming up behind her. How long had he been there? How much had he heard? She hadn't noticed that Lyndsey had fallen asleep either; her mouth parted slightly. Her breathing slow.

Lyndsey's father pulled up the chair next to her. His kind face took her back to all those days when she'd run round to her friend's house, seeking comfort in a calm household without her mother's ranting and raving.

'You poor child,' he said, his eyes milky. 'What a terrible experience for you to go through. Mavis and I were both so worried when you just disappeared like that. But Lyndsey kept saying that you'd done it to get away from your mum. She was hurt, mind, that you didn't send so much as a postcard.'

He nodded his head; this time as though agreeing with himself. 'But I can see why now. You were scared you were going to get arrested.'

Georgie nodded, too horrified to speak. Yet at the same time she was relieved. Someone who had known her since childhood now knew what had happened. Well, part of it. Not just someone. A man whom she'd always revered. He understood! But that didn't mean Sam would do the same.

'My mother,' she began.

Lyndsey's father's face darkened.

'What happened?' said Georgie urgently.

There was a shaking of the head. 'She married that ne'er-do-well. You were right to be suspicious of him. Spent all her money, he did. Broke her heart.'

'Did I ... did I ...'

She stopped, unable to go on. For years she had told herself she'd done the right thing in ending contact with her mother – especially after she'd had Nick. What kind of a woman treated her daughter the way Mum had treated her? Always screaming at her. Always telling her that she should never had had her.

It made Georgie shiver to think about it. But now, faced with the people who had known her then, she began to have some misgivings. What if her mother – instead of being relieved that she'd gone – had had some sort of breakdown as a result?

'Did you play a part in breaking your mother's heart?' Lyndsey's father voiced her own thoughts.

His face softened. 'Your mother had her own demons, dear. You mustn't be hurt.'

'So she didn't miss me?'

He glanced tenderly at his own daughter who was still sleeping, her lips closed now. 'She may well have done in her own way but she never talked about you. Now she's in the home ...'

'She's in care?'

'Her mind began to go a few years ago.' He patted her hand. 'It's very nice, actually. Top class, in fact. Lyndsey and I go and see her every now and then.'

'Do you talk about me?'

He gave a sad smile. 'Not so much. We've had to move on. Just like you.'

Georgie felt a stab of hurt. Then again, what else could she expect?

'Mind you, lass. There are times when it's hard to move on if you've got the weight of the past on your back. Does your husband know what you've been through?'

She shook her head vehemently. 'He mustn't. He thinks he

married Georgina Peverington-Smith. Knows nothing about the real Georgina or the old me.'

The old man nodded. 'Thought as much. Maybe it's time to tell him the truth.'

A wave of panic caught her. 'But I can't.'

'Can't? Or won't?' There was a steely edge to the voice now. As if in unison, they both looked at Lyndsey. Her eyes were flickering as if she was about to wake up.

'Write him a letter,' said Lyndsey's father quietly. 'It's a good way to tell people something. None of your emails, written in haste and repented at leisure. If he loves you, he'll understand. You'll be surprised how much easier it will be for you to shed your load.'

Tell Sam everything? No way. How could she risk losing her life as she knew it? Georgie edged away. She shouldn't have said anything.

'Actually,' added Lyndsey's father, 'talking about a letter reminds me of something. When I was in the canteen just now, a young lad came up and gave me something to give you.'

'Give me?' Georgie felt another flicker of unease. 'How did he know we knew each other?'

'That's what I wondered. Then I thought he must have seen us talking here.'

They both looked at the envelope which had the name *MRS HAMILTON* neatly written in capital letters.

'Is it anything to do with my girl?'

Georgie was already ripping it open. Reading the first few lines, she let out a small gasp.

'What is it?'

Lyndsey's eyes were open now. Wide open as though she hadn't been asleep at all.

She couldn't worry her friend. Not in the state she was in.

'It's nothing,' she said hurriedly, standing up and shoving the letter into her bag. 'Nothing important.'

Both looked at her. Neither, she could see, believed her.

'We're always here for you,' said Lyndsey. She spoke as

157

though she understood that her father knew the truth too.

Georgie bent down to kiss her friend on the cheek. It felt cold. 'It's more than I deserve.'

'No, it's not.' The old man's cheek was wet as she kissed that too. 'You'll always be our Georgie. Won't she, love?'

'Please,' Georgie whispered. 'Please be careful what you say.' She gave Lyndsey one more hug. 'I'll be back later. I promise.'

Then, walking briskly down the corridor, she made her way to the car. Only when she'd locked herself in did she read the letter more carefully.

IF YOUR HUSBAND WANTS HIS MONEY BACK, YOU'LL HAVE TO TELL HIM THE TRUTH ABOUT THAILAND.

That was it. No name. No signature. It was typed too, so no handwriting to go by apart from the capitals on the envelope.

If she went to the police, they'd ask her what it meant.

The truth about Thailand.

How did the writer know. And who was he – or she?

Sweat began to break out over her brow. Then she jumped as her mobile bleeped. It was a text.

'*Don't be late for our meeting with Charles.*'

That was it. No kiss. No word of comfort.

Still, what did she deserve? No more than this, surely. In fact she'd been lucky to get as far as this. No. Don't think like this. Don't give into blackmail, she told herself sternly as she started the car and headed for town. You've blagged this out before. You can do it again.

The meeting with Charles wasn't pleasant. Again and again, he made her tell him what had happened as if he was trying to catch her out.

'So you left the car outside your client's house but it was outside your home when you got back?'

She nodded. 'I know it sounds strange but ...'

Charles took off his glasses as though it might give him a better view of her, and then put them back again. 'It does,

158

rather.'

'Georgie's had an appointment with the doctor about it,' said Sam crisply.

'Identity fraud is a very complex business,' said Charles, as if she hadn't learned that already. 'But I have to say that this one seems different. Usually it's someone emptying an account in small dribs and drabs so the holder doesn't notice. Or it's a large one-off payment. You appear to have had several of the latter. Then of course, there's the added complication of the appearance on CCTV.'

He slid the latter sentence in so fast that Georgie didn't feel it until it had hit her. 'It wasn't me,' she said furiously.

'I didn't say it was,' added Charles smoothly. 'Although I must say that it's odd, given that you were in the same place at the same time. A hospital, wasn't it?'

'You know damn well it was the hospital,' retorted Georgie furiously.

'Georgie,' said Sam warningly.

'It's all right.' Charles smiled at her. 'I'm only asking these questions in the same tone – or thereabouts – as a lawyer would do on the other side, in case we have to take your bank to court. It's maintaining that you took the money out yourself. We need to prove it was someone else.'

There was a dangerous pause. '*If* it was someone else.'

'Come on, Georgie. Why would my wife want to steal her own money?'

Georgie sat back, a satisfied look spreading over his wide features. 'You did say she was seeing the doctor over memory loss.'

That was it. She didn't have to take any more of this. Standing up, Georgie pushed back her chair so that it fell on the ground. Both men looked at her startled. 'I'm sorry ...' she mumbled. Then she opened the door of the office and walked. Briskly at first, past the surprised look on the receptionist's face, and then faster. By the time she reached her car, she was out of breath.

There was a note on the windscreen! Her hands shaking, she read it swiftly. It was typed, this time.

I HOPE YOU'RE TAKING MY ADVICE.

That was it.

Someone was watching her. Someone had been watching her in the hospital – how else could Lyndsey's father have been given the note? – and now someone had followed her to this meeting.

For a minute, Georgie felt like running back to the hospital and asking Lyndsey's father his advice. Yet somehow she knew what he'd say. Tell Sam. Tell him the truth.

Maybe they were right. Maybe they weren't. Maybe she should go back to Charles' office and apologise. Maybe she should drive home – or to a café – and write a letter.

Getting into the car, Georgie put her head back into the seat and closed her eyes. All she could see was a young girl. Her younger self. Sitting on that fisherman's boat. Clutching her dead friend's passport in one hand with the shell in the other. And hoping that no one was coming after her.

The piece of paper that was poking out of Georgina's passport on the boat was a driving licence. Part of Georgie, the part that wasn't shaking with terror, recognised that this might come in useful. The more identification she possessed, the better chance she had of getting out of this awful country.

Even better, there were some Thai bank notes inside the passport. Enough, it turned out, to get a train up to Bangkok. It was a long, horrible, dusty journey crammed with laughing backpackers as they bumped into each other when the train rattled round bends. But Georgie barely noticed the sort of discomforts she might have done otherwise. Instead, all she could see was Georgina, lying flat on her back, her eyes open; staring up to the sunlight.

If she hadn't slept with Joly, her friend wouldn't have run off like that. Wouldn't have run into the shrubland. Wouldn't have been bitten by the snake. Wouldn't have been murdered.

As for the others and the police, that was awful. But it wasn't her fault. They'd been the ones dealing drugs. It had had nothing to do with her. Then she thought, with a shock, of the small parcels Joly had given her to leave in that isolated spot on the beach. How naïve had she been? She thought too of the joints she had smoked. Both might be enough to put her in jail.

Georgie began to shake so violently that one of the other backpackers noticed. 'Are you ill?' asked a tall, gangly boy next to the window.

'I'm not sure,' she answered truthfully. The scenes she had just witnessed had certainly made her feel dreadful. Even though it was stiflingly hot in the carriage, she couldn't stop shaking with the type of coldness that fear brings on.

'Take this,' he said. He opened his rucksack and pulled out a sky-blue jumper.

His kindness made her want to weep.

'What's your name?'

Georgie, she was about to say. And then she remembered the passport she was still clutching. Better be safe. 'Georgina,' she said. 'Georgie for short.'

'I'm Rufus.'

Rufus? Another posh name.

'Do you live here?'

She almost laughed at the thought. 'No. I'm … I'm travelling.'

'No luggage?'

'No. No … I … I lost it.'

'Poor you. Aren't you with friends?'

So many questions! So many answers that she had to find without having had time to work them out. 'I … I lost them too.'

Rufus indicated the group around him. 'You can come with us if you like. We're going to visit my brother Sam in Bangkok. He's a banker there.' He made a mock wry expression. 'The clever one.'

'Come on, Roof. That's not true and you know it.'

161

A pretty blonde was tugging at her sleeve. She glanced at Georgie with a hint of suspicion. He was already taken, said the look.

Don't worry. She wasn't making that mistake. Not twice.

'That's very kind but I'm sure I'll be all right,' she said. Then, making her excuses, she moved onto the next carriage. Found a quiet spot. And tried to go to sleep.

Eventually she fell into an uneasy doze. Before she knew it, someone was nudging her. 'Wake up. We are here.'

It was a train guard. Already, a sea of people were surging in from the station, keen to get on before the train left again.

She was here! Now what?

Bangkok was bustling. A crazy mixture of spice smells, and sweat, and bodies that pushed you one way and then another in the street. Shops had clothes spilling out on rails with signs in broken English inviting you to purchase. Everywhere were bikes laden with five or six members of the same family – or so they seemed – along with an assortment of fruit or straw. The river stretched out before her, packed with barges festooned with petals.

'It's a festival,' she heard another backpacker say as she walked past.

By now, Georgie had formulated a plan. She'd try to get work – any work – to save up for a ticket to Australia. There was no way she could return to England. She might get found. Someone might trace her. Her mother would disown her if she was convicted of dealing drugs. As for what everyone else would say ...

But what kind of work? She tried approaching several restaurants but it had been difficult to make herself understood. Meanwhile, she needed somewhere to stay for the night.

Georgie began to get increasingly anxious. If the worst came to the worst, she could always bed down by the river. Almost immediately, a vision of the swamp came back to her and Georgina's staring eyes. Where were the others now? Maybe, she told herself, Joly had talked them out of trouble. He would

162

be good at that. Perhaps the police hadn't found the drugs. Perhaps ...

'Good evening.' A sing-song voice came from the doorway. The most beautiful girl Georgie had ever seen stood there, beautifully tall and erect. Her face was immaculately made up with long eyelashes (false?) and jet black hair that fell onto her bare shoulders. Her dress was dark green. 'You want massage?'

Georgie almost laughed. 'I want a job,' she said. 'Sorry. I can't afford a massage.'

'You wait there, please.'

Uncertainly, Georgie hovered, her hand in her pocket, holding the shell for reassurance. Maybe she was going to offer a cheap deal. Even so, she didn't have enough money to spare for such a luxury – although it would be nice if someone rubbed all this awful tension away that was throbbing through her.

'Please. Come in.'

The girl had returned and was beckoning her. Georgie followed her in. It was a smallish room with a display of plastic flowers on a desk and some tinkly music coming from a cassette player in the corner. At the side, a small indoor fountain ran into a pool with pebbles at the bottom.

'You are American, yes?'

Georgie's attention was diverted to another tall, beautiful girl in a blue dress.

'No. English.'

'English.'

The voice took on a keener note. 'You want a job, yes?'

'I do.' She glanced through a side door where there was a bed. 'But I can't do massages. I'm an art student – at least I was. I've graduated now ...'

'You speak English well, I think.' The woman was looking at her appraisingly. 'It does not matter about the massage.' She grinned suddenly, revealing a row of gold teeth. 'We need nice lady for front desk.'

A job! She was being offered a job!

'That would be lovely. How much are you offering?'

'Money? You want to know about money?'

There was a chuckle. 'The money she is very good.' Then she named a figure which meant nothing to Georgie. It was so hard to work out this currency!

'I'll need to think about it. I have to find somewhere to live first.'

'You have no room?'

The girl frowned and then hurriedly whispered to the first girl. 'There is room here,' she announced. 'If you start now, you can sleep there tonight.'

Start now? But she had nothing nice to wear. Georgie looked down at her grubby shorts and T-shirt. She still had that kind boy's jumper on, she realised. Too late to give it back now. She seemed to be rather good at taking things that didn't belong to her. Including a life …

'*If you hadn't upset Georgina, she wouldn't have run off …*' Wasn't that what Jonathan had said? He was right. Georgie might not have been responsible for the wounds that had killed her friend, but she had good as murdered her with her actions.

Suddenly the shell felt threatening in her pocket, rather than reassuring.

'You have bath and then we give you clothes.'

The second woman was definitely the one in charge. There was another toothy gold grin. 'We give you massage too.'

Feeling as if she'd stumbled into another world, Georgie allowed herself to be led into the side room she'd seen. In the corner was a large bath with yellow and white petals floating on top.

'You wash,' said the first girl.

Georgie waited for her to leave but she just stood there, smiling. Embarrassed, she scrubbed herself fast with the loofah and then dried herself with the large white towel held out to her.

'Now you lie on bed. Not that way. Face down.'

She did as told. The girl's hands worked their way into every sinew as if they belonged to a lover who knew her well. Georgie's eyes closed. She was back in Joly's arms. Giving herself up to his hands, his mouth, his body.

The past blurred into oblivion as, dimly aware that the massage was finally over, she fell into a deep sleep, clutching Georgina's precious shell inside her right hand.

That spark of suspicion had gone now. Instead, she had this inexplicable certainty that the shell would keep her safe.

TWENTY-FIVE

Don't write many letters, myself.

Didn't know how to write until I had my first stretch. There was a prison officer there who helped me. Fancied me, she did. I quite fancied her too.

Anyway, she got what she wanted. And I got what I needed.

'Didn't you go to school?' she asked.

I shrugged. My mum hadn't made me. And when I went to my foster parents, they didn't know when I started to skip classes.

So they put me in a different school. It was my fourth one. By then I was eleven. Some of my mates were on their sixth or seventh.

They still can't write.

Just goes to show that not all prison officers are scum.

But don't tell anyone I said that. Or my mates will think I've gone soft.

TWENTY-SIX

She didn't need much, Georgie told herself firmly as she glanced around the beautiful home she'd made with Sam after returning to the UK. If she stopped to agonise over which clothes or which precious possessions to take, she'd never get away.

Often, in the past, when watching refugees on television make their lonely path across a dusty, war-torn battle ground, she'd wondered how many of those women had had to leave behind items that meant a great deal to them.

Now she knew it didn't – couldn't – matter. Besides, hadn't she done this once before, already? It might have been years ago but it felt almost like yesterday …

'You will need something to wear,' the girl in the green dress had announced when Georgie woke from her sleep.

It was morning, judging from the rays of sun that were streaming through the curtainless windows. How had she got here? It wasn't the same room where she'd had her massage. It was a smaller one with lots of knickknacks on the dressing table: mainly brightly coloured cats in that glossy, lacquered material which she'd seen in markets.

Someone must have moved her here. The girl in front of her? The one handing her a dress in a colour similar to her own? 'I had a friend to make it in your size,' she said, smiling.

'How did you know my measurements?'

The girl grinned again. 'I just look at you.'

A wave of embarrassed heat washed over her. She was still naked under the sheets after the massage, she suddenly realised. That was what was different. So this woman had appraised her, run her eyes over her sleeping body and then got her friend to make this dress. The type which she would have worn to a ball at home if there had been such a thing to go to.

'Please. You try it on.'

Her new boss stood there, watching. Still grinning. 'Please may I have some privacy?' Georgie wanted to say.

But it seemed rude and the longer she waited for the woman to go, the more awkward it felt.

'You put it on.'

The smile had gone now. The eyes narrowed.

Hot with shyness now, she slid out of the bed and into the dress as fast as possible. There was no offer of underwear.

The grin returned as fast as it had disappeared. 'Perfect fit,' she announced. 'Look.'

Taking Georgie by the hand, she led her to a long thin mirror that was hanging by the door. She gasped. For a minute, she saw Georgie standing there. Tall. Confident. Elegant. Beautifully dressed. This dress was far better than one she could have made herself.

Then she frowned. Suddenly Georgina was there in her place.

'Do not frown,' the woman instructed. 'The clients. They do not like it.'

Clients! That reminded her. After all, this dress was her uniform. 'When do I start work?'

A lazy smile crept across the woman's face. 'Later. You have breakfast now. Then you rest. Then you work.'

Something didn't feel quite right.

'First you take off dress.' A long, thin, brown arm stretched itself out expectantly to take it.

'But what will I wear?'

For a minute, Georgie had a horrible vision of being expected to eat breakfast naked.

'I have other.'

As if by magic, there was a rustle of more material and a pair of thin black trousers and a white top appeared from a bag by the door. Once more, they fitted perfectly. The trousers felt cool in the heat, which was already beginning to take over the day. They ended halfway between her knees and ankles. There was a pair of beige flat shoes too. A perfect fit.

'We will have high heels for the dress by evening,' announced her benefactor. 'It is being taken care of now.'

Georgie felt as though she had stepped into Cinderella's life. She was about to ask for a more detailed breakdown of her job description when there was the sound of a little bell in the distance.

Her companion took her hand, almost roughly. For a woman, she had a firm grasp. 'Come. We must go.'

Through one door and then another. The massage parlour might look small from the outside but it was a veritable labyrinth behind, she thought as they came to a small courtyard garden, and the woman who'd worn the blue dress the previous night was already sitting by the small pool in the middle. There was a young boy too who watched her keenly. On a table in front of them were small bowls filled with a steaming, brownish-green liquid. There were two other places set too, waiting.

'Good morning. How was your sleeps?'

Sleep, Georgie wanted to say. It's sleep, not sleeps. Yet she held back fearing this might sound rude.

'Very good, thank you.'

'You like the massage, yes?'

There was an all-round giggle which made Georgie blush.

'Thank you. It was very relaxing.' Then she hesitated. 'Please. Can you tell me what you are called and also what I am expected to do?'

All three faces turned solemn. The woman in green spoke first. 'You may call me Emerald.'

She turned to the other. 'My sister is known as Sapphire.

171

The boy, he is just "boy".'

The youth remained impassive. Georgie wondered if he even spoke English.

'As for your duties, you are to meet the customers as I said last night. You welcome them. Give them green tea.' She gestured to the small bowls in front of them. 'Talk to them like your Queen. Make them feel at home.'

Like your Queen? Georgie resisted an urge to giggle.

'You are hostess,' added Sapphire more kindly. 'If they like you, they come back for more.'

'More massages?'

The two women burst out laughing. The boy followed although Georgie suspected that he was only doing so because everyone else did.

'Of course,' said Sapphire, taking a sip from the bowl in front of her. 'What else?'

The thought had crossed Georgie's mind that this might be a brothel. Then again, the bed which she had lain on had been a proper massage table – didn't that make them seem legitimate?

'Too many questions,' continued Sapphire with an edge to her voice that Georgie hadn't heard before. 'You drink now. And eat.'

At the word 'eat', the boy jumped up, only to return in seconds with a bowl of fruit and a large dish of something which tasted like natural yogurt.

It was too hot to eat much. In fact, she was already feeling sleepy, which was strange since she had only just woken. 'We rest now,' said Emerald.

Taking her by the hand, she led her back to the small room where Georgie had woken up in. Before she knew it, she was dreaming again; running along the beach hand in hand with Joly ...

There was a knock on the door. Beano was barking furiously. Just the postman. That was all right then. Beano? How could she think of leaving him behind?

Georgie buried her face in his fur. 'I'm sorry,' she whispered. 'I wish you could understand.'

Then she carried on writing. Writing the letter which Lyndsey's father had put in her mind. Writing the letter which she would leave for Sam to find when he returned home.

It was just the basic facts, but he deserved some kind of explanation.

Georgie's first client arrived at 7 p.m. Before that, there had been a flurry of preparations which reminded her of the one and only school play which she'd been in. Sapphire and Emerald fussed over her as if she was a famous film star. One did her hair, putting it up in such a way that Georgie had to admit flattered her face. The other brushed powder onto her face, accentuating her cheekbones, and then succeeded in making her eyelashes twice their natural length.

Georgina stared out at her from the mirror. Georgie could barely look.

'You are beautiful, yes?'

Georgie didn't know how to answer that. A yes would have seemed too boastful. Yet a no would clearly have been a lie.

'You are very clever,' she murmured.

Both women preened at the compliment. Then it was their turn. Georgie could only sit and watch in amazement as they stepped behind a screen to shed their light cotton trousers and top and stepped out, wearing different dresses from the previous night but in the same colour. Tonight's outfits had more modest necklines.

Wordlessly, they proceeded to sit down at the mirror and do each other's hair and make-up.

The whole transformation took less than ten minutes.

Then there was the sound of the bell: similar to the one which had announced breakfast and then later, lunch.

'You must go.'

Emerald pushed her out of the door towards the reception desk. At the doorway, the boy was speaking to a pair of local

173

businessmen, small and dapper in their suits.

They seemed uncertain.

'You must welcome people in,' Emerald had said firmly, her gold front tooth glistening as if to make the point.

'Good evening.' Georgie glided across the floor, as if someone had stepped into her skin. 'May I help you?'

Both men looked her up and down. 'You speak English?' one of them asked in perfect diction.

She smiled. 'I am English.'

Immediately, relief spread over both their faces. 'My friend and I, we would like a massage,' said one, glancing over his shoulder as he spoke. 'Do you have any appointments free?'

Georgie thought of the appointments book which Sapphire had shown her earlier. It was blank for tonight.

'I am afraid we are fully booked,' she said reluctantly.

Disappointment spread over both men's faces.

'However, if you can give me a minute, I will see what I can do.'

Hardly knowing what she was doing, Georgie slipped back into the room where Sapphire and Emerald were waiting. 'What you doing?' said the latter crossly. 'Why are you not out there with the client?

Georgie held a finger to her lips. Then she walked, in tight steps because that's all the dress would allow, back to the door. To her relief, both men were still there. It had been a gamble but it might be worth it.

'You are in luck, gentlemen!' She smiled warmly. 'I have persuaded two of our finest practitioners to free their diaries so they can accommodate you.'

Both men beamed. As she'd thought, anticipation was part of the game. Then Georgie put up a warning hand. 'There will, however, be a special fee for this.'

'No problem. No problem at all.'

'Wonderful. Now, gentlemen, please follow me.'

She sat them down in the waiting room and poured two cups of green tea from the pot which the boy had made. Both drank quickly, glancing at the door as if worried someone would see them.

Better take their money fast in case they went. 'Gentlemen, before we go further, I must request payment.' She held out her hand. 'It is a rule of the house.'

She named a price; a little over the one which Sapphire had given her. One of them handed over a pile of notes without quibbling.

The boy was nowhere to be seen, noted Georgie. There was nothing to stop her from taking the extra. But that wouldn't be right.

Behind her, the door opened. Sapphire stood there, resplendent in blue. At the same time, a door on the opposite side of the hall opened. Emerald was breathtaking.

Both men drew in their breaths audibly.

'Enjoy your massages, gentlemen,' said Georgie.

She didn't need to tell them twice. The doors closed. And Georgie was left alone at the desk. The boy had materialised swiftly. This time he was grinning. Toothlessly.

'Very good.'

He nodded again in case she hadn't understood.

'Very good.'

Beano barked again. Sweating, Georgie looked up from the letter. It was one of her neighbours, a staunch member of the local flower club. She wouldn't answer. She couldn't. Not in this state.

To her relief, there was the sound of the letter box. A request for the rota, perhaps. Or maybe a flyer for the flower show.

Beano's barking subsided but the interruption had taken her away from Thailand all those years ago. Now she was back in the real world with two options open to her.

Stay and face the music.

Or flee.

IF YOUR HUSBAND WANTS HIS MONEY BACK, YOU'LL HAVE TO TELL HIM THE TRUTH ABOUT THAILAND.

How exactly would that happen? How would the writer know when she had told her husband?

Georgie's head spun. It was so hard to make sense of all this. But Sam had rescued her. It was her turn now to make amends.

She had to go on. Even if she was caught.

TWENTY-SEVEN

I ran away from prison once. It was one of those open prisons. I only got six months. It wasn't for anything much. Just a video machine I nicked from this bungalow.

Well, the back door was open. What did they expect?

It's easy to run away from open prison. Nothing to stop you getting out apart from the cameras. And you can dodge those if you know what you're doing.

Some of the men in my block were allowed to go out anyway, to work.

The rest of us were meant to stay put.

'It's a test, see,' one of the prison gaffs had told me. 'If you do what you're told, you'll be considered fit to re-enter society.'

'Re-enter society? What kind of language did he speak?

I might have listened but it was my mum's birthday, see. July 12th. I thought it would be nice to visit her grave. She'd died when I was inside, see. The bastards wouldn't even give me permission to go to her funeral. And they weren't going to let me go for her birthday either. So I just went.

They got me before I reached the end of the road.

Maybe that plan for dodging the cameras hadn't been so foolproof after all.

I got shipped out that night. To a different prison. One where you couldn't go in and out.

It would be a lesson, they said.

But all I could think about was my mum's grave. Overgrown. Because there was no one else to look after it.

TWENTY-EIGHT

By the end of the first month, Georgie had really got into a routine. The girls were so pleased with her knack for enticing clients that they not only bought her a second dress (exactly the same style but in a fuchsia pink) but they also raised her wages.

Slowly but surely, she was managing to save a little every week to put towards a plane ticket. But that didn't stop the pounding terror each time someone came into the shop, in case it was someone from the island.

'You are worried about something,' remarked Sapphire sharply one evening.

They had met for the usual early evening repast of fruit and cheese by the pool before work started. For some reason, Georgie felt particularly twitchy and kept glancing back towards the main door.

'No,' she lied, using the opportunity to sip the green tea and find a second to compose herself.

Sapphire's eyes narrowed. 'Yes. I think so.'

Both Sapphire and her sister had firm views on what kind of clients they were happy to 'entertain'. Every now and then, she saw them turn men away with a 'So sorry. I have no appointment. Big mistake.'

When Georgie had later expressed surprise, the boy had laughed. 'Not good men. Sapphire and Emerald, they know their business.'

Now it seemed that Sapphire was also trying to know hers. It didn't help that Georgie was aware of flushing deeply. 'You can tell me.'

Sapphire laid her hand on hers. For a minute, Georgie wondered – as she had done before – why it was only men and not women who entered, looking for a massage. Yet occasionally, she had seen both women at work through a door that was not quite closed, and all they were doing was massaging the clients.

Slightly thrown by the familiarity, Georgie found herself talking. 'I had … I had a bad experience with a friend. I do not want him to find me.'

It was not that far from the truth. If Joly or any of the others came across her, they would accuse her – rightly – of having left them to face the music with the police. And then there was the fact they thought she had killed Georgina.

Georgina. Beautiful Georgina whose face still haunted her dreams despite the metal gate which Georgie succeeded in putting up around those thoughts during the day.

'You are scared of the police too.' Sapphire's tone indicated a statement as well as a question. 'Yes. Do not deny it.' She reached across to the pond and gently dipped in her hands, rubbed them together, and then scattered drops over her bare skin to cool herself down.

Maybe she had done so to give Georgie time once more to think of a reply. She was about to come out with one, a hastily-concocted tale about having a visa check. But then she felt Sapphire's eyes burning into her. A lie would not wash with this woman, Georgie felt instinctively. Only the truth would do.

Or part of it.

'Yes.' This time it was her who reached across to the pond and splashed herself with water. So refreshing in the heat. 'I am.'

Sapphire nodded, satisfied. Then both her hands reached out for Georgie's. They held them for longer than was strictly necessary, yet it was not unpleasant. Nor was it merely comforting. There was a strange sensation of heat passing from the other woman's skin into hers. A strength which made

Georgie feel that her problems were – despite the odds – solvable.

'You do not need to worry.' Then she grinned, revealing those gold teeth which everyone had around here. 'We have the police in our pockets, as you English say.' Then she laughed, a deep, throaty laugh. 'Indeed, I have one tonight. So you must not worry when he arrives.'

A policeman was coming here? A hard ball of fear formed in Georgie's throat. It was all very well Sapphire saying that she didn't have anything to fear. But the police on the mainland would surely have been informed of Georgie's death and of the drugs raid. They'd be on the lookout.

'I must go,' she said quickly.

'No.' Sapphire's grip on her arm was firm. 'You will stay. Have faith. We will look after you. Now go. Go and change.'

Shaking, Georgie did as she was told. As soon as there was an opportunity, she told herself, she would run before the evening customers arrived. Out of here along with the savings she had squirreled away. But Georgie hadn't reckoned on the boy. He was waiting by the door, arms folded as if he had been posted there on sentry duty.

'You cannot leave.' His voice was kinder than before. 'They will find you. Do not worry. I know about this.' He pointed to his ears. 'I hear things. But I tell you this.' Moving close to her face, he whispered, 'You might be scared of the police but it is Sapphire and Emerald you should fear. They need you here. You English. Classy. You bring in clients. If you go, they will …'

Then he made a gesture as if someone was slitting his throat with a knife.

Georgie stood stock-still. 'Surely you cannot mean …'

He nodded. 'They may not kill your body. But they can make sure that you will not be able to live outside a prison. I have seen it before. You hear Sapphire. The police are good clients. They work hand in hand. If they wish, they can make up accusations. Be careful. Be very careful.'

Then he held out his hand. 'I give you good information. Now you pay me.'

That was outrageous! Yet not liking to offend in this strange world she had found herself in, Georgie found herself dipping into her pocket and giving him a note.

He shook his head. 'Not enough.'

She handed him another. He gave both notes a scornful look and then stopped, like an animal detecting a human. 'Someone is coming. Go. Behind the desk.' He grinned. 'Time to be English queen again.'

Reluctantly Georgie did as she was told. The boy was right. He was talking to a man on the threshold. A man in full police attire, complete with gun in his belt. She could hardly breathe with fear.

The boy was smiling and grinning as he led him in, gesticulating that Georgie should take over.

'May I give you some tea?' she asked in a strangled voice.

The man, thick-set with a stocky gait, eyed her. Her heart began to pound so loudly that she was certain he must hear it. 'You are new,' he stated.

She nodded.

'You are the English girl.'

Again, she nodded. How stupid she had been! Why had she allowed herself to be brow-beaten by Sapphire? Why hadn't she run when she'd had the chance?

Fingers sweating, she gripped the edge of the table, almost knocking over the vase of artificial flowers.

Then there was a grin. A broad grin, suggesting he had enjoyed playing mind games with her. 'You like it here?'

Another nod.

'You are shy.' He gave a shake of a head that displayed approval rather than displeasure. 'This is a good quality. Rare amongst those who do not live here.'

He sat down expectantly. 'The old girl, she know I do not have tea.' He nodded at the curtain behind the desk. 'I take something stronger. Then I see Emerald. She is ready?'

Georgie wasn't sure. But she didn't care. Instead, relief was flooding her body. He hadn't arrested her. Yet.

Diving behind the curtain, she grabbed a glass and a bottle of white liquid. Emerald had told her earlier that this was for the customers who declined the green tea.

But when she emerged, with the glass, the policeman's chair was empty. Instead, the boy held out his hand. 'He has gone in already to Emerald.' Seizing the glass, he knocked the liquid back. 'We must not wait.'

Then he held the half-empty glass back to her. 'You taste.'

Not wishing to drink from his side, she turned it round. It burned her throat but immediately, she felt a similar strength to the one she'd experienced that afternoon with Sapphire's hand.

'Do not fear,' said the boy, his dark eyes glistening. 'Whatever you are hiding is safe here. As long as you stay.'

Over the next few weeks, Georgie learned to feel safer. The women looked after her and, after that evening with the policeman, the boy had become kinder too.

Yet all the time there was the sense of entrapment. Yes, she was 'allowed' to wander out to the markets to buy fruit or fish, but always the boy was sent out with her. When she paused at a clothes shop, he told her that he would be 'waiting outside'.

It was almost like being a slave, she told herself, yet at the same time, a pampered one. Besides, where else could she go? It would take a while to save up for a plane ticket. She was saving as much money as possible and keeping it in a secret pocket she'd sewn into her haversack. If Sapphire and Emerald knew she was planning leaving, they wouldn't be very happy.

Occasionally, she wondered about ringing home to tell her mother everything. But she wouldn't understand. In fact, she'd be horrified and possibly call the English police to 'help'. That wouldn't do at all. Georgie had heard enough backpacking stories to know that she could, all too easily, end up in prison. This was even more likely if she annoyed Sapphire and Emerald.

So instead, she carried on with this rather sleepy pattern of green tea round the pool; resting in the heat; and exploring the back alleys of Bangkok, always with the boy in attendance. Again and again, she sought refuge in the bales of cloth, the colours, the feeling of the fabrics as she ran her fingers down them. They seemed to soothe her. Tell her it would be all right.

'You like?' the boy would often say.

She'd nod. 'I like.'

At times, his constant presence irritated her. At others, she was glad of his protection. Once, a rowdy crowd of Australians tried to chat her up as she bought vegetables in a market. 'We'll buy you a beer,' one of them said.

Instantly, the boy had slid in between them. 'Leave her alone,' he snarled.

It did the trick. The police officer turned up three times a week, but he never gave her any trouble.

Three weeks later, Georgie was changing into her dress – the pink one – when she heard voices outside in the reception area.

'Too early,' she heard the boy say. 'You come back later.'

'Can't you make an exception?' The voice was cultured. Well-bred. English. 'It's my brother's stag night. We've got a full evening ahead and we wanted to start here.'

Georgie froze. That was Joly's voice. She would have known it anywhere! He was here. Joly had come to find her. All thoughts of Joly being angry flew out of her head. Maybe he'd understand if he saw her. She would explain. No, she shouldn't have run away from them. She ought to have stayed and faced the music. As for Georgina, that wasn't all her fault. It was Joly's too. Surely he'd understand that?

Desperation won against common sense. Hastily fastening her dress and leaving her hair loose, she pushed open the door.

The tall, good-looking boy with sandy hair pushed back to one side stared at her. His eyes ran up and down her body, taking in her dress and false eyelashes.

'Good heavens. What are you doing here?'

It was the boy on the train. Rufus. The one who had lent her the sky-blue jumper. Instantly, a deep flush vied with her pink dress. 'I work here.'

Her voice came out apologetically.

The boy's eyebrows raised. 'As a masseuse?'

Conscious that the boy's eyes were on her and that Sapphire and Emerald were, quite possibly, listening, she tried to sound confident. 'I'm front of house, so to speak. I book in clients.'

There was a whistle. 'That's very enterprising of you, I must say.'

Enterprising? She didn't see it that way. It was a job, something that young men like Rufus – and Joly – didn't need with their trust fund money.

The boy coloured up. He was almost, she observed with more sympathy than earlier, as embarrassed as she was. 'I'd like to make an appointment with Sapphire.' Another blush. 'It's not for me. It's for my brother. He's on his stag night.'

Georgie – trying to remember she was really Georgie – took a look at the book. They were genuinely busy that evening. It was impossible to fit anyone in.

Rufus' face fell. 'That's a shame. This place has a great reputation. That's why I was surprised …'

His voice trailed away and he flushed. Then a thought seemed to strike him. 'What time do you get off? Would you like to join us?'

Georgie glanced at the boy. There was no need for him to even shake his head. 'I'm sorry. I don't finish until midnight.'

Rufus nodded eagerly. 'We'll still be there. At the club on the corner of the road – the one with pink neon lettering. Do you know it?'

She did. It was a very expensive place, frequented by wealthy ex-pats.

Again, she felt the boy's dark eyes on her and his heavy, sullen disapproval.

'I'm afraid I have to get up early. Another time, maybe.'

Rufus' disappointment was as clear as the unspoken

approval from the boy. 'See you around, then. It would be great to catch up. We've been travelling since I last saw you but came back for my brother's stag do. The wedding's next month and we're flying back in two weeks.'

'I hope it goes well.' Her voice came out stiff. It wasn't fair. Why did she have to be cooped up here? Why could she just not say 'to hell with it' and go? Yet there was a darkness here; one which was beginning to feel increasingly oppressive since Rufus had come in.

'I've still got your jumper,' she suddenly realised.

Rufus put up his hand. 'Please. Leave it. It might give us a chance to meet again.' But no sooner had he left, than both women materialised silently behind her. 'I will take over now,' said Sapphire smoothly. 'You are needed with Emerald.' Her lips were unsmiling. 'She is going to teach you.'

'Teach me?'

There was a grave nod. 'You are very lucky. We have decided to train you to be a masseuse.'

Beano was barking again. There was just time to take him for a walk and then go. Georgie looked down at the scrawled pages in front of her. She'd leave part of the letter and then go. The rest would have to wait.

'I'm sorry,' she said, kneeling down to rub noses with the dog. 'I'll come back. Providing everyone understands.'

This was the only way, she told herself.

IF YOUR HUSBAND WANTS HIS MONEY BACK, YOU'LL HAVE TO TELL HIM THE TRUTH ABOUT THAILAND.

Could she trust this person? Hadn't life showed her already that she'd put her belief in others, only to be betrayed?

Yet something told her, as she called for a taxi to take her to the station, that this was the only choice she had.

'Going anywhere nice?' asked the driver, glancing at her light case.

'London,' she replied, before realising that she should have made up another place. 'To see a friend.'

186

That part wasn't true, of course. But already a plan was forming in her mind, rather as it had in Bangkok after bumping into Rufus. She would find somewhere to rent. Get a job. Finish the letter to Sam.

Then he would finally know the truth about her past. If he forgave her, they might move on. And if he didn't ...

Georgie could hardly bear to think about that.

She'd have to find a way of explaining her decision to the children. And as for Lyndsey ...

Georgie took out her phone, scrolling down to the number her friend had given her. '*Have had to go away. But will visit soon. I promise.*'

TWENTY-NINE

I was locked up once. At a special sort of school. They said it was for my own good. But it didn't feel that way.

One night, I got out. Shimmied down the drain pipe and bruised my leg into the bargain. Not that that mattered.

I'll never forget the feeling of freedom. No one to tell me what to do. No one to make me learn things I didn't want to learn.

But before I had even reached the gate, I felt a hand on my arm.

'Where do you think you're going?'

Do you know, those words still strike terror into me?

Childhood can do some terrible things to you. It leaves marks which no one can ever scrub away.

People like you wouldn't understand that. You've got everything. And we've got nothing.

When I had my kid, I told myself I'd make it different for him. But I couldn't. Not unless I did things I didn't want to do.

I don't like stealing. Others get a buzz from it. But not me.

I'd really like to work in a shop. A clothes shop. Then I could try stuff on and pretend I'm someone else.

That would be cool. Really cool.

THIRTY

It wasn't easy writing on the train as it bumped and jolted its way across country towards London. Georgie's hand slipped several times as a result, making the ink splodges look like apologetic exclamation marks. That wouldn't do at all. She screwed up the page altogether – to the fascination of the elderly woman opposite – and had to begin again.

Maybe, she wondered, it was fate telling her to keep quiet. But she'd left the first part of her story at home, on the kitchen table for Sam to find when he returned. There was no going back now. She would simply have to send the next part when she got to London.

Rufus, with his kind face, unsettled Georgie. He was a reminder of what she had run away from. Yet at the same time, he brought back the freedom she'd had. Yes, she had been terrified at the thought of the police chasing her. But now she was almost a prisoner of Sapphire and Emerald, albeit a willing one. After all, where else could she go?

During the following weeks after Rufus' visit, she found herself searching for him in the market. On more than one occasion, she caught sight of a group of well-spoken English boys, but when she walked past to investigate further, none was him. She took to sleeping with the jumper under her pillow (along with Georgina's shell), though she could not say why. It wasn't as though she was attracted to Rufus but she felt certain – so strange! – that she would see him again.

Meanwhile, Georgie was kept busy under the beady eyes of Emerald and Sapphire. Training as a masseuse was more complicated than she'd realised. No one had warned her how much it hurt your hands, or that enormous strength was required to knead someone else's muscles and sinews. Hour after hour, she practised on both girls, who unashamedly stripped down to their waists. But never, to her relief, further down than that.

By the time it came to her evening duties as a hostess, Georgie was exhausted. Seeming to recognise this, the women paid her extra. All the more to put away for the flight to Australia – providing no one questioned her passport. Georgie's heart beat so fast when she thought of this that she considered staying here longer. Emerald and Sapphire would look after her; she was certain of this. As for the police, if they were in the women's pockets as the boy had suggested, she was possibly safer here than risking deportation.

Then one day – when the boy who usually came with her was on another errand – about five weeks after Rufus' visit, she heard a voice shout out across the floating market.

'Georgie!' it seemed to say, but when she shaded her eyes from the sun to see who was calling, it was hard to make anything out amidst the sea of brown faces and barges, filled to the brim with fruit and vegetables and lace and knick-knacks of every description. The stench of the river and the fish together with the heat made her feel she was living in another world. How she would have loved to have shared this with Lyndsey. But it was too dangerous to send a postcard. Why, oh why, had she ever allowed herself to get mixed up in the world of drugs? She could be at St Martin's by now, learning the art of design. Pursuing a safe, 'proper' life.

'Georgie?' repeated the voice.

This time, she could see a tall, fair-haired boy waving from the other side of the river. It was Rufus. Next to him was another boy. Or rather man. He was a different colouring – dark – but taller and slightly stockier.

'We're coming over,' called out Rufus and before she could

think of making an excuse, he leaped onto a boat, followed by his companion. They jumped over the next vessel and the next so that before within a few seconds they were standing in front of her, laughing, accompanied by furious shouts from the boatmen behind.

'I've a feeling that we night just have done something illegal,' said the dark-haired one.

Rufus laughed. 'That would be a first for you.' He turned to Georgie. 'My brother's a stickler for the rules. Sam, this is Georgie, the girl I was telling you about.'

Brother? But they looked so different.

Georgie felt a little flutter. Partly because of what Rufus had said – hadn't she broken the rules big time? – but also because it was hard not to stare at the brother. He didn't take her breath away as Joly had done at first glance, but there was something about him that held her gaze; made her feel that this was a man who she could be comfortable with.

Yet he was married! After all, the last time she'd seen Rufus, it had been for his brother's stag night.

'How was your wedding?' she asked.

Instantly, Sam turned away.

Rufus was shaking his head. 'Wrong question!'

What had she said?

'It's all right,' said Sam quickly, turning back. 'I'm going to have to get used to this.'

Rufus snorted. 'I told you, bro. If a girl hasn't got a sense of humour, she's not worth it.'

Georgie was becoming increasingly confused, something that neither boy could fail to spot.

'She didn't like her fiancé cavorting with a ladyboy,' grinned Rufus.

'You know there was more to it than that.' Sam shook his head again, as though telling himself off.

'For pity's sake, Sam. It was your stag night. If you're not allowed to let your hair down, when can you? Besides if anyone's to blame, it's me!'

He grinned again; just like a naughty schoolboy. 'We paid a ladyboy to be handcuffed to him for twelve hours. By the end, they were both nearly killing each other.' There was another grin. 'Can you imagine it? They even had to go to the loo together and ...'

'That's enough.' Sam's face was puce.

How horrible. Georgie shivered at the image this evoked.

'Then we took him to one of those ping pong clubs where the girls put ...'

'Rufus.' Sam's eyes were shining with anger now. 'I said that's enough.'

'OK. Keep your hair on. Pity you didn't do the same with your clothes ...'

'*Rufus!*'

Shrugging, the younger boy turned to her. 'Do you get lots of stag dos at the parlour?' He placed a good deal of emphasis on the word 'parlour'.

Georgie shook her head. 'We're not that kind of place.'

'Are you sure?' Rufus' grin was wry this time instead of beaming with amusement.

'No. Sapphire and Emerald just do massages.'

Sam's colour seemed to have died down. 'That's not what I've heard. My brother told me you were working in a massage parlour. We've both been really worried. There are quite a lot of European girls who get sucked into that kind of thing, you know. Ladyboys can look very convincing.'

Suddenly, Georgie's head began to whirl. Ladyboys. She knew about them, of course. You couldn't work in Bangkok without being aware of strong, muscular-looking women with deep voices. Apparently taking the right hormones could produce their convincing-looking breasts.

But Emerald and Sapphire were women. They looked feminine, every inch of them. Except ... her mind wandered to the massage sessions. 'Not below the waist,' Sapphire had giggled. Was it really possible ...?

And what about the police officer who turned up three times

every week? Had she been incredibly stupid? Was that why they didn't like her going out too much or having friends? Because they were running an illegal brothel? A homosexual one?

'Maybe, I've been a bit naïve ...' she began.

Rufus laughed but Sam was serious.

'There's another thing.' He glanced around nervously. 'The firm's got close links with some consulate staff out here and word has it that there's going to be a big clean-up of places like ... like the one you're working for. The bank has got a spare flat for visitors. I'm sure that I could get permission to put you up – keep you out of all that.'

Why was he concerned? He hardly knew her.

Sam seemed to read her mind. 'I don't want you to think I'm being pushy. I'm aware we've only just met. But it doesn't seem right that a nice girl like you should be in a position like this.'

Rufus raised his eyebrows. 'Ever the gentleman, my brother. Apart from when he's shackled up to a ladyboy, of course, or chatting up a ping pong stripper. All right, I'll stop there.' Then he too looked serious. 'Actually, Sam's right, Georgie. You do need to be careful.'

'I know that.' Her voice came out more abrasive than she'd meant it to. 'But I need a job.'

'We can help you out.'

But what would he want in return?'

'No strings attached,' added Sam quickly. 'Please, Georgie, at least think it over. You don't want to get mixed up with those kind of places. I've heard some horror stories. There are some people here who prey on vulnerable girls. They suck you in and won't let you go.'

Georgie didn't want to say that this is exactly what she was experiencing. But even so ...

'Look, here's my number.' Sam pushed a card into her hand. 'Call any time you need to.

Then, almost as fast as they had arrived, the brothers went, swallowed up in the crowds. But when Georgie looked back through the crowds in the market, she could see Sam looking back too.

'You been gone long time.' Sapphire's eyes were dark with disapproval. 'You say one hour.'

Georgie felt as though she was late for school.

'I'm sorry. There was a long queue at the market.'

There was an impatient cluck of the tongue. 'You talk to friends. You were seen.'

Her repentance was replaced with annoyance that she'd been followed. The boy. She should have known.

'I'm entitled to have friends if I wish.'

The eyes narrowed. 'We pay you to work.'

'I am entitled to time off.

Never before had Georgie stood up for herself like this. The effect wasn't what she'd hoped.

'You lucky we keep you here.' This time it was Emerald who spoke. 'You not who you say. We know.'

A cold fear shot through her. How could they know?

'Your passport name, she does not match the other names in your bag.'

The other names? Suddenly Georgie remembered the nametape which was sewn into her shorts. The same ones she had worn when she'd run away from the others back on the island. The girls had taken them away from her, washed them. They would have seen it. Georgie Smith. Not Georgina Peverington-Smith.

'I don't use all my names all the time,' she said, shrugging.

'Or maybe you have someone else's passport,' retorted Sapphire snidely.

No, Georgie wanted to say. But the lie stuck in her throat. There had been too many lies already.

Then the woman's face softened. 'You be good to us and we be good to you.'

After that, Georgie felt even more scared than ever. But

196

what could she do? On more than a few occasions, she considered ringing the number which Sam had given her. Yet each time, she thought of the policeman client. What if the women reported her? It was too scary to think about.

Over the next few days, and then weeks, she felt increasingly frantic. Trapped. But on the outside, she had taken care to remain calm as if she enjoyed working for the women. Certainly, she was learning the tricks of the trade. She had proved to be an adept masseuse. At the same time, she had tried to use the opportunity to see if Rufus and his brother were right. Was it possible that Sapphire and Emerald really were ladyboys? But each time she tried to massage below their waists they pulled her up sharply.

It was as if they knew that if she found out the truth, she would go. They needed her, that was certain. The Englishwoman, as she was known, was ringing in more and more custom. 'Even better when you do massage,' grinned Sapphire.

Georgie felt a sense of panic. As long as she wasn't expected to do anything else.

Eventually, her patience paid off and she was finally allowed out to the market once more. 'One hour and no more,' instructed Sapphire.

Feeling like a prisoner out on bail, Georgie took care to keep an eye on the time. She had learned to do this without her watch, which she'd lost during the tussle with the boy who'd killed Georgina. There were always clock chimes she could follow from somewhere.

Sapphire couldn't be cross this time. After all, she'd reached the street just as the bronze hand on the clock in the square reached five. Plenty of time to get ready and …

What was that noise! Aghast, she stared at all the people milling outside the parlour. There were police there too – but they didn't seem to be acting like clients. Instead, they had guns in their hands and were shouting. Some of the crowd was cheering them on. Others were yelling words that, although incomprehensible to Georgie, sounded like abuse.

Out of habit, she touched the shell in her pocket for safety. Then she froze. Four more policemen were escorting two women out of the parlour. Sapphire and Emerald. The boy was behind them too, handcuffed. He spat twice on the ground as he was pulled along and pushed into a car.

'Word has it that there's going to be a clean-up of places like yours.'

Sam's words came back to her. So he hadn't been exaggerating. Her bosses were being shoved into another car now, behind the boy. There was a rev of the engine as it sped past. But as it did so, two faces looked out of the window. Straight at her. Sapphire. And Emerald. And from the identical glare, it was clear that they thought she was responsible for this.

Meanwhile, the crowd were teeming in through the door, coming out with armfuls of costumes: beautiful dresses which the women had worn, including Georgie. There were wigs too. Long, dark wigs. She'd always thought their hair was natural.

The chanting grew louder and louder. Georgie found herself being pushed from one side to the other. There was no way she could stay here: no way she could spend the night in what she had come to see as 'her' bedroom. What was she to do?

Shaking, she felt inside her pocket. There was her passport – or rather, Georgina's – which she carried everywhere. And there was the phone number which Sam had given her. Turning her back on the crowds, she wove her way through the streets to the bakery where Emerald and Sapphire would often send her to buy the morning bread.

'Please, I need to use the phone,' she gasped.

The baker, who had a soft spot for her, silently handed her the receiver. The chant outside was growing louder and louder. He looked scared. 'Be quick. I must close door.'

Her finger shaking, she misdialled twice before someone picked up the phone. It was a woman. His secretary, perhaps? 'May I speak to Sam Hamilton, please?'

Shaking even more, she held on for what seemed like ages.

Outside, the crowds got louder and louder. 'You must go now,' urged the baker. 'I do not want foreigners in here. I get into trouble.'

'Hello?'

The baker's voice was so persistent that for a minute she didn't hear Sam.

When she did, she was almost too scared to talk. 'It's me, Georgie. I'm in trouble.'

His voice was steady but firm. Exactly the kind you needed in a crisis. 'Can you meet me by the floating market?'

Desperately, she glanced outside. The crowd were swarming up the street now. She had a few minutes at the most. The baker's face was drawn and he was gesticulating towards the back exit.

'I'll try.'

The baker almost pushed her out. Reeling, she pounded down one lane and then another, not sure where she was going. Then – miracle! – she rounded a corner and there he was. Sobbing, she fell into his arms.

'It's all right.' Sam's arms were around her. Without warning, he lifted her up and carried her down another back street. As he ran, she closed her eyes. It was Joly. Joly carrying down the beach as in her dreams.

'Jump in.'

It was a taxi.

'Where are we going?'

She began to shiver with cold and shock.

'To the airport.' Sam's mouth was set. 'Rufus is already there. This whole place is going to explode by the end of today. There's a massive uprising against the brothel closures.'

'Brothels? But I worked in a massage parlour.'

His hand closed over hers. 'There's no time to worry about that now. The most important thing is that you're safe. Damn.'

'What is it?'

'You might need to go back for your passport.'

'I've got it.'

'Good.'

She began to shiver again. 'The only thing is that my paperwork might not be in order.'

'We'll face that when it comes. The British consul will be there.'

That was even worse. He'd know about Georgina's death. He might arrest her for her involvement with the drug dealing. They might …'

She had to get out of this somehow. 'I don't have anywhere to live in England any more. My mother re-married and I don't want to go back.'

Sam's arm tightened around her. 'Then come to Australia with me.'

'Australia?'

'I'm being transferred there by the bank.'

'But …'

He took away his arm and she felt a curious sense of loss. 'I don't mean come with me in that sense. I mean come with me until I can help you find a base.'

A base? With a tall, handsome man who was a real gentleman? But what if she was stopped before she could leave?

'We're here.' Sam indicated the large, glass airport building. 'Stick with me and it will be all right.'

It was too late to do anything else.

'We will shortly be arriving at Paddington.'

The station was packed. Loud. Hot. People were pushing her. Walking through her as if she didn't exist. Georgie took a deep breath. It had been months since she'd been here, when she'd come up for an interior design trade fair.

Maybe she should start looking for a flat there. Her hands closed around the wodge of notes she'd taken from the safe – cash that Sam kept there for 'emergencies'.

It should be enough for a month. Hopefully, this weirdo who was blackmailing her might have returned the money to Sam.

200

And if not?

Georgie couldn't think that far. It was too terrifying. Just as it had been at the airport in Bangkok all those years ago.

THIRTY ONE

I got stopped at a train once. It was when I'd absconded. Big word for me, I know. But believe me, it's a word you soon get to hear.

Most of the men what absconded got caught and sent to somewhere worse. But a few got away for a few weeks. Sometimes months. Occasionally years.

Why bother, you might say. Why do something daft if it's going to increase your sentence?

I'll tell you why. Cos you can't put a price on the smell of fresh air. The taste of freedom. Seeing trees. Looking through shop windows. Sleeping in doorways instead of on a hard cell bed.

That's why I hit the guard. Turned out he was just questioning my ticket. But I panicked, see. Only broke his nose. But it was enough for the cops to get me at the next station.

And back I went. Another twelve months.

Now I'm careful. I let other people do the dirty work.

And by the way, if you see me again, I've never met you. OK?

THIRTY TWO

The last time Georgie had been at the airport was when she'd arrived, over a year ago, on her way to the island. If only she had known what was to happen. She would have got straight back on the plane; back to the safety of England. She could have started her degree; finished her first year around now; hung out with Lyndsey during the summer.

A difficult mother and a stepfather she didn't care for were nothing compared with the situation she was in right now.

'Hold tight,' instructed Sam.

His voice, normally so calm and assured, scared her. If he was worried, then she had every reason to be. All around them, people were pushing and shoving and snarling in a bid to get to the check-in desk.

'Everyone's desperate to get out,' added Sam tight-lipped. 'But if you stay with me, we'll be all right.'

He patted his breast pocket. 'I've got tickets here.'

'How did you book mine?' she asked. 'Didn't you need my details?'

Sam gave a slightly smug smile. 'The firm has a contact with the airline.'

The firm, it seemed, had contacts with everyone. Certainly, there were quite a few people in the crowd who now stood back as Sam – still holding her tightly – fought his way to the front. 'Hi, Sam,' said one man.

'Don't forget to keep up,' added a girl, a few lines on. She glanced at Sam admiringly and then gave Georgie a dirty look.

Sam was clearly someone of importance, even though he was – what? – only about five years older than her. It struck Georgie that she didn't know his age exactly. Yet here she was, agreeing to go with him to a place that was on the other side of the world from home.

Home. A place she could never go back to now in case they found her.

At last, they'd got to the check-in desk. Georgie began to shake as she handed over her passport. She had a desperate urge to go to the lavatory – even the usual hole in the ground which she'd learned to accept in the camp. Yet at the same time, she knew she had to try to look calm.

It would be fatal to arouse this woman's suspicions.

'You are travelling together,' said the woman at last, after staring at Georgie's passport details for some time. Georgina Peverington-Smith. Georgie Smith. Who was she anyway?

Sam nodded. Then he put his arm around her. 'This is my fiancée.'

Fiancée? Georgie nearly opened her mouth to say 'very funny' but then saw Sam's eyes. Don't say anything, they warned.

The girl nodded. 'Very good. Nice to see you again, Mr Hamilton.'

Then the woman raised her eyebrows. 'No luggage?'

The remark was addressed to Georgie. Sam had a neat, small suitcase in expensive brown leather.

'No.'

This time, her voice came out as a distinct tremble.

'My poor darling didn't have time to pack.' Sam's arm tightened protectively around her. 'She got caught up in the crowds so we arranged to meet here.'

The girl nodded, her sharp features softening slightly. 'It is all very regrettable,' she murmured. 'We hope to see you again when the current trouble has died down.'

At last! She handed them their boarding cards. 'I don't need to tell you the way to Security,' she smiled.

Clearly Sam was a frequent flyer.

'This way,' he said. Then he cursed under his breath.

A bolt of alarm shot through her. There was a problem. Of course there was. This had all been too smooth. 'What's wrong?'

'Rufus. Little blighter said he'd be here but he hasn't turned up. I can't go without him – Mother would kill me – but I can't leave you either.'

'I'll be all right.'

'No.' He shook his head. 'It's time he stood on his own two feet. I'm tired of looking after him ...'

Yet still he stood, scanning the crowds, clearly loath to leave without his brother. This was a good man ...

A sharp, metallic tannoy voice broke through, announcing their flight.

Sam's face was distraught. 'Where *is* he? Wait there. By the news seller. I'm just going to ask around.'

Georgie tried to do as she was told, but it was hard. Everyone was pushing and shoving. Behind her, the old woman selling papers was clucking her tongue and staring at her with beady eyes.

Then Georgie froze. The ex-pat newspaper that the old woman was selling ... there were pictures on the front page. Pictures of Joly. Of Vanda. Of Jonathan. And of her ... below it was the headline.

Three Europeans standing trial for drug smuggling. A fourth – a woman – is being sought in connection with the same crime. She is also wanted for suspected murder.'

Oh my God. That was her. A picture of her laughing on the beach. She remembered Vanda taking it.

But she hadn't murdered Georgie. That was the boy. The boy in the woods who had tried to attack her. The boy whom she had stabbed in a desperate attempt to get away.

Yet she'd had blood on her hands ... Blood on her clothes ...

Georgie tried to move away from the newsstand but her legs

were like jelly. She couldn't afford to wait for Sam. She'd have to go. Then she remembered. He had her boarding pass. She couldn't get on the plane. She was stuck …

'Found him!' Sam's voice was both furious and exultant at the same time. He was dragging his young brother much in the way that he had been gripping her earlier.

'I don't know what the fuss was about.' Rufus, ever jovial, was laughing. 'This is just one of this country's usual silly scares. It will all die down in a moment and …'

BANG

For a second, the entire airport stood still. Then someone screamed. Someone shouted. 'He's been shot. My God, he's been shot.'

'*Who's* been shot?' said Georgie in a strangulated voice.

But no one replied. Instead, Sam grabbed her left hand and Rufus her right. Together they ran through Security. No one bothered to check their bags or their persons. Everyone else was running too. Down a corridor and then another and finally into the opening up the steps into a plane. The air hostesses were clearly fearful. 'Fasten your seatbelts, please. This aircraft is about to take off.'

Sam was white-faced. So too were all the passengers around him. Even Rufus was subdued.

'Looks like we just made it.'

'No thanks to you.' Sam glared at his brother while putting his arm round Georgie. 'You risked all our lives.'

'I'm sorry.' He sounded like small boy.

Sam nodded, his tone softening. 'You're here. That's what matters.' Then he reached out and patted his brother's shoulder.

Once more, Georgie thought what a good man he was.

For a minute, Sam looked as though he was going to kiss her. Instead, he squeezed her hand. 'Are you all right?'

She nodded, still convinced that at any minute someone was going to jump on the plane and haul her off. Someone must have seen that newspaper article. Someone must recognise her.

But they were off. Flying up through the clouds. Away from

the carnage below. She was safe, Georgie told herself. Then the hostess asked if she would like something to drink. Her eyes rested on Georgie's for more than was absolutely necessary. She's recognised me, Georgie told herself, waiting. I've had it now.

Putting her head under the blanket, she pretended to go to sleep; but all the time expecting a hand on her arm. But when, after an hour, nothing had happened, she opened her eyes. The two boys on either side of her were asleep.

The air hostess walked past and smiled.

Maybe this time she had done it. It was more than she deserved.

Then Georgie fell into a deep sleep, in which Sapphire and Emerald and Joly and she were all running along the beach. Georgina – a furious Georgina – was racing behind, barefoot. With a gaping red wound in her chest.

Earl's Court wasn't what she'd thought it was. Central London, to Georgie, had always seemed a smart place to live, compared with Yorkshire. Knightsbridge – where she had been once with Lyndsey's parents when they had taken her to London for a birthday treat – had always stuck in her mind. How wonderful to live in the capital! A place where everyone dressed beautifully and smelt of perfume counters.

She'd assumed Earl's Court would be similar. After all, when she'd gone through it by taxi to the last trade fair, she'd been struck by the handsome, white stucco, Georgian buildings. But now, after hours of browsing estate agents' windows and finally summing up the courage to go in and talk to them (expecting her husband to be following any minute), she was beginning to wonder if she was in the right place.

Rents were so expensive!

'You might find something that's more suited to your budget somewhere like Kilburn,' murmured a girl who was barely more than Ellie's age.

Really? She knew central London rents would be steep but

she hadn't realised they were this much. 'I'm afraid I'm a bit out of touch when it comes to the rentals,' said Georgie apologetically. 'We live in the country.'

The girl looked envious. 'How lovely. We get a lot of people here looking for second homes so they can stay in London during the week for work. I wish I could escape somewhere rural at the weekend.'

'Actually, this isn't a second home. It's ...'

Already she'd said too much. The girl's face grew curious. She glanced at Georgia's left hand. Her wedding ring still shone there. Defiantly. Even though it had no right to be there. Her past had caught up with her. Quite how, Georgie didn't know. But she was certain of one thing. When Sam finished reading her letter, he wouldn't want her back.

Drugs were a big no no in his world. He'd been against them, ever since she had first met him And what if he found out she might be wanted for murder?

Sydney was so hot! She should have been used to the humidity after Bangkok but as she stepped off the plane, it hit her with a force after the air conditioning.

But that's where the similarity ended. Instead of being surrounded by the babble of an incomprehensible language, she heard English words. Not English accents, granted. But words which made sense.

It was all too much. Unable to help herself, she burst into tears. 'It's all right,' said Sam softly. 'We're safe now.'

Rufus held her too. Together, the three of them clung to each other. They'd been scared too, she realised.

'But what will I do now? I don't have anywhere to live.'

Rufus laughed. 'Me neither. I'm a gap-year student, remember? But don't worry. Big brother here will sort us out. He always does.'

'The company has a flat,' began Sam.

'The company always has a flat,' laughed Rufus. 'I tell you, Georgie, this brother of mine landed on his feet after uni. More

210

than I will.'

Sam flushed while looking pleased with himself at the same time. 'Don't be so hard on yourself. All you have to do is knuckle under. I've told you before.'

'Hah! Like you knuckled under with that girl from the ping pong bar ...'

'SHUT UP!'

Georgie was taken aback. She'd never heard Sam shout like that before. Rufus clearly felt he'd overstepped the line too. He was mumbling something about not taking any notice of what he'd just said and that he was only being an idiot because he was relieved they'd got here.

But it worried her, even after they'd got into a taxi and were threading their way through this incredible mixture of old and new buildings that was Sydney.

'Maybe I can find a hostel to stay in,' she ventured.

'Nonsense. You can stay in the company flat,' said Sam. 'My brother will stay with me until he's ready to move on.'

'Is that a hint?'

'I promised Mum I'd keep an eye on you.'

Rufus snorted. 'I'm not going to get into trouble like those idiots in the paper.'

Georgie's chest tightened. 'Rufus was at school with one of them, you know,' added Sam. 'Jonathan, he was called. Stupid idiot. He deserves to be put inside for years. There's no excuse for drugs. Never has been and never will.'

Rufus raided his eyebrows. 'My brother can be very conservative. I hope you're prepared for that.'

He spoke as though their relationship was a given arrangement. All she could do was smile nervously.

'What about you, Georgie?' added Rufus. 'Where did you go to school?'

Her background was clearly so different from theirs that she felt inferior. 'A girls' grammar.'

'Clever,' said Rufus admiringly. 'I was only able to get into a minor public school. My brother of course, went to one of the

211

biggies. He was at …'

'Rufus,' Sam groaned, 'please.'

'All right, all right. I'll shut up. Looks like the taxi's stopping anyway.'

'You go on, Rufus.' Sam's voice was commanding. 'I'll get Georgie sorted. Help her settle down and show here what's what.'

They climbed up to a first-floor apartment, and as coming in, Georgie felt as though she'd stepped into another world. There was an oatmeal sofa, a huge double bed, a bathroom with clean, white, fluffy towels, and a kitchen.

'I'm worried you'll be a bit lonely,' said Sam after he'd shown her how the shower taps worked. Slightly unnecessary in her view but he insisted.

'I'll be fine. All I need to do is get a job to pay for the rent and then …'

'There's no rent. I'm allowed to let clients and friends stay here.' Sam bit his lip. 'As for the job, you might find that harder than you realise. You'll need work permits. That sort of thing.'

Georgie thought of Georgina's driving licence and passport. Would those be enough to apply?

'There is another option.' Sam was moving closer. 'I know we haven't known each other very long but I'm drawn to you, Georgie. And I suspect, if that doesn't sound forward, that you might feel the same about me. You could be my girlfriend. Let me look after you. Don't say no. Just think about it.'

Isn't it too soon after your broken engagement, she wanted to say. It was certainly too soon for her, after Joly.

But before she could say anything, a startled Georgie found herself being wrapped in Sam's arms. His kiss wasn't like Joly's. Nothing like it. But it was safe. And besides, Joly was lost to her. For ever.

All she had left of that life was her memories. And Georgina's precious shell, now hidden in a small box under her side of the bed.

'I'll take it,' Georgie said to the girl, trying to imagine what the flat would look like with new curtains.

'Really?' The girl looked troubled. 'It's very small and there's a bit of damp on the ceiling. I'll try and get the landlord to fix it but …'

'I can afford it,' said Georgie firmly. And that's what matters. After that, I'll need to find a job.'

The girl hesitated. 'My mother found herself in your situation,' she said kindly. 'It was after my dad left. Actually, I did wonder whether you have any office experience. My boss is looking for someone to help out in the office. Not terribly demanding, I'm afraid. Just answering the phone and doing some paperwork.'

She was an interior designer, Georgie reminded herself. A woman who'd been successfully running her own business. A vision of Mrs R-R's house came back to her. The decorators would be hard at work now on her plans.

But how could she do that now, in London, without her contacts? And more importantly, how could she return to Sam? He knew now that she had been living a lie for the last twenty odd years. She hadn't been Georgina Peverington-Smith at all. She'd been plain Georgie Smith. Drug dealer – well, accomplice – on the run. Suspected murderer.

'Answer the phone?' she repeated, wondering how she'd managed to fall on her feet so easily. It was all too reminiscent of Bangkok, and look how that had turned out. 'I can do that. And I'm used to paperwork. Thanks. I'd love to apply for the job.'

THIRTY THREE

Once, when I was in an open prison, they allowed me out into town for a day. It's meant to help you get readjusted to life on the outside when you're finally released. I thought it would be wonderful.

But it wasn't.

I'd walk down the street expecting someone to tap me on the shoulder any minute and haul me back.

The noise of the traffic made my head ache. You couldn't hear them from inside the prison. So I went into a pub for some peace and quiet.

That was worse. Everyone looked at me as I sat at the bar, nursing a pint.

After a bit, they stopped staring and began talking about themselves. Might as well have been talking in a foreign language. They talked so fast about things I hadn't heard of. Stuff that had happened in the news. Celebrities I didn't recognise.

Just when I'd decided to go, this girl came up to me. 'Hi,' she said.

She was big. Blonde. Busty with a T-shirt that was a definite 'hello'. Before I knew it, I'd found my tongue again. In more than one sense. By then, we'd found our way to the playing field at the back of the pub.

Shit. Was that the time? If I didn't rush, I'd miss curfew and then all my privileges. That meant losing my next day out for starters.

'Aren't you going to ask for my number?' she said, disappointedly.

I felt bad for her. She was nice. Really. Not just the physical bit if you know what I mean. But the talking.

'Your number?' I repeated, feeling stupid.

Maybe I should have told her the truth there and then. That I was going back Inside where you had to queue up for hours to use the phone and where no one could ring you. I also had the distinct feeling that she might not want to date a con.

'I'll be back,' I sat, pulling up my trousers. 'Maybe this time next month. OK?'

I carried the pain on her face with me; all through the next four weeks. It's exhausting, pretending to be someone else. Maybe I should just come clean with her after all.

When I made my way to the pub on my next day out, she was there all right. With another bloke.

'Hi,' I said.

But she carried on talking to him at the bar as if I didn't exist.

Don't blame her, really.

I'd probably do the same.

See? We have feelings too. So don't think we're totally heartless. We're just doing our job. Like you.

It's just that the rules are different.

THIRTY FOUR

She needed to work. This was driving her mad! To begin with, it had been all right. The relief of being safe in Australia – so far – was so great that Georgie would have gratefully accepted a small poky room to have lived in.

But the flat was amazing. So was Sam. He insisted on buying her clothes; stocking the fridge; suggesting places for her to visit while he was working; and taking her out to dinner where he would quiz her about her day.

At first, this was a novelty. 'The aquarium was amazing,' she enthused and Sam grinned with pleasure, rather like an indulgent parent who had given a child a present.

On another day, she went on a ferry to Manley, where she sat on the beach surrounded by families having picnics and waited for someone to arrest her. No one did. She returned to the flat with a growing sense of confidence. Maybe it would be all right after all.

Quite often, Rufus came round. Together they would explore the city. Darling Harbour was another of her favourites. She loved just looking at the water and imagining what it would be like to get on one of those beautiful boats and sail off into the sunset.

Away from the constant fear of being caught.

'I couldn't live here,' said Rufus suddenly during one of their trips – this time to the zoo where they watched a mother kangaroo carrying her 'joey' with fascination.

'Really?' She was still staring at the baby. Cocooned in its

217

mother's body, it looked so safe.

Rufus gave her a sharp look. 'Could you?'

'Maybe.'

'I thought you said you had a uni place to go back to?'

'I deferred it.'

The lie came out smoothly. Much easier than admitting she hadn't contacted them and that her place would now have been taken by someone else.

'What are you going to do then?'

They were walking on now. Heading for a cafe – she was dying for something cold to drink! Later, Rufus promised, they'd do a tour of the Royal Opera House – such an extraordinary roof! – where it would be cooler inside. It was so hot, even after Bangkok. This was a different type of heat: one that was dry. So dry that there were fires, apparently, raging through the Blue Mountains a few miles from here.

At home, it was winter. What would her mother be doing? A vision of her in bed with that man made her shiver. What would Lyndsey be doing? Laughing over a hot chocolate with new friends at uni. Confiding in them instead of her. For a moment, a pain flashed through her. Then she reconsidered Rufus' question. What *was* she going to do?

'I don't know,' she replied truthfully. 'I can't rely on your brother's kindness for ever.'

He didn't disagree. Had she hoped he would? Told her, perhaps, that Sam had plans for a future together? Of course, she'd thought about it. But every time she did, a picture of Joly came into her head. Followed by Georgina ...

'What are *you* going to do?' she asked as they passed a small crowd gathered round one of those motionless human statues who stood on the street, coated with face paint with a bucket for money at their feet. The things people did to survive. Things she knew about all too well.

'I'm too thick for university. Sam's going to try and pull a few strings so I can join "the firm" at a junior level.'

He said 'the firm' in a slightly mocking manner. Then he

laughed. 'What would we do without my brother, eh?'

The conversation worried her all day. When Sam arrived to take her out to dinner that night, she was quiet and not as responsive as usual when he kissed her.

'What's wrong?' he said, sensing immediately that something was up.

'Nothing,' she lied. But over dinner, she did tell him.

'Please don't think I'm ungrateful.' She took a sip of sparkling water, eyeing the wine bottle on the table. Wine which he had paid for. In an expensive restaurant which she would never have dreamed of going into before she'd met him. Her mother's voice rang out in her head. 'No better than a kept woman but without the sex. That's what you are.'

It was true. Georgie pushed her plate away, her salmon steak half-eaten. Suddenly she didn't feel hungry any more. 'I can't carry on living here for ever. I need something to do.'

He nodded. 'I know. But you don't have a working visa. The only way ...'

Sam stopped as a well-dressed couple swanned up to them. 'Sam!' squealed a small, dumpy woman with little sense of style, judging from that sack of a dress.

'Great to see you,' said her partner, reaching across Georgie (so rude!) to shake Sam's hand. Then they launched into a rapid conversation involving cocktail parties and a yacht in the harbour. Clearly they weren't short of money.

Eventually, the woman turned to her. So far, her conversation had been directed at Sam. 'It's so hard to find anyone to decorate out here, don't you think? The Australians have little sense of culture.'

'I could help.' Georgie found the words coming out of her mouth. 'I'm not bad with colours.'

Sam looked up, startled. Suddenly she realised she'd never discussed this with him. In a way, she'd wanted to keep it a secret. It was part of the old her. Yet here it was, escaping.

'I was going to do a fashion design course in London but ... well, I stayed out here instead.'

She smiled at Sam. He smiled back at her. Somehow she'd managed to re-write her past in a few sentences. The implication was that she'd stayed out here for him.

The woman was drawing a card out of her handbag. 'Maybe you'd like to ring me.' She glanced at Georgie's outfit appreciatively. It had been one of the expensive dresses which Sam had bought for her but Georgie had chosen the colour. Coral. Simply cut. But elegant. 'I like your style. Ring me and we'll see what happens.'

Sam was quietly pleased as he took her back to her flat afterwards. 'They like you,' he murmured.

Georgie sensed this was important.

His pleasure (which also sounded like relief) was evident in the way he was unzipping her dress. Until now, they had just kissed and – occasionally – gone a little further. So different from Joly when they had almost devoured each other within a few minutes. No. She couldn't think of that now. Couldn't allow herself to think of Joly who would right now, be languishing in prison, furious with her because she'd got away.

If only she knew what had happened to him. But the news – which she'd been scanning – had been silent on the fate of the three English backpackers in Thailand. Maybe it wasn't so important over here.

Thinking of Joly distracted her as Sam explored her body further. Suddenly she was aware of his bare skin on hers. It was different. Smoother. Too smooth.

'I've waited as long as I can,' he said, leading her to the bed.

Georgie waited for the excited rush; the fireworks; that incredible wave of passion that had happened with Joly. Nothing. Just a feeling of being entered and then hanging on while he squirmed and writhed and eventually let out a small moan.

'That was amazing,' he said, tears in his eyes. 'I love you, Georgie. I really do.'

'I love you too,' she found herself saying out of politeness. And then it was too late to take it back.

Georgie found it curiously appealing to work at the estate agent's. The cut and thrust of London and the office routine distracted her from the real world. The one in which Sam would, even now, have read part of her letter. He'd had plenty of time to ring her. To say that he understood. But there had been nothing.

Ellie had gone away for two months with friends – how wonderful that academic life allowed you to do that. And Nick was travelling too, with his friends. It was almost as if she'd never had a family. Often, Georgie stayed late working in the office, something that her boss commented on with appreciation. In reality, it was so she didn't have to return to the one-bedroom flat with the damp on the ceiling.

If it had been hers, Georgie told herself, she would have done it up. Got someone in to do a damp course. Painted the walls sage green with a cream carpet. Put in white shutters instead of curtains to maximise the light …

Stop. This wasn't her home. It was a make-shift. Until something happened. Meanwhile, she spent her spare hours wandering round galleries – there was a great exhibition at the National Portrait – and browsing round Fenwicks and Selfridges, knowing she couldn't afford to buy anything. It was like being a poor backpacker all over again.

Meanwhile, underneath was that constant current of fear. What if the unknown blackmailer still hadn't given Sam the money back? What if she had done this for nothing?

Word spread around Sydney's ex-pat circles. The dumpy American with the gold chain was so thrilled with the 'transformation' (as she put it) of her apartment that she recommended Georgie to all her friends. Even better, Sam's boss got to hear about it and he commissioned her to oversee the 'revamping' of the board room and the offices of senior members of staff.

'We can't pay you because of the permit situation,' he

explained. 'But you'd be doing us a favour if you could lend your eye.'

At first, Georgie was daunted by the challenge. Yes, she was good at colours. But she'd been lucky so far. If she hadn't managed to spot just the right shade of curtain fabric in the market for her first client, it might have been a different matter. The friendly fabric seller had put her in touch with a warehouse that specialised in unusual paint colours and wallpapers.

Her outlandish mix for the boardroom (apricots with yellows and reds) had met with some raised eyebrows from the warehouse staff, but Sam's boss had loved it! 'That'll wake them up, that's for sure,' he'd chuckled.

Meanwhile, Sam was thrilled at her success. 'They love you,' he said, interlacing his fingers through hers during a rare evening out alone at a local restaurant. Since coming to Australia, she'd discovered that very few people ate in within their circle – usually they were in a group of 'friends'. The latter were Sam's, of course – none of the other women appealed to her as kindred spirits. Oh how she wished Lyndsey was here. She missed Rufus too, who had been sent to Singapore.

'It's a great opportunity,' he'd said excitedly. Then his face had darkened. 'But – and I know this sounds awful – I'd rather have done it off my own back instead of Sam's.'

She knew exactly what he meant. Yes, she had a flair for decorating. But if she hadn't had Sam's contacts, none of this might have happened. Still, at least she was busy. Busy enough to almost forget the horrors she had left behind. Then, four months after she'd arrived, three things happened in one week.

On the Monday, Georgie began to wonder why her period was late. It was quite often three or four days behind, but it had been nearly ten days. She reassured herself with the thought that she didn't have sore breasts or felt sick like her current client, who was three months pregnant and keen to tell her about her symptoms. But it was late, nevertheless.

On the Wednesday, Sam came home early with a strange

expression. He knows, she told herself, appalled. He knows what I did. Someone's told him about Georgina. About Joly. About the drugs. He's going to turn me in.

In a funny way it was almost a relief. At least she wouldn't have to hide any more.

'Please sit down.'

He led her to the sofa with a degree of courtesy that exceeded even Sam's beautiful public school.

Georgie's heart threatened to burst out of her throat. And then he began to speak. 'My boss called me in today. He wants to promote me.'

'That's wonderful!'

Relief made her voice come out in a squeak. So this wasn't about her. It was about him. That half-hope that she might be discovered (if only to put an end to this constant looking over her shoulder), vanished. In its place was an all-encompassing gratitude that she wasn't being thrust into prison after all.

Sam's fingers drummed on her shoulder. They felt curiously irritating. 'In one way, yes. It is wonderful. But in another, it means change.'

Change? A change that involved her? Or which shut her out. Every now and then, Georgie had wondered about leaving Sam. Much as she cared for him, she never had the fireworks she'd had during that one night with Joly. There had to be more out there. Yet at the same time, it was safety which counted. Wasn't it?

'They want me to move to Hong Kong.'

Hong Kong? Of course! It was where all Sam's friends went, the ones who'd been promoted. It was seen as the next step up.

'That's wonderful!' she said, stammering as she tried to take all this in. 'Congratulations.' Then she looked around at the flat with the furnishings that she'd made her own. How she'd miss it! 'Would it be possible for me to stay on here a bit?'

'Stay on here for a bit?' Sam shook his head. 'For someone as lovely as you, you have an amazing lack of confidence. I want you to come with me, Georgie.' He dropped to his knee and pulled out a box from the inside of his jacket. Georgie's heart raced and sank at the same time. Out of all the options which had been flying round her head, she hadn't been expecting this.

'Georgina Peverington-Smith. Will you marry me?'

For a minute, she almost corrected him. I'm plain Georgie Smith, she nearly said. Not the posh one. I'm the girl they're looking for. The drug smuggler with a warrant for suspected murder.

Her voice wobbled. 'I'm not sure I can.'

Sam's face fell.

'It's not that I don't love you – I do. But it's so fast.'

He stood up, disappointment spreading across his face. 'Of course it is. I'm sorry.'

His tone reverted to the type he used when speaking to a business colleague.

'Please.' She leaped to her feet. 'May I just think about it until the end of the week?'

Another stiff nod. 'That's when I have to tell them my decision. I don't want to leave without you. But I need to think about the future, Georgie.' His eyes looked sad. 'I want a wife and a family. And I think you will fit that role perfectly.'

Fit the role? If only he knew! For the next few days they tiptoed around each other. Still her period didn't come. Most women would have leaped at the chance of a proposal from a man like Sam, especially in her situation, Georgie told herself firmly. But the memory of Joly lingered. It wouldn't go away as she advised clients on wallpaper and colours. And it wouldn't go away in her dreams.

Then on the Thursday – the day before her deadline! – she went into the market to look for more silks. Glancing at a newspaper stand, she froze.

Three British backpackers jailed for ten years. Hunt still on for the fourth.

Her mouth turned dry and she wanted to vomit right there, on the ground. That could be her! Instantly, she reproved herself for being selfish. Poor Joly. Poor Vanda and Jonathan. Even though she didn't like the last two, the thought of them being sent to a Bangkok prison was too awful to contemplate. Yet what could she do about it? Handing herself in wouldn't reduce their sentences. At the same time, it was too dangerous to stay here. Someone might follow a lead from the airport. Someone, somehow, might track her down.

It was time to run again.

Turning round quickly, she headed for the medical centre. By the time Sam came home from work, she was ready. Poor Georgina's shell was no longer in its box under the bed. It was in her pocket to give her strength as she spoke.

'Is your offer still open?'

They might have been negotiating a contract in the boardroom.

He nodded.

'I'm pregnant.'

The words came out starkly. She didn't feel like messing around.

His face broke out into a grin. 'That's amazing.'

She studied his face. 'Really?

Understanding broke out over his face. 'So that's why you wouldn't accept my proposal immediately. You were worried it was for the wrong reasons.'

Georgie certainly hadn't thought of it that way but if that was how he wanted to see it, that was fine.

'So will you accept me now you know I'm thrilled?' he asked, gently touching her slightly rounded stomach.

She nodded. 'Yes.' Thank you, she murmured under her breath. 'When do we leave for Hong Kong?' she said through his chest as he enveloped her in his arms. Smooth arms under the shirt. Not tough and hairy like Joly's.

'In a fortnight.'

Happiness rang through his words.

'Is there any chance of leaving earlier?'

He paused, loosening his grip, and looked down on her.

'Why the rush? A few days ago, you weren't certain you wanted to go.'

She felt a quickening of panic. 'I just don't want people to see that I'm pregnant, and I want to get married in another country.'

He nodded. 'I can understand that. But what about your mother? She'll need time to come over.'

Georgie's mind worked fast. 'She doesn't travel.' Standing on her tiptoes, she forced herself to kiss him. 'Besides, I just want a quiet ceremony. Is that all right?'

He kissed her back. A too-wet, too-slobbery, keen kiss. 'If that's what you want, my darling. The sooner the better, in my view. I can't wait for you to be Mrs Hamilton.'

Georgie Hamilton.

Two names that had nothing to do with her.

Two names that might just help get her out of the mess she was in.

'Georgie Hamilton?'

The south London voice at the other end of the phone was slightly rough at the edges, jerking her back to the present.

Georgie was used to this. You got all types, she discovered, looking for rental properties. There were the young rich who didn't bat an eyelid at the ridiculous prices being asked for one-bedroom near-slums. There were professional couples who still couldn't afford to buy. There were women like her: shy, embarrassed, clearly unused to asking the right questions about rentals. Georgie had learned to recognise them immediately. Bolters. Women who had left their husbands and now needed somewhere to live.

And the rather rough-spoken, self-made type who referred to her as Georgie on the strength of one appointment. One had even asked her out to dinner the other night despite the fact that she still wore her wedding ring, even though Sam had still failed to get in touch. There'd been nothing from the police either. Only an answer-phone message from the computer man, saying he was 'still working on the gremlins'.

'Is that Georgie Hamilton?' repeated the voice impatiently.

'Sorry.' She was jolted back into the present. 'Yes. It is.'

'I'm ringing on behalf of a friend. Be outside the Royal Academy at 6.30 p.m.'

'Who is this?'

'Don't be late. You finish at six so you should have plenty of time.'

Then there was the sound of a receiver being replaced.

This person knew what time she finished! How weird ...

'Are you all right?' asked the girl working next to her.

Georgie nodded. 'Yes, thank you.'

Her private life had to stay private. But instinctively, Georgie was certain that the phone call was about the missing money.

THIRTY FIVE

I got into private security, as I like to call it, when I was Inside.

Easy money, said the bloke in my cell.

Varied too. You never get bored.

Sometimes you follow someone.

Sometimes you make a phone call on behalf of the client, like. It might be to check that someone's in the office. We get a lot of wives who want to know that.

Sometimes it's to make an assignation, like.

'Why can't the client do it themselves?' I asked.

'Cos they don't want to be recognised, 'course.'

Didn't sound too difficult. And it isn't.

Provided you're careful. Sometimes though you feel really sorry for the person you're taking in. I felt that way about this woman I've just spoken to. She sounded scared. Really scared.

I've been there. I know what it feels like.

To be honest, I felt sorry for her.

And that's when I knew it was time to get out of this game. The trouble is that too many people know what I do. Sometimes you just can't escape your past. So you have to do the next best thing.

You have to embrace it.

THIRTY SIX

The Royal Academy had always been one of Georgie's favourite haunts. She'd discovered it soon after they'd returned from Hong Kong with two irritable teenagers in tow. London was a good place for day trips and – desperate for some European culture – she'd dragged a rebellious Nick and Ellie round several galleries and museums.

But it was the RA, with its beautiful yet welcoming architecture, which always drew her. Was it coincidence that the anonymous caller knew that Georgie was familiar with it? Or was it just a convenient place to meet?

As Georgie walked through the streets, trying not bump into people or be walked into by others, she tried to work things all out in her head.

'Georgie Hamilton,' the voice had said. The tone had suggested the caller knew her. 'I'm ringing on behalf of a friend.'

Who? A friend of hers as well as the caller? Or was it not a friend at all? An enemy. Someone who somehow knew enough about Georgie to have her work number.

Someone who maybe, if her instinct was right, was connected with the threatening notes about Sam and the money.

None of it made sense. Then again, hadn't she been waiting for something like this to be happening for most of her adult life? You couldn't live a lie – couldn't steal someone else's life – for as long as she had, without expecting it to catch up with you.

In some ways, it was almost a relief. Or would it be?

Where had she felt that mixture before? Back in Australia when Sam's sudden proposal had shown her that, despite everything, she was still scared of being discovered. Instead, she wanted to be rescued. And that's exactly what he had done.

The wedding took place quietly, just as she had requested, at a small church in Hong Kong – shortly after their arrival there – followed by dinner at the Jockey Club.

Sam and Rufus' mother had flown out for the occasion. She was a widow – their father, Sam had explained soon after meeting, had been much older and had died when the boys were still teenagers.

'It's one of the reasons I feel responsible for my brother,' he'd added. She could understand that. Not for the first time in her life, did Georgie wish she had a brother or sister to give her support.

'Such a shame your family couldn't be here,' Sam's mother kept saying pointedly during the celebrations.

Georgie, who didn't care for Sam's mother's sharp features and condescendingly cold manner, was getting tired of saying the same thing. 'I don't have much of a family left any more and besides, my mother doesn't like travelling.'

'You must wish that your mother was here,' Sam's mother had persisted.

'Not really.' She waited until the attentive waiter had finished serving them. 'We're not particularly close since she married again.'

Sam's mother's thin lips, which were perfectly coated with a pale pink creamy colour, pursed. 'What a shame. I do dislike family arguments. I always feel that whatever one's differences, one should put them aside where blood is concerned.'

If Sam's mother knew her family better, she might think otherwise.

It was a relief when her new mother-in-law flew back home shortly after the ceremony, via Singapore where she was staying with friends. She could just imagine the conversation there. 'Poor, dear Sam, wasting himself on some girl who had neither breeding nor education. I wouldn't be at all surprised if she was pregnant. In fact, I'm almost certain that she was showing ...'

Indeed, it had been difficult to hide that little bulge underneath the ivory dress she'd had made up – in only forty-eight hours! – by one of the clever seamstresses she'd found in the dressmaker section of Hong Kong. So much better than she could have done herself ...

Within a few months, she was as 'big as a house', as Rufus put it when he visited. 'Fantastic!' he beamed, patting her tummy without asking permission first. 'I've always wanted to be an uncle. Can't wait to see what fatherhood does to Sam. Really loosen him up with any luck.'

Just as well her husband wasn't in the apartment at the time. 'Actually, he's being really attentive,' defended Georgie. 'I can't move anywhere without him asking if I'm all right.'

'Exactly what I mean.' Rufus helped himself to a glass of wine from the huge fridge which the maid stocked every day. 'There's a difference between loosening up and being a control freak, you know.'

Then his face got serious. 'Seriously, Georgie. I do worry for you. Sam's a good chap. Too good. He expects perfection; not just in himself but in others too.' He rolled his eyes and the joker Rufus returned. 'It can be very wearing.'

Georgie shivered. She was already learning this herself. Sam got upset if the maid put something in the wrong place or – as happened the other day – placed a coffee cup on a book cover, leaving a stain.

What on earth would he say if he knew about her past? Thankfully, she hadn't seen any more headlines about Joly and the others. Maybe it would die down in the press. But it could never die down in her heart. As she grew larger and larger, so did her imagination. At night, she would wake screaming with terror at a nightmarish picture of Joly in a filthy Bangkok prison with cockroaches crawling up his legs …

'Shh,' Sam would say soothing her. 'I've told you. Don't eat strong cheese. It's renowned for nightmares. What were you dreaming about anyway?'

'I can't remember,' she'd lie. But Joly's face continued to haunt her. Sometimes it was Vanda's too, and Jonathan's. She hadn't liked them but that didn't mean she couldn't feel pity for them. If she hadn't left them to it, she would have been there too.

'Be grateful,' she told herself firmly. Put it all behind you. Maybe it was time to put Georgie behind her too, as well. A new baby. A new life.

The shell, warm in her hand, seemed to agree.

She was here now. Georgie walked across the beautiful courtyard of the Royal Academy as she had done so many times before. But this time was different. Which of these people she was passing was the one who had called her?

Was it the man with the walking stick by the fountain who had given her a sharp glance?

Or the boy in the orange anorak who was sitting on one of the outside café chairs, staring at the ground?

'Be outside,' the voice had instructed.

But had he meant by the doors or in the café area?

Unsure, Georgie ordered herself a latte and took a seat. Her mouth was dry and her chest felt tight with apprehension. Maybe she should have told the girl in the office that she was meeting someone here. It might have been sensible. Just in case …

'Georgie!'

She jumped as a tall, slim, confident woman slid into the seat opposite her. For a minute Georgie couldn't place her. The Hon. Mrs David R-R belonged to a different part of her life. It threw her. Made her babble with nerves and stammer slightly.

'What a coincidence! Look, I'm sorry I haven't been in touch about the house. I hope it's going all right. I had to come to London unexpectedly for a few weeks and …'

'It's not.'

She stopped. 'I'm sorry?'

'It's not all right and it's not a coincidence.'

Mrs R-R's eyes hardened. At the same time, a cold tendril of fear wrapped itself round Georgie's heart. 'What do you mean?'

Without speaking, she undid her purse and placed a small piece of paper in front of her. It was a receipt. A bank receipt, showing that a large sum of money had been paid into an account. Sam's account.

'He won't be able to trace it,' she said, showing a neat row of pearly teeth in a small smile. 'We're good about that kind of thing. But it's there all right.'

Georgie could only stare. 'You? It was you? But why … how?'

There was a shake of the head. 'You still don't recognise me, do you, Georgie?'

Recognise her? From where?

'We met before we were "introduced" in Devon. But then again, the surgeon did a good job.' Her face hardened. 'He had to after what I went through in prison. Thai prisons aren't like British ones, you know. '

Georgie's heart began to race. 'I don't understand …'

'Oh, but I think you do.' There was another click of the handbag opening. This time it was a small black and white photograph that was being pushed across the table. A group of youngsters grinned back at her. Joly. Vanda. Jonathan. Georgina. And herself.

'We all looked rather different then, didn't we, Georgie? After the guards slashed my face and I was finally released, my parents paid for plastic surgery. I used the opportunity to get my nose fixed. Never cared for it.'

Another small smile. 'Rather thin, if you remember. Unfortunately they couldn't do much with my ankles. "Lumpy", I think, was the term you and Georgina referred to them when you hadn't thought I was listening. '

Vanda? The Hon. Mrs David R-R was Vanda? No wonder she hadn't allowed her to use her first name. Georgie could hardly find the breath to breathe. 'How ... I don't understand ...'

Mrs R-R sat back, a satisfied expression creeping over her face. 'At first it really was a coincidence. Your husband mentioned to mine that his wife was an interior designer. He knew I needed help.' Another smile. 'Statistics are more my forte than art, although I appreciate the latter. Then when you arrived, I recognised you immediately.' The smile went. 'You always did have an incredible similarity to poor Georgina.'

A lump rose into her throat. 'I often think about her –'

'Don't.' The face grew fierce. 'You murdered her.'

'I didn't –'

Ignoring her, Vanda went on. 'You ran away, leaving us to carry the can, and then you ratted on us about the drugs –'

'That's not true –'

'You told the police about where we kept it.'

'No.' Her voice came out choked, attracting the attention of a well-dressed couple at a neighbouring table who eyed them curiously. 'I wouldn't do that.'

The face that met hers was steely. 'How else would they have known? Joly was always so careful.'

'Is this why you are punishing me?'

'What do you think?'

'But how did you do it ... the car ... my car that disappeared and my handbag ...'

Another satisfied grin. 'That was nothing to do with me. All I did was recognise you – especially when you showed such interest in the Thai paintings – and then I told my husband. Sam had already told him about living in the east. So we made investigations. Somehow you had to be made to pay. It wasn't difficult to get access to your husband's account – it was clear he had no idea of your past from the glowing way he talked about you.'

She snorted. 'You might look like Georgina but you're

nothing like her in spirit. She wouldn't have harmed a fly.'

'I've told you,' whispered Georgia through gritted teeth. 'I didn't kill her. It was a boy. A boy who ran away after he tried to hurt me.'

Vanda snorted. 'Tell that one in court.'

Georgie's head was still reeling. 'I still don't see how you got into Sam's account.'

A pigeon flew overhead. As it did so, a passing Japanese tourist let out a little startled cry. For a second their conversation was interrupted, teasing out the reply.

'Because they work together. You still don't get it, do you? Jonathan is my husband. We got married soon after we were released.'

'But he's called David ...'

'That's his real name. The one he was christened with. The one on his paperwork which your husband would have been familiar with. All his friends call him Jonathan – one of his middle names.'

Someone tried to squeeze past her chair. Automatically, Georgie put out her hand to check her bag was safe while trying to take all this in. The fear of being robbed was always with her thanks to the stolen car. But this was different. This was a different kind of theft.

Jonathan was David Romer-Riches? It struck her that she hadn't even known Jonathan's surname when they were all together. That sort of thing hadn't seem that important.

'So,' she murmured disbelievingly, 'you planned this as a revenge.'

Vanda's face darkened. 'Why should you have it all when you murdered Georgina and then dropped us in it? After what they did to me...' Her voice dropped. 'After what they did to me, I couldn't have children.'

Georgie gasped. 'I'm so sorry.'

She laughed shortly. 'I had mental issues too.'

I know about mental illness. Wasn't that what Vanda had said when they'd met in her house? Hadn't they all? Wasn't that

237

one reason why she, Georgie, didn't drink any more? If she and Joly hadn't had so much wine, they might not have got together and then Georgina wouldn't have died …

She'd sworn after that not to touch a drop again.

'I know what you mean,' she said slowly.

'Then you accept responsibility, do you?'

'No. No! It wasn't me who murdered her –'

'I don't care if you're lying or not. Because the fact remains that you left us and stole Georgina's identity. Now you know what it's like to have yours taken too.'

'So you were responsible for my credit card and the YouTube video and –'

There was an impatient wave. 'I told you. Nothing to do with me, although I did take a certain pleasure in the gossip about that. Just as I am taking a pleasure in the fact that your husband now knows the truth about your past.'

'He's told you about my letter to him?'

'He told Rufus.'

Rufus? Rufus who had stayed in Singapore and had, against the odds, done very well for himself?

'They were at school together.' Vanda smiled. 'Ours is a small world, Georgie. We stick together. And we seek revenge together.'

'But why take the money from Sam's account?'

There was a crocodile smile showing those rows of tidy, pearly teeth. 'Because it threw you off the scent. You thought it was related to the other frauds. In fact, it was the handbag and card incident that gave us the idea. You'd assume it was part of the whole complex web of deceit. If I'd just told you to tell your husband about the past, you might not have done it. But we put him in a vulnerable position and made you capable of being his saviour.'

The crocodile smile faded. 'This time you've dug your own grave. Just as the local undertaker had to dig poor Georgina's.'

She got up. 'My job is done. Good luck with the future. Maybe you'll make it up with your husband. But from what

Rufus has told me, it's unlikely. Goodbye.'

'But wait.' There was something else they hadn't talked about. *Someone* else.

'What about Joly?' she gasped, catching up with her by the fountain.

Vanda's eyes gleamed. 'You always did have a thing for him, didn't you? I wonder what your husband would make of that.'

Then, throwing Georgie a nasty look, she marched off, disappearing into the crowds.

THIRTY SEVEN

I was Inside with a bloke who got promised a new face. 'Before they let me out,' he told, excitedly, 'they're going to make me different. Then no one can get me.'

Made me feel sick, I can tell you. We all knew what he'd done. I don't usually agree with capital punishment but I would for this bloke.

The irony is that a week before he was having his face changed, someone else did it for him.

After that, he didn't need any more help.

Boiling water and sugar is highly effective on the skin.

Do I need to say more?

THIRTY EIGHT

After Vanda left, Georgie wandered round the RA in a trance.
The exhibition of pre-Raphaelites which would, at any other
time, have taken up her attention, now faded into memories of
the island, Vanda, Jonathan, Joly (always Joly), and poor
Georgie.

Then, rounding the corner, she came across a large painting
of a bride by Singer Sargent. The subject wore a look which
might be interpreted as either fearful or slightly arrogant at her
lot. Judging from the plaque at the side, the woman had married
a traditional wealthy member of the aristocracy. An outsider
might say that she, Georgie Smith, had done the same.

Sitting down on a bench seat, opposite the painting, Georgie
allowed her mind to wander back to those early days of her
marriage in Hong Kong.

Pregnancy suited Georgie. She didn't have morning sickness or
indigestion or sleeplessness. This appeared to disappoint the
other women in the new ex-pat community in which Georgie
found herself.

What they didn't know was that her internal turmoil more
than compensated for the lack of usual pregnancy symptoms.
As she grew bigger, Georgie became more and more convinced
that there would be a phone call or a knock on the door or an
official letter, summoning her to justice.

Every time she opened the little postal box at the bottom of
their building, her heart raced. But there was never anything for

her.

'Don't you and your mother write to each other?' enquired Sam at the beginning.

She had shaken her head. 'Mum's not a great correspondent.'

He'd raised his eyebrows, clearly disappointed that her family wasn't the same as his. His own mother wrote once a week in perfectly-scripted handwriting, on Basildon Bond notepaper with the family address embossed on it. What would he say if he knew that her mother didn't know where she was?

Not that it really mattered. Mum had lost any right to filial love years ago – a fact undeniably demonstrated when she'd refused to 'bother' the doctor and consequently put her daughter's life in danger. She still found it hard to forgive her for that. But Georgie's heart did ache for Lyndsey. If she was able to write to her friend, without telling her where she was and blowing her cover, she'd have described this incredible city with the silent men and women who did tai chi in the park; the tailors who ran you up a dress in a day at a fraction of the prices at home; the muggy atmosphere; the rooftop pool in their apartment block; the parties; the boat trips; and the fortune teller she had taken herself to one day on the Star ferry.

The last had been a grave aberration on her part. One of the other women had spoken about him with great reverence. He'd told her that her sister would finally get married and, lo and behold, there was a phone call the next day from England to confirm this. Another woman had also been: one who was trying to get pregnant. She was told to expect a happy event in six months' time. In fact, it had turned out to be eight but as the woman said, joyfully, he was right in the end.

Tempted, despite that warning voice inside, Georgie went on her own. The fortune teller only set up his stall in the evening market. Fortunately, Sam was working late again. All the way, on the boat, Georgie thought about turning back but some unseen pull inside her chest took her almost straight to his stall.

He was older than she'd expected, although that might have

244

been the sun which made everyone age prematurely unless you carried a shade and applied lotion liberally like the other ex-pat wives.

Scared, she sat down in front of him after parting with her money. He wasn't cheap. She'd expected some preamble, something obvious that might apply to anyone such as 'You are far from home'. But instead, his words rocked her.

'You are running away,' the old man said to her, taking her palm in his. 'One day your past will catch up with you.'

She'd snatched her hand away then, making to get up. But he hung on fast. His grasp belied the fragility of his bones. 'Your husband too, he has a secret.' He smiled. A rather sad smile in milky blue eyes. 'It might save you both.'

Sam had a secret? 'My husband isn't like that,' she said fiercely.

The smile slipped away. 'Who is *anyone* like?'

The truth of the words threw her just as his previous declaration. Shaking, Georgie stood up. This time, he made no attempt to detail her.

'Be careful,' he added. 'Trust no one.'

Then he glanced at her protruding bump. 'You will have a boy.' He grinned. 'But you will also have a daughter.'

Then he closed his eyes and seemed to slip into a type of reverie. Georgie hovered, not sure if she should go or not. Had he finished? Suddenly, he opened his eyes. 'You are still here?' he said. His face tightened and there was an impatient wave in the air. 'You must go now. That baby will not be long.'

All the way back on the ferry, her unborn child kicked with an insistence it had not shown before. She should not have gone, Georgie told herself. The fortune teller had unsettled her and this had spread to the baby. *One day your past will catch up with you ... Your husband too, he has a secret.*

The phrases pounded again and again in her head. By the time she got home, after taking a tuk-tuk from the port, the kicking had given way to a strange, dull ache.

'Where have you been?'

Sam's meeting, it appeared, had been cancelled. He had come home early to take her out to dinner and been concerned by her absence.

'I went to the other side of the island,' she faltered. 'To explore. But now I don't feel well.'

Instantly, his initial annoyance gave way to concern. She must lie down. Put up her feet. But as he helped her into bed, there was a sudden gush of water. Georgie knew from the doctor and the ex-pat women what this meant.

'I'm three weeks early,' she cried all the way to hospital, appalled to be met by a team of doctors clad in white theatre outfits 'just in case'.

'It's all right,' soothed a midwife. 'You're in good hands.'

Your past will catch up with you. Your past will catch up with you. The soothsayer's words drummed in her head. Did he mean that something would happen to the baby; something bad as punishment for her part on the island.

'I'm sorry, I'm sorry,' she moaned as the pains got worse and the urge to push increase.

'My darling,' said Sam's voice as she felt a hand on her forehead. 'You have nothing to be sorry for.'

'But I have,' she began. 'I need my shell.'

'Need your shell?' questioned Sam.

'She's hallucinating,' said someone. 'It's quite natural with the gas and air.'

And then the urge to push became so great that the words were stuck in her mouth, just as the baby was stuck. 'Bear down,' urged the midwife. 'Bear down ...'

There was a high-pitched cry. At first she thought a woman was shrieking.

'Is it all right?'

That was Sam's voice.

There was an agonising silence and then another cry.

'You have a son,' sang the midwife as she placed a small, slippery bundle on her stomach. 'You have a baby boy!'

'Excuse me but is this seat taken?'

The question came in a soft American accent. Georgie glanced up as a good-looking man about her age stood in front of her in the gallery.

Reluctantly, she was brought back to the present.

'No. Please.' She indicated that there was room for more than one.

'Stunning, isn't it?'

It took Georgie a few seconds to realise he was referring to the wedding painting. 'Yes, beautiful.'

She was still half in her head. Still remembering ...

Nick had been born seven months to the day after her own wedding. Luckily, his premature arrival had allowed Sam's mother to twist the dates on behalf of her friends.

'Make sure you are strict with feeding hours,' she wrote. 'Too many young women nowadays feed whenever Baby starts crying. You do not want to spoil him.'

Not spoil him? Not give in to everything that this incredible, tiny being demanded? How could she not? To her surprise, motherhood came so naturally to Georgie that the other women were once more disappointed. Even though she fed him exactly when he wanted, Nick had not become 'obese' as her mother-in-law had warned. Instead, he excelled at all milestones.

'He's crawling,' she announced excitedly one night when Sam returned from another late meeting.

By the time he was eleven months, he was walking. Or rather, staggering from one table leg to another. It required every ounce of concentration on behalf of her and the maid to keep an eye on him.

'If your mother doesn't want to come and visit him, perhaps we should visit her,' suggested Sam after his own mother had been to stay.

Georgie took a deep breath. This pretence couldn't go on for ever. Yet at the same time, she couldn't tell him the truth.

Holding Nick, almost as a defence between them, she put on her most beguiling look. 'To be honest, darling, I'd rather not see her.'

He was shocked. 'I know you've never got on but surely ...'

'She has her own life now.'

That was true enough. Was her mother worried that she hadn't heard from her? Georgie only hoped that her mother hadn't contacted the British Consulate.

'Maybe you'll feel different when Nick is a little older.'

Sam's voice was gentle; reassuring; not wanting to upset her. He had been like this ever since his son had been born.

'Maybe.'

Georgie went along with it. It was easier. Yet if she had known this was the peace before the storm, she might have acted differently.

'Do you come to this gallery often?'

Once more, Georgie was reluctantly dragged back to the present day. It occurred to her that this handsome American in the smart navy jacket might just be trying to chat her up. It was almost amusing, given her circumstances. Romance was the last thing she needed. It was only Sam she wanted. Sam, whom she'd married out of convenience at the beginning. Sam, whom she'd learned to love over the years but always with the sense that she wasn't good enough for him.

'It's my favourite.'

Then just to make things clear, she added, 'I used to bring my son and daughter here when they were small.'

He nodded approvingly. 'I come from Boston. We have some beautiful galleries there.'

Boston. She and Sam had taken the children there once. Nick had been three. Ellie had been four. They had only been a family of four for a few months. A holiday, Sam had said desperately, might help.

Nick had been a year old when Sam came back from the office, his face drawn even more than usual. Immediately she knew something had happened. Another move, perhaps. It happened all the time. One of the other ex-pat women was excitedly packing for New York.

'All those theatres and shops,' she had enthused. 'Decent food too.'

Georgie was hoping for a city that was less high profile. Anywhere where she might not bump into someone from her past.

Every day, she scanned the papers for news of three British backpackers in a Thai prison. Nothing. Then again, what did she expect? People like that disappeared for years. The old dreams had started to come back too. Visions of Joly and the others, with one meal a day if they were lucky. Perhaps that was why she'd lost so much weight. The appalling luxury of her new life had consumed her with guilt.

'Can you sit down?' Sam said.

Just like last time! But somehow, Georgie had a feeling that this was more than a move. Her body went very still. He'd found out. He knew what she'd done. He was going to divorce her. Take away Nick who was, even now, sleeping peacefully in his cot.

'I'm afraid I've done something I shouldn't have done,' he said in a quiet voice.

Georgie froze. *Your husband too, he has a secret. It might save you both ...*

'What?' she managed to say, her voice cracked.

Sam had his head in his hands. 'Before we met, I went to a bar for my ... for my first stag night.'

First? In fact, he hadn't had one for their own wedding; had firmly declined one. Now, Georgie was to find out why. 'I'm afraid I ... I went too far with a girl in a bar.' His face was contorted with wretchedness. 'One of those ping pong bars.'

She'd heard about them, of course. Girls who did unspeakable things to their bodies with ping pong balls and worse.

249

'It appears that she had a child.' He raised his face now in an obvious effort to look at her straight. It was like viewing a stone gargoyle. 'A few months before Nick was born. A daughter.'

Georgie could only stare. *You will have a boy but you will also have a daughter.*

Suddenly she felt powerful. Sam, always the perfectionist, had slipped. Broken the rules of his own kind. Had a child out of wedlock.

'It's all right,' she said. 'These things happen. We can support her. You can see her regularly and ...'

'This girl found me – through the phone book, can you believe – to say she cannot afford to keep her.' Sam's head was back in his hands now. 'She says I have a responsibility. I must look after her now.'

How could a woman give away her child, even if she couldn't afford to keep it? And how could Georgie take on a child that wasn't hers? Of course! Suddenly it became clear. This is what the fortune teller meant. *It might save you both.* This was her opportunity to tell Sam about her past. 'I've done something wrong too.'

The words were almost on her lips.

Then she stopped. Drugs. Suspected of murder. Both were far bigger than a chance encounter in a bar. They weren't even comparable. Sam might even end up with custody of both children. He was repentant now but he had a far tougher side. One that she had seen both at work and when he was ranting on about drugs from newspaper stories.

Then again, none of this was as important as a small child who didn't have anyone to love her. Of all people, Georgie knew that.

'Of course we must have her,' she said softly. 'I'll love her as my own. She'll have a ready-made family and it will be good for Nick.'

Instantly, Sam's arms enveloped her. 'I can't believe you've just said that,' he said, his eyes wet. 'Thank you. Thank you.'

It was arranged that baby Ellie would be flown over two

weeks later. 'We will tell everyone else that we adopted her,' she told Sam, with the imagination of an accomplished liar. 'We will say she belonged to a maid of ours who needed help.'

His face was etched with anguish. 'They won't believe us.'

'It doesn't matter. But as far as we're concerned, we will treat her as our own flesh and blood.' Flushed with this new power, she held Sam by his collar, forcing him to look down on her. 'She's ours. Otherwise it will be too difficult.'

Inside, however, Georgie was quaking. How would she feel when she really saw this baby who had nothing to do with her? Yet when she and Sam stood, tremulous, at the airport arrivals, and she saw an air hostess approaching, carrying a scared little girl with smooth, dark skin and huge brown eyes, she fell in love instantly.

A daughter! A daughter! Only now would she allow herself to admit how much she had secretly yearned for a daughter to dress up and go shopping with. Besides, Ellie was living proof that her husband wasn't perfect. Georgie was shocked to find that the calculating part of her realised that one day, this might come in useful.

'Come on little one,' she soothed, taking the child into her arms. 'You're home now.'

'I was just wondering,' said the American stranger on the bench next to her in the gallery, 'if you'd like lunch.'

Her head was so full of the past that she almost didn't take in his words.

'No, thank you.' She blushed furiously. 'Actually, I'm married.'

He cast a nod at her wedding ring. 'I know you are. But would it make a difference if I told you that Joly sent me?

THIRTY NINE

I never wrote letters till I got sent Inside. Then I found they were more important than anything else. You can spend hours queuing up for the corridor phone, aware that everyone else is listening in.

But letters are sacred. They are personal. You can pour out your heart. And the other person can tell you stuff that she can't always manage on the phone.

Letters tell you more about the feelings of the writer than a call when someone can put on a voice or tell you that they can't speak now because they're busy – as if you can ring back any old time.

I know how important letters are because in five years, I only received one.

And then I wished I hadn't.

FORTY

Joly? Joly had sent this quiet, good-looking American to talk to her?

'I don't believe you,' she stuttered.

It had to be a scam. Just like the stolen money which hadn't been stolen at all. Well, not all of it. It had been a complicated trick organised by Vanda and Jonathan to 'pay her back' for something that wasn't all her fault.

The quiet American nodded gravely. Both had forgotten the beautiful, large, Impressionist painting which had brought them together in conversation only a few minutes ago. 'He thought you might say that.'

Handing her a letter, he moved away, towards a different painting. This time, one of a mother and a child. The former was gazing adoringly at the latter and they were both eating cherries from the same dish.

Dear Georgie,

It has taken us a long time to find you. How clever you have been to deceive us by pretending to be someone you weren't.

I wonder if you thought of us as often as we thought of you.

We could, if we chose, contact the police. It wouldn't be the first time that a murderer has been caught after years have passed. However, something inside me makes me doubt that you could have committed such a crime. So I have persuaded Vanda and Jonathan that we will allow you to state your case. To us, rather than the authorities.

I cannot – will not – return to the UK. So that leaves one option. You must come to me. My friend will give you details.
   Joly

The words flew round in front of her. None of them made sense. Yet in another manner, they all fell into place. *Won't return to the UK.* 'Where is he?' asked Georgie, walking over to the American, who was gazing at the bowl of cherries as if trying to work out how they had been painted with that dark red tone contrasting with the pink inner flesh.

But even as she asked the question, she knew the answer. 'The island you were on.' The man turned and faced her, his eyes glued to hers. For the first time, she noticed a small, silver scar on the top of his right eyebrow. 'Despite everything, Joly chose not to leave.'

Then he put his hand in his right pocket and drew out an envelope. 'Tickets,' he said simply. 'You leave on Wednesday.'

His next words came out clear and crisp. 'If you don't board the plane, we will call the police.'

Of course, she couldn't possibly go. It was ridiculous! How could her life change so dramatically in the course of a few months? Not long ago, she was running a respected interior design company with a loving husband, a son, and a step-daughter. Now she had lost the first two. She would also lose her children too when the truth came out.

As she walked briskly away from the Royal Academy, threading her way through the crowds towards Green Park tube station, Georgie's mind whirled. Go to the other side of the world to defend herself? What if they didn't believe her? What if they called the police and she found herself imprisoned in a hellhole just as they had been?

'If you don't board the plane, we will call the police,' the American had said.

Who was he anyway? In the shock, she had stupidly failed to

ask his name.

'Sorry.'

A man bumped into her as she fumbled for her mobile. This had gone on for long enough. She had to ring Sam.

Don't go through to answer-phone, she silently begged. Don't. She needed to explain in person.

Or was that the wrong thing to do?

Please go through to answer-phone. Please. She was too scared to face the music.

Answer-phone.

'Sam,' she began, conscious of a middle-aged woman eating chips out of a bag beside her on the park bench. Green Park itself seemed a better place to make a call than outside the tube station.

Then, her courage failing her, she pressed End Call.

The woman finished her last chip, scrunched up the paper bag, and threw it on the ground. At any other time, Georgie would have said something or at the least, put it in the bin.

Then her phone rang of its own accord, startling her. *Sam,* said the screen.

Shaking, she pressed the green answer button.

'You rang.' His voice was so stiff that it might have been speaking to a cold caller.

'Yes.' Her own voice wobbled audibly. 'I wanted to explain.'

'Your letters did that.'

'Don't you want to know more?'

There was the sound of disgust at the other end. 'More? What else do I need to know. My wife passed herself off as a dead woman in order to hide her past. A past which consisted of drug running and – oh yes – a murder charge.'

His voice got louder and angrier. 'For nearly twenty years, you have pretended to be someone else and I – idiot that I am – believed you. You only married me for safety – to escape the past. No wonder you didn't want to see your mother. She doesn't even know where you are. Now I understand why you were so nervous when we came back to England and why you've never wanted to make contact with her. You're a fake, Georgie or Georgina Peverington-Smith or whoever you are.'

'Wait, wait,' she cried desperately. 'It wasn't like that.'

'I don't believe you.' His voice was hurt now rather than angry. This was worse. 'Just as I don't believe you know about the money. All that nonsense about the car going missing and then our accounts being emptied. You made it up. You've got the money squirreled somewhere in a private account.'

'No, no,' she protested, aware that people were looking at her. 'That's not true.'

'True? There was a bitter laugh at the other end. 'What do you know about truth? Luckily, I have good friends to help me. David Romer-Riches has put his own security people onto your latest trick. He's managed to get my money back, although he's still working out how you did it. Frankly, if it wasn't for the children, I'd go straight to the police ...'

'Don't. Don't.'

Her voice rose in pain. 'Give me two weeks. I've – I've got to go somewhere. When I come back, I'll be able to prove everything.'

There was a silence. 'Come back from where?'

'Thailand,' she said, more quietly now. It wasn't until the words came out that she realised this was the only option open to her. If she could persuade Joly that she wasn't responsible for Georgie's death, maybe – just maybe – the others would understand too. Until then, she didn't want to explain the full story to anyone, including Sam. He was in such a state that she might only have one chance to do this – and she couldn't blow it.

'I didn't kill anyone,' she added quietly. 'It wasn't me.'

'But what about the drugs? You know my feelings on that. Just look at Ellie. People like you were responsible for young kids ruining their lives.'

'I know,' she said numbly. 'I'm sorry. But I didn't

258

realise ... I just went along with the others ... I simply carried a few parcels ...'

Silence. Dead. He'd put down the phone. Wiping her eyes, Georgie leaned back on the bench, her eyes closed. At the same time, her phone bleeped with a mixture of new text messages and emails.

One from Ellie in Turkey with her friends, asking if she was 'OK' because she hadn't heard from her. 'Staying out here another week.'

Good. The longer she was away, the better. Georgie couldn't bear the thought of her daughter knowing her past.

Another from Nick. 'Sicily is great.'

Once more, the longer he was away travelling, the better too. Then a new term would start at Durham. Now that seemed more like a blessing than it had before. He wouldn't be around to witness the fall-out.

There was a missed call from Lyndsey's mobile.

Lyndsey. Her old friend who knew her better than anyone else – despite everything. Lyndsey, who was the only person, apart from Sam, who knew the truth.

The phone picked up immediately.

'Are you all right?'

No need for preambles. The test of a true friendship, they'd agreed, was the ability to slip right back.

'Brilliant. The treatment is working.' Her friend's voice was brighter than usual. 'But I was worried about you. You've been away for weeks. How's the job? Have you spoken to Sam yet?'

'Just now. He doesn't believe me.'

'Then we have to think of a way to make him.'

We. The plural gave her strength. 'Actually, there is a way.' Falteringly, Georgie told her friend about the American in the art gallery. 'It's a gamble,' said Lyndsey when she'd finished.

'I know.' Georgie began to watch a mother playing ball in her toddler on the grass opposite the bench. The child fell and cried. The anguish on the mother's face was painful. Why did life seem difficult at times when actually it wasn't = because

259

there was so much worse to come.

'Would you take it?' she asked suddenly.

'Yes.' Lyndsey's voice rang out clearly. 'Yes. I would. Besides, you need to see Joly again. Reading between the lines, Georgie, he's a ghost that needs to put at rest.'

'Passengers for Flight 7173 must now go to Gate Number Fourteen ...'

She could still leave, Georgie told herself. She could still go back through security and say that something had happened. That she needed to go home for an emergency.

But home wasn't home with Sam any more. It was a decrepit, one-bedroom flat with a job that wasn't anything to do with interior design. Except there was no job now. She just couldn't go on living another lie. Even so, their disappointment at her resignation letter was curiously gratifying. 'You had potential,' her boss had said. 'I was thinking of training you up as a negotiator.'

She'd been touched but explained that she had friends in Thailand who needed to see her. Then the boss had said something about coming back if she ever needed a job.

It might well come to that.

'Gate Number Fourteen,' reminded the tannoy.

'We will contact the police if you do not get on the flight,' the American had said.

It had to be done.

Showing her passport, Georgie experienced a momentary flicker of panic as she had done in the past. Since moving back to the UK, she'd persuaded Sam that they didn't need to holiday abroad – it was nicer to explore Cornwall and Devon. Anywhere where she didn't need to show her paperwork.

Thank goodness technology hadn't been as hot all those years ago as it was now.

The girl at the desk smiled. 'Have a pleasant flight.'

As she went through, Georgie turned round. She couldn't see anyone but there was a distinct feeling of being watched. Sam had retrieved the money from his own account but that didn't explain the other frauds, including the plundering of her friend Jo's account. Was that a coincidence or was someone else after her too?

Taking her seat next to an elderly woman, Georgie tried to calm herself by taking deep breaths. Was it really possible that in sixteen hours' time, she would be seeing Joly again?

'You don't like flying?' Her neighbour's powdery face wrinkled with kindly concern as she misinterpreted the cause of the deep breaths. 'Me neither. I'm visiting my son in Bangkok. He's just been promoted, you know …'

Georgie allowed the woman to natter for the next hour. After that, she feigned sleep. After changing planes at Abu Dhabi, she was placed next to a mother with a sleeping child. Her heart contorted, taking her back to the early days with the children. People had been curious of course, to see her with one white son and a daughter who was darker. Georgie made a point of not offering an explanation unless someone was bold enough to ask.

'My daughter is from my husband's first marriage,' she would say. 'But I see her as my own.'

Marriage? Another lie in a complex tapestry of deceit.

Finally, there was a bump as the plane landed. 'The temperature in Bangkok is 27 degrees,' announced the pilot.

Georgie's body felt the heat as she stepped outside. Not just of the place itself, but of what lay before. 'A taxi will be waiting,' the American had said. 'It's a five-hour drive to the ferry.'

When she'd done this before, it had been a van crammed full of backpackers. This car was a luxury with its air conditioning, she told herself, leaning back into the seat. Outside, the crowds bustled past. There was the palace. There was the floating market where Sapphire and Emerald had sent her to buy food. Were they here still? What were they doing now? And what about the boy, who would be a man now?

The driver grinned at her. 'You are here on holiday?'

She shook her head, swallowing hard. 'No.'

A trickle of sweaty fear ran down her back. 'I'm here for business.'

FORTY ONE

I had a holiday once. It was when I was in the first children's home after that trouble with the foster family.

A whole week in Southend! We ran round for days beforehand, giddy with excitement. When we got to the caravan, we couldn't believe it. There were loads of other kids there too. All from foster families.

Susie was in the one next to us. She was fourteen. I was . twelve.

At night, we'd all sneak out together when the adults were having a smoke or a bonk in their tents.

I don't need to tell you what happened between Susie and me. Or maybe I do.

Let's just say I got sent home early. But every time I drive past Southend, I think of Susie and what she's doing now. There are some people whom you simply can't forget in life.

Sometimes I think that's what made me into the kind of bloke I am now.

Just in case you're wondering about the letter, it was from my nan. Granddad had died. She wanted me to come to the funeral. To show respect and prove I was sorry for everything I'd done.

It was dated six weeks earlier.

FORTY TWO

The ferry. Georgie sat upright in the back of the taxi, suddenly awake after hours of bumping along dark roads. She remembered the ferry!

In those days, she had been one of those backpackers she saw now; scurrying past the lines of waiting cars, eager to get onto the boat and discover the island which beckoned tantalisingly from the other side of the water.

Now she was a middle-aged woman with a Louis Vuitton handbag which hid the fact that she was almost as broke as the backpacker she had once been.

'You hungry?' asked the driver, gesturing to a shop on the harbourside.

She was. But she had to watch her savings, which had taken a bash from living costs in London and she'd been too proud to ask Sam for more when she'd spoken to him.

Joly's letter kept ringing round and round in her head. *'How clever you have been to deceive us by pretending to be someone you weren't'.*

Well, here she was, trying to make amends. Maybe, if she saw Joly, she could persuade him that she hadn't had anything to do with Georgie's death. Then perhaps Sam might take her back.

The taxi jolted as it lurched forward onto the ferry. Don't be daft, she told herself angrily. That still wouldn't take away the fact that she had stolen someone's identity and hidden it from her family. How would she feel if Sam had done that?

'Your friends, they meet you on other side?' asked the driver.

It was one of those ferries where you could stay inside the car as it moved. Georgie began to wish she could get out to avoid conversation.

'I told you,' she said slightly snappily. 'I am not meeting friends. It's a business meeting.'

He grinned again as if he didn't believe her. But that's what it was, Georgie told herself firmly. Joly didn't want to be her friend any more than Sam wanted to be her husband any more.

Then again, what did Joly want? To hand her in to the police? To question her about what happened? To tell her about his own experiences in prison so she'd feel even more guilty?

Georgie was beginning to feel really sick. Then again, it might be the waves which were slapping up over the ferry and hitting the side of the ferry.

'The weather,' said the taxi driver, his eyes narrowing. 'She is behaving very strangely.'

The island was getting closer now. Georgie could see the outline of roofs. Small ones. Large ones. Something that looked like a hotel. From the looks of things, the island had become more developed since she'd been here.

There was another lurch. Another slap of waves. The ferry had stopped and the taxi was moving. 'Where shall I go now?'

Georgie took out the piece of paper she'd folded neatly in her handbag. It had been in the envelope with the flight tickets that had been handed to her by the American.

On it was the name of the hotel.

The driver nodded. 'Very nice place,' he declared approvingly. 'Very nice.'

So Joly wanted her to meet him in a hotel? Georgie felt her mouth going dry. Was that because it was a public place and she couldn't make a scene? Or was it because he had booked a suite and wanted to talk intimately?

Sweat began to pour down her back. Glancing in the passenger mirror, she saw that her eye make-up had begun to run too. What would Joly think of her? What did that matter?

They were climbing up a steep hill now. On either side were clumps of bushes and trees overlooking a river down below. Parts looked familiar. Others didn't. Had her nineteen-year-old self been here before? Or was it her imagination playing tricks the way it did when you were abroad and saw people you thought you knew from home? It was all about creating security, she had read once. Hah! Security. Something she'd been trying to find all her life. But every time she caught the tail end, it slipped out of her grasp. And now was no exception.

Every twenty or minutes or so, they passed through shanty towns with run-down shops selling vegetables and tin-roofed houses. Men sat on the steps, smoking and staring. Women clucked after their children. Someone walked beside an elephant in a field, as it carried something in its mouth. There was a smell of sewage in one hamlet. Swiftly, Georgie put up the window even though the air conditioning wasn't working. The driver smiled as if taking enjoyment in her discomfort.

Suddenly, he took a sharp left. The road in front narrowed but the surface was smoother. There was a sign for a hotel. Private. Georgie's heart quickened just as the taxi pulled up outside a substantial three-storey pagoda-style building in green and red brick. It could be a private house.

'We are here,' he announced.

Georgie sat, rooted to the spot. Why had she done this? Why expose herself to more danger? Joly could be waiting here with the local police. She might be dragged off. She could be …

Then a tall figure emerged from the side of the house. Slightly stooped but tall nevertheless. Dressed in a crisp, white shirt and tailored trousers, gold chain round his tanned neck. Blond. A face which was plumper than she had remembered. Eyes which were crinkled. On any other face, they might have suggested a smile. But not this one.

'Georgie,' said Joly solemnly. 'Thank you for coming.'

It was like arriving at the hotel as a guest. One who was being treated by the host. It was clear that he either owned this place or managed it. After shaking her hand – such formality! – Joly tipped the driver handsomely, judging from the satisfied look on the man's face. Then he called a boy to take her luggage.

'I've put you in the green suite,' he said as if she was already familiar with the place. 'Shall we meet downstairs in, say, half an hour for a drink?'

He consulted his watch as he spoke. A gold one with the kind of discreet numbers that suggested serious money. She nodded, aware that she had hardly spoken since getting here. It was too much to take in. Joly had only been out of prison for ten years or so, from what Vanda had said.

Yet he had not only stayed in the very country that had imprisoned him, but he also appeared, both from his surroundings and appearance, to have done rather well for himself. More worryingly, he was neither angry nor pleased to see her. What was going on?

You should have asked him when you arrived, she told herself crossly, looking into the mirror.

Her worried face stared back. A face that she had seen before, all those years ago. Her old nervous self. The one that had been so glad to be accepted by a cool crowd that she hadn't asked the right questions. Hadn't followed that gut instinct inside her that had said it was wrong to help Joly with those bags of white stuff.

She shivered. Wasn't that how Ellie had felt? Wasn't that why her daughter had resorted to taking drugs? Because she had been different with that beautiful dark skin. And wasn't that why Georgie had stood up for her against Sam, arguing that they needed to understand everything she was going through?

Now she could only hope that Ellie would understand when all this came out. As for Sam, she had a horrible feeling that this was beyond him.

Quickly, she showered and changed into a cool, blue cotton dress that – miraculously – hadn't creased in her bag. Briefly, she glanced in the mirror. She looked better now. At least from the outside. Inside, she was still quaking.

Her eye fell on her mobile. Should she text Sam to say where she was? No. He didn't want her any more. It was no more or less than she deserved. Instead, she texted Lyndsey.

Here safely. Meeting Joly for drink. Not sure what to expect.

It felt good knowing that someone somewhere knew what was happening.

More than I do, she murmured to herself, making her way down the wooden stairs and the shiny handrail, which someone clearly polished regularly.

Joly was waiting in a comfortable, square room that might have passed as a drawing room in Sussex. It had two sofas facing each other in sage-green silk. The drapes at the window were quintessentially English too. Yet there was also a definite far-eastern touch in the carved sideboard stacked with drinks and wooden statuettes. There were huge shells too, she noticed with a pang, on another table. None were as lovely as the little shell which Georgina had given her. Once more, she felt a lurch of loss.

'What can I get you?' He gestured to the bottles.

'Just something soft, please,' she said awkwardly. 'I don't drink any more.'

He laughed and for a moment she saw a flash of the old Joly. The one who had charmed her. The one who had charmed everyone. 'Me neither.' Then his eyes grew steely. 'What made you give up?'

'Us.' The word flew out of her mouth before she could take it back. 'If we hadn't drunk too much that night it might not have happened.'

His eyes grew even steelier. Instantly she realised she'd said too much. Assumed too much familiarity before it was time.

'Is that what you think? That we made out because we'd had too much to drink?'

Made out? Was that how he saw it? For her, it had been love …

She nodded. 'Why else would you have wanted me when

269

you had Georgina?'

He turned away, facing the windows. Beyond was a dry patch of grass and beyond that, the sea sparkled. 'You never did have any confidence, did you, Georgie? Was that why you killed her?'

'I didn't.' Any pretence at dancing round the subject was gone. Desperately, Georgie grabbed Joly's arm. The touch of his skin against hers was electrifying. Both sprang apart, horrified at what she had done. 'I didn't murder her,' she said tightly. 'It was some boy. I tried to explain at the time. He attempted to kill me too.'

'You had blood on your hands.' He spat out the sentence as if it was venom.

'I was trying to stop Georgina's wound. And some of that blood was his – the boy's. I cut him. With the knife. It's him you should have chased.'

He narrowed his eyes. 'Describe him.'

This was her only chance. She had to seize it. For all she knew, the police were on their way now. 'He was small. Dark. Like all the others. And he had a limp. Yes, that's right. When I – when I cut him, I got his face. And then he ran off into the forest ...'

Those lips which had once pressed itself against hers, curled with disbelief and scorn. 'He had a limp? Then how could he have got away? The police combed the woods. After they arrested us, that is.'

His face was almost black with fury now. ' Do you know, they tried to pin her death on me? Then they found the drugs. Hard evidence. Something that was guaranteed to put us all in prison – including you, except you had run away.'

He grabbed both her hands and pulled her down onto the sofa next to him; forcing her to look at him. His eyes were wild. His face flushed with anger. 'Do you have any idea what it was like in there? We were starving most of the time. Desperate for water. They kept us in isolation so we couldn't talk to each other. Vanda was ... Vanda was abused ...'

His voice trailed away so she had to strain to catch his words. 'We could hear her through the walls.'

Now his eyes were ablaze with fury and wet with pain at the same time. 'It was hell. Pure hell.'

This was worse than she'd imagined. Georgie put her head in hands. 'I'm so sorry.'

'I don't blame you for running away.' This last part was so unexpected that she lifted her head to look at him. 'But I do blame you for killing Georgina. My beautiful Georgina. I know you must have been jealous of her but your own sister ...'

'What?'

Georgie felt as if she'd been dealt a blow to the head. Then she shook herself. He must mean 'sister' in the general sense.

'That's right.' His words were crisp and clear. 'Your own sister.'

Joly stood up and walked towards the mahogany desk by the window. Opening a drawer, he removed a small wooden box and handed it to her. 'I found this amongst her possessions when they let me out. I knew about the adoption, of course. She'd told me years ago.'

'What adoption?'

The thought flitted through her mind that Joly and Georgina might have had a child together. It wasn't beyond the realms of possibility, yet she found herself hoping that wasn't so. Quite why, she wasn't sure.

Joly's eyes were steely. 'Open the box. Then you'll understand.'

There was a birth certificate. A mother's name. Angela Smith. Her mother? That was surely impossible. Underneath the title of father was an empty space. Then there was an adoption certificate.

'I don't understand,' she wavered.

'Read the letter,' commanded Joly. His voice scared her.

My darling Georgina,

One day when you read this, I hope that we might have been reunited. But if not, I need you to understand why I had to give you away. I wasn't married to your father. In those days that was a sin, especially in the Catholic faith. There was a middle-aged couple at church. They were rich. They could give you everything you need. But they only wanted one of you. I had to choose. My parents made me.

I didn't know which one to give them. Forgive me. You were both so alike yet you had more of a knowing air about you, even at such a young age. I felt you might survive adoption better than your twin who was smaller; sicklier; and yet the mirror image of you in almost every feature.

I made one stipulation. You were to be called Georgina after my grandmother: the only person who said I should be allowed to keep you. I insisted you were to retain your surname – that of your father. Smith. I also called your sister Georgina. It was the only way I could keep you girls together.

I know that I will never get over the guilt. I am aware, already, that I can never love your sister as much as I should. Forgive me, Georgina. You will always be with me.

Georgie felt her body shake as if it wasn't her own. 'My mother had twins? She gave one away? That's impossible. It's too much of a coincidence. Besides, my father died when I was young. This suggests she wasn't married at all …'

Joly shrugged. 'It was a common excuse for unmarried women at the time. As for the coincidence, that's what I thought when I first read it. But they happen in life.'

Joly turned away but not before she saw the pain etched on his face. 'She'd spent her life searching for her other half, as she called it. That's why she attached herself to you at the airport. "Joly," she said to me. "I think I've found her. She's so like me that she *has* to be!" She wanted to ask you outright instead of probing into your background with the odd question about your mother. But I told her not to. I told her to wait. I was worried you might pretend you were her sister just to get your hands on

272

her inheritance.'

There's something I need to ask you.

Wasn't that what Georgina had said, on the evening she'd been feverish? Dear God. The shell. It wasn't just a sign of friendship. It was a gift between sisters. But neither of them had known it.

Georgina had suspected it, though. She could see that now. All those odd remarks about secrets. Maybe she thought Georgie knew about her missing twin and was trying to coax the truth out of her.

Then there were the questions about her mother and where she'd grown up. Whether she had brothers or sisters. Questions which seemed innocuous on the surface but which clearly had a hidden agenda.

I also called your sister Georgina. It was the only way I could keep you girls together.

How tragic. How utterly tragic …

'You were alike yet different,' continued Joly. His knuckles were clenched, she noticed. 'That's what different upbringings do to you.'

It was true. Horribly true. If none of this had happened, they would each have gone their own ways and been none the wiser. Georgie wanted to howl. She'd always wanted a sister. Or a brother. Anyone to share her mother's wrath with. To think she'd had a twin. To think she'd laughed with that twin. Enjoyed her company. Admired her. Revered her, almost. Wished that she could have had the confidence that made the real Georgina so special.

Then his face hardened again. 'And you were jealous of her. That's another sisterly trait, isn't it?'

That was true, too. Much as she hated to admit it, she had been jealous of Georgina. It was so unfair, she'd often thought, that one person could have so much and the other so little. How weird that the slightest difference in appearance – the kink in her nose, the small gap in her teeth – could make the difference between beautiful and merely pretty.

273

'She had the better deal,' Georgie now spluttered. 'She had parents who loved her.'

Joly snorted. 'Hippy cocaine-heads who should never have been allowed to adopt in the first place.'

'But did they love her?'

'Sure.'

'My mother disliked me.'

'Yet now you can see why. The letter told you. She felt guilty.' Joly's tone was slightly softer. Then his face tightened. 'But that still doesn't excuse murder.'

Georgie heard her voice come out in a shout. 'I DIDN'T KILL HER! When will you believe that?'

Flinging herself down on the floor, she began to pound the carpet like a child. 'And now I've lost her. I've lost my sister. Not just once, with her death. But twice because of what you've just told me. And if this is true, I've lost my father too. Mum always said he'd died before I was born but this – this makes me feel I don't know who I am any more.'

His face faltered. She could see the uncertainty in his face. 'I did tell them you were innocent,' he murmured. 'But they wouldn't believe me.

'Who? Vanda and Jonathan?'

His face confirmed her suspicions. 'They always disliked me,' she said, the tears still wet on her face. 'Jonathan had made a pass at me. He was cross because I turned him down. And Vanda wanted you. Don't you see? Now they've ruined my life. They blackmailed me into telling my husband everything about my past. Now he wants nothing more to do with me. Any minute now the police will come and ...'

Joly stiffened. 'What do you mean?'

'Well, isn't that what you're going to do? Get me arrested? Vanda said I had to pay. I presume the police are still looking for me. I had blood on my hands, remember? I was trying to stem Georgie's blood but no one will believe that.'

She sank onto the sofa, tears gushing out. 'Now they'll put me in prison, just as they did to you ... I'll never see my children again ...'

'Shhh, shhh.'

Joly's arms were around her. Stroking her back comfortingly. His voice was assuring like a parent. 'I'm not going to call the police. As far as they're concerned, it's a closed case.'

'Why?'

He moved away and she felt a pang of loss. 'Because I did a deal with them.' He gesticulated to the furnishings in the room. 'How else do you think I've managed to buy a hotel? Why else do you think I have stayed here? Everyone's crooked in this place. I promised to keep my ear to the ground; help the police if they wanted to know something about the locals or visitors. In return, they grease my palms provided I grease theirs.' He shrugged. 'It suits me.'

It didn't seem right and yet ...

At that moment, a beautiful young girl with olive skin passed by the window. She exchanged looks with Joly. Instantly, Georgie suspected there was something between them.

'So why did you want me to come here if you didn't want me arrested?' whispered Georgie.

'Because I wanted to see if you were guilty. Wanted to see it in your face when I showed you Georgina's things.'

It was beginning to make sense now. 'You thought that if I'd realised I'd killed my own sister, I might confess to it.'

'Something like that.' He put his hands in his pockets awkwardly. 'Or maybe show me in your face that you were lying.'

'So I've passed the test?' Her words came out mockingly.

'Yes. Not like before.'

Her skin prickled. 'What do you mean?'

Joly's eyes shifted. He wasn't looking her straight in the face. 'I wanted to test you, back then. See how loyal you were to Georgina.'

Suddenly she realised. 'That's why you kissed me. Because

a good friend – or sister – would have rebuffed you.'

Silently, he nodded.

'So I failed. You're not telling me anything new.'

'Actually, we both failed.'

Georgie was so wrapped up in self-loathing that she almost didn't catch the implication of what he'd just said. Had she got that right? 'You failed,' she repeated, 'because …'

'Because I wanted you.' His eyes met hers this time. They were wet. 'It wasn't an act. That's why I got so angry with you. It's me I hate. It's me who caused Georgina's death. Not you.'

It was true. Why deny it? Georgie watched as Joly shook his head as though nothing made sense any more and then strode over to the sideboard with bottles. For a moment, he stood looking at the bottle of whisky and then seemed to think better of it. Instinctively she knew why there was drink there. It wasn't just to offer to guests. It was to test himself. To make sure he was strong enough to resist.

Her *sister!* None of this seemed real.

'But why now,' she said urgently. 'Why bring me out now to see you?'

'We tried to find you after we were released,' he said slowly. 'We all did. But we couldn't find you. In the end, it was pure coincidence. When your husband started to do some business with Jonathan, he told him about working in Bangkok. He mentioned that his wife had been there too. At first it seemed like one of those many ex-pat crossovers but as they got to know each other better, Jonathan began to realise that you might be Georgie. We suspected you'd taken her passport because yours was still there and hers was gone.'

It was almost too much to absorb. But he was missing something. Something vital. 'Vanda and Jonathan broke the law too,' she broke in. 'They took our money. It's an imprisonable offence.'

Joly shrugged. 'That's their problem. But knowing Jonathan, he'll have covered his tracks. He'll have had others doing the dirty work for him. Credit card fraud is a Godsend for some.'

'That's awful!'

His face tightened again. 'Who are you to talk? You committed identity theft.'

It was true. Yet if her sister had been here, Georgie felt pretty certain she would have given her approval. She was about to say so to Joly when he cut in. 'Look, I'm sorry it's caused trouble with your husband. But now you can go back and say it's all been sorted.'

'No.' She shook her head. 'He has a thing about drugs. Rightly too. He won't forgive me for being mixed up in them.'

'But we were kids.'

'It doesn't matter in his book.'

Joly shrugged. 'Hasn't he ever done anything wrong in his life?'

She thought of Ellie. Could her beautiful stepdaughter be seen as 'anything wrong'?

'Not like that.'

'Then that's his loss.' Joly looked thoughtful for a moment. 'Presumably you're in no hurry to rush back then.'

'Not really.'

He nodded. 'Then make yourself at home here for a few weeks until you decide what to do next.'

A few weeks? Her ticket was open-ended but she'd promised Sam she'd be back in a fortnight.

'You're going to accept I'm innocent of Georgie's death just like that?

He nodded. 'I like to think I'm a good judge of character. Besides, what Vanda doesn't know is that I wanted you back for another reason.'

Her heart quickened. 'What?'

He gestured to the box. 'That. I felt you deserved to know the truth. You didn't get on with your mother. I always remember you telling me that. Maybe, when you do go back, you should make up with her.'

FORTY THREE

I've got a brother I've never seen. Two sisters too. My dad had them before me. After he left us, he had three more kids.

I don't know where any of them are.

Sometimes I wonder. Suppose I slept with my sister without knowing we was related?

What you don't know doesn't hurt you.

I try to tell myself that when I think of my own kids. One boy and one girl. That's what I've got. Five and six, they are.

When my solicitor said I wanted to get in touch, he got another letter back from my baby's mother's solicitor. Now I'm not allowed to contact them. Not till they're eighteen.

How's a kid meant to grow up without a dad?

It isn't right.

Maybe that's another reason why I do what I do.

One day, I'll earn enough money to make them all happy. I'll buy them toys and stuff. Then they'll love me.

FORTY FOUR

The heat. The colours. Rich pink silks. The stunning greenness of the grass. The sea. Warm, even in the morning. Her room with its subdued lighting – electricity seemed less bright here and more tranquil as a result. The food (wonderful exotic fruit which she couldn't name). And of course Joly himself.

All these ingredients rolled into one like Chef's mouth-watering concoctions, conspired to make Georgie feel as though this was the real world now. And that everything she'd left behind was a haze that didn't matter any more. Even Georgina – her sister! – didn't seem real. Her memories were so hazy of that short time they'd spent together that it was as if she hadn't existed.

How could coincidences like this happen? Or was it simply one that had bided its time? As Joly had said during one of their many long evening talks about Georgina, children were adopted all the time. Sooner or later they would bump into brothers or sisters, usually without knowing of the connection.

'I don't know who I am any more,' she told Joly on the veranda where they had fallen into the habit of spending some time together before dinner. 'I'd got used to being Georgina. But now I'm not sure.'

His hand gently replaced a stray golden strand of hair which had fallen over her face. 'You'll always be the same young, shy girl to me, who simply didn't realise how lovely she really was.'

Then she'd moved away, flushed by the gesture, confused as

to whether it suggested an intimacy or a concern based entirely on friendship rather than anything more.

At night, her dreams brought everyone to her. Her mother bolting the door so she couldn't get in the house. Ellie and Nick as small children at one of the many international schools they'd attended. Sam and Georgina chasing her, hand in hand, even though they'd never met. At times, her husband's face was clearer. At other times, her sister's. Sometimes it was Georgina calling for her. Telling her that she loved her. At other times it was Sam. Begging her to come back. But when she woke in the morning, there was nothing. No text. No message at the hotel even though she had told him where she was going.

Oddly, the hotel was very empty. Every now and then, a guest would arrive to stay for a night – usually a man or, occasionally a couple – and then be gone in the morning.

'We're not a family concern,' Joly explained. 'More of a stopping place. Many of my guests are businessmen with concerns in the islands.'

Of the tall, dark-skinned girl, whom she'd spotted soon after she arrived, Georgie saw nothing.

The days went by. Before she knew it, Georgie had been there a week. Soon, the children would be back from their various trips. They would want to know where she was. Sooner or later, she was going to have to tell them – if Sam hadn't done so already. Maybe, Georgie told herself as she went for what was becoming her usual morning walk across the white sand, he had done so already.

Perhaps their silence indicated not just disapproval but a cutting off. Like Sam. They would be shocked. Horrified. Disapproving. Dismayed. Their own mother had been living another life. A lie. She'd helped deal in drugs – even if she hadn't known for certain what was inside those parcels. She'd been accused of murder even though this hadn't been proved. Was it any wonder that there had been no communication from them? Or was it because emails were hit and miss due to the poor Wi-Fi connection?

'There's no rush to leave,' Joly told her as if reading her mind. He had been good at that all those years ago, she remembered. It struck her that this man might understand her better than her own husband. 'Although I do wonder why you don't want to visit your mother before it's too late.'

Too late?

'She's getting old. People don't last for ever.' There was a tinge of bitterness in his voice. 'My father died last year, just after he had finally agreed to forgive me.'

They were having breakfast on the terrace – another habit which they had fallen into so easily that it was like putting on an old glove again. Yet at the same time, it was very different from the shared breakfasts on the beach all those years ago when they'd make do with a banana or a bit of stale bread.

'Did your family visit you in prison?' Georgie asked, still unsure how far she should probe about that time.

Joly nodded. 'How else do you think we managed to get out in ten years? It would have been thirty if the old man and his lawyers hadn't persuaded the police to do a deal.' He looked out over the grounds to the sea and for a moment, Georgie could see a much younger Joly. One who still had the world at his fingertips without a care in the world.

Then his expression darkened. 'Didn't mean he forgave me, though. Probably would have let me rot here if my mother hadn't made him help.'

Georgie took a sip of the fresh orange juice that was constantly topped up by one of the maids. 'Motherhood makes you forgive things you would never do in another life.'

He looked sharply at her. 'You have a son, I heard. That must be wonderful.'

She was surprised by the envy in his voice. Joly did not seem to be the kind of man who would welcome such responsibility.

Yes, it is. I have a daughter too.' Another sip. 'Ellie isn't strictly speaking mine. She's Sam's, from a previous relationship.'

283

There was a short, sharp silence. 'He had a thing with a girl in a Bangkok bar before we were married and had a daughter whom he didn't know about. Her mother traced him a little while later and said she didn't want to look after her any more. So of course, she came to live with us.'

A keen look of interest flitted across Sam's face. 'So you have forgiven him. Yet he cannot forgive you.'

Instantly, Georgie felt protective of her husband. 'The two are very different. He thinks I was a professional drug dealer. A murderer too.'

To her surprise, a hand stretched out across the table, briefly clasping hers. The bolt of electricity was as great as the one which had flashed between them when she'd caught at his arm on the first day to gain his attention.

Yet this time, Joly's hand stayed firmly in place. 'But I don't think you're a murderer any more. And I've told Vanda and Jonathan that.'

'They believe you?'

He shook his head. 'No.'

'So why do you?'

The hand moved away. Once more, Georgie felt a mixture of disappointment and relief. 'I told you. I wasn't sure at the time. It wasn't you. And now you're here, I'm even more certain.'

Standing up, she moved to the edge of the veranda to give herself breathing space. 'How do you know who I am, Joly? I told you, I'm not even sure myself.'

There was a presence behind her. One that melted her just as it had done all those years ago. 'Because I knew you at the beginning of your grown-up life. I saw the young girl. The one who desperately wanted to be like the rest of us. The one who was running away from a background which didn't belong to her. A kind girl. Who didn't yell at Jonathan and tell him to get off when he made a pass. Or scratched Vanda's eyes out when she was catty. A girl who was a friend to Georgina ...'

She turned round. His eyes were wet. 'I still miss her ...'

Georgie felt a rush of envy and compassion. 'Me too. She

284

was my sister yet …'

'You hardly knew her.' Joly's face was red. 'We met when we were thirteen, for God's sake. She was my first. I was hers. She was different from anyone I'd ever met. Different from everyone except …'

His voice fell away. At the same time his arms encircled her. 'Except you.'

Suddenly, before Georgie was even aware this was happening, his mouth came down on hers. Hard. Meaningful. Rough, yet at the same time with a smoothness about it that made her yield. Melt. Succumb to this energy that was so hot that her body felt it was burning into his.

She couldn't have stopped even if she had wanted to.

'I'm sorry.'

Joly stepped back, wiping his mouth as if erasing what had just happened. 'I didn't mean to …'

This was awful.

'It's just that you look so much like her. It's as though she's still here after all this time.

Georgie gripped the rail of the balcony for strength. 'She was my sister,' she repeated. 'Yet I didn't know her. All I do know is that during the brief time I knew her, she was kind to me. Yes, I was jealous of her because … because I wanted what she had. And then I hurt her because you and I both allowed ourselves to do … to do what we've just done now.'

'Don't,' implored Joly. 'It hurts too much.'

'But I had to,' continued Georgie ignoring him, 'make a life for myself afterwards. I had to survive. And I did. I built another life. I got married. I had children. Made a career.' Her hands tightened on the balcony. 'Until one day, you and your friends decided to pull all that down.'

She whipped round, feeling an anger she hadn't done before. 'And now look where I am! Stuck in some fantasy land. Far away from my husband and family who now think the worst of me. Did you know that this all started with one of my credit cards being stolen? '

Joly shook his head.

Did she believe him? It was so difficult to know. 'Then one of my client's accounts was hacked. Vanda's very clever, isn't she?'

Joly shook his head. 'I wasn't aware of that. I just know that she and Jonathan said they had found a way to get you out here.'

Georgie laughed. 'They did that all right. But you know what? I'm going to go back and face the music. If they can't forgive me, fine. I'll start again. I've done it before.'

A look of admiration crossed Joly's face. 'You're more like your sister than you realise, you know.' Then he caught her hands. 'Please don't go. Stay. Stay with me.'

He's mad, she suddenly realised. He wants me here because I look like her; the sister I never knew. The girl who was kind to me. Was that why she'd shown such friendship? Had the real Georgina felt deep down that they were connected?

'I'm sorry,' she said simply. 'But I can't stay. None of this is real.'

As she spoke, a stout black woman bustled in to refill the orange juice. Something about her made Georgie stop. The half-smile on her lips didn't match the hostility in her eyes. 'You want me to organise taxi,' she said to Joly. Clearly she had heard the conversation.

'No.' Joly was pleading with her again.

Silently, she waited until the woman had left.

'I need to find out the times of the flights first,' said Georgie quietly. 'I've fulfilled my part of the bargain. Told my husband all about my old life. And I've come here as you asked. Now it is time to wrap up the past and go.'

Suddenly that kiss seemed like a huge mistake. Another big error on her part. It was Sam she loved. Not this man whom she'd idolised over the years. Now she'd said those words, it was clear this was what she had to do. Go home. To be with her real family. Even if they didn't want her any more

'Mum, where are you?'

'Mum – Dad says you're away. Where? He won't tell me. What's going on?'

'Georgie – are you all right? I'm home now. Until the next treatment. But I'm worried about you.'

The stream of texts and emails from Ellie, Nick, Lyndsey, and even Jo poured into her inbox as Georgie sat in the back of the taxi on the way to the airport. Clearly the reception here was better than it had been at the hotel.

Nothing from Sam. The stark absence of any message physically hurt her chest.

Was it really only an hour ago that Joly had kissed her goodbye formally on both cheeks? 'Come back if it doesn't work out,' he'd murmured.

Through one of the upstairs windows, Georgie had glimpsed the tall, dusky young girl she'd seen some days earlier. No need to fear for Joly. He would find comfort elsewhere. He was that kind of man.

'On way home,' she texted back to Ellie. *'Need to talk.'*

They'd have a family meeting, even if Sam didn't want it. Without him, if necessary. And she would see her mother. There was a lot of explaining to do. Georgina ... Georgina ... not her. The real one. The sister who'd been taken from her and then, through life's cruel fingers, been shown to her briefly before being taken away.

And yet, despite this, Georgie was aware of a great burden being lifted from her shoulders. At last, after all these years, she didn't have anything to hide. 'I don't know who I am any more,' she had told Joly. But her husband knew. He was aware now, thanks to her confession, that she was plain Georgie née Smith.

Yet what would the children say? And supposing Vanda and Jonathan, still convinced of her guilt, called the police? Even now, they might be waiting for her at the airport, ready to quiz her about Georgina's death. She might not be allowed out of Thailand. She might be flung into the same kind of hellhole

287

prison as the others had been.

For a moment, Georgie almost asked the driver to stop so she could be sick with nerves. But he seemed distracted. There was some kind of hold up. Another stream of cattle, perhaps, crossing the road in yet another shanty town, like the others they'd passed through. Georgie looked out through the window, momentarily distracted from her thoughts. It was market day. There were cages of birds – ugh – and platters of brightly coloured vegetables. But in the middle some kind of argument was going on. A policeman was holding the arm of a tall, thin man with partially-shaved black hair. The man was trying to push him away. Another policeman came to hold him.

The driver shook his head. 'That is Joshua. Bad man.'

Georgie shivered.

'He is son of housekeeper,' added the driver. 'Master Joly kind to him.'

The fight was getting worse now. A third policeman had arrived.

The driver shook his head. 'This not good. Must call Master Joly before they take him away again.'

Taking out his mobile, he proceeded to talk rapidly. As he did so, the police dragged the man in front of the taxi. Georgie froze. The man was limping. That in itself was not unusual. In a country where medical treatment was scant, many had limbs that were missing or didn't work. But it was his face that caught Georgie's attention. The scar. The jagged white scar along the side of his face.

Stop, she had yelled all those years ago. Stop.

Picking up the knife, she had lunged at him, anger coursing through her veins. This man had killed Georgina. Her friend.

The man had screamed as the knife had sunk into his flesh. Repulsed, she had dropped the weapon, appalled at what she had done, shocked it had been so easy to mark a man like this.

The horror had haunted her. So badly that until now, she hadn't allowed herself to think about it. Had pushed it to the bottom of her mind. No, she hadn't murdered Georgina. But she could so easily have murdered her sister's attacker ...

Could it be ... was it possible that Joshua, staring at her now through the taxi window, was that man ...?

'You know him, miss?' asked the driver sharply. 'Because he sure seems to know you.'

FORTY FIVE

My father got picked out once in an identity parade. When I was a kid, I used to like that word. Parade. It suggested a fair like the one in town once a year. Made me all excited.

I remember jumping up and down and asking if there would be candyfloss and if I could go too.

Got a sharp slap across my face for that, I did.

I can see why now.

Still, at least with identity parades there was a chance you'd get off. Now there's nothing you can do about it unless you change your fingerprints.

We used to say that as a joke but there was a bloke in Wandsworth who managed to do that. Or so it was rumoured. Cost him a lot of money. But it worked.

Rumour has it that he's living the good life now. In Australia. Or somewhere like that.

I'd like to go abroad one day.

All I need is to nick enough money.

FORTY SIX

'Turn round,' Georgie instructed the driver. 'I need to go back.'

The man frowned in the cracked mirror. 'You don't want to go to airport now?'

Yes. Of course she did. But she also needed to tell Joly what she had just seen. The man who limped. The scar down his cheek. Then again, there were probably lots of men like that around here.

Besides, she'd miss the plane if they didn't carry on. The three policemen were pushing the man into a car now. For a minute he seemed to catch her eye and scowl. Another trick of her imagination?

'You're right.' She sank back into her seat, hot and sticky in the heat. The air-conditioning didn't seem to be working in this car either. 'Just carry on.'

He made a sound that suggested she was not the easiest of passengers. At the same time, her phone bleeped again. Another message from Ellie.

Mum, ring. Please.

She couldn't. Not until she'd got back to the UK. Some things were better done, face to face. And this was one of them.

When Georgie had arrived at the airport nearly two weeks ago, she'd been terrified of being recognised. Now, as she checked in, that fear returned to her. True, her passport had been under Sam's surname for years. Her face had changed beyond all recognition. But technology was so different now. Supposing she was recognised as the teenager who had fled all those years ago?

She breathed a sigh of relief when the girl at the desk – so beautiful with her immaculate make-up and dark skin – handed her back her passport with a smile along with her boarding ticket and told her to proceed to Security.

Meanwhile, Joly still hadn't replied to the numerous messages she'd left. 'Please call,' she'd said. 'I need to tell you something.'

Suddenly she became aware of a hand on her arm. Georgie whipped round. Her heart literally filled her mouth as she took in two military men with guns at their holsters. 'Mrs Hamilton?'

She nodded, unable to speak. Had something had happened to the children? Or Sam. Or Joly …

'Come with us.'

To her horror, Georgie found her right arm being taken by one man and her left by the other. In front of a wide-eyed group of family tourists ('What's happening to that lady, Mum?'), she was marched across the shiny-floored departures lounge and into a small, officious-looking room off the side.

'I don't understand,' she spluttered after they'd motioned that she should sit down.

On the other side of the desk was another man. Also in full uniform.

'I think you do.'

He pushed across a faded yellowing newspaper. On the front page, a girl stared out of it. A young girl.

'You have been here once before, have you not, Georgie Smith?' He spoke good English, with a curl of a smile at his lips. 'How foolish of you to return.'

For a moment she could hardly breathe. Her throat had swollen with such fear that it was difficult to get the words out. 'No. No. You've got it wrong.'

He shook his head. 'I do not think so. We have been looking for you for a long time.' Then his face darkened. 'Murder is punishable by death in this country, you know.'

Cold beads of sweat broke out down her back. Her arms. Her face. 'I need to ring someone,' she said, struggling to find her voice. 'That's my right.'

Even as she spoke, Georgie was unsure if this was the case in this weird, unknown land. But the man opposite had a resigned look on his face, as if he'd been caught out. He gestured at the large phone on his desk. 'Use this.' Then he shook his head at the mobile in her hand. 'Not that. You will give your phone to me please. And your passport.'

Pick up, she prayed. Please pick up.

'Hello. This is Joly ...'

Frantically, she turned to the policeman again. 'It's not answering. Please. There's another number I can try for this person.'

To her surprise, he smiled. 'If you wish. I do not think it will help.'

He spoke as if he knew something she didn't.

Somewhere, she had the number for the hotel. Yes. Here. On the pad of paper.

'Hotel Kho Chang Kho. May I help you?'

Yes!

'Please. I need to speak to Joly urgently.'

He isn't here, she expected the girl on the desk to say. He's in a meeting. He is not available. Then she realised. What if Joly himself had set her up. Of course. How stupid of her! He didn't believe her at all about Georgie. He, Vanda, and Jonathan were behind all this. She was being arrested for a crime she hadn't committed ...

'Hello?'

Joly's voice, so normal, so assured, made her want to weep.

'They've arrested me.' She could barely speak. 'I suppose this is your doing. I thought you believed me, Joly. I thought ...'

'Wait.' He interrupted her. 'What happened exactly?'

Now the words poured out of her mouth in terror. The market. The man with the limp. The scar down his cheek.

'That was me,' she said weeping. 'I tried to stab him when I was still trying to save her. Remember I told you?'

Horribly aware that all this was being written down by the policeman opposite, she continued. 'The driver said it was your housekeeper's son.'

'Joshua.'

It was a statement rather than a question.

'But now they've got me here and I'll never get home. I ...'

'Your time is up.' The policeman brought his hand down on the phone, cutting off the call. At the same time, she found herself being hauled to her feet.

'Where are you taking me?'

'To a cell until your case is brought to trial.'

'But I need to speak to a solicitor first.'

There was a tight polite smile. 'You have had your phone call. That is enough.'

Georgie had seen a film on television once about a teenager who'd been 'slammed up', as they called it, in some third-world country where no one was allowed a lawyer or fair trial.

He'd been forced to share a cell with several other men, many of whom hit or abused him. She'd been unable to finish watching it but Sam had been riveted. 'It's important to know what goes on in these places,' he'd said.

Now, as Georgie was escorted through the airport – all those stares again! – and into a waiting car, she had a horrible vision of what lay in front of her. By the time the car had stopped – after zigzagging through the city past the floating market and all the other spots which she had once known in a different life – Georgie found to her embarrassment there was a damp patch on the seat below her. She had wet herself with fear.

The men's face showed disgust as they pulled her out. It wasn't necessary. She was disgusted enough at herself. Furious too. How naïve she had been to have come back. If Joly wasn't responsible for this, Vanda and Jonathan certainly were. Someone had tipped off the police ...

'In here.'

She was being marched into a building with red-tiled floors. Past a desk manned by more officious men. Down a corridor. A door was being opened. Georgie braced herself. What kind of hell hole were they going to throw her in?

It was one room. No one else there. Just a mattress on the floor and a small window. She breathed a sigh of relief.

'You stay there.'

And with that, the door was slammed shut. She was alone.

Without her phone or access to an outside line, there was no way of telling the children where she was, let alone Sam. They'd think the worst when her plane arrived without her on it.

Then again, would anyone be there to meet it? She'd told Sam the arrival details but would he have passed those to Ellie or Nick? How stupid to even imagine that her husband had forgiven her enough to be there himself.

In comparison, the stolen credit cards at the beginning of this nightmare had faded into insignificance.

Georgie's stomach gurgled. She must be hungry but she didn't actually feel it. There had been a bowl which had been pushed through the door a few hours ago. A disgusting mix of something which made her want to vomit. The water had been welcome, though. Now, as the early morning light streamed in through the window, she used the last bit in the bottle to wash herself. Thankfully they'd allowed her to keep her spare travelling underwear in her bag. Yet her accident seemed nothing compared with what lay before her.

Was this what Vanda and Jonathan and Joly had felt when they'd been thrown into prison? She could imagine Vanda's voice in her head. *'It was far worse.'*

She could almost hear Vanda's voice ringing in her head.

In some ways, she didn't blame them. They wanted her to go through what they had.

Vanda was abused, Joly had said. Abused …

Georgie wanted to retch. At first she'd been relieved she was in a room on her own. Now the silence was making her feel mad. The heat was becoming unbearable. The flies were everywhere. What would happen next?

If Joly had really been on her side, he'd be here by now. If ... if ... The thoughts rambled round and round her head until she could bear them no more. Slumping down in a corner of the cell, she drifted off into an uneasy dream. Georgie was holding her hand. Telling her it would be all right. but Ellie was screaming. 'Mum! Mum! Mum!'

'Wake.'

Georgie woke to find herself being shaken roughly by a man in uniform. He wasn't the same policeman as yesterday. He was younger. Harder in the face. Leaner.

'This way.'

Once more, she found herself being frogmarched down a corridor. 'I need to see a lawyer. It is my right.'

The man shot her a nasty sideways look. 'You are not in England now.'

Another door opening. Another desk.

On one side, the same policeman as yesterday. On the other, two men. One dark. One blonde. She didn't know the first. But the second ...

'Joly!'

The warning look in his eyes prevented her from falling into his arms with relief.

'Are you all right?' he stood up, taking care, she noticed, to keep a distance between them.

'Yes.' She tried to recover herself. 'I mean, no. I didn't do it, Joly. I thought you believed me. And the man in the market ...'

Joly held up another hand. 'Don't say any more. It might not help.' He gesticulated to a man on his right. 'This is my solicitor. He is going to sort it out.'

The tall, lean, blond man stood up and shook her hand. 'Mrs Hamilton.' He spoke with an Australian accent. 'Nice to meet you.'

He cast a look at the policeman on the other side of the desk. A sharp look. One that meant business. 'As agreed, I should like some time alone with my client.'

It was the housekeeper who had tipped off the police, apparently. She had seen Georgie and guessed who she was. She'd found out about Georgina years ago, and been terrified that Georgie was going to recognise her son. So she'd packed him off to another shanty town where – as Georgie had seen – he'd got into trouble again.

Now Joshua was being held.

'Naturally, he's denying it,' said the Australian who'd instructed her to call him Mac. 'It's his word against yours. Joly has a great deal of influence in these parts. He has managed to get you off the drugs charges by insisting that you didn't know what was inside those parcels. But ...'

His shrug said it all. Georgie's hopes, which had shot up wildly, now plummeted to the ground.

'If the murder ...'

Georgie flinched as he said the word...

'If the murder had been recent, we could use DNA evidence. But we have nothing left that belonged to the victim. Nothing that could link the two ...'

Georgie felt a shoot of electricity. The box. The box which the police had taken away from her when they'd arrested her. The box with her mother's letter and some small belongings from her sister.

'It might help,' said Mac doubtfully. 'But we actually need something that Georgina was wearing when she died.'

'Then that's no good.' Her head fell back into her hands.

'Actually,' said Joly from the corner. 'I've just had an idea.'

He'd been so quiet that she'd almost forgotten he was there. 'I couldn't bear to let Georgie go completely.'

His eyes were wet.

Hating herself, she felt that old jealousy.

'I pulled some hair from her after... after we found her.' His hand went up to the gold chain around his neck. Taking it off, he opened the small box-shaped locket and withdrew a tiny clear packet. Inside were some strands of hair. Very blonde. 'Don't ask me how but I managed to keep them safe, even in prison.'

Tears were streaming down his face now. 'I used to smell it. It still had her fragrance for a time.'

'May I have it?' asked Mac gently.

Georgie couldn't stop crying now. Her sister's hair. Exactly the same colour as her own. A reminder of what she had lost, without even knowing at the time, that she had it.

It was a thin hope. But the only one they had. There was a possibility, a very remote one, that the labs could do something. Not the police labs. Mac didn't trust those. But he and Joly had connections …

Another night in the room on her own. But this time – did she imagine it? – she was treated with more respect.

At lunch time she was taken down a corridor into yet another room. Joly was waiting. His face was drawn. He cares, she realised. He really cares. Not just for Georgie but for me too. That was more than Sam.

'Good news. Joshua has been told that his DNA matches some skin cells on the hair.'

He said the word *'hair'* as if he wanted to distance himself from it.

'It does?'

'No. We just told him that.'

'But that's a lie.'

Joly sighed. 'Don't be naïve, Georgie. It's how these things work. We might not even need to prove it in court. But the great thing is that it prompted Joshua to confess.'

His voice suggested he was furious with himself. 'I should have guessed. The boy always had a thing for Georgie. She'd laughed about it. Said it was flattering for a thirteen-year-old kid to run after her like a lap dog.' He groaned. 'Even

300

encouraged it by giving him things.'

'But I don't remember him being there.'

'He wasn't. Not during your time. His mother had sent him away to be with his father because he was too much of a handful for her. Apparently, according to his confession, he was coming back when …'

He paused as if trying to recover his composure. 'When he found Georgie wandering in the woods.'

'She'd run away because of us.'

He nodded. 'Exactly. When he tried to kiss her, she lashed out at him. Then, scared, he … he attacked her and then …'

'Then I appeared.'

Another nod. Tight lips. A slight wobble, indicating he was doing everything he could to hold himself together. Instinctively, she knew he couldn't talk about this any more. His short, almost brusque words confirmed this.

'Mac is next door waiting. I hope you have a good journey back.'

Her mind whirled in confusion. 'They're letting me go?'

'Yes.'

She flinched at the lack of emotion.

'Just like that?'

'Please Georgie, no questions.' He passed a hand over his face wearily. 'Let's just say I have still have some influence in these parts.' Another wry smile. 'I just hope this doesn't come back and bite me too.'

FORTY SEVEN

Confessions! I could tell you anything you want to know about confessions. One of the other kids taught me in my third foster home.

'On telly, you see people saying "I didn't do it",' he told me.

I already knew that!

'But you don't do it that way. Otherwise they can disprove it, see.'

No, I didn't. But I was ten. Nearly a man. So I tried to listen carefully.

Everyone looked up to this boy. He was always stealing stuff and getting away with it. No one could catch him. If anyone was going to help me through life, he was.

'What you've got to do,' he added, 'is say "No comment". That's what my dad taught me.'

I felt jealous then. This boy had had a dad who'd bothered to teach him stuff about life. Mine had just buggered off before I was born, leaving Mum and me in 'the system'.

'If you keep saying no comment, they can't do nothing, like. Then you have to get your lawyer.'

'How?' we all asked. There was a group of us then, listening. But we got called right then to 'supper': bread and marmalade, which you wolfed down in seconds even though the foster couple swore to social that they gave us meat every night.

In the morning, I woke to find that the only possession I owned in the world – a photo of my mother – had gone from the wobbly cupboard next to my bed.

'Have you seen it?' I asked everyone.

Their faces went blank, to a boy. 'No comment,' they said.

That's when I stabbed him. The one who had started all this. The one with the dad.

I stabbed him with a fork. A fork I'd been saving under my bed.

He was all right.

But I got sent to one of those juvenile places.

Been out for five years, I have. But it's hard to change old habits. I might not stab. But I steal. Bags, cards, phones, identities.

I just can't help it. It's not my fault. It's because I never had a dad.

Everyone needs one.

But like they used to say to me in the home, 'Need doesn't get.'

FORTY EIGHT

She'd have to sign something, Georgie was told, to promise she'd come back for the trial. A witness statement wouldn't be enough.

That wasn't all. 'There might be publicity both here and in the UK,' Joly's lawyer had warned.

Georgie gripped the sides of the plane's seat with apprehension at the thought. But it had been the only way they'd allowed her to go.

And she had to get back.

'Arriving Heathrow tomorrow,' she'd texted Ellie. *'Will explain all.'*

She had to. There had been too many lies. It was time now to face the truth. To absorb the revelations she'd had while over here ...

She'd had a sister ... A twin! If only she'd known, they could have had time together. Special time to tell each other about what had happened to them since they'd been pulled apart. They could have gone, arm in arm. to their mother ... Perhaps forgive her. To ask too, what had happened to their father ...

'Please note that the seatbelt sign has now been switched on. We will be entering an area of turbulence shortly.'

The pilot's voice – not European – was silkily reassuring. Yet unlike her neighbour who began crossing herself, Georgie felt quite calm. In some ways, it might help if she never came back. Then again, she thought, looking at the baby across the aisle, wrapped up in a shawl against her mother's chest, that wasn't fair on everyone else in the plane.

It was time she began to think of other people now. Not just saving her own skin.

Slowly, the tablet which Joly had given her ('to help you sleep during the first leg'), began to make her feel drowsy. When she woke, it was to see her neighbour looking much chirpier and paying for a bottle of duty-free perfume with a credit card.

Credit card.

The sight of the red and white plastic card began to bring it all back. That was how it started ... Vanda and Jonathan had a lot to pay for.

'We have now landed at Heathrow airport. Passengers in transit ...'

The stewardess' chirpy voice broke into Georgie's deep dream in which she was chasing Vanda and Jonathan, with the computer man in hot pursuit. All four of them were clutching credit cards, the same red and white design as the one with which her neighbour had paid.

The latter was heaving her small bag out of the luggage compartment above them. Other passengers were rushing past, keen to get out. Georgie's heart began to race again. What would be waiting for her out there?

She'd deliberately not given Ellie her flight details. I need time, she told herself, to think. Joly had insisted on giving her money which would cover a modest hotel in London for a couple of nights. She'd use it as a base before working out what to do next.

One thing was clear. Ellie and Nick had to be told ...

Feeling sick at the thought of them knowing the truth, she stood up to help the woman with her case overhead.

'It's all right, thank you.' The older woman was flushed. 'I can do it.'

Was she merely independent? Or didn't she trust her? Did

she look like the kind of woman who would take someone's bag? Or murder her sister?

Feeling like a criminal, Georgie took her own bag and headed for security. Once more, her heart began to race. Supposing this was a trick? Supposing they refused to let her back into her own country ...

But the man with the neat black haircut merely nodded. 'Had a good holiday?' he asked almost chummily.

Georgie could merely nod; too scared to talk.

Her bag was first out on the conveyor belt. That had never happened to her before. She'd have welcomed the delay if only to give herself more time to think. In Bangkok, all she had wanted to do was to get out.

Now it was time to face the music, she simply wanted to crawl into a hole. Everything she'd had had gone. Including someone she hadn't even known she'd had.

Georgie's mouth set as she passed through Customs and out into Arrivals. Forget the hotel in London, there was somewhere else she had to go first.

'Mum?'

A small, pretty, dark-skinned girl dived under the barrier and wrapped her arms around her. 'Mum. You're back. You're safe.'

Georgie could only stand in surprise as Ellie held her, oblivious to the other passengers walking around them.

'How did you know my flight?' she began.

Ellie took a step back. Her eyes were wet too. 'Lyndsey and I worked it out together. This was the first flight today. If necessary, we'd have waited for all the others.'

Lyndsey? Yes. Her friend was waiting there too. Rather pale and leaning on a stick.

'You shouldn't be here,' she said, ducking under the barrier herself to hold her friend.

'Please stay in line,' barked an official.

She was breaking rules already ...

'I had to.' Lyndsey's eyes travelled from her to Ellie. 'I

needed to know you were all right. We were so worried about you.'

We?

'I'm sorry.' Lyndsey's gaze faltered. 'But Ellie came to see me in hospital.'

'I had to,' burst out Ellie. 'None of your friends seemed to know where you were and Dad wouldn't tell me. Then someone told me about Lyndsey so I went to see her.'

'Where's Dad?'

Ellie shook her head.

So he'd given up on her. Just as Ellie would when she knew the truth.

'Have you told her what happened?' Her voice was harder now as she faced Lyndsey.

'No. That's for you to do.'

She turned to Ellie. 'And your dad hasn't said anything?'

'Said what? Come on, Mum. You can't go on being secretive. Lyndsey said you went to visit an old friend in Bangkok.' Her face clouded with uncertainty, reminding Georgie that her daughter might look like a young woman but was still a child beneath. 'Are you having an affair? It's all right. I can deal with it. I know Dad's a complete prat at times. But I just need to know …'

There were at the station entrance now, the one to Paddington. The quick route. 'I'll explain on the way.' Then she glanced at Lyndsey. 'Shouldn't you be in hospital?'

There was a wan smile. 'I'm in remission. I can go where I like, within reason. Including Yorkshire.'

She understood!

'Why Yorkshire?' demanded Ellie.

'Because,' answered Georgie slowly, 'that's where your grandmother lives.'

She explained on the train, in a hushed voice, hoping no one else would hear. Lyndsey insisted on buying first-class tickets, which helped.

Both listened, spellbound, with the occasional 'I don't believe it' or a gasp, as she took them back down the years. Georgie was determined to leave nothing out. The fear but excitement of travelling abroad for the first time on her own. Her surprise when someone glamorous like Georgina befriended her in the Arrivals queue. Her admiration for this beautiful girl. Her crush on Joly – she could see that Ellie didn't like that. The vague knowledge that they were all dealing with drugs even though it didn't seem that wrong, out there. (A deep inhaling of breath there from Lyndsey).

And then the dark bit. Georgina finding her in Joly's arms. That panic when they found her missing. Running into the scrubland. The blood. The knife ... The boy ... The running ... The police ... and then meeting Sam in Bangkok.

'You were so brave, Mum,' said Ellie. Her eyes were wet again. So were Lyndsey's.

'So strong,' added her friend, shaking. 'I couldn't have coped.'

No. Georgie brought her hand down on the table as though slicing away the lies. 'I didn't tell the truth. I pretended to be someone else. That's why your father can't forgive me. And I don't blame him.'

'But you had to,' cried out Ellie. 'You were just trying to survive. I'd have done the same.'

Lyndsey nodded. 'Me too. If I'd had the guts.'

Georgie took her friend's hand. 'You've got more guts than any of us.'

There was a quiet silence. Then Ellie broke it. 'It's a bit weird to find out that I've got an aunt who died. And a grandmother in Yorkshire. What are you going to tell her?'

Georgie looked at Lyndsey. 'I'm not sure yet.'

Her mother was in a home now. Her mind wandered and she wasn't very steady on her legs. It was a nice place with a good reputation. She seemed happy. Lyndsey used to visit regularly before she moved down. Her father still did.

Her friend told her all this in the taxi as they headed out of York Station – just the same as it had been in her time with its vast dramatic ceiling – towards the moors.

Ellie's eyes were wide. 'I've never been this far north before. It's freezing.' She shivered. 'But beautiful.'

Georgie hardly heard. All she could think about was her mother. What would she do? What would she say …?

By the time the taxi pulled up outside a pleasant, red-bricked building, she was wondering if she'd acted too hastily. Maybe a letter would have done instead …

No, said the real Georgina inside her. She owes us this.

Funny. Ever since she'd discovered she'd had a twin it all seemed to make sense. That feeling that half of her was missing. That desperate need for a friend …

'She's been expecting you,' said the kindly woman who opened the door. 'Been talking of nothing else. You're her daughter, aren't you?'

Georgie nodded.

'Down here and to the right. Like a cup of tea, would you?'

Her accent reminded her of the warmth up here, despite the climate. Tea. Hospitality. All so very different from this woman who was sitting on the chair, staring at her.

Mum.

She hadn't changed. Her hair might be grey. She was thinner too. But that look, that disapproving look, was the same.

'You've brought me the wrong one.'

Her voice rose in a cry.

'You've brought me the wrong one. Don't you think I can tell, even after all these years?'

Lyndsey and Ellie both shot her agonising looks but Georgie knelt down next to the old woman. Then she took both her hands in hers. 'It's all right, Mum. I understand. You did what you had to do.'

None of this was what she'd had in mind. She was going to berate her mother. Accuse her of breaking them up. To demand why she couldn't have kept both. But now, perhaps because she had Ellie next to her, she felt differently.

A mother had to do what she felt best at the time.

'Georgina wanted to come but she couldn't,' she said softly.

Her mother's eyes softened. 'She was busy, I expect. Got lots of friends, has she? Going to parties, I expect. Georgina was the lovely one, you know. I knew she'd be all right.' Then her face sharpened again. 'I suppose that's why you left. Just like that. Not a word. Not a letter.'

This was awful. 'I couldn't come back, Mum. I – I got into trouble.'

'What kind of trouble?'

Georgie now felt angry. 'Do you really care? You didn't seem to do much of that when I was at home.'

'That's because I had to hide my feelings. If I did, I couldn't have coped.' The old woman's voice trembled. 'I gave away your sister. They would only let me keep one of you. All your life I resented you for that. Wasn't fair of me, I know. But it's the truth.'

So much for her mind wandering.

'Now where is your sister? You said she was outside. Bring her to me.'

This was terrible.

'She's not outside,' chipped in Ellie softly. 'She's ...'

Mum's face jerked up. 'Who are you?'

'My daughter,' said Georgie firmly.

'Your daughter? But she's not the same colour as you. I suppose you've married one of those ...'

'Mum. Stop.'

Ellie's face was red. 'It's all right.'

'No, it's not.'

'BRING GEORGINA. I WANT GEORGINA NOW!' roared the old woman.

There was the sound of a bell being pulled. Feet running. Two staff. Lyndsey slumped on the chair as though it was too much.

'I think you'd better go now, if you don't mind,' said the

kindly northern woman who had opened the door. 'Come back another time, eh?'

Wait. Georgie hadn't finished. 'Who was my father, Mum? Please. Tell me. You owe me that.'

Her mother's eyes went distant for a minute. 'Your father? I hardly knew him. Here one minute. Gone the next.'

'So those stories,' spluttered Georgie. 'All those tales you told me about him ...'

'All made up.' Her mother's voice was clear. Certain. Not like before. 'I spun you a yarn, lass, to save your feelings. He had his own family. He didn't want you two as well.'

This couldn't be right. Her mind shot back to the photograph on the mantelpiece of a handsome man with a moustache and upright stance. It was the only one they had. We weren't ones for taking pictures, her mother used to say.

'But the photograph. Dad's picture.'

Her mother made a snorting noise. 'That wasn't your father! Do you think he'd let himself be compromised that way? That was some old snap I found in a junk shop.'

A junk shop? So for years, she'd been worshipping a picture of a stranger? Putting her hands to her mouth, Georgie let out a huge sob and ran from the room.

'You mustn't blame her,' said Lyndsey on the train home.

Georgie, still reeling from the revelations about her father, shook her head. 'You think I should have got in touch with Mum earlier.'

Lyndsey's mouth tightened. 'If I'd had a daughter, I'd have been devastated if she'd just left like you did. Think about it. For years, she didn't know if you were dead or alive.'

'For years, she lied to me, you mean.'

'She had to. In those days – especially in Yorkshire – it was a disgrace to have a child out of wedlock.'

Such old-fashioned words.

'Maybe she just made it up,' suggested Ellie.

Lyndsey shook her head.

'You knew all along, didn't you?' Georgie suddenly realised.

This time, her friend's voice was softer. 'Mum always said there were rumours. But they couldn't prove anything.'

So everyone else suspected, apart from her. It was all beginning to make sense now. 'Your dad didn't have any family,' her mother used to say when she asked.

'I'd like to trace him,' she said, looking out of the window at the fields racing by. He'd be old by now. But he might still be alive. The thought was so impossibly exciting that she could scarcely breathe.

Lyndsey sighed. 'I knew you'd say that. But it will be difficult getting anything out of your mother. It would upset her too.'

So what? Didn't she owe her? Or rather, them?

'At least she's in a really nice home,' Georgie couldn't help pointing out.

'Who do you think pays for that?'

'It's not state?'

Lyndsey smiled. 'Definitely not.'

'Who *does* pay, then?'

'Georgina.'

'Georgina?'

'She had a trust fund. And, luckily she left a will. After she was found dead, your mother inherited.'

'So Mum knows she's dead?'

'Theoretically. But over the years, her mind has blocked it out. That's why she talks as though your sister is still alive.'

It was all too much to take in. Good, kind Georgina who apparently knew she was adopted and who could still forgive her birth mother for giving her away.

Would her children be so forgiving towards her? Ellie's hand was firmly linked in Georgie's, just as it had been from the minute they'd got on the train. 'I don't know how you managed, Mum.'

'Then you forgive me? For lying?'

313

'Absolutely. I'd have done the same. I did, didn't I? And I didn't have the reason to do so, like you. Nor does Nick ...'

'What do you mean?'

Nick was still travelling. His latest text had said he was in Morocco.

'Nothing.'

'Ellie ...'

'Please Mum. Not yet. It's not important anyway. Not compared with what you're going to do next.' She looked away. 'Dad gave me this letter for you.' She handed over an envelope. 'I wasn't sure whether to give it to you earlier or not. Sorry.'

... house will be empty when you return so you can stay there ... going to spend some time with Rufus ... you're not the woman I married ... it's not the drugs ... I might be able to cope with that ... Or that girl's death ... I can't believe you were responsible ... It's the fact that you have lived this lie for so long ... that you were someone else ... that I am married to someone I don't know ... as for going to Thailand to stay with a man whom you used to love ... how could you do that? I know I am rambling ... how I feel at the moment. Please don't try to contact me ...

Sam

FORTY NINE

I'm doing another job now. At first I was worried they weren't happy with me. But then I was told it was cos the fraud squad were sniffing around our trail.

That made me feel sick. But also excited. Crime's like that. You know what the risks are – anyone who's been in Wandsworth can tell you it's not worth it. But when you're on the Out again, it's just too tempting. Addictive. Just look what I earned from the last job.

'We're going to try our best to help you get a proper job,' my social worker told me after I got released the last time.

But I don't want a proper job. I'm not the type that could be stuck in an office, day in and day out.

I like this life.

I'm prepared to take the risk in return for my freedom. Even if it means I lose it every now and then.

We're all aware of the risks. Sometimes I wonder how many of us there are in this.

'Ask no questions,' said my boss.

Don't worry. I won't.

It's not worth the risk. Not if I want to keep my face looking the way it is.

FIFTY

The house seemed so strange without Sam. It made Georgie realise how much she needed him. How much she loved him. All those years when she'd silently regarded him as 'second-best' compared with her naïve passion for Joly ... Only now did she realise that there was no substitute for that steady love that was built slowly over the years, based on the foundation of children and gas bills and quiet evenings in.

He might have his faults – like his obsession with perfection – but didn't they all?

If she'd told Sam the truth in the first place, she told herself, as Ellie now sat with her in the sitting room watching television (her daughter had insisted on moving back in 'until Dad comes back'), none of this would have happened.

He wouldn't have married a girl on the run. He might even have handed her over to the police for a crime she hadn't committed. But then she wouldn't have had Nick or Ellie. What an awful thought ...

Meanwhile, there was still no word from her husband. *'I've left you enough in the bank to manage,'* he had added in his letter.

Presumably he would continue working from Hong Kong. Hadn't he always said he could work anywhere? As for Rufus, Georgie felt hurt that her brother-in-law hadn't kept in touch. Although they usually only saw each other at Christmas – and not always then – they'd always got on well.

Perhaps he now thought as badly of her as Sam himself.

Meanwhile, Nick's emails had been brief and infrequent.

'That's boys for you,' Ellie had reassured him. 'I don't think Dad has said anything.'

Meanwhile, Georgie tried to pick up the pieces of her old life, aware that it wasn't just Sam and Nick she had to worry about. It was the threat of the trial hanging over her head. Sooner or later, she would need to return to Thailand to give evidence.

'There will be publicity,' the lawyer had warned her. 'You're an intelligent, attractive English woman with a well-off husband. The papers will love it.'

The very thought made her quake inside. But it had to be done. Her sister's killer had to be brought to justice. Often, as Georgie began reviving her network of clients through word of mouth ('I'm back now') and publicity in the local paper, she found herself wondering why she was bothering.

The children. That was why.

The only important thing in life was family. Her mother might have rejected her out of guilt for giving away her sister – a sister whom she'd failed to recognise. But she still had Ellie.

'You didn't give up on me when I went off the rails,' her daughter kept saying. 'I'm not going to give up on you, either.'

Still, there was one huge relief. Vanda and Jonathan's house had a For Sale sign outside. 'They've gone to their home in France,' Jo had told her when they met up for coffee during her first week back. 'It was very sudden, apparently. Not long after you went.'

In a way, she didn't blame them. Perhaps they should be allowed some peace now, after everything. Those years in a Bangkok prison didn't bear thinking about.

Her old friend eyed her with undisguised pity. 'Are you all right? Do you want to tell me about it?'

It was the question everyone wanted to know. Why had she just taken off for nearly two months? Why had she come back? And where was Sam?

'We're having a break,' she said, stirring her latte so she

wouldn't have to look up at her friend. 'That … that fraud business. It caused a lot of tension between us.'

Jo stiffened. 'I can understand that. My husband wasn't too happy either when our account was emptied.'

This time, Georgie *had* to look up. 'I'm sorry.'

Jo shrugged. 'It's all right. Made me more aware, actually. I hadn't realised how prevalent personal fraud is. Did you ever find out who was behind yours?'

She tried not to flush. 'Yes and no. It's partly why I was away.'

Jo frowned. 'I don't understand.'

Already, she'd said too much. 'Nor do I. Please, Jo. I don't want to talk about it.'

'But have you heard from the Fraud Squad?' her friend persisted.

'Every now and then. They're still making investigations apparently.'

It was true. Amidst the pile of post she'd had to wade through upon getting back, had been a letter to this effect. But what if they found out that Vanda and Jonathan were behind the theft from her husband's account? And had Vanda been telling the truth that she'd had nothing to do with her own missing money, which still hadn't been returned? It was all too complicated …

'That's modern living for you,' said the computer man when he came to sort out another problem the following week (something to do with a password that kept popping up and demanding to be confirmed). 'I don't do banking online any more.'

He flashed a sympathetic look. 'Not after what happened to you.'

Weeks went by. They turned into a month. Then two. Every now and then, Sam emailed. They were always to the point. He was paying the bills by direct debit but she was to let him know if she needed anything else. Was the roof all right in the storms

319

he'd read about? How was the dog?

Practical. Emotionless, apart from that question about the dog and a reference to the fact that he rarely heard from Nick. Join the club. Still, maybe the time to worry was when they were always with you.

Then there was Lyndsey. Lyndsey whom she thought she'd lost. It was a mark of true friendship, they told each other, that they could pick up again, just like that. She'd had to tell her husband, of course. 'I gave him a sanitised version,' her friend said quickly. 'Something about you changing your name for a fresh start. He accepted that. After all, he knew your mother had been horrid to you for most of your life.'

'And your dad?'

Georgie couldn't bear the idea of that kind man thinking the worst of her.

'I told him you'd been accused of something you didn't do.' Lyndsey's voice tried to make light of it but Georgie knew her all too well.

'Everyone will know when the trial comes up, won't they?'

'Not necessarily.'

But they both knew that wasn't true. More importantly, Lyndsey's treatment seemed to be working. She looked better than she had for a long time. Georgie's phone was also beginning to ring again. Old clients wanted to update their old look. New ones responded to her ads in the paper. And – irony of ironies – the new buyers for Vanda and Jonathan's home wanted 'a complete overhaul'.

She told them – truthfully – that she was booked up for the next six months. The thought of going back to the place where her life had begun to tumble down was all too much.

'It is weird though, Mum, isn't it?' said Ellie when they talked about as they so often did. 'Your bag turning up like that at home … You know, I still think Dad doesn't believe I had nothing to do with it.'

Georgie felt a rush of love. 'But I do,' she said, squeezing her daughter's hand. 'And that's what's important.'

The phone call came when she was least expecting it. Bang in the middle of redesigning a conservatory for some new neighbours of Jo's. (The latter had recommended her, perhaps as a sign of forgiveness.)

'Georgie?' said Mac's voice, distantly down the line.

Georgie froze. 'Will you excuse me?' she said to the new client; a small mousey woman who hung, rather gratifyingly, on her every word.

Hand shaking on her mobile, she went out into the garden for some privacy.

'They've fixed a date for the trial.'

'So soon? You said it would take months.'

'That was before the latest tidy up.' Mac's Australian twang belied the severity of the situation. 'The government is having a crackdown and is bringing everything forward. We need you out here next week.'

Next week! That was ridiculous. 'But I've just started working again,' she began to say, before stopping. This was her sister they were talking about. Their chance to nail her killer.

'But what if they don't believe me?' she faltered. 'Supposing I go back and they put me into prison.'

They won't, she expected Mac to say. But instead, there was a short pause. 'I guess that's the risk you have to take.'

For a minute, Georgie stood looking at her client's lovely garden with its beautiful copper tree shining in the autumn sun. If she went back, she might lose all this. The police were corrupt. Mac had told her that. They might reject her evidence. Put her in prison.

Or else they might send Joshua there instead.

That man had to pay for her sister's death. She owed it to the real Georgina Peverington-Smith.

'I'll be there,' she said simply.

'This is incredible,' murmured Ellie beside her, gazing out at the green fields where a woman sat astride an elephant. 'Such a mixture of ... of everything! That shanty town we just passed

321

through. So basic compared with last night's hotel.' Her lips tightened. 'It doesn't seem fair.'

Her daughter had insisted on coming with her. ('You're not going out there alone, Mum.') Of course she'd tried to talk her out of it, but deep down, Georgie was relieved to have the company. She also suspected Ellie might have an ulterior motive ...

Sam had expressed disapproval through a text but had failed to offer to accompany her himself. So here they were. Heading for Joly's hotel.

If Sam didn't like that, it was too bad. She felt different now, Georgie told herself. Any feelings she'd had for Joly in that direction were gone now. It was justice she needed. Justice for her sister. Justice for herself.

'You came.' He was waiting for her outside the hotel, his eyes taking in Ellie at the same time. Georgie felt a jolt of alarm. 'This is my daughter,' she said, putting an arm around her.

Joly's eyes expressed an interest that made Georgie feel decidedly uneasy. 'Very good of you to offer support.'

Ellie's face was blank. 'She's my mother.'

Thank goodness. So Ellie hadn't been taken in by his charm.

Mac was waiting for them inside. 'The trial starts in two days.'

'It's been brought forward?' gasped Georgie.

'Probably to throw us,' intercepted Ellie.

'My daughter's reading psychology,' added Georgie, feeling the need to explain.

Mac's face showed he was impressed.

'I don't know if you've been to a trial in the UK ...'

Georgie shook her head.

'Well, it's very different here. More informal. People shout out.' His fingers began to drum the table. 'You'll have to be prepared for that. All we need you to do is tell the truth.'

He looked at her. They all did.

'Can you do that?'

322

She nodded.

'There's just one other thing.' The fingers began to drum faster. 'The DNA on the hair ...'

Joly visibly winced, as did she. The blonde hair ... her sister's hair...

'The lab results aren't as conclusive as we had hoped.'

Both men looked at her. 'That's why your testimony is so important,' said Joly softly. 'If the jury don't believe you, we're stuffed.'

The court wasn't what she'd expected. After Joshua had given evidence, his supporters from the side began applauding him. Someone close to Georgie spat at her. This was awful.

Mac's face was grim. 'Welcome to the third world.'

Joshua's mother was speaking now. Angrily in a language that neither Georgie nor Ellie could understand. But from Mac and Joly's faces, it didn't look good.

'She says you're trying to pin the murder onto her son,' whispered Mac. 'That you killed Georgie because you were jealous of her.'

Georgie felt the old fear pass through her.

'But what about the hair and the DNA?' whispered Ellie. 'Don't they count for anything?'

'Their lawyer had discredited it, just as we feared.' Mac's mouth was tight.

Suddenly there was another roar from the gallery. 'It's your turn now.' He placed a hand on hers. 'Just tell them the truth.'

Her heart pounding in her ears, Georgie walked across the court floor. Someone threw a banana at her. It hit her cheek. Desperately, she looked back at Mac and Joly and Ellie sitting where she had just been.

'You can do it,' mouthed her daughter.

She had to. For her family. She had to persuade this hostile jury if she was going to return for the children. She had to get justice for the real Georgina.

The shouting was getting louder. For a moment, Georgie

froze. Then she reached inside her bag and brought out the photograph. The black and white photograph which the nursing home had found for her in her mother's private possessions, when she'd written the other month. She held it up.

'This was me and my sister when we were babies,' she said.

The shouting dropped. The crowd appeared to understand. They were bemused. What did this have to do with a murder? 'Georgina was my sister.'

Someone yelled out. Someone else told that person to shut up.

'I didn't know that at the time. But I do now. It was one of those strange coincidences. But even if I had known it, I would never have hurt Georgina.'

For a moment, the courtroom blurred. 'She was the kindest, nicest person I have ever known ...'

'Then why did you sleep with her boyfriend?' yelled out a voice.

Georgie nodded. 'You're right. I shouldn't have. But who here hasn't done something they shouldn't have done?'

There was a brief silence. She had their attention now. 'It didn't mean I killed her.' She looked directly at Joshua. 'When I found Georgina that day, she was already lying on the ground.'

She closed her eyes, gripping the flimsy rail for support. 'Her chest was bloody. She'd been stabbed ... By the boy who was standing over her. That man.'

She jerked her head at Joshua. Immediately there was a tidal roar.

'He tried to stab me too but I grabbed the knife.'

Every minute was coming back to her. 'I cut him. That's why there's a scar on his cheek.'

'Prove it. Prove it.'

The chant was getting louder now. Mac and Joly were looking increasingly worried. Fear was written all over Ellie's face.

'It's true,' continued Georgie desperately.

A man jumped up. Joshua's lawyer, Mac had pointed out earlier, although he too was in shirt sleeves. 'She's lying. This rubbish about her sister is a lie. She is saying that to gain sympathy. This is the woman who should be imprisoned. Not my client.'

The crowd surged forward. They were going to lynch her. Someone had to do something.

'Joly!' she called out.

Then, all of a sudden, as if someone had switched off a light, the noise stopped. Hardly daring to look up, Georgie was aware of a different atmosphere around her. A presence.

Four men were entering the courtroom. Two she didn't know.

The other two, she did.

Rufus. And Sam.

FIFTY ONE

My lawyer.

My barrister.

When you're Inside, you notice men using these words as though these people work just for them and no one else.

It's like it gives them false airs of pretension.

But you've got to have that, see, 'cos you need hope in prison.

You need to wake up every day, thinking that this is the one when they'll tell you that you can launch an appeal or that they know you didn't really do it.

Not all of us are guilty, you know.

When I was Inside last, we had two men who were always in the library. Always poring over books to prove they were innocent.

We used to take the piss out of them.

But it turned out they were right. They found stuff in those law books that their own lawyers didn't find. Precedents, they called them. Don't ask me what that means.

All I know is that those men walked free.

The rest of us had to serve our time.

Then, when you get out, no one will give you a job 'cos you've got a record. No one wants to rent you a room in case you don't pay the rent. Friends won't even give you a corner to sleep in case you nick their stuff. And your old lady doesn't want to know because she went off with someone else long ago. Your kids are that bloke's kids now.

So what do you do? The only thing you can. You take other people's things. Strangers' stuff. And you hope no one catches you. But if they do, at least you know you'll have a roof over your head.

Some of us get caught on purpose. Just so we get fed.

And then all we want to do is get Out.

Don't make sense, does it?

FIFTY TWO

'They're here,' breathed Mac.

His relief was palpable.

But Georgie only had eyes for Sam. Her husband was here, in a stiff tweed jacket that looked out of place but curiously comforting. He'd come to support her after all! Initial relief was replaced by fear. He wasn't even looking at her. Instead, his head was down as he sat in the public gallery as though he didn't want to be there.

'Dad,' breathed Ellie. 'So he did it, after all.'

Rufus was gesticulating. Mouthing something. Then she realised. He wasn't making signs at her. He was making signs at Mac.

'We request an adjournment,' he said leaping to his feet.

The judge sighed heavily. 'Is this really necessary?'

At the same time, Joshua's lawyer began jumping up and down like an impatient child. 'He's buying time,' he yelled. 'Don't give it to him.'

What was going on? Georgia felt as though she'd wandered into a weird fairy story where her very existence depended on the uncertain outcome. She didn't know much about legal proceedings apart from the odd drama on television. She didn't understand how, having come in as a witness, she was now being treated as a suspect.

But something told her that if Mac didn't get his adjournment, all might be lost. Besides, an adjournment would give her time to talk to Sam.

'Please,' she said, leaning forward so her eyes met that of

the judge's. 'Please.'

For a minute, he faltered. It was enough. Quite why, Georgie never knew. Until then, she'd been certain that he was against her; choosing instead to side with Joshua.

'Very well.' He nodded, giving Georgie a tight 'You owe me' smile. 'Two hours for lunch, everyone.'

'That means three,' hissed someone behind her but Mac was already on his feet.

'Take her to that bar on the square. The quieter one. Ellie, come with me if you don't mind. You might be needed. '

None of this was making sense. 'But what about my husband?' She shot a pained look up to the gallery where Sam was still sat, head bowed.

'Trust me,' said Joly quietly for the first time. 'He'll talk to you when he's ready.'

She stared at him. 'You knew he was coming?'

Joly moved closer. For a minute, she thought he was going to hold her in his arms. No! That wouldn't do. Not in front of Sam. Or in front of anyone else, for that matter. Any feelings she'd had for him in the past had gone. Especially now she knew Sam cared. He must do, mustn't he? Otherwise, why else would he be here?

'Go, now,' added Mac, almost pushing them out.

So they went.

It seemed ridiculous that Sam had come all this way and yet here she was, sitting in a bar only a few feet – potentially – from her husband without any sight of him.

'You've got to see it his way,' Joly said to her, buying her a large glass of orange juice while knocking down a stiff whisky himself. 'Men are proud creatures. He'll think you've been having an affair with me.'

He said it in such a smug way that Georgie wanted to get up there and then. 'No. Stay. Listen. You want to know why he's here? Because he still loves you and – more importantly – good old Rufus has come up with something. I knew he would when

I emailed him.'

'You emailed him? Why?'

But even as she spoke, Vanda's words came back to her. Know it through Rufus ... at school with Jonathan ... Close-knit circle ...

'Because Rufus, despite being as thick as two short planks, knows people.' Joly, despite the severity of the situation, tapped the side of his nose, knowingly. 'He put out feelers in Bangkok, where young Joshua had been holing up since his last attack.'

Attack?

Joly looked around furtively. 'They were just rumours. Unsubstantiated rumours. But unless I've read Rufus' face wrongly, I think we might just have the evidence we need.'

'You're wrong,' she said suddenly as a crowd of men came in, jostling and hustling their way to the bar.

Joly's eyes sharpened. 'How do you know?'

'You're wrong about what you just said.' Her eyes were on the men, who had begun to point loudly in her direction. 'More importantly, you said. More importantly, Rufus has come up with something.'

She moved towards the exit. 'The most important thing for me = whether they try and convict me instead – is that Sam is here.'

'Wait,' said Joly sharply, jumping up. 'You can't just go like that. It's not safe ...'

But she was already threading her way through the crowds, searching, scouring the sea of faces for a pale European one. A tall, dark-haired man who, despite his former ex-pat life, looked lost in this world so far removed from Devon.

Yes. There he was. Sitting by the river. Only a place like this could have a stinking river bank running behind the courthouse with young boys fishing.

'Sam.'

She sat next to him.

He said nothing. Sweat poured down his face. The heat? Or the strain? Both, perhaps.

'You've got to believe me.' Her hand stole out towards him but then retreated, knowing this wasn't the right time or place. 'I didn't have an affair with Joly.'

Still silence.

'It's you I want. Not him.'

At last. His face was turning towards her. Instantly, she wished it hadn't. His expression was black. Furious. Just like he had been when Ellie had admitted to doing drugs.

'I saw the way he looked at you in court,' he said slowly.

His voice rasped with pain. There was no denying it. Georgie had seen it too. 'But I don't feel the same way.' Her voice trembled. 'I just want us to go back to the old life. The one we had before my card was stolen. When everything was normal.'

He moved away. 'When you were lying to me, you mean. Pretending to be someone else.'

She shook her head. 'I didn't know what else to do. I was young, Sam. Not much older than Nick. I was scared.'

'So you latched onto me for safety?'

She hesitated. Momentarily. But it was enough.

He moved away further. Desperately, she caught at his sleeve but he shook her away. 'I did love you, Sam. I learned to love you. I know it's not the way it should have been but it's a more long-lasting love than something that's just built on ... well, lust.'

His face saddened. 'Like the lust you had for him, you mean.'

'Maybe.' He winced. Well, he wanted the truth. 'But is it right that a nineteen-year-old should have to live the rest of her life judged for a wrong decision? Would you make Nick eternally responsible for something that he did wrong?'

She could see she'd touched a nerve. Emboldened, she carried on. 'And what about Vanda and Jonathan? They're adults but they continued to break the law.'

He frowned. 'What do you mean?'

Did he not know? Somehow she'd presumed that Rufus –

332

part of this tight-knit group – would have told him. 'Your precious clients. The Romer-Riches. His first name might be David but he's known to his friends as Jonathan. He and his wife were in the group, here, all those years ago. They blackmailed me. They're the ones who stole the money from your account.'

'No.' He shook his head. 'They helped me get it back.'

'Only because they took it in the first place. They blackmailed me – except that I didn't realise it was them at the time. They told me that if I didn't tell you about my past, you'd lose all your money.'

His face was beginning to clear. 'So you wouldn't have told me – would have gone on living a lie – if they hadn't made you?'

Instantly, Georgie realised she'd said the wrong thing. 'I'm sorry.' Her voice came out desperately. 'Please, Sam, listen to me.'

There was a cough behind them. Joly! For a minute, she stood there, looking at the two men. Each so different. Joly, blonde, still athletic despite a slightly chubbier look. Sam. Tall. Dark. Wiry. The man she had had a child with.

'We've got to go back to the courtroom now.' Joly spoke with an assured steadiness that almost managed to carry a 'Sorry to interrupt' tone at the same time.

Sam nodded curtly before turning on his heel and leaving Georgie alone with Joly.

'Looks like things are a bit difficult for you,' he said quietly as they fell into step back to the court building.

She nodded.

'You know,' he continued, 'if it doesn't work out, you could always stay here.'

What she would have done for that suggestion twenty-odd years earlier!

'Thank you,' she began, 'but ...'

'Mum!' Ellie was running towards them, pulling her hand and casting dirty looks at Joly as if she knew what he'd been

333

saying. 'You've got to come. Now. You'll never guess what Uncle Rufus has found out.'

Rufus' networking of contacts had paid off. He'd unrooted a web of deceit. Everyone had been in cahoots. Even the police, who had hidden Joshua's long catalogue of assaults on other women. Why? Georgie concentrated on the rapid speech and dramas played out before her. The men admitted that yes, they could prove that the police were being paid to keep quiet in return for 'favours'. Large sums of money had been handed over to the men who controlled Joshua and other key figures in their drug rings.

Georgie watched, shocked, as a list of attacks was read out. Attacks which Joshua was accused of.

'Prove it,' he spluttered.

So they did. Photographs were produced. Blood samples. DNA. It was as if all the evidence had been sitting there, waiting to be used.

'They would have been prepared to save their own skin,' muttered Mac. 'This way, they'll get a lighter sentence even though Joshua will be hung out to dry – no more than he deserves.'

Georgie shuddered as the list went on and on. Rape on four accounts. Missing girls. Blood discovered in his rented room in Bangkok ...

A memory of her sister's battered body swam in front of her.

'This could have been Mrs Hamilton,' thundered Mac, pointing to her. 'If she hadn't managed to fight him off, Georgie might have been another of this man's victims.'

Georgie? Georgie Hamilton? Or Georgie Smith? Or Georgina Peverington-Smith? It was so hard to know who she was now, in this strange country where her old self swapped in and out of the elaborate façade she had built up over the years.

'This lovely woman – this wife, this mother – is lucky to be standing here today,' continued Mac.

All eyes were on her now. The jury's faces seemed more

sympathetic. A couple of women had tears in their eyes. And was it her imagination, or was Sam looking across at her instead of staring at the ground?

Georgie felt Ellie's soft hand creep into hers.

'Yes, she stole another woman's identity,' continued Mac in a softer voice. 'But which of you would not have been scared at the age of nineteen?'

He was addressing the jury directly now; making the same defence plea that she had made to her own husband a few minutes earlier.

'Which of you might have done the same in Georgie's situation?'

There wasn't a sound in the court now. Only the screech of motorbikes outside.

'Georgie Smith – now Georgie Hamilton – has been living a lie for twenty-two years. Isn't it time we allowed her to shed that guilt?'

There were some nods.

'And isn't it time that the real culprit had to pay for his wicked offences?'

A sea of nods.

'He's good, isn't he?' whispered Ellie.

Was her daughter rather taken with this good-looking lawyer? Georgie batted the thought to one side as the court erupted. Joshua's mother glared at her, her eyes spitting stones. She'd tried to protect her son by tipping the police off at the airport, Georgie reminded herself. But could she really blame her? Wouldn't a mother do almost anything for her child?

'Silence, silence,' roared the judge.

No one took any notice. Shocked – surely this would never happen in a British court – policemen marched Joshua off without so much as a show of hands. Around them, people were clapping and cheering. One man even leaped over the edge of a bench and shook her hand. 'You are very brave lady.'

Mac took her arm and also that of Ellie's, leading them to the front of the court. He was smiling as broadly as if he had

335

won a sports match. Maybe that's what he had done. It was a game for him; one which a lawyer needed to win in order to prove his or her worth.

But for her, it was her life.

Sam was nowhere to be seen.

Nor was Joly.

'He's gone,' said Mac, after he'd shepherded them inside a taxi which had, miraculously, appeared out of nowhere.

'My husband?'

Her chest hurt as if someone had lanced it.

'Joly.'

Mac's face had gone solemn again. 'He had to.'

'Why?'

'You don't get it, do you?' He shook his head. 'The police who were covering up for Joshua … some came from round here. They were also protecting Joly's interests.'

The hotel? The quiet hotel where she hardly saw a guest? It was beginning to make sense now …

'Joly was always into some sort of scheme.' Mac smiled fondly. 'The police turned a blind eye in return for a payment. But now we've blown their cover with Joshua and his cronies. So they'd have gone for Joly.' He glanced at his watch. 'With any luck, he'll be on the boat by now.'

Ellie's voice broke in. 'He's given up his life – as he knows it – for Mum?'

Georgie couldn't speak. Only listen.

'He reminded her of the woman he had loved.' Mac's voice was so soft that she could barely hear him. 'Georgina Peverington-Smith. He never stopped feeling guilty about betraying her.'

Georgie winced.

'He'd have done anything to turn back the clock.' Mac stopped. Then he made an expression, suggesting he was reassuring himself. 'But Joly will be all right. Men like him are survivors.' He glanced at Georgie. 'You're the same, if I'm not mistaken.'

336

'Am I?'

Her voice came out in a strangled cry. 'I've lost my husband. I've lost my children ...'

'No you haven't.' Ellie linked her arm through hers. 'I understand, Mum. And Nick will too.'

'But Dad ...'

Ellie was stroking her hand now, like a parent might do to a child. 'Just give him time. He needs to think about it.'

They couldn't get a flight until the next day. All Georgie wanted to do was get home but there was no option but to wait.

'We could use the time to look around,' suggested Ellie pointedly.

She'd wondered when that was going to come up. Ellie was in her birthplace. It was natural she'd want to try and find her mother. Her real mother. Just as it was vital that Georgie didn't show how much that hurt inside. Hadn't her mother given her away? Then again, her own mother had done the same to her sister and lived to rue the day.

This ping pong girl from the club all those years ago might well still be here. In Bangkok. In this pool of people; jostling, hustling, waiting, watching from doorways. Was it possible too, that Emerald and Sapphire might still be here?

'Do you think I'd recognise her if I saw her?' asked Ellie after hours and hours of walking the malls and markets, their eyes peeled for anyone who might look just a bit like Ellie with her long, dark hair and almond eyes.

She had to be honest. After years of lies, it now seemed imperative to tell the truth about every little thing.

'I don't know.'

They were sitting now at the coffee shop in the foyer of their hotel. Their feet were sore and their minds were fried. 'Do you want to stay longer to give it a better chance?'

Even as she spoke, Georgie prayed Ellie would turn down her offer.

It seemed a while before she answered. 'No.'

Georgie looked across the foyer at a family who'd just arrived; two children and a middle-aged couple. Luggage. Laughter. A shared past.

'I've had to accept that my father isn't dead,' she said flatly. 'I don't suppose I'll ever find him. I suppose he may even have died by now.' She gave a sharp laugh. 'My mother isn't very forthcoming with any details.'

Then she reached out for her daughter's hand. 'But you know what?'

She stopped as a tall man with short, dark hair stood over them.

'Dad!' Ellie rolled her eyes. 'About time.'

Stunned, Georgie watched as he pulled up a seat next to her. 'I thought you'd gone home.'

He shook his head. His eyes met hers. 'I couldn't get a flight. And besides, I needed time to think.'

He stretched out his left hand to take hers. With his right, he grasped his daughter's. 'I wish you'd told me the truth. But Mac was right when he asked the jury if they were incapable of making a mistake at nineteen. Rufus has helped me see that too.'

He bit his lip. 'What really matters is that we stay together as a family. I've missed you.' His voice was strangled. 'Really missed you.'

Georgie felt tears pricking her eyes. Exactly what she'd been about to say to Ellie before Sam had arrived.

'Shall we try to start again?'

He was frightened, Georgie realised. Scared of losing what they had, just as she was. From the relief spreading over Ellie's face, their daughter felt the same.

'Yes. Yes, please.'

She wanted to laugh. To jump up. To hug him. But his face was still solemn. There was something else, she realised. Something he wasn't telling her.

'What is it?' she began.

He looked at her. 'It's Nick.'

FIFTY THREE

They want me to do a different kind of job now. In fact, we've all been put on something new, apparently. It sounds very complicated, but that's technology for you.

Always on the move.

Glad I specialised in this. It was all down to this man I was banged up with in Durham.

He taught me how to find my way round computers. The irony was that we were encouraged. Got lessons, we did. Taught how to navigate our way through the system to get a certificate.

It might help us get a job when we were released, they told us.

But not the way they imagined.

In the old days, you could lock up your stuff. But now you can be a virtual thief. Steal things online. It's much safer than mugging a woman for her bag.

At least, it is if you're part of a group. There's safety in numbers. It's one of the few things I remember from school.

'There are loads of us in this outfit,' my boss is always saying. 'If one of us goes down, we take the rest with us. So no mistakes. OK?'

That's the only thing I don't like. It makes me shit scared, to be honest, when I think that my safety is in the hands of some kid, right at the bottom of this pyramid.

I just hope he's got his head screwed on.

Cos if not, we know how to remove it.

FIFTY FOUR

Sam's bombshell spun round her head for the entire flight. Words still kept diving in and out of her thoughts, making it impossible to doze like the snoring woman in front of her whose reclining chair was digging into her knees.

The fraud squad had found it out. They'd tracked her missing secret, emergency card which Nick had 'borrowed'. They'd found out that he'd made the withdrawal in Edinburgh. The furthest place he could think of, apparently. After that, he'd come home – when they were all out – with his spare key and returned it.

And why? Because he'd been gambling. Gambling! It was all the rage amongst uni students, apparently. Some of them make a fortune, Sam said grimly. Others end up in jail.

But Nick had never been the gambling type, she'd protested. Then again, did any of them really know each other?

'There was some old CCTV by the checkpoint, apparently,' her husband had told her. 'It should have been checked daily but it hadn't been – goodness knows why. Then a new manager took over. The police were looking for something else but they got suspicious when this kid keyed in two sets of digits before getting lucky with the third.'

This *kid*? It made him sound like a common or garden thief rather than their son.

'How did he get the right numbers?' she asked numbly.

Sam made a rueful expression. The kind one might make when you'd just agreed to try again and didn't feel inclined to say I told you so. 'You used your birthday dates.'

Ellie rolled her eyes. 'Mum! I've told you before. It's too obvious. People can find that kind of stuff out from Facebook.'

Her daughter was right. She should be more careful. Yet after everything that had happened, it didn't seem as significant as it should have been.

Even so …

'He admitted, on the phone this morning, that he found the card in your hiding place and thought he'd put it back in your purse to make you think you'd used it yourself,' added Sam.

No wonder his emails had been so sporadic. He probably felt guilty. As well he might.

'It all sounds so devious –' she began.

'Clever.' Ellie was grudgingly admiring. 'There's a name for that in psychology. It's called …'

'We don't need to know,' said Sam, tightly. 'As if we didn't have enough on our plate.'

He was right. There was still so much that needed tidying up.

'Did he have anything to do with the first card that was used?' demanded Ellie. 'The one you thought I'd nicked?'

Sam had the grace to blush. 'He says not.'

'And what about Jo's account? Had he hacked that?' Georgie began to feel her pulse racing. 'Hang on. What about the YouTube video? He told me about that in the first place.'

Wasn't that what the guilty did? Alerted you to the very crime that they had committed in the first place?

'What YouTube video?' demanded Ellie.

'Nothing,' they both said. Clearly she wasn't convinced by their denial so they had to tell her.

'That's an invasion of privacy,' she thundered.

But wasn't that what the modern world was all about now? It wasn't just her, the police had said. There were others in the area who'd been targeted. No one was safe any more.

And now, here they were, having changed planes in Dubai and on their way home to face their son who'd now come home.

342

It wasn't the best way to try and start a new life together, Georgie told herself. Hadn't she always told him to steer clear of drugs and be careful about the company he kept? But she hadn't said anything about stealing. Wasn't that something so obvious that it didn't need talking about?

Yet, parents made mistakes too. So who was she to cast stones?

'Georgie, look this way!'

'Georgie, how do you feel about being let off a murder charge?'

'Georgie, was your family shocked when they found out about your past?

None of them had been prepared for the onslaught of questions; the flashing of cameras; the sheer volume of people who waited for her at Arrivals in Heathrow.

'I wasn't exactly on a murder charge,' she wanted to say. 'They called me in as witness and then tried to pin it on me.'

But Sam had taken her arm and was marching her through the crowds. Ellie was close behind. Every now and then, she looked back to check their daughter hadn't been lost in the sea of heads.

'Keep going, Mum,' she heard her say.

So she did. It was the only way.

After all, Joly had given up his lifestyle for her. He had traded his comforts for her freedom. She owed it to him. She also owed it to Georgie. And she owed it to her husband.

This was no time to be a victim.

She had to stand up for herself.

FIFTY FIVE

I've got a bad feeling about this new job. It feels I'm being watched.

'Losing your nerve,' one of the others said to me.

No one accuses me of that. So I kept going even though my fingers shook over the keyboard.

I should have stopped.

Should have listened to that voice inside me.

'Never break the law,' my gran used to say to me. 'Then no one can get you.'

She knew what she was talking about. It's why she brought me up instead of my mum. She was doing time in Holloway.

At first I listened. But when I got a job at the factory after leaving school, I began to realise why Mum had done it.

You just can't seem to pay the bills with an ordinary job.

That's why, even though every bone in my body is warning me that something's going to go wrong, I'm still doing it. Still doing the only kind of work I know.

FIFTY SIX

Six months later

'How was your mother?' asked Sam as she walked in the front door, tired and sticky from the long drive.

'Much the same,' Lyndsey answered for her with that bright, cheery smile that made Georgie determined to count her blessings rather than have a moan. If her friend could smile her way through remission, she could put on a brave face about a mother who blew hot and cold.

'One minute she accused our Georgie of running away as a kid. Fair enough. But the next, she told her that she didn't want her living at home any more because ...'

'Because I wasn't my sister,' finished Georgie.

Sam gave her a cuddle. One of his wonderful hugs which made her feel instantly better. Things like this, she decided, were more important than the Other. That part had only recently started to come back. Both had been wary. Both still needed time.

But now it looked as if it might be all right.

As for Nick, he'd been suitably repentant. 'I know it was wrong,' he kept saying. 'But everyone gambles. I kept thinking that if I went on, I'd win enough to pay off my debts.'

Then he'd given her a look which made her blood run cold. 'I asked you for a loan, Mum. Remember? If you'd given it to me, none of this would have happened.'

Sam had been furious. 'Was that why you picked on your mother? Because you felt she'd let you down?'

He'd shrugged. 'Sort of.'

Was this her son? How could he have changed so much?

So they'd sat him down and had a family discussion about the importance of honesty. Even Sam had held up his hand. 'We all get it wrong at times, son.' For a man who constantly tried to be perfect, this was a big deal.

Yet Nick was still adamant that he hadn't had anything to do with the other card thefts. He was so convincing, swearing his innocence! Surely she had to believe him.

Sam wasn't so sure. 'There's more to this than meets the eye,' he kept saying.

Georgie had another saying. 'The young are not yet wise.' It was one an aunt of hers often used. And it was true. Nick was young. He'd made a mistake. Just as she had. But it wasn't a matter of life and death as it had been with her. He knew he'd done wrong. And a parent's role, as she kept telling Sam, is to forgive as well as educate.

He also allowed them to talk to his tutor. 'Fat lot of good that will do,' said Sam. 'Personally, I blame student loans. They get thousands at the beginning of term and think they're rich.'

Meanwhile, the headlines had disappeared, thank goodness. The press had long left them alone to chase other stories. But the old adage 'Any publicity is good publicity' seemed to be true. Georgie had had several phone calls from prospective clients after the trial, many of which had borne fruition as commissions. She'd even had to take on an assistant.

'Don't you want to move?' Sam had said on more than one occasion.

She'd shaken her head. I'm tired of running. I just want to stand still. Grow roots.'

'I understand that.'

For a minute, he looked as though he was going to kiss her before changing his mind. Georgie swallowed the hurt and reminded herself of what Lyndsey had said. 'These things take time.'

She only hoped her friend was right. After all, how would she feel if Sam confessed he'd stolen someone else's life? To forgive something like that was a big ask ...

Then Ellie had come downstairs one day with a strange smile on her face and asked if they could possibly lend her the fare to go to Perth. There was a psychology conference which her tutor was speaking at and it just so happened that Mac, the Australian lawyer, was going too.

Both Georgie and Sam had exchanged knowing looks. They made her feel warm. United. Almost like a proper family again.

But all of this paled into insignificance with the knock on the door one evening. It was the computer man.

Shifting awkwardly from one foot to the other. 'Sorry to bother you,' he said. 'But I've just been reading about a new scam on what the wife calls my geeky online forum site.'

There was another shifting from side to side. 'Mind if I take a look at your computer again?'

FIFTY SEVEN

'Amanda Jones. You are accused of computer hacking on twenty-three counts and conspiring to rob ...'

No comment. No comment.

FIFTY EIGHT

Twenty-three-year-old single mother convicted of hacking nineteen online banking accounts and stealing thousands of pounds.

Amanda Jones – known as Mandy – turned out to be part of a wider ring, involving computer experts and 'runners' from all over the country. They had been preying on small businesses for the last four years.

Other personal stolen possessions were also found, including jewellery and photographs, said to be of a sentimental nature.

Extract from The Times

FIFTY NINE

There's only so long you can go on saying 'No comment'. Besides, I got fed up in the end. I'm a mother now. The other jobs were before I had Ryan.

'Why did you do it?' my lawyer asked me.

''Cos it's a job, isn't it?'

And 'cos people are so vulnerable. I didn't tell him that bit. But they get careless. They lose their credit cards = cash machines are the best place to look – and someone in the team copies them.

It's their own fault. They shouldn't keep details of other people's accounts in their bags for anyone to nick.

Or else they're carrying too much stuff and they drop a car key in the road. If you're alert – like me – you pick it up.

'Thank you,' that blonde woman with the Volvo had said, as if I was doing her a favour. It was like picking a plum off a tree.

Still, I'll be out soon. They have to = or else someone will come and get me for splitting.

It's worth the risk. I'm getting a new name. Fresh documents. And a place of my own.

Then I'm going to turn straight. Anything to get my kid back. He's in care now. Someone else is putting him to bed. Waking him up. Getting him dressed. Teaching him his letters.

Shit. I can't talk any more.

I just want him with me. I just want to be a good mum with enough money to give my boy a nice life.

Amateurs! Bloody amateurs.

If it wasn't for that girl blabbing our names, we might have got off.

Stupid little cow.

Five years I've got. But I'll be out.

Then there'll be more computers to hack. More unsuspecting middle-aged women. More victims.

Including that girl if I find her.

Watch this space.

SIXTY

'I still don't quite get it,' said Lyndsey.

They were sitting on the hotel's private beach overlooking the Amalfi coast: a girls' weekend in Italy. Georgie was reflecting. Lyndsey was doodling on a sketchpad as part of her cancer rehab therapy to help her relax.

It had been Stephen's idea. 'My wife needs a break after everything she's gone through. And something tells me you could do with one too.'

Sam backed him up. 'Get away from all the publicity. By the time you're back, it might have died down.'

There were certainly enough headlines.

'Massive UK crime ring cracked'.

'Kids as young as 12 swept up in identity fraud.'

'British housewife from Thai murder case was victim along with hundreds of others'

The papers – keen to have some good news for a change – had been ecstatic.

But the actual mechanics were all so complicated to explain! Georgie poured out another glass of fresh lemonade for them both before starting. 'Our computer man – who used to be a techie hot-shot in the City – came across a new scam in America.'

Lyndsey moved back into the shade, reminding Georgie that you couldn't be too careful; anything could take you by surprise in life, whether it was illness or betrayal. 'I know that bit. It's the next part I don't understand.'

Georgie shrugged. 'Nor do I, really. That's because identity fraud is what they call a "constantly-evolving crime". Kevin explained ...'

'Kevin?' Lyndsey raised an eyebrow. 'We're on first-name terms with the computer man, are we?'

'Yes! When someone has saved you thousands that were stolen from you in the first place, a surname seems far too formal. Anyway, Kevin managed to tap into a ring of fraudsters by pretending to be one himself.'

'Stolen identity again?' Lyndsey was scribbling it down. 'It seems to be all the rage.'

'Thank you.' Her friend's comment stung. Even now she was terrified that Georgina's adoptive family might contact her – even though her parents were dead. She'd have to tell them the truth. Admit that she'd borrowed someone else's identity.

That was, she'd explained to Lyndsey, why she hadn't wanted to come back to the UK a few years ago. A hidden ex-pat life had been safer. There had been less risk of bumping into people who knew her past.

'Sorry.' Lyndsey looked repentant. 'I didn't mean to be thoughtless.' Her eyes gleamed, as though she was a mischievous teenager again. 'Georgina is far too formal, anyway. Georgie is much more you.'

Even her mother, who had slipped very fast into a rambling incoherency during the last few months, no longer talked about the old Georgina. It was as if the return of her surviving daughter had laid the ghosts to rest.

In a strange way, Georgina Peverington-Smith had merged into her own body now that her killer had finally been caught and justice done. Perhaps, she sometimes mused, her sister had 'sent' her old friend Lyndsey back to her. For the first time in years, she felt comfortable in her own skin. As though her identity had been restored to her.

Until now, she hadn't realised just how important one's true identity really was. Without it, you were nothing.

Just as important, she and Sam were slowly but surely

rebuilding that wall of trust. They'd gone beyond the cuddling stage now ...

'Kevin managed to get evidence on this ring,' she continued, 'by pretending to be one of them. It was incredible. There are all those people out there who surf the net, looking for idiots like me who use their pet's name as a password or who answer unsolicited emails that pose as genuine questions about your private details.'

Lyndsey sucked in her breath. 'But what about the car being moved and the credit card inside the handbag?'

Georgie still felt stupid over that. 'It's what they call an "opportunist ruse". Thieves bump into you in the street and apologise while taking your purse in the confusion. Or, in my case, they look out for anyone who drops their bags or needs help getting off a train or crossing the road. That's been going on for a while, but Kevin says it's become more sophisticated. Sat Navs are often used to find out where the real owner lives. All you have to do is punch in "Home" and the address comes up. Luck comes into it too.'

She drew a deep breath, thinking of the slim woman in jeans and trainers with the pushchair. No tattoos. No earrings in her nose. Barely any make-up. Shoulder-length mousy hair, tucked behind her ears. Hardly your average image of a female thief – whatever that might be.

'I assumed that the mum with the stroller was just being kind when she helped me pick up the things I dropped outside Vanda's house. But she hung onto my car key. Apparently her brother – who's a bit of a computer geek – had dragged her into this ring. I can't help feeling sorry for her. She must have been desperate. Maybe that's why she was the first one who crumbled, so she'd get a lighter sentence. If it wasn't for her, the police told me, we wouldn't have got the other names.'

Lyndsey wrinkled up her nose sympathetically. 'You don't expect a woman to do this kind of stuff, do you?'

'No. You don't. In some ways, that makes it worse.' Georgie still felt terrible about it. 'Who's going to look after her child when she's in prison? '

She stopped, remembering the little bundle in blue with a globule of snot running down its nose. He might have to go into care. Then the whole spiral might start again. And what would happen when the girl got out? Would someone try to hurt her because she'd 'grassed'? Or would the police give her a new identity?

So many questions. Not enough answers.

'I still don't see,' mused Lyndsay, 'how your card could have been used when it was still in the bag when you got home.'

It was clever, Georgie had to admit. Very clever. 'Apparently, this Mandy Smith's brother rang someone else in the ring. He copied my card on a special machine and then drove the car home.'

'But why?'

'Apparently it makes some people think they're going mad – that they hadn't gone out in the first place.' She gave a short laugh. 'It did it for me. It also buys the thief more time to use the card because you don't realise that a duplicate has been made.'

'How devious.'

'Apparently that's the way it's going.'

She gave a short laugh 'There also the so-called business friends, like Vanda and Jonathan, who use their "privy information", as it's known, to empty your account.'

'Were they ever caught?'

This was still a bone of contention. 'Sam refused to take action. He said it would lead to more publicity and we'd had enough of that. Besides, I'm not sure where Vanda and Jonathan have gone. Rufus reckons it might be Australia. But according to my computer man, they were the ones who'd put that awful thing on YouTube. They were trying to discredit me.'

'Don't you want to sue them?'

Georgie had thought about that. 'I think they've suffered

enough.' She went silent for a minute, wondering – as she'd often done – what hell it had been in a Bangkok prison. How could she take their freedom away again?

'So many people were involved!' added Lyndsey, cutting into her thoughts. 'I bet there are some stories behind them all.'

'Probably. They all work for someone at the top, like a proper business. But very few of them know each other. It's called organised crime.'

She breathed out deeply at the complexity of it all. 'Then, apparently, acquaintances – and even friends of the victim – latch on. Vanda said it was when I told her about my handbag and the missing car that she and Jonathan thought of pretending to be me and emptying my husband's account.'

'What about the man who used your card? Right at the very beginning? The first one who took money from Jo's as well?'

He still haunted her, to be honest. Maybe she shouldn't have gone to the trial. His defence had spared no details in eliciting sympathy. 'He came from a really bad background. You could say he'd learned credit card fraud at his mother's knee. He was in goodness knows how many foster homes. And then he fell into bad company. Apparently, the man towards the top of the chain was the pillar of his local community. Everyone thought he'd made his money through his company but it turned out to be a front for the huge fraud ring. There were loads of others too. Goodness knows what their backgrounds were.'

'And Nick?'

Georgie felt a lurch at the pit of her stomach. Out of everything, this was the biggest betrayal. 'He, too, got the idea from the other card thefts when he ran up those gambling debts. Ellie had unwittingly told him about it because she was upset. Sam thought it was her, you see. Like I said earlier, the police said it often happens like that. Others – connected to the victim – think they'll cash in. I just didn't think my own son would do that kind of thing.'

'They say we never really know each other, don't they?' Lyndsey was still scribbling in the shade, under the striped parasol. 'You could write a book about it.'

'Is that what you're doing?' Georgie sat bolt upright. Her friend had always wanted to be a writer as a little girl. Teaching had clearly been a safer bet.

'I'm thinking of a children's spy novel, actually.' Lyndsey coloured up.

'Will I be in it?'

She shrugged. 'Only as a nine-year-old girl. Don't worry. No one will recognise you.' Her eyes grew dreamy as she stared over the sea towards the horizon where a white sailing boat could just about be seen. 'I thought it might take my mind off the next hospital appointment.'

How could she deny her friend that? Even so, it made Georgie feel a bit uneasy.

Just like the computer man's warning. 'Be careful every time you go on the net or hand over your credit card in a shop or buy something on the phone. You never know who's going to be the next victim.'

Georgie shivered. Then her hand closed over the small, hard object in her pocket.

'Did you find anything else?' She'd asked the policewoman when they'd rung to say they'd found some 'goods' at the home of Mandy Smith. She'd glanced at the Boots card, wondering if the girl had used all the points on it. 'I know this sounds silly but there was a small shell in my bag that had great sentimental significance.'

'Like this one, you mean ...?'

'That's pretty.' Lyndsey now leaned over to take a closer look. Her friend's hair was growing back again. It was a slightly darker shade of red but colour could change apparently, after chemo. It rather suited her.

'Where did that come from?' she added.

The small pink and white shell lay in the palm of her hand. It whispered of an island; heat; and a beautiful young woman who had found her at the airport.

'My sister gave it to me.' As Georgie spoke, she could

almost hear Georgina's voice. *'There's something I need to ask you.'*

'She gave it to me,' she added, 'years ago. Before I knew of our connection. And I've always kept it. It sounds silly but I always felt, despite everything that happened, it was a lucky charm.'

'That doesn't sound silly at all.' Lyndsey took her hand in hers. Lyndsey. Her childhood friend. The one who had always been there for her.

'You know,' she added gently, self-consciously touching her hair, 'one of the doctors told me something at the hospital that's stayed with me.'

Georgie waited.

'He says that if someone dies, he always tells the person that's left behind that no one – not even death who is perhaps the biggest thief of all – can take away the memories.'

A huge lump rose in her throat. 'That's lovely.'

Lyndsey smiled. 'It is rather, isn't it?' Then she reached across for her glass. 'To Georgina.'

Georgie swallowed back the tears. 'To Georgina. The real one.'

'By the way,' added her friend. 'When did you say you were going to visit your mum again?'

'I didn't. But actually, I'm going to drive up next weekend. And Sam's coming with me.' She paused. 'There's something else, too.'

There was a nod. 'I thought there might be.'

'Sam's found someone who specialises in finding people. And we've got a lead.' Georgie could hardly speak. 'It's not definite but it's a possibility ...'

'Your dad.' Lyndsey spoke flatly.

'Actually, no.'

She'd given up on that one a long time ago. Her mother's memory was either deliberately obtuse or simply not there. There were some things, as Sam said, that just had to be accepted.

'Who then?' Lyndsey was frowning.

Georgie twisted her fingers. 'Ellie's mother. Yes, I know it's going to be difficult. But it's something that Ellie wants. And I don't want my daughter to go through life without understanding her roots, like I did.'

Lyndsey reached across for her hand. 'You're a good woman.'

'No.' Georgie felt embarrassed. 'But every person is entitled to know who they are. And no one has a right to take it away.'

She shivered. 'Now how about a top up?'

Anything for a distraction. Georgie's hand shook as she poured out the lemonade. She'd just been about to give away something, had almost confided in Lyndsay that she'd received a postcard, just before they'd left. A postcard in an envelope with a Philippine stamp.

On one side, were the words of a poem she had always loved. Kipling had got it spot on.

'If you can keep your head ...

And at the end, had been a single initial, indicating the identity of the sender.

J.

Of course there was nothing in it. Joly might seek solace in the breast of a dusky maiden but he would always love Georgina. Just as she had learned to love Sam and leave Joly behind.

Yet the postcard had sent a warm feeling through her; a message that the only person she really needed to be true to, was herself.

'No need to tell anyone that Joly's got in touch,' she could hear Georgina saying in her head. *'After all, every girl needs her secrets.'*

Finally, she could see why! A secret is the one thing that no one can steal.

But only if you keep it safe.